JENNA TERESE

IGNITE

IGNITE DUOLOGY BOOK ONE

This is a work of fiction. Names, characters, places, and incidents either are the product of the author's imagination or are used fictitiously. Any resemblance to actual persons, living or dead, events, or locales is entirely coincidental.

First paperback edition July 2021

Book cover design by ebooklaunch.com

ISBN (paperback): 978-1-7367481-0-7

ISBN (ebook): 978-1-7367481-1-4

To the Gift Giver

"As each one has received a special gift, employ it in serving one another as good stewards of the manifold grace of God."
1 Peter 4:10

CHAPTER ONE

The news channel shows it in chilling detail.

Smoke billows from the half-crumpled building as people struggle to escape the flames. Screams of terror and panic fill the air. It looks like a war zone. I can almost taste the fear, feel it raise the hair on the back of my neck. The camera recording the scene jostles, like the man behind it wants to join the others running for their lives.

The noise of the TV drones on under the sounds of the small ice cream shop. I strain to hear beyond the hum of conversation, the noise from the back kitchen, and the scrape of tiny spoons against paper cups. My own ice cream sits forgotten, the cup chilling my palm while I watch the replay unfold on the TV.

The news channel ends the replay and flips back to the two white-faced reporters sitting behind a glossy glass desk. The woman brushes her shaky hand over her already flawlessly curled hair and clears her throat.

"That was a replay of yesterday's events," she says, a slight tremor in her voice as she folds her hands over the sheets of paper before her, "when a superhuman attacked this small town of Hermosa, South Dakota."

My town. I gulp. My throat tightens as I glance around the

shop. People pretend to not be listening to the TV, but the tightness in their shoulders and the ways their eyes dart to the screen betrays them. I turn my attention back to the screen. I can't believe the sirens I heard that day were because of all this.

"Locals are still reeling from the attack. Some mourning loved ones and others demanding their safety be ensured. Especially since authorities haven't been able to find the attacker as of yet. Here's what some of Hermosa's own have to say about this."

The screen switches to a balding reporter in a blue collared shirt, holding a microphone in front of a woman in a stained grey sweatshirt standing on her overgrown lawn.

"This is ridiculous," she says. "The government said they were going to handle this problem. That's why they built that facility over there in Wyoming. To keep the superhuman freaks locked up and away from us. Seems to me the government's not doing their job right."

I nod in agreement as fear tickles my gut. The Superhuman Containment Facility was supposed to fix things. It was supposed to keep us safe. But instead supers are crawling everywhere, like ants over a dropped hotdog. There are still attacks and crimes committed by these superhumans almost every week. Most of them probably from Rapid City, where there are so many of them that the government can't handle it. And that's only twenty minutes from my town. A shudder runs down my spine. How many supers are hiding in my own neighborhood?

"Scarlett? Hey, Scarlett!"

I jolt and look across the table at my younger brother. Dylan only meets my gaze briefly before digging back into his vanilla ice cream. He spoons a generous bite into his mouth. "Daydreaming again?"

Next to him, Ian Henley smiles, but his grin falls as he studies my face. My little sister wriggles happily beside me, taking quick, tiny bites of her pink sherbet. My fingers tighten around my melting bowl of ice cream. Ian's gaze lingers on me, but I can't say anything out loud with Hannah listening in. I look at Ian again and nod toward the TV hanging in the corner of the shop.

He follows my gaze and frowns at the screen. Dylan finally takes his attention off his dessert, glancing between both of us, then looks at the TV too.

Hannah follows his lead, scooting in her chair just as the news channel shows another replay.

Dylan's brow furrows. "They always make the supers look bad," he mutters.

I clear my throat loudly, glancing around the shop to make sure no one heard. The other customers scattered between the small cafe tables don't pay us any heed, though several gazes are fixed on the TV. "Let's not talk about that right now." Or ever.

Dylan sighs and turns his attention back to his cup, but with a little less gusto.

Ian's gaze lingers on the screen before he tears himself away from it. "Right. We're supposed to be celebrating summer break starting tomorrow. Only one more year of high school to go."

Dylan groans. "Lucky for you guys. I've still got three years."

Hannah looks up at me, sherbet smears around her mouth. "How many years do I have?"

I chuckle and flick her braid over her shoulder. "Plenty."

Despite my efforts to turn the conversation away from the TV, we fall silent again, eyes straying to the screen.

They've finished showing enraged citizens giving their two-cents worth. A tall man in a white lab coat stares at the camera with piercing blue eyes. Bright lights above him highlight the white desk and white-walled office, and shine off his gelled blond hair, combed to perfection.

"...and the people don't know how hard we are working to fix this," he's saying with a smooth, business-like voice. "Attacks will still happen, yes. What happened in Hermosa was terrible. But improvements are being made, and we have been able to drastically cut down the population of superhumans in our country."

The screen flicks over again and the reporters at the desk nod. The woman shifts her papers on the desk, tilting her head. "And what about the criminal supers in Rapid City? What's being done about that?"

A flicker of irritation pinches between the doctor's brows. He shifts his jaw. "I assure you, plans are being made to gain control over that area."

The reporter nods and offers a polite smile. "Thank you so much, Dr. Bailey—"

A burst of laughter from a nearby table drowns out the next words. I cast a discreet glance at the table next to us, where Ian's parents and mine sit with their ice creams. Their conversation has fallen silent too as they pretend not to be watching the news —spoons swirling in their dessert and heads bent, but gazes drifting toward the screen.

Ian's mother, Mrs. Henley, leans around her husband to get a better look at the TV. As soon as I see her face pinch in frustration, my stomach knots and I frantically think of a conversation topic. Before she goes off again about superhuman politics. I don't want that to break up our gathering. Again.

"Hey, Ian, I got some new sheet music yesterday." Still, my fingers tap a nervous rhythm on my knee under the table.

I find him looking at the TV again. "Cool. You know I'm gonna ask to borrow it."

I chuckle. "I know it. Saves you money on music."

He grins and shrugs. "Why spend my hard-earned cash on sheet music when I can just borrow from a friend down the street?"

I roll my eyes, but can't keep from smiling. The conversation at the parents' table resumes, and some tension releases from my shoulders. "I might not be around forever you know. When you're a big music star and I'm stuck here in Hermosa..."

Ian tosses his spoon in his empty cup, licking the remains of strawberry ice cream from his lip and shaking his head. But as he opens his mouth to speak, his mother's voice escalates.

"No, Tim!" Mrs. Henley clutches the small pink spoon in her fingers. "I think it's appalling how they're treating the supers. Just because they're different doesn't mean—"

"Now, honey." Mr. Henley sighs, rubbing his wrinkled forehead and discreetly scanning the shop. "Let's not get into this again."

I flick a glance at the table on our other side. The middle-aged couple sitting there doesn't seem to notice us, but I shrink against my chair, poking at my final scoop of chocolate ice cream.

"It's people that don't want to talk about it that are to blame for the way supers are being treated." Mrs. Henley scoops her last bite of dessert into her mouth and tosses the spoon on the white tabletop. "They need someone to stand up for them!"

Now a few heads turn our way. I catch Ian's soft groan and he covers his face with his hands. My toes curl in my sneakers, willing Mrs. Henley to just be quiet. Didn't she listen to what they were saying on the news? Supers shouldn't be left free, it's dangerous. How can we feel safe with those freaks roaming around?

"Rachel, not so loud." Mr. Henley looks around again before leaning closer to his wife. "Let's just talk about this later, okay?"

My parents glance between each other before looking at us too. They throw pleading gazes at Mrs. Henley.

Mrs. Henley lifts her chin sharply, but lowers her voice. "Well...the kids should hear this. They should be informed. To make their own decision."

At that, my parents shift uncomfortably in their seats.

"Really, Rachel," Mom says with an exasperated sigh as she leans across the table and lowers her voice to a whisper. "Is this really the time or place to go off again?"

Mrs. Henley presses her hands on the table and stands, chin still lifted. "Now is as good a time as any."

Her husband pulls her back down to her seat as more customers cast concerned glances at us.

Dad leans his elbows on the table and laces his fingers in front of his nose, muffling his next words. "You saw the news the same as we did. What that super did was wrong, Rachel, there's no doubt about that."

I doubt Mrs. Henley will see Dad's sense, but I'm thankful for him saying it anyway. Voicing opinions like hers can draw unwanted attention. Besides embarrassing her son.

Ian's face is already pink and I can feel strangers glancing our way. Dylan huffs and props his elbow on the table to rest his chin in his hand. "Boy. What a summer celebration this turned out to be," he mutters.

Ian groans. "I'm sorry, guys. I really thought she'd keep quiet this time, especially after what happened." He nods toward the TV.

Dylan shakes his head. "I didn't mean it like that, Ian."

"Yeah," I wipe the stickiness from Hannah's cheek with a napkin. "It's not your fault."

Hannah pushes my hand away. "Did they catch the bad guy, Lettie?" she whispers.

Ian, Dylan and I share a look. I rub the six-year-old's back and force a smile. "They will. Don't worry."

She nods, but wrinkles her freckled nose as she frowns at the table. I bite my lip, wishing I could clamp my hands over her ears against the noise from the TV.

Ian sighs deeply as his eyes narrow at his empty ice cream cup. "You think she's crazy?" he asks, barely above a whisper. He glances briefly at his mom.

I hesitate. "Did somebody say that?"

He shrugs and stacks his empty cup with Dylan's. "I don't know, some people say she is." He chuckles softly through his nose. "You guys are basically the only people who are still friends with us."

I cross my arms. "It would take more than a couple of rants to get rid of us." I wink.

Dylan doesn't play off my attempt to lighten the mood, looking tentatively at Ian. "Do *you* think she's crazy?"

At first, Ian doesn't even look like he heard. He just chews his lip and stares at nothing. I raise my eyebrows and lean forward to look Ian in the face. "You don't mean you actually believe her."

"I...don't think so." Uncertainty laces his words.

I gape at him. "But—"

"What if she's right?" Dylan interjects softly.

I snap my head toward my brother. Even Hannah looks up at him, her big blue eyes shifting between all of us, catching the thickening tension.

Dylan continues to stare at the table, avoiding our shock. But I recognize that look on his face. His brow furrows as he gazes unseeing at his reflection on the glossy table surface, working his jaw. He's been thinking about this a lot lately, asking questions that shouldn't be said out loud. Not that I told anyone.

But I'm not about to get into another debate with him. "You saw the same news I did," I mutter, gathering their trash to the center of the table. My remaining lump of ice cream sits in a brown puddle at the bottom of my cup.

Stabbing my spoon in the soft ice cream, I watch Dylan as he distractedly ruffles a hand through his messy brown waves. We hardly ever argue, but when it comes to superhuman politics, we agree to disagree. He thinks supers need a chance. I think they should be kept somewhere where the rest of us will be safe.

I turn my attention to the parents' table again. Mrs. Henley's voice has returned to a normal level, but tension still hangs in the air as she continues in a lower tone.

As she pauses for breath, Dad leans his elbows on the table, almost glaring at her. "This isn't the place to discuss this," he says firmly.

Dylan and I share a glance. We know that tone of voice all too well.

Mrs. Henley's face turns as pink as Hannah's sherbet and I quickly turn the tide of the straining tension at our table.

"Hey, Ian, how's that song coming?" I ask, loud enough for the parents to hear.

Ian sits up straighter, but his smile doesn't quite reach his green eyes. "Pretty good, I think. At least I've got the chorus figured out." He smirks. "Graduated past that puny ukulele of yours to an actual instrument yet?"

He's been trying to get me back into guitar for years. But ever since I discovered the fun of a soprano ukulele, I've been hooked. "No, not yet. Ukulele's fun, you should try it."

He fake gags. "Ukuleles are for the weak," he says in a deeper voice.

I chuckle. "I'm just trying new things. Don't you think musicians should do that, hmm?"

"Well, sure, but you won't catch me playing a mini piano."

"A guitar and ukulele aren't the same thing!"

"Oh, sure. They're just the same shape and you play them the same."

I sigh dramatically. I'll probably think of a clever comeback later.

Ian chuckles and shakes his head. "How you ever got stuck on those little things I will never understand. How many do you have now, fifty?"

My face reddens. "No!" I clear my throat. "Just four."

He hides his grin behind his hand.

"They're small!" I protest.

He and Dylan laugh and shake their heads like I'm a lost cause, but say nothing more. I pretend to be mad and scoot away to cross my arms and pout. Hannah giggles at me.

"Ah, don't be mad," Ian says. "I have some news that might cheer you up."

"Yeah? What?"

"I got my first gig."

I gasp. "We've been together most of the evening and you

never told me? Rude."

He shrugs one shoulder. "I guess I forgot about it after...you know." He flicks a glance at the parents' table.

Heaviness threatens to return, but I push it away. "Fine, you're forgiven. This time." I lift my chin. "But when I get my first gig I'm not going to tell you right away."

"Oh, please. Who's going to hire someone who plays a *ukulele*?" He says the word like it's sour on his tongue.

I groan and roll my eyes, angling away slightly toward the front window, and hooking my arm over the back of the chair. The darkness outside creates a perfect backdrop for the mirror image of the brightly decorated shop in the glass. I can barely see past the reflection of the white tables, customers, and modern decor in the store's blue and pink colors.

So Ian has his first music job. I know it's probably just a small event, but still...it feels official. Like his dreams are starting to come true. And mine haven't even gotten off the ground yet.

I shake my head to clear it. The last thing I want is to get jealous of him. I should be happy for him.

"So when's this gig?" I ask. I can't help that a little excitement has leaked out of my voice.

"Two weeks. It's just a birthday party. Not that big a deal."

"Not that big a deal? First it's playing at a birthday party, then it's on to touring the world. Like, maybe next month."

He chuckles. "Yeah, I wish. College first though, huh?"

I wave a hand. "Eh. Who needs education?"

A sharp gasp brings me toward the parents' table again. Mrs. Henley leans forward, glaring at my dad, who must've said something to upset her. Her strawberry blond hair almost dips into her ice cream cup, but she doesn't relent the staring match. "How dare you!"

Without looking away from Mrs. Henley, mom tilts her head toward me. "You guys can wait for us outside," she whispers. "We'll be leaving soon."

I sigh softly, but nod.

Ian scrubs a hand over his face as Dylan stands and reaches for the empty cups. "I'll take care of the trash."

"I'll help you," Ian says, crumpling some napkins in his fist.

As Dylan carries the cups to the trash can, Hannah scrambles after him. Probably to make sure her cup was licked clean properly. Ian follows them.

I grab my cup and spoon and head toward the door. The cheerful celebratory mood may have been snapped, but I still want to enjoy the rest of my ice cream. Even if it has turned to soup.

Warm summer air hits me as I step outside and my fingers curl tighter around the cup, relishing in the residual coolness. Tilting the cup to collect the remaining dessert on my spoon, I settle on the bench under the shop's front window. The old wood creaks under my weight as I lean back on it.

Wind cools my skin and car headlights sweep the road as the vehicles pass, and the stars multiply overhead. I look over my shoulder to the scene inside. Dylan and Ian squat near the trash can, frantically picking up trash dropped on the tiled floor. An employee in a hot pink apron hurries over, wet rag in her hand ready to mop up droplets of melted ice cream. Hannah stares guiltily at it all, pink spoon in her hand. What'd she do, knock all the cups out of Dylan's hand trying to find hers? Didn't know she liked sherbet *that* much. I chuckle and shrug, turning my attention back to my own ice cream and polishing it off in a few more spoonfuls.

A jarring metal crash makes my heart jump to my throat. I still, tongue freezing mid-lick of my lower lip. It sounded like it came from behind the shop. I scoot toward the other end of the bench near the corner of the building and strain for any sound beyond the road noise. Nothing.

Probably just someone taking out the trash, right? Yet my hand trembles, shaking the spoon clutched in my fingers. I give my head a sharp shake as if to clear it before my imagination runs wild. No super would be here around so many people.

Everything's fine. I scrape the tiny spoon along the edges of my cup to get the last miniscule bits.

A loud rustling makes me pause again, spoon on my tongue. I frown and quietly set my cup and spoon on the bench and lean around the edge of the building.

The shop building blocks most of the street light, and I squint into the splotchy blackness. I lean a little farther, not yet willing to get off the bench. All seems still and quiet.

Wait...

My eyes strain deeper in the darkness. Subtle movement shifts in the shadows. I hold my breath, listening for the smallest sound. Maybe a shoe scuff. A sniff. Something to tell me what's in there. I swallow against my suddenly parched throat.

A faint meow calms some of my tension. I let out a breath. It's just a cat. Now I get off the bench and crouch beside it to face the shadows. Ian would call me delusional for trying my hand at cat whispering again, but I don't care. Even if I've gotten a fair number of scratches in the past. I'd give the stray my ice cream if I had any left.

Now that my eyes are adjusting, I can make out dark masses where the dumpsters are as I scan the area for the cat. When I don't hear anything more, I stand to take a few slow steps forward.

Behind me, a car turns into the parking lot, headlights illuminating the darkness for a moment.

There's no cat.

Just the thin form of a man leaning over the open dumpster.

My spine stiffens. *No, relax.* It's probably just an employee or something. Nothing more. Not here, not with all these people around. A super wouldn't chance getting caught. Especially if it's the same one from the news.

That last thought makes me shudder, and I could kick myself for thinking it and sending my heart into a nervous flutter. I don't want to scare the man, so I slowly take a step back. My heel scuffs on the cracked asphalt, and his head jerks up.

His eyes glow like fire.

My breath cuts short and my throat constricts as I stare into the fiery orbs. *Move!* My mind screams. *Run!*

Before I can get my legs to work, the man leaps down off the dumpster and grabs my shoulders. I open my mouth to scream but he clamps a grubby hand over my face.

My muscles finally listen and I try to twist away. His grip is like iron on my arm, bruising instantly as he whips me around to the back of the building and slams me against the wall. My head smacks brick and stars swim across my vision.

I bare my teeth under the sweaty pressure of his bony hand and kick at his shins. He gives my shoulder a squeeze so sharp that I flinch and go still.

"*Shh*," he hisses, his breath hot on my face. "Just...don't scream. Please." His voice trembles and the hand over my mouth shakes.

I nod: a complete lie.

He hesitates, then slowly lowers his hand from my mouth. His glowing eyes are wide, frantic. They dart everywhere. When his gaze finally settles on me, I shrink back. "I'm not going to hurt you if you just—"

"Dylan!" My call for help is cut short by another hand-clamp.

He shoves me and my back scrapes along the brick as I fall to my side. I press my palms against the rough asphalt to stand, but another shove against my ribs knocks me down again. He crouches over me, and I press against the ground, tilting my face away from his rancid breath.

"I told you not to scream!" he hisses. He glares at me, his hands trembling at his sides. His fingers curl into tight fists as his skin begins to glow red. The light in his eyes grows brighter, like flames flickering in his irises.

I open my mouth and take a breath for another scream.

The man's eyes widen and he thrusts his glowing hands toward me.

Flames burst from his palms.

Fire engulfs me. Fear chokes me. I cover my face with my arms, but the flames are everywhere. Devouring me. Consuming me. My hands clamp over my ears against the roaring of the fire, like a raging river. Heat flares through my whole body, eyes burning, skin tingling.

Is this how I die?

In the midst of the roar of the flames, I hear screams. My screams. Screams of my name. The flames falter for a moment and I hiccup a breath, choking on smoke. There's more yelling, then the fire disappears all together.

I lie paralyzed, curled in a tight ball, quivering and stiff. My mind fogs and my eyes ache with how hard I squeeze them shut. Voices surround me, sounds that should be loud but are turned to molasses beneath the pounding in my ears. Dylan yelling my name again. Ian's panicked voice. Hannah crying. But I can't move. Only a nauseating flare of panic clutches my gut, telling me to scream at them to get away in case the criminal is still around.

Shoes scuff the ground all around me. Someone places a hand on my arm but jerks it away.

In the absence of the fire, the cool air caresses my burning skin. I can't stop shaking. Waiting for the searing pain. Waiting for my mind to realize what's happened.

I feel a soft breath on my ear. No one tries touching me again.

"Lettie." Even though he sounds like he's underwater, I can tell it's Dylan. His voice shakes. "It's okay. You're okay now. We're getting help, just hang on."

I want to nod but my muscles won't loosen. Heat pulses through my body. Sounds begin to dim even more as my mind shuts down. My muscles slowly release. Somewhere, far away, I hear an ambulance siren. Something like panic pokes my gut, but soon fizzles out.

All sounds disappear as I slip into unconsciousness.

CHAPTER TWO

Fire and ice.

That's what I felt when I woke up. Even now heat still boils inside my body and the icy air conditioning in the hospital room chills my skin.

My skin that isn't burned.

I was afraid to look at myself, in case the pain sank in. But when I came to, Mom and Dad hovering over me, I barely had a scratch on me. Mom said it was a miracle, but something about it makes me queasy.

Fire is supposed to burn.

"And you said you couldn't see what the man looked like?"

I blink, jolted out of my thoughts. The broad police officer stands at the foot of my bed, staring at me with narrowed eyes as he waits for my answer. Another officer, a thin woman with kind eyes and a round face, stands just behind him with a small notebook.

I swallow and wince. Before I can even ask, Mom lifts a cup of water to my lips. I take a couple gulps. "No," I croak. "It was too dark for me to see much." All through this questioning my throat has just become dryer and rougher. I try to clear it, but that only irritates it more.

Dad rises from his chair. "Don't you think that's enough, officer? She needs rest."

The man frowns and opens his mouth to reply, but the woman touches his arm. He shifts his jaw, glancing between the three of us and the other officer before nodding. "All right. We'll leave for now, but we may need more information from you in the future. Understood?"

I nod.

As soon as they're gone, Mom lets out a sigh. She moves from her chair to sit on the edge of my bed. "How are you feeling, Lettie?" She smooths some hair away from my face, brows furrowing over her clear blue eyes.

I try to give her a smile. "Better."

Dad leans his elbows on the bed and studies me. I give him a smile too. "Really. I am feeling better."

As silence passes between us, both of them stare at my arms. I know what they're thinking. I should be charred, but my skin is normal, except perhaps a little pink.

I finger the rough weave of the light blue blanket covering my legs as Mom rubs my other hand, blinking back tears. She opens her mouth to speak, but the door opening cuts her off.

Two women in business slacks and blazers stride inside, heels clicking on the floor. The taller of the two smiles at me and adjusts her navy blue jacket, a short lock of hair curling over her forehead. "I'm Amanda Blake," she says, "with the local news—"

"Nope." Dad stands abruptly and she blinks at him, taking a step back. "No more reporters. We've had enough of that." He gestures toward the door. "Please leave."

Both women glance at me, as if for support. I look away. Without another word of objection, they turn and walk out.

Dad sighs and rakes a hand through his hair as he shakes his head. "Surely we can get this room off-limits." He rounds the bed to head out the door, calling for the nearest nurse.

I take another sip of water before trying my voice again. "Dylan and Hannah...they're okay, right?"

Mom offers a tight smile and nods. "They're okay. Just a little shaken up." She chuckles and strokes my cheek. "You really gave us all a scare."

"And Ian?"

She nods again. "He's all right. Concerned, of course."

I let out a breath. I'm just glad that superhuman decided to run away when he heard their voices, instead of turning his attack on them too. I don't know what I'd do if they were hurt.

After only a moment, Dad comes back in. "Well, now that that's taken care of..." He sits back down and takes my hand. "I guess you're gonna get the royal treatment for a bit, huh?" He grins.

I chuckle, loosening some of the tension in my shoulders. "Sounds good to me."

The door clicks open again, and Dad's cheerful mood snaps. He drops my hand and stands, the chair screeching back. "What in the world..."

A man in a dark grey suit and black tie steps through the door, shined shoes creaking. A woman in a black pencil skirt and burnt orange blouse follows him.

Dad points a finger at the man. "You're gonna have to leave, sir—"

The stranger holds up a hand. "We're from the Superhuman Containment Facility. Here to ask a few questions."

Dad freezes, then slowly lowers back down into the chair.

"W-what do you want?" Mom asks, glancing between them both.

The woman steps forward, folding her hands and smiling stiffly under sharp cheekbones. "Just a few questions, ma'am." She addresses Mom, but doesn't take her eyes off me.

This time, Dad just blinks at the strangers. I shrink against the pillow tucked behind my back as the man and woman step closer. The woman slips a sleek phone from her pocket and types something.

The man adjusts his tie and the clip glints in the white light overhead. “Miss Marley, can you describe the powers the superhuman attacked you with?”

I swallow, struggling to keep his intense gaze. My palms dampen with sweat and I slide them under the blanket. “Um...sure.”

He nods. “Good.”

My pulse quickens as I remember the darkness and the figure standing over me with glowing eyes— I shove the fear down and concentrate on the information these people want. “I don’t know what else to say besides fire,” I begin. “It was thick. Consuming. I couldn’t... see through it.” My brows draw together as I stare at the blanket, trying to remember everything. “His eyes glowed.” I shrug, the motion a little shaky. “I’m sorry, that’s all I can give you.”

The woman types effortlessly as I speak, keeping up with every word. When she finishes, she looks up at the man.

He leans his hands on the footboard and tilts his head, a stubborn ringlet falling over his forehead. “And you came out uninjured?” His eyes narrow.

I shift. “That’s right.”

“Hmm.”

Heat rises to my face as he studies me. “And have you experienced any odd symptoms since the attack?”

Now my eyes narrow. What does he mean? “Like what?”

“Like, say, symptoms that could seem almost like superpowers, or something similar.”

“I think that’s enough.” Mom settles a glare at the man. “She’s fine. That’s all you need to know.”

Both strangers stare at Mom, but she doesn’t shrink. After one more glance at Dad and another narrow-eyed study of me, the man turns on his heel and marches out the door, the woman close behind. A nurse in purple scrubs comes in just as they leave, and she gives them a confused look as they brush past.

She stops at the foot of my bed and smiles. "Well, we can't find anything really wrong with you, Scarlett. So you're free to go home."

Mom and Dad smile at me, relief written on their faces. I return their smiles and let out a breath. I'd much rather recover at home, where it's warmer and there aren't any reporters or officers. Or strangers from the SCF asking uncomfortable questions.

"Here, honey." Mom offers her hand to help me out of the car.

I clutch one hand to my head against the headache that developed on the way home, and slip the other into hers. Her hand feels cold against mine, so mine must be so hot, but she gives me a strong hold.

On shaking legs, I slide out of the car and Mom wraps her arm around my shoulders and brushes some of my hair away from my face. "Let's get you into bed."

I manage a small nod. Exhaustion drags at my body and I just want to sleep and forget. Not just this headache...but the thoughts of consuming fire, alive and devouring, all around me. And the fact I came out without so much as a blister.

When Mom ushers me into my room, I glance at the digital clock reading *5:15am.* I can't even concentrate to find some clothes to change into, so she helps me and settles me into bed. After a soft kiss on my forehead, she quietly leaves the room.

I pull the covers over my shoulders, but promptly throw them off when I get too warm. I slide out of bed to crank the ceiling fan on high. But I still feel feverish inside even though the room's cool enough to fall asleep. Great. A fever? Maybe I caught something from the hospital.

My breath stills as Mom and Dad's hushed conversation drifts in from their room across the hall. I can't decipher any words, but the hum of their voices finally lulls me to sleep.

I wake up the next morning with my stomach churning and a headache still pounding in my temples. My clothes and sheets have hard wrinkles like I was pouring sweat and tossing and turning all night. I sit up in bed with a groan and press a hand to my head until the world stops spinning.

It sounds like the rest of the family is already up. I can hear Dylan and Hannah chatting from the kitchen coupled with the sound of a knife on a cutting board. Mom must be making breakfast.

My stomach heaves. *No, don't think about breakfast.* I glance at the clock. *12:46pm.* Okay, lunch, then.

I slide out of bed—not bothering to make it—and pull a sweatshirt over my head. When heat pulses underneath the fabric, I take it off, but shiver and put it back on again. I grimace at the cold-and-hot combination still warring within me.

I shuffle out of my room and down the hallway toward the bathroom. Wincing against the hammer in my skull, I clutch my hands over my ears against Dylan and Hannah's loud chatter until I've closed the bathroom door behind me. I lean my hands on the sink and sigh at the coolness that it brings to my palms. I don't even want to see what I look like right now, but I lift my eyes to the mirror.

Yikes. I look as bad as I feel.

My hair's a mess—is my scrunchie even still in there?—my eyes are bloodshot, and my cheeks are flushed. My stomach gives an unsettling churn. Did I get food poisoning from the ice cream too?

I try to swallow against my parched throat then splash some water on my face. I half-heartedly brush my teeth before stumbling out of the bathroom and down to the kitchen. All conversation stops when I enter the room.

Dylan blinks at me. "Wow. You look terrible."

I sigh and purse my lips. "Thanks a lot."

Mom sets down a jug of orange juice and circles the island to me. She frowns as she studies my face. "Feeling bad, sweetie? Maybe you're getting sick..." Something I can't read flickers in her eyes. I don't why, but the man in the hospital from the SCF flashes across my mind.

I try to swallow again. "Guess so," I mumble.

She presses a wrist to my forehead but only holds it there for a second. She tilts her head, frown deepening as her eyes bore into me. "You're warm. Very warm." She hurries off toward the bathroom. "I want you to take your temperature," she says over her shoulder.

I nod then wince at the throbbing it causes in my skull.

Hannah lifts a half-eaten sandwich, dropping bread crumbs on her pink leggings. "Hungry?"

I hold my stomach and press my lips together. "No, no. Thanks though."

I can feel them watching me as I shuffle into the living room and collapse on the couch.

My phone rings from my bedroom.

I groan and half-sit up. "Dylan...?"

"On it." He hops off the island stool and rushes to my room, then comes back to hand me my phone. "It's Ian."

My head throbs even more at the thought of talking on the phone. I clear my dry, parched throat. I should've gotten some water. I sit up and squint against the headache and tap the green phone icon. "Hello?" I croak.

A pause. "Scarlett?"

I clear my throat again. "Yeah, it's me."

"How are you doing?"

There's a soft tap on my shoulder and I look over to find Hannah peeking over the top of the couch. "Are you thirsty?" She holds up a swishing glass of orange juice.

I quickly steady the glass before she spills it. "Just water, please. Thanks."

"Okay." She disappears again.

"Scarlett? Are you there?"

"Yeah, sorry. I'm here."

"You sick?"

"Mhm. I think I caught something from the hospital."

"Man, that came on fast. You sound terrible."

I roll my eyes. "You and Dylan are my biggest supports at times like these."

Mom comes back with the thermometer and I slip it under my tongue.

Ian pauses again. "So other than being sick...are you okay?"

I take a deep breath and close my eyes as the events of last night flash through my mind as fast and furious as a forest fire. Fear lingers in my gut. I take a deep breath. "I think I'm okay." My tongue knocks the thermometer against my teeth and I readjust it.

"You sure you're not hurt? Mom said you weren't burned or anything..."

I gently rub my aching eyes with my fingertips. "Yeah, that's the weird thing. I'm fine. And I should be...burnt to a crisp." Even the doctors at the hospital couldn't give me an answer. Neither could the tests they ran.

"Hmm... that is really weird."

I sigh. "You're telling me."

Mrs. Henley's voice comes distantly on Ian's side, and he pauses to talk to her. "Hey, my mom said we should come over and cheer you up. And I don't think she's taking no as an answer."

I chuckle around the thermometer. With memories of last night vying for my mind's attention, maybe having them over would be a nice distraction. "Cool, fine by me. As long as you guys aren't afraid of catching what I got."

Ian huffs. "You kidding? Mom will equip us with so many of her natural remedies that we'll be invincible."

I laugh and the thermometer almost falls out of my mouth. "Right."

The line falls silent for a moment and I bite my lip wondering if Ian had to endure another rant from his mom after she found out about what happened to me. I don't know how she'd defend the supers in this case, though.

"Hey, Ian?"

"Yeah?"

"You mind if I hang up now? I think I just need to rest."

"Oh, yeah of course! Get better soon. See you later."

"Thanks. Bye."

As I drop my phone on the couch cushion, I slip the thermometer out of my mouth and squint at the results. *118.4.* I frown. It must be broken. "Mom?"

"Yes?" Mom comes around the couch and sits next to me.

I hand her the thermometer. "I think it's broken or something."

Her eyebrows fly up. She blinks and tilts her head. "Hmm...I guess it is." She goes silent for a moment. "Because we know you're not at 118.4," she says with a chuckle.

"Yeah, that'd be weird." I definitely don't *feel* like I'm that hot.

Mom frowns at the thermometer, falling silent again.

"Oh, Mom, can the Henleys come over? You know, to cheer me—"

"Hang on, sweetie." Eyes still on the thermometer, she stands and rounds the couch. "I'm just gonna test this on your brother real quick." She calls for Dylan, voice disappearing as she goes down the hall to his room.

I spend the next hour on the couch, not wanting to exert the energy it would take to get back in bed. Mom gets on the phone with Mrs. Henley and starts pumping every natural remedy under the sun into me—per her recommendation—and Dylan and Hannah generally avoid me for fear of catching what I've got. With the TV on softly, I drift in and out of sleep.

Late afternoon, Mom gives Mrs. Henley a call to confirm the time they can come over for dinner. At that, I force myself off the couch on achy joints and shuffle to my room to fix my knotted hair and change into a clean outfit. From lounge clothes to more lounge clothes. I don't have the energy for more effort than that. I decide to return to the couch to watch TV until the Henleys get here.

The old 60's show is just finishing when the doorbell rings. Hannah skips through the living room to the door before anyone else can and throws it open.

"Well, look at you!" Ian laughs. "So grown up you're answering the door now, huh?"

Hannah giggles and hugs him around the knees. With the girl still gripping his legs, he waddles over to me with a smile and lifts a bright bouquet.

I smile and stand to gently peel Hannah off him.

"Mom thought you'd like these," he says, handing me the cluster of sunflowers.

I finger a soft petal and smile past him at Mr. and Mrs. Henley. "Thank you. They're beautiful."

Ian's parents smile and nod. Mom and Dad come from the hall in time to say hellos and give hugs and the house fills with friendly chatter.

At Hannah's tugging on his t-shirt, Ian hoists her up on his back. She stifles a giggle and immediately starts trying to braid his hair.

I chuckle. "I told you you should keep your hair shorter."

He blinks. "Why? What's wrong?"

"She's braiding it."

"Hey!" He twists his head around, groaning in protest. But it only makes Hannah laugh harder and continue to knot his hair. He gives up his struggle with a weary sigh. "Glad I don't have sisters."

"Yeah. Otherwise you might've even had to learn some manners."

"Why, I take offense to that, young lady," he says in a British accent. "No man is more polite than I."

"Dinner time!"

We turn toward the kitchen at Mom's call. I'm surprised when my stomach gives a little hungry grumble as she pulls the lasagna out of the oven.

Hannah wiggles off Ian's back and runs into the kitchen. Ian grimaces as he attempts to untangle his hair. "Where's Dylan?"

"Dunno. I'll find him." I leave the flowers on the coffee table and go to Dylan's room. The door's open, so I don't bother knocking and stick my head in. "Hey, Dylan, we're ready to eat."

Dylan, sitting at his desk with his back to me, jumps at my voice. When he turns, I catch a glimpse of his laptop screen. A video. There's that SCF doctor again. What was his name? Dr. Bailey?

I raise an eyebrow. "Whatcha watching?"

"Uh..." He glances at the screen then back at me, then closes the device. "Nothing. Food, you said?"

I stare at the closed laptop. "Uh, yeah. The Henleys are here and it's time to eat."

"Okay." He stands and squeezes past me.

I stare at his computer a moment longer before following him to the kitchen. Mom and Mrs. Henley are already sliding generous squares of lasagna on plates, while Dad pairs each with a hunk of garlic bread. Ian cracks open a box of cinnamon rolls.

I gasp. "Cinnamon rolls?"

He grins. "Told you it'd cheer you up for us to come over." He reaches for one of the glorious desserts.

"Not before dinner, son," Mrs. Henley playfully slaps his hand and flips the box closed.

"Aw, come on. Scarlett wants one now too, doesn't she?" He beckons frantically at me with raised eyebrows. "And she's sick so she gets whatever she wants, right?"

Mom hands Ian a plate and smirks. "Nope."

I shrug. "Nope."

Ian sighs and pokes at the blue lid on the dessert box. "Guess I'll just leave room for dessert."

Everyone laughs. Because we all know he'll eat everything on his plate, go for seconds, and still have room for two cinnamon rolls. I just hope he won't eat us out of house and home.

Once everyone has a plate, the parents branch off to eat in the dining room while the rest of us congregate in the living room. I let the others take the couch and sit in the armchair on the other side of the room, just to be safe. The plate of lasagna warms my lap and the rich flavors filling my mouth makes me forget that I feel sick. Not a word passes between us as we hunch over our food and fill our stomachs.

Midway through the meal, Mrs. Henley comes rushing out of the dining room, staring at her cell phone. "Ian, turn the TV on!"

He swallows a mouthful of garlic bread and scowls. "What for?"

She doesn't take her eyes off the phone as she scrolls with her thumb. "Just turn it on. Big news."

I don't miss Ian's sigh as he exchanges his plate for the remote on the coffee table. After a few moments of button-pushing, he gets the national news blaring from the TV.

Mr. Henley, Mom and Dad follow Mrs. Henley from the dining room, all frowning at her.

"What are you doing, Rachel?" her husband asks wearily.

Now she glues her gaze to the TV screen and waves a hand dismissively at her husband. "News, honey, news. Look!"

Everyone goes quiet when that doctor from the SCF comes on screen. He stands with his hands clasped in front of him in the same office I saw him in yesterday on the TV in the ice cream shop.

A reporter with a shock of red curls and nails to match shifts the mic from him to herself as she offers a question. "Dr. Bailey, there have been some rumors about a potential cure in the works. A cure for superpowers. Anything to say on that?"

Mrs. Henley purses her lips and plants her hands on her hips.

The doctor shifts his jaw and hesitates. "There's really not much to say—"

"Can you confirm or deny these rumors?"

"Well..." He fidgets with the smartwatch on his wrist. "There is something in the works, yes. Of course we're always trying to find a way to make this a safer country." When the reporter opens her mouth for another question, he holds up a hand to stop her. "But that's all the information I can give."

As the reporter wraps up the interview, Mrs. Henley throws her hands in the air. "I can't believe this! They talk like it's a good thing. It's like...like...coming up with a cure for having freckles or something."

Hannah wrinkles her freckled nose.

I slide my plate onto the coffee table and knot my hands in my lap. I can feel Ian watching me as I curl my toes against the tan shag carpet and listen to Mrs. Henley rant. You can't compare superpowers with freckles. It's not like that. Freckles can't kill people. Superpowers are a dangerous defect, and nobody wants those.

I look back at the screen in time to catch Dr. Bailey's blank, placid face before it switches to another news story. If there was a cure then attacks like mine wouldn't happen. There are plenty of people who don't come out as lucky as I did. I rub my hands along my arms.

Mr. Henley grabs his wife's wrist to stop her lightning-fast rant. "Honey, I think that's enough for now." He glances briefly at me.

Mrs. Henley doesn't seem to get the hint, but when she opens her mouth to hurl words again, Mom cuts her off, "I think a cure would be a wonderful thing." Her face flushes as she glares at Mrs. Henley. She gestures to me, her voice rising, "If there was one sooner then my daughter wouldn't have been attacked by a superhuman."

Dad places a hand on her shoulder. Mrs. Henley glances at

me. Everyone else does too. Warmth rises to my face and I look away.

Mrs. Henley softens her voice a little. "Yes, what happened to Scarlett was awful. But she could've been attacked by a person without powers just as easily."

As Mom's face reddens even more, eyes sparking, Mr. Henley holds out his hands. "Okay. I think maybe we should just go home now."

Mom turns away and Dad rubs the side of his face while the Henleys prepare to leave. Mr. Henley guides his wife through the front door before turning back to say a timid goodbye to us. Ian's the last to leave, and Dylan, Hannah and I follow him to the door.

He rubs the back of his head and looks apologetically at us. "I'm sorry—"

"Don't worry about it," I say.

He smiles sadly, then looks past us for Mom and Dad. They've already disappeared to their room. Ian swallows and doesn't meet our eyes. "Well, enjoy those cinnamon rolls."

Hannah bounces on her toes. "We will very much, thank you."

We chuckle and Ian offers one last goodbye before closing the door behind him. While Hannah goes to climb onto a barstool at the kitchen island and reach for the cinnamon rolls, Dylan and I stare at the door in silence.

"What was that video you were watching about Dr. Bailey?" I ask quietly, eyes still fixed on the door.

Dylan glances at me, then he clears his throat and slides his hands into his pockets. "It was nothing." Before I can say anything else, he turns away. "I'm gonna go to bed. I'm kinda tired."

"You don't want one?" Hannah says through a mouthful of dessert. She holds out a cinnamon roll to Dylan, her half-eaten one crumpling and dropping crumbs on the countertop.

Dylan shakes his head and half-heartedly grins at her. "Not tonight. You enjoy it though."

I stare after him until he disappears into his room. Replaying the evening in my mind, I settle onto a stool to keep Hannah company. Her endless chatter rolls right over me as I absent-mindedly pick at the last piece of garlic bread on the island. I don't even notice she eats a second roll until she says her stomach hurts.

When Mom and Dad appear again, they don't say a word as they send Hannah off to change into her pajamas and start cleaning the kitchen. When I ask if they want help, they send me to my room too. To rest. But I know they want to talk alone.

I close my door softly and relish in the quiet darkness of my room. But in the quiet, Mrs. Henley's words replaying in my head just seem that much louder. I grimace, thinking of Mom's face as I tug my hair out of its ponytail. Tumbling thoughts infusing exhaustion in my muscles, I shuffle over to my desk, lean my hands on the smooth surface and sigh. Blinking the sting from my achy eyes, I look up at the mirror—and freeze.

A fire-like light glows faintly in my irises.

My breath stills. Mouth hanging open, I lean closer to the mirror and blink several times. It doesn't go away.

I squeeze my eyes shut and rub them with my fists. This can't be possible. I look back at the mirror to find no change. Still the faint orange glow, like a small match flame. I clench the edge of the desk until my knuckles pop. What is going on?

My hands shake as a warmth spreads from my core through my body. I turn away from my reflection, fanning my suddenly heated face. I turn my ceiling fan on high and lie on the floor, spreading my arms and legs out. I close my eyes and let the breeze cool my skin and focus on deep, even breaths.

I'm imagining things. Just imagining things.

But the image of my burning eyes is seared into my mind.

I don't know what time it is when I wake in the middle of the night, still on my back on the floor, arms and legs spread out. The shadowy mass of my ceiling fan smears across my vision, and I try to blink away the blurriness. My muscles tremble as I push myself into a sitting position and look at my clock. *2:13am.* My fingers grope for the edge of my desk as I struggle to my feet. I keep my back to the mirror.

But I can't keep myself from turning. My muscles move against my will, and I slowly look over my shoulder, my stomach already knotting.

No circles of fiery light pierce the darkness. Only the faint outline of my body in the reflection, barely visible in the dark. My eyes are normal.

A breath whooshes out of my lungs, and I fully face the mirror to lean closer. The dim light from my clock casts an eerie red glow on my face. But the fire-glow has disappeared. I touch a hand to my cheek. And I don't feel broiling hot either. Maybe it was all just a dream.

I turn, bringing an onslaught of dizziness, and stumble the few steps to my bed. I collapse into the mattress and sigh at the coolness of the sheets. Sleep takes me again.

My body soaks in the rejuvenating sleep, and I wake late again, after lunch time. Hannah and Dylan surprise me with a special spot set up in one of our comfy armchairs. They gathered blankets, a glass of water, books, the TV remote, and my guitar. I'm not even mad about hands other than my own touching my instruments. This time.

The leather of the armchair feels gloriously cold against my skin, and I sit there enjoying it until it warms. My eyes still ache a little so I don't pick up any books and my muscles are too shaky to pick up the guitar—ukulele would've been better, anyway—so I turn on the TV. It goes to the news and I lean my head back, letting it distract me from the memories of last night.

Surely that was just a dream...

The doorbell chime makes me jump and I open my eyes to see Dylan rush to the front door and open it.

"Hey, Ian!" he says. "Come in."

"Hi. Scarlett around?"

"Yeah, she's in the living room."

"'Kay, thanks."

Ian comes around the door, guitar in hand. He smiles when he sees me. "Hi there."

I hold up a hand. "Don't say I look terrible. I already know."

He chuckles and steps over to sit on the couch across from me. "No, you're looking better." I turn down the TV volume as he sets his guitar on the coffee table between us.

The leather squeaks as I shift to sit up straighter. "So, what's up?" He's got that excited songwriter-on-a-breakthrough look in his eye.

He rubs his hands together and glances between me and his guitar. "Well, I think I..." He breaks off, mouth hanging open.

I blink. "What?" Is it my eyes? My hand creeps to my face.

He points at my guitar still propped up against the wall by the armchair. "You...you're playing guitar again?"

"Ian—"

"You've finally given up those ukuleles? Oh, how I've prayed for this moment!"

"Ian!" I smack his arm.

He flinches away, laughing. "Ew, don't infect me!"

I bite the inside of my cheek to keep from laughing. "You'd better tell me what you came to tell me before I hit you with your own guitar."

He snatches his guitar from the table and holds it against his chest. "Okay, okay, just don't touch Gibson."

I sigh and rub my forehead. "Gotta stop naming your instruments..."

He settles the guitar on his leg and slides his fingers over the fretboard. "Anyway, as I was saying before my prayers were answered..." He clears his throat over a chuckle as I roll my eyes. "I think I finished that song I was working on."

I scoot forward. "Really? Can I hear it?"

He grins and settles his fingers on the strings. "That's what I came over for. I was thinking about playing it for my gig, but only if you think it's good enough."

"Okay, I'm all ears." I turn off the TV.

"Alrighty." He gets his hands settled and clears his throat.

I close my eyes to listen, like I always do. He begins his original song timidly at first, then grows more confident when he reaches the chorus. I find myself tapping my foot to the upbeat tune.

A wave of heat across my body makes my smile fade. My eyes flutter open. The living room swims before me, a soft red haze surrounding my vision. I blink several times and press a hand to the side of my head. The sound of Ian's song grows muffled and all the notes blur together.

I'm so *hot.*

I swipe shaky, sweaty palms on my pants. "Ian..." I breathe.

He looks up, still strumming. Then his hands freeze. "What's wrong?"

"I just, uh..." I give my head a jerk as my thoughts jumble. "Can you get my mom?" My words slur together.

"Sure." He sets down the guitar and runs off, calling for Mom.

My vision tints more red by the time she rushes to my side. Her hand feels ice cold against my cheek as she turns my face toward her. "What's wrong, Lettie?"

I swallow against my dry throat and lick my lips. "Can I have some water?" I resist the urge to recoil from her cold touch.

Almost immediately the rim of the cold glass is against my lips. I shiver as the water slides down my throat and settles like ice in my insides.

Mom sets the glass down and grabs my arms. "Come on, let's get you back in bed."

I can feel Ian watching me as I lean against Mom. "Sorry, Ian. You'll have to play it for me again some time soon." I try to smile, but my cheek just twitches. "I'm sure it's great."

He smiles back, but it doesn't reach his eyes. "Don't worry about it. Just get better, okay?"

I nod. "I'll try."

I hear Ian and Dylan talking for a few minutes as Mom settles me back into bed. She disappears and returns with my glass of water and the thermometer. "I want you to take your temperature again."

I take the thermometer from her. "Isn't this the broken one?"

She sets the glass on my desk and stares at the thermometer in my hand.

"Mom?"

She jolts. "Hmm?"

"Isn't this one broken?"

"Um, yes, but let's just see what it says, okay?"

I nod and set it under my tongue. Mom fluffs my pillows and gets me comfortable until the thermometer beeps. I slip it out and blink sore eyes at the digital face.

120.3

My heart gives an odd flutter. Without warning, the image of my glowing eyes flashes across my mind. Panic clutches my gut. I close my eyes and take deep breaths. Everything's fine. Last night was a dream and I'm just sick. That's all.

Mom takes the thermometer from me and stares at it, forehead wrinkling. She slowly turns her back to me, studying the device. She tosses it in my trash can.

"Mom?"

When she turns around, she plasters a smile on her face. "Well, Scarlett, for now I just want you to try to sleep and rest, okay?" She smooths a hand across my forehead. A flicker of worry crosses her eyes. "I'm sure you'll shake this in a few days."

I nod and let my eyes drift closed as she leaves.

The next several hours pass in a confused haze as I drift in and out of sleep and wrestle with the fever. At some point Mom and Dad came in to check on me. I didn't open my eyes, but I didn't feel any warm sunlight from my window so it must've been nighttime. Their voices sounded muffled, like my ears were plugged, so I didn't catch much of what they said. But I did hear the word "doctor." Mom says something hurriedly after that. At some point a hand is laid on my forehead. I suck in a breath at the cold of their skin and they pull it away.

That's all that happens. I catch snatches of conversation, people touching me, sometimes blurry visions of someone walking past my doorway and peeking in.

I wake with a jolt in the middle of the night. The house is silent except for my huffing breaths. I lay there for several long moments, blinking at the ceiling. Why do I feel so wide awake?

My hands tingle, but for once my skin doesn't feel on fire. I struggle out of the sheets twisted around my legs. I expect the room to tilt with the dizziness, but my head only feels a little light. The ache behind my eyes has all but disappeared.

I gingerly slide out of bed to test my head, and catch a glimpse of my clock on my way to my desk. *4:13am.* I lean my hands against the desk, staring at my fingers. They still tingle.

A faint orange glow covers my hands and the desk. I almost didn't notice it, it's so faint. I narrow my eyes, brow furrowing, and it dims. My eyes shoot wide open again and the light brightens. My jaw clenches.

No. I'm imagining things.

I have to calm down and go to bed, stop acting paranoid and letting my fears make me hallucinate. But against my will, my gaze lifts to the mirror. Two glowing orbs meet me, the fire-glow so bright that it glints in the reflection. I blink once. Twice. It doesn't go away.

My hand clamps over my mouth. What's wrong with me?

This...this can't be related to the attack. Right? I choke

against the tightness in my lungs, trying to find my breath. Maybe something really is wrong. I give my head a hard shake. No. Everything's fine. Maybe these are just some side effects from the attack. Yeah, that's it. It'll go away soon. Just side effects...

But my breath quickens as I turn, dazed, from the mirror and lean against my bedroom door. I've never heard of someone getting powers from being attacked by a super. They just...get hurt. That can't be possible. No one's ever heard of that before. At least, I haven't. I glance at the mirror again. If it's impossible then how do I explain my eyes?

I lick my chapped lips and slide my hands over my arms, over the skin that should've been burned when the fire engulfed me. Still trembling, I crack open my door and peer down the hallway both ways. All the bedroom doors are closed and the house is dark and still. I slip out and pad down the hall.

My socks swish across the kitchen tiles, coolness seeping through the fabric into my skin. With a shaking hand, I swing open the cabinet to the right of the sink and grab a matchbox.

My fingers try to slide it open, but I'm trembling too hard and I lose my grip. The box clatters onto the floor, and the matches scatter. "Great." Hoping no one heard, I pick up the matches and pile them and the box on the counter.

I light one match and a flame bursts to life.

The flame flickers as my hand shakes. A wave of dizziness washes over me, and I press my eyes closed until it passes. My throat stings as I try to swallow. My body begs for water, but I ignore the thirst for now.

I hold the side of my free hand over the small flame. The warmth spreads over my skin, but the fire hasn't touched me yet. Small tendrils of smoke curl around my palm.

My teeth clench until my jaw aches. I lower my hand into the flame.

Nothing.

It doesn't burn.

Stinging tears start to run from my fiery eyes as I run the match over my hand. No searing pain, but a deep warmth spreading through my hand and spreading up my arm. It almost feels...good.

No. I throw the match into the sink and turn on the faucet. The water soaks the small piece of wood until it darkens with moisture, the flame long extinguished. I clutch the faucet head and let the water run. As if it will wash away what just happened.

Finally, I turn off the water and lean both hands on the sink edge. A few strands of blonde hair tickle my cheeks and I shove them away. I stare at the sopping, dead match sitting at the bottom of the sink and bite my trembling lip. This can't be happening.

Slowly, timidly, as if tip-toeing into a dark room, my mind lets in the thoughts I've been shoving away.

What if...the attack changed something? What if it changed me?

I sniff hard and straighten. My reflection meets me in the window above the sink. Two fiery, glowing orbs stare back. With a suppressed growl, I dig my fists into my eyes. *Go away.*

When I drop my hands, my eyes are the same. The flame is still there.

My hands clench into fists. I want to smash that window until all that's left is glassy dust and bloody knuckles.

I force myself to turn away from the window and take a deep breath. My neck aches as I roll my shoulders, trying to release some of the tension clutching me. I just need to calm down. Yeah, this is weird, but it's got to be just strange side effects from the attack. It'll go away and I'll be just fine.

My hands tremble, but I force them to pick up each match, put them back in the box, and put it away. Then my shaky legs carry me back to my room, and I close the door firmly behind me. I slide into bed and rub my hand. The hand that should have been burned by the match.

I try to control my thoughts and the trembling overtaking

my body. But my explanations and excuses snap like over-tightened guitar strings.

My stomach twists, sickened, as my thoughts deadend at reality: my life is spiraling out of control, and I don't know how to stop it.

CHAPTER THREE

When I wake up, my head is clearer, my eyes don't ache as much, and my temperature feels closer to normal. But none of that is on my mind.

Familiar fear slowly squeezes the air out of my lungs as I lie limp in bed. Worries and what-ifs line up in my mind, as if readying to run a dizzying sprint in my head. I squeeze my eyes shut, forcing my mind to go blank.

A soft knock makes me jump. Dylan peeks his head in. "Hi. You're awake." He grins. "How are you feeling?"

I roll over to my stomach to keep my eyes glued to the carpet. What if they're glowing again? I swing my legs over the edge of bed and pretend to rub sleepiness from my eyes. "Better, I think."

"Do you need anything? Breakfast?"

My stomach still feels a little unsettled, whether from panic or whatever's going on in my body, I don't know. I keep rubbing my eyes. "Orange juice?"

I peek through my fingers to see him nod and snap a mock salute. "Right away, ma'am." He disappears.

I take a deep breath and push myself off the bed. Dizziness only lasts for a moment as I cross my room to the mirror on shaky legs, tugging my hair out of its messy, knotted bun. I force myself to look at my reflection.

My eyes still glow. It's faint, like a dying ember, but it's there. I bite the inside of my cheek and glance at the door, hoping Dylan didn't see. He couldn't have. He would've said something. Clenching my jaw, I close my eyes while I wrestle my hair into a ponytail.

I know I should tell Mom and Dad about this; they still must think I caught something at the hospital.

But I'm afraid. Afraid of what will happen if I tell someone. Will I be sent to the Superhuman Containment Facility? The rumors I've heard about that place make me shiver. Cold, dark cells. Isolation. Torturous tests run by doctors trying to figure out how powers work.

A shaky breath passes my lips as I wrap my arms around myself. Maybe this will pass. There's no reason to make a big deal out of this if it's temporary. The glowing is just a side effect of the attack, and it will go away eventually. And maybe my skin will burn again too. Like a normal person.

My hands freeze in the middle of smoothing back my flyaways. I bite my lip as I stare at the faint glow in my irises. My breath quickens as tears sting my eyes. Why can't this just go away *now*? I don't want to be some sort of freak that the world hates. I don't want to be one of *them*. I don't want to be locked up in a cell, dreams crushed and forgotten.

A wave of heat rushes through my body so fast and furious that I stumble back. Beads of sweat dot my face and my vision clouds, the edges tint red as the room tilts. I trip and fall to the carpet on my back.

A small flame bursts from my hand as I hit the floor.

My lungs freeze, a gasp caught in my throat as I stare wide-eyed at the ceiling. I clutch the shag of the carpet under my fingernails and try to control my panicked breathing. My jaw aches as I clench my teeth and squeeze my eyes shut. *No. That didn't just happen.*

Slowly, the heat inside my body dissolves. My sweaty hands let go of the carpet. I swipe my wrist across my slick forehead and sit up.

Dylan stares at me from the doorway, orange juice in hand. His cheeks are pale and his wide eyes search mine. We stare at each other for a long moment.

"Dylan," I breathe. How much did he see?

He takes a half step back. "Lettie, what..."

I bolt to my feet, pull him in, and close the door. Once I take the juice from him and set it on the desk, I grab his shoulders. I look intently in his eyes before I remember the fire-glow still in my gaze.

He recoils.

I tighten my grip. "Listen to me." My voice rasps in my parched throat. Thirsty again? "You can't tell anyone."

He yanks out of my grip, staring at me. "Are you crazy? We need to tell Mom and Dad *now*!"

I grab his wrist, afraid he'll run off before I can convince him. "No, listen to me." I dab my wrist across my forehead again. "You can't tell them. At least, not yet." When my voice quivers, he softens a little. "I...I don't know what's going on." My voice cracks as tears clog my throat, and I swallow hard. "It's probably just some weird side effects of the attack. It'll...go away soon."

His blank stare makes a jolt of panic zip through me. He doesn't believe me.

"Right?" I fight to hold back my sobs, stuff them down, but the tears come anyway, running down my cheeks.

Cautiously at first, Dylan wraps his arms around me and gives me a squeeze. When he pulls away, his eyes are glossy. "Lettie..." He shakes his head. "We need to tell Mom and Dad. Why don't you want to?"

"I just..." I close my eyes for a moment and swallow again. "I need to figure this out. It might pass. We don't have to scare everyone if this is just temporary." I pause. "I don't want to go...there."

His forehead wrinkles under his mop of waves, then understanding crosses his face. "The SCF."

"Just give me some time to figure this out. Maybe it'll go away."

"So you think it's just side effects from your attack?" His voice sounds limp. Unsure.

I nod. "Yes, exactly."

He turns away, chewing his lip. "I don't like this, not telling Mom and Dad."

My fingers knot together. "I don't either. But if it turns out that this is temporary...then there's no need to worry them, right?"

After a long moment, he looks back at me. "I don't want you to go to the SCF either," he says softly. He sighs. "I won't tell them under one condition: that you will tell them yourself eventually. Okay?"

I let out a breath. "Okay, agreed." The word rolls off my tongue before I've made up my mind that I actually will tell them.

He studies me for a while. I can't tell if he's trying to decide if I'm going to keep my end of the deal or looking at the fireglow in my eyes.

Without a word, he turns and opens the door.

"Thank you," I say, reaching toward him.

His face is unreadable. He nods once, then disappears.

I stand still as stone for a long moment before closing the door. My breaths echo through the small room as I lean against the wood, resting my head back on it. What am I doing?

Guilt already hangs on my conscience about keeping this a secret from my parents, but a deep part of me is terrified of telling them. Like actually talking about it makes this more real, more frightening. My heart beats as fast as my worried thoughts fly.

I collapse onto my desk chair and hold my head in my hands. My palms are unusually warm, so I pull them away from my flushed face and flip open my laptop. I don't like all this uncertainty about my body. I need to do some researching.

I log into the computer and minimize the songwriting software I'd left up and open a new tab in the browser. My fingertips hover over the keyboard as I try to think of what I want to search. Not sure what else to do, I type "superhumans on the news" into the search engine.

Countless results pop up. The first video shows more coverage of the attack on the city. With a trembling hand, I move the mouse and click on it. I turn the volume down to a whisper as the video starts playing. I pull my knees up under my chin and wrap my arms around my legs as the events unfold.

The reporter is rigid and fidgety with fear as she covers the attack. People run past her with pale fear plastered on their faces. Her eyes dart to each passersby, as if at any moment she'll drop her microphone and join them.

A pillar of thick smoke rises in the distance.

I squint, searching the background of the grainy video for the superhuman responsible for the attack. A man emerges from the smoke, flying through the air. Balls of fire surround his hands, and his eyes glow bright like twin suns. Something about his thin, raggedy clothes clinging to his bony frame looks familiar. He hovers midair and surveys the chaos under his feet as people scream and scramble away and police yell and point their weapons. Where are the SCF forces? Don't they handle these things?

The super's eyes lock onto the officers. For a moment I think he's going to surrender as the fireballs diminish. He seems dazed as a police officer orders him to land and give himself up.

A shot is fired, and he slaps his hands over his ears as it whizzes past his head. His muscles coil, and the flames flare again as anger twists his face.

As a river of fire shoots from the super's hands toward the officers in the streets, the camera jolts and falls. The reporter and cameraman's footsteps scuff across the rubble as they run away.

I tilt my head, still squinting at the video, now sideways. My fingers knot together as the fire consumes the police officers. I refuse to let my eyes search the flames for human bodies. The fire probably burned them. Unlike me.

My eyes focus on the super as the flames falter. They fizzle out like water drops on hot coals. He slowly descends, head lolling to the side and hands going limp. His descent quickens until he crashes to the top of a building in a puff of dust.

I close the video and bite my nail until I reach skin. The destruction and pain in the video lingers in my mind. I close my eyes and shudder. For a split second, an unexpected flare of anger rises against Mrs. Henley. How could she think superhumans are just like everyone else? I don't care what she says; I hope the SCF finishes that cure soon.

I stare at my trembling hands. Maybe I need the cure too.

With a weak groan, I force myself to turn back to the laptop. I scroll through the other results from my search. There are countless articles about supers: personal encounters, news stories, political stances, and information about the SCF when it was started several years ago. That was long after people decided they were terrified of the powers supers had. They wanted them snuffed out.

My eyes go out of focus as I stare at the screen and my shoulders slump. Does that mean me? Is the world afraid of me? Will everyone I know hate me?

I shake my head to clear it. No, these are just symptoms of the attack. They'll go away. I'm not like them. *I'm not.*

I click on a blog post about a woman's encounter with a super. My eyes ache as I try to read the red font on the purple background. The blogger uses too many exclamation points as she recounts her trip to another city and being held up. Turns out a super came to her rescue. Didn't even ask for money, and she wasn't hurt. A super saving people? That doesn't happen. That's for the comic books.

I skim some more. The writer even goes on to defend supers, saying in all caps, "GOD MADE SUPERS TOO." I huff. I don't like calling people naive, but really. I always hear people say that God is good, so why would He create something so destructive?

I turn away from the blog post to slip my phone out from under my pillow and pull up my social media apps. It only takes a few minutes of searching, scrolling and reading to come to a definite conclusion, one I already knew.

The people scorn superhumans.

I pick at the cracked edge of my phone case. It seems odd that there would be such a void of people who support supers. Mrs. Henley can't be the only one advocating for them. But judging by everyone's reaction to her outbursts, maybe people are too afraid. Maybe it's too dangerous to make such controversial views public.

I drop the phone to turn to the laptop again. My fingers pause over the keyboard. Maybe I can punch in my symptoms. Maybe I'm not the only one who has experienced this kind of thing after an attack from a super. But I don't want that in my search history.

I slap the laptop closed and cross my room toward the door. My hand freezes on the doorknob and I glance at the mirror. My eyes look normal now. Good. I let out a breath.

I try not to act guilty through the rest of the day. Dylan is uncharacteristically quiet and generally avoids me. My temperature still feels high, but I don't feel like I have the flu anymore. The fire-glow doesn't come back, and I keep my hands closed in fists whenever I can. If I don't...well, I'm scared what could happen.

Mom takes Hannah grocery shopping later that afternoon. Apparently the Henleys are coming over for dinner again so she had to run out to get some things. Before she left, she told me I could rest in my room while they're here. What she doesn't say is that Mrs. Henley probably invited herself over to talk about superhuman politics, even after how things ended the day before yesterday. That part I read on Mom's face.

I'm already in my room by the time the Henleys get here. My ears strain to listen to the mixture of voices as they greet each other and move to the living room. I busy myself with cleaning my room to give my hands something to do. The evening is unusually cool for summer, but I quickly get too warm, and I open the windows to let some fresh air in. When I wipe my wrist across my forehead I realize how much I'm sweating.

It's okay. I'm fine. Sweating is a normal thing.

I straighten a stack of sheet music on top of my bookshelf, pausing to slide one off the shelf and let my fingers brush across the handwritten notes. The paper crinkles as I press it to my chest and look up at my ukuleles hanging on the wall.

What if this threatens everything? What if this doesn't go away and I can't become an indie artist? A weight presses down on my shoulders, a knot forming in my throat. If I burn my own ukuleles when I try to play...

I glance at the door. Muffled conversation drifts through; a burst of laughter follows something Ian said. I'm glad they're laughing. Especially after our arguments. Things quiet when Mrs. Henley's voice cuts through.

I bite the inside of my cheek and turn away from the bookshelf. I wonder if I could confide in Mrs. Henley. She's definitely not so opposed to supers like the rest of the world, so maybe I could—

Wait. I can't do that. I slide a hand in my hair and grab a fistful. I can't tell *anybody*. Dylan was an accident.

I collapse on my newly made bed and shiver against the wind drifting in and tickling the back of my neck. I slide the window closed and curl up on the covers, my ponytail spilling over my face. I blow a few strands away with a deep sigh. Why is this happening to me?

My chest tightens and I press the heel of my hand to my

forehead until it aches. Why did I have to let my curiosity lead me to that fiery attacker? Why can't these symptoms just go away? Why am I keeping all this a secret?

I keep it a secret because I don't want my life to change.

I sit up, trying to ignore the warmth building inside me as my thoughts spin faster. The fading sunlight glints off the gloss on one of my ukuleles. I sigh again, long and weary, like it's my last breath.

This problem will just go away. Then I can go back to normal, and this will all be forgotten, like a bad dream. I can go back to writing songs and planning my future. I don't want to be locked away in a cold cell the rest of my days. I don't want to lose my life, my family.

It hits me that I haven't heard Dylan's boisterous laugh through my door. I bite my lip. If only he hadn't seen my flames. I didn't want to add my burden on him, a secret to keep. My chest aches that it makes him smile less.

An invisible weight drags at my shoulders as I push off my bed and press an ear to the door. Silverware clinks against plates, the conversation more sparse as they eat. I wish I was with them but maybe they're safer with me in here.

I listen for a long while, catching snatches of their conversations and pretending I'm a part of it. Mrs. Henley's voice is the easiest to hear. From her I get words like "supers," "cure," "Dr. Bailey" and "outrageous." When the conversation gets drowsy and quiet, Mom's and Mrs. Henley's voices drift as they clear dishes from the table and take them to the kitchen.

A tear forms in the corner of my eye and I press my fist against the door until my knuckles pop. *I just want this to go away.*

A wave of warmth under my skin just makes fists clench harder, trembling with fury. I whirl at the mirror, too upset to notice the dizziness coming back again. I let the anger, the frustration, fester. Heat builds up in my insides, and the room blurs around me. I lean against the dresser under the mirror to keep my balance. My choked panting fills the space.

Heat pools in my palms, and I jerk them off the dresser. Faint char marks dot the wood where my hands were. I suck in a breath and jump away, scowling. I lift a hand to my face and trace my fingers along the lines on my skin. The heat continues to grow, like a burning energy that needs to be released. It swells up, rushing through my veins and making my skin tingle. It grows and grows until I want a way—*need* a way—to release it. Get some relief...somehow...

I tilt my hand so my palm faces up, and I wait...for what? I don't know. I just want the heat to stop, to get relief from the pressure.

In a blink, a small flame bursts to life. It flickers softly, resting in the deepest part of my palm. Energy surges through my body and releases in my hand. The veins on the underside of my wrist glow faintly orange. Pressure, energy, slowly seeps out through the fire. I let out a breath.

My body begins to tremble as I watch the fire. It trembles with me. Now how do I get it to stop? My breath hitches. I raise my eyes to the mirror. The flickering light of the fire casts warping shadows over my face. My eyes glow along with the flame in my hand. I squeeze my eyelids shut.

A soft knock to my left makes me jolt and the door squeaks open. Ian looks in. "Hey, I just thought I'd see—" He stops short, breath frozen. He gapes at my hand.

I whirl around, turning my back to him and biting my lip hard, trying to *will* the fire to go away. My jaw clenches. *Go away.* Finally, I snap my hand into a fist and the flame fizzles out. I slowly turn to Ian.

He doesn't come any farther into my room. Just stares at my closed hand, blinking. "W-what..." He backs away a fraction of an inch.

"Come in," I hiss, glancing over his shoulder to see if anyone's near.

He doesn't move.

I beckon him sharply. "Come on."

He slowly steps in, leaving the door open a crack. His jaw hangs slack as he stares at my eyes. I look away, stepping past him to shut the door.

We stare at each other for a long moment, our heavy breathing echoing off the walls.

"Lettie—"

"You can't tell anyone."

"What?" He croaks. I shush him, but he doesn't quiet. "What are you talking about? When did this start?"

"After the attack."

His mouth opens and closes several times before he finds words to say. "You haven't told anyone?"

My fingers knot together as I shake my head. "No." I pause. "Well, Dylan knows."

His hand trembles as he rakes it through his honey-blond hair. "So you're telling me you haven't told your parents."

Fear makes my heart flutter. "No. They can't know."

Ian's face twists in confusion. "Why?"

"They just...can't." I launch into my next words like it's a script, one I've memorized and replayed over and over. Because I have. "This could be temporary. You know, just weird side effects from the attack. It could go away soon. And if it does, there's no reason to scare everybody."

He huffs, shaking his head and throwing up his hands. "I'm already scared." He shakes his head again. "I don't know about this, not telling anyone. It could make things worse."

I press my eyes closed. "Just trust me." I just want to figure this out without people going crazy.

I've already gone crazy.

Ian shakes his head. "Scarlett, I don't know—"

"Promise me you'll keep quiet."

He hesitates, tapping his fingers rapidly on his leg and biting his lip as he studies me.

"Just for now," I add.

He sighs. "Fine." He points a finger at me. "But you have to tell someone someday. Even if this goes away—"

"It will."

He raises an eyebrow. "If it does, people still need to know."

Ian and I both glance at the door when Mrs. Henley's voice drifts through as she says something loudly to her husband. Ian stares at the floor for a long moment, eyes somber. When he lifts them to mine again, I can't quite read what's going on behind them.

He drops his voice. "Are you sure this is a good idea?"

It's the best one I've got right now. I lick my lips and nod.

He holds my gaze for a long minute, brow furrowed. When he sighs, his shoulders sag. "Okay. Now tell me how this started."

CHAPTER FOUR

I don't want to tell Ian everything. I want to keep it all bottled inside and believe that I'm just paranoid or imagining things. I want to believe that I just have a regular flu and maybe some after effects from the attack that will go away. But once I start, it all gushes out. I start from the beginning, relaying all the details after the attack up until now.

The whole time Ian just listens, silent and unreadable. I try not to let his stiffness stop me; I let the words flow until there's nothing more to tell.

At the end, he takes a half-step back.

My hands twist together. "Please just tell me I'm paranoid or something."

He just rubs his jaw and looks everywhere but at me. I stare at my socks.

"Scarlett..." He shakes his head. "I don't know what to say."

"You promised you wouldn't tell," I say abruptly.

He holds up a hand. "I know, I know. I'll keep my promise. I just...don't know what to think about all this."

I swallow. "Me either."

He finally looks at me. I can tell he's struggling to hold my literally fiery gaze. "I'm sure it'll pass. It's probably just some temporary side effects."

He said the words I wanted to hear, but anxiety still twists my gut. Because the dullness of his voice tells me he doesn't believe it and the glint in his eyes tells me...he's afraid. Of me.

He bites his lip for a moment, studying me. He glances at the door, then lowers his voice even more. I lean closer to catch his words.

"Look, maybe..." He bites his lip again. "Maybe it wouldn't be so bad if you *were*, you know..." He shrugs.

I gasp and take a step back. "Are you kidding? Of course it would be bad if I was superhuman."

He winces. "Keep your voice down."

My voice matches his whisper, but still holds its bite. "How could you even say that? This could ruin my life." It's ruining it right now.

He grimaces and rubs the back of his neck. "I'm sorry. I shouldn't have said that. Just forget it, okay?"

Words escape me, so I just swallow. He turns toward the door.

I reach out. "Wait."

He doesn't stop until the door's between us, leaving only his head to lean in. "What?"

I bite my lip and shrug. "I don't know...Thank you."

He nods, then leaves.

I need to tell them.

I toss and turn in my bed all night, twisting the sheets around my legs. The longer I wait, the harder it will be to tell Mom and Dad about what's going on. I untangle the sheets to yank them over my head and curl into a tight ball.

I don't want them to look at me like I'm a monster. I don't want to see them trying to hide the fear on their faces and tell me lies that I want to hear. I don't want my life to change. I just want to finish high school and go to college for music and write songs. My jaw clenches thinking about how I might have to give that all up.

When I get too warm under the covers, I throw them off and scramble out of bed to sit at my desk. My fingers find my laptop and I flip it open and login. I should try to get some sleep, but I know I won't be able to. My eyes sting from the bright screen as I do more research about superhumans.

I pull up another article and start skimming it. My gaze snags on a sentence.

...nearly killed by her brother's newfound powers, more powerful than anyone could've predicted...

My eyes widen, heart in my throat as I read slower.

Someone discovered they had powers...and nearly killed a family member on accident.

Pictures follow, intermingled with the text. I recoil at the images of a young girl, skin pale as the moon and bloody wounds lining her body in a pattern like lightning. I turn my chair, breath hitching as I swallow. My hand shakes as I raise it to my face.

Could I hurt someone? What am I thinking? Of course I could. I can't turn anywhere without finding stories of supers hurting people. Suddenly Hannah replaces the girl in the picture. I give my head a sharp shake and go back to the laptop, hoping I can find something else that will get that article out of my mind.

I click on another video, a news interview with that scientist from the SCF, Dr. Bailey. He sits too close to the camera, slicked hair shining in the white light and blue eyes piercing. He folds his hands on the desk, resting stone still as the reporter asks him about the scientific progress from their superhuman research.

"We're discovering more and more about superhuman powers," he replies. "Here at the SCF, we're not only keeping the citizens of the country safe, but we're also doing as much as we can to learn more about superpowers to better control them."

The reporter nods. "Some citizens of our country have

expressed concerns as of late, especially after the attack in Hermosa, South Dakota. They're concerned about their safety and the government's job of handling the situation. Any thoughts on that?"

He stares at the camera, unblinking. "Like I said before, we're doing as much as we can to learn more about powers to better control them. The more we learn, the more we understand and can work toward a solution for this problem."

"The solution you're talking about, is that the cure for superpowers?"

He hesitates only a split second. "It could be."

They go on to talk about the state of things at the facility and Dr. Bailey's opinion about other current events. At the end of the interview, despite the reporter's insistence that they're out of time, Dr. Bailey looks intently at the camera to say one more thing.

"Do your part. Superhumans are dangerous and can't be trusted. If you witness superhuman activity, report it. If you are a superhuman," He pauses and his jaw shifts a fraction, "turn yourself in. It'll make things that much easier on you and your loved ones."

My eyes blur out of focus as the video wraps up. Minutes pass and the laptop screen falls asleep. Darkness blankets my numb body. The red light of my clock casts its glow across the room. I can't move. Can't breathe.

I can't stay here.

My heart squeezes as I stand. I run my hands through my hair and my breath returns in a panicked flutter. What am I thinking? Leave my family and my life? That's crazy. I don't need to be so extreme.

Warmth spreads through my body and channels toward my hands. I clench them into fists, glaring at the faint glow in my veins. Why does it always seem this fire surfaces just when I least want it?

"*No*," I croak. "This will go away. Go *away*."

The fire inside me strengthens as my emotions spin farther out of control. The more I frantically try to control it, the more it pulses into my hands until flames seep through my clenched fingers. When the room tilts, I close my eyes and take a deep breath to steady myself.

I can control it.

Flames writhe between my fingers.

I can control it.

My veins brighten with fiery energy.

I *can't* control it.

I need to leave.

I can't try to hang on to my normal life and risk the safety of my family. The soft flames flicker around my closed fingers. The energy releasing through my skin makes my heart steady and my breathing even out.

I *am* one of them. As if spent and exhausted, the flames die out like my last hope of normalcy.

I look at my computer. That doctor said to turn yourself in if you're a super. I force myself to return to the laptop. My finger trembles, hovering over the touchpad. Should I look up how to turn myself in? My stomach gives a nauseating lurch, and I press my lips together. I can't bring myself to type that in. My hand shakes as I slowly scroll more of my search results. I land on an article about Rapid City. My fingers clench at the thought of that city—overrun with illegal supers—so close to my hometown. The article includes some grainy helicopter shots. The streets are empty and dirty and a lot of the buildings are reduced to rubble.

How can people live here? Surely the SCF would've figured something out. But all we're told is that they're not equipped to handle such a large number of superhumans. I study the helicopter photos again. What would that be like, living in Rapid with a bunch of other supers, knowing that their numbers keep them safe?

I shake my head. Nope, don't even think about it. I'm going

to do this right. The SCF is my only option. I'm not going to have my family shamed because I decided to live as a criminal.

When I slowly close the laptop, the clock blinks *5:13am.* My thoughts still spin like a tornado, but I need rest. If I'm sleeping, at least I know I won't panic, and the fire won't come.

I'll think about the SCF tomorrow. I want to talk to Dylan and Ian about it. I don't know why. Maybe because this decision is too big to make on my own. Sheets rustle softly as I crawl into bed, pull the covers over my head and tuck my knees under my chin. I blink at the darkness. I can't believe I'm doing this. Is this a mistake? Is it really necessary?

The image of the girl injured from her brother's powers flashes through my mind. Yes, I have to do this. A tear escapes my eye.

Sleep eludes me. All I do is stare into the dark. My mind jumps between different solutions but always returns to turning myself in.

The girl's scars plaster my mind, but I see Hannah's face in the place of the stranger's.

Despite my lack of sleep, I feel pretty good the next morning. My muscles ache with weariness, but that's all. This gives me a little hope as I enter the kitchen at breakfast time. Maybe I won't have to go through with it.

Mom looks up from cutting fruit on the kitchen island. "Good morning, Lettie. Sleep well?"

I manage to smile back. "Yeah. I feel pretty good."

Mom crosses the kitchen to press her wrist to my forehead. "Hmm. Your temperature feels normal now, from what I can tell." She studies my face for a moment before turning back to chopping apple slices. "Looks like you're finally past it."

"Yup." I watch her pile the fruit on a plate. I'm hungry too. That's a good sign, right?

"Morning!" Hannah tackles me from behind, squeezing me around the knees.

I chuckle and pat her back, then jerk my hand away. *Don't touch anyone.* "Good morning."

She doesn't let go of me when she looks up. "Are you hungry?"

I resist the urge to wiggle out of her grip. She shouldn't be touching me. It's dangerous. I give a nervous chuckle. "Sure am."

"Good," Mom says, pulling a carton of eggs from the fridge.

I watch Mom and Hannah set up for breakfast. Dylan comes in halfway through the preparation. He doesn't look at me as he goes to the cabinet for a glass. "Feeling better?" he asks.

I nod, watching him. "Yes."

The three of them chat while they finish preparing breakfast. I just watch, my feet rooted to the living room carpet. My hands clench tighter at my sides as I focus on taking deep breaths before my emotions get too out of control.

I can't stay here. I can't endanger them like this.

"Scarlett?"

I look up. "Huh?"

Mom frowns at me, looking over her shoulder from stirring scrambled eggs. "You okay?"

I force a grin. "Yeah, I'm fine." I pause. "Um, can we invite the Henleys over for dinner?"

She pauses, frown deepening. "Tonight?"

The sooner the better. "Yeah."

She turns back to the stove and gives the eggs a couple more stirs. When she drags the pan off the hot burner and stares at the wall, I think she forgot my question. Finally, she straightens her shoulders and glances over her shoulder at me. "Okay, I think that would work."

My heart beats faster as my stomach churns. Warmth begins to pool in my palms. "I'll be right back," I blurt and hurry back to my room.

When the Henleys come over, Ian's all smiles when they come in until he takes one look at me. He frowns when he sees my face, then catches Dylan's quiet mood too. I try to put on a more cheerful front all through dinner. Just as the others are finishing their dessert and chatting, I make an excuse to pull Dylan and Ian through the back door.

"What's the matter?" Ian asks as soon as the door closes behind us.

I huff. "Really? You can't guess?"

When he looks down at his shoes, I sigh. "I'm sorry, Ian. I'm just a little anxious."

"It's all right. I know."

Dylan crosses his arms. "Really though, why did you drag us out here?"

All the news, articles, and videos I skimmed over last night flash through my mind at a dizzying speed. That girl's wounds... Suddenly second thoughts creep into my head. How can I leave my family like this?

Dr. Bailey's face fills my mind instead. I *have* to turn myself in. It's my...duty, I guess. At the SCF the world will be kept safe from me. The world and my family.

"Lettie?" Dylan reaches for me. As soon as his fingertips touch my skin, he flinches back.

I stare at him. He looks with wide eyes from his fingers to me.

"I...did I..." I look down at my hands. My veins glow faintly in the night. Tears sting my eyes when I look up at my brother. "Did I burn you?"

Dylan holds my gaze and tucks his hand behind his back. "No. You didn't. I'm fine."

Out of the corner of my eye I see Ian take a half-step back.

I close my eyes and take several deep breaths. If I can keep myself calm, maybe the fire will go away. It always seems to come when my emotions get the best of me. When I open my eyes again, both of them are staring at me. I'm glad the darkness mostly masks their faces. I don't want to see what they're thinking.

I huff a sad laugh. Bitterness laces it. "I guess that kind of explains things."

"Explains what?" Ian asks, softly.

I force myself to meet their eyes. "Explains why I have to leave."

The night silence is deafening.

"What are you talking about?" Dylan's voice turns low.

I bite my cheek and wince. "I mean the SCF."

His eyes widen as his jaw goes slack. "You can't mean—"

"Yes."

"That's crazy!"

"*Shh!*"

He begins to pace. "Lettie, this is ridiculous. That's too extreme."

I jerk my hand up. "Is it?" As if on cue warmth flares inside me and a small flame bursts to life in my palm. I grit my teeth and snap my hand closed.

He stills, staring. "We...we can figure this out. We'll tell Mom and Dad, figure out some way to—" He breaks off and presses a hand to his forehead. "We can figure out a way you can stay."

More tears threaten, and I clench my jaw hard and blink until they dissipate. Still, all I can do is shake my head.

"Do whatever you want to do, Scarlett." Ian's voice is soft like the night, carrying something underneath. Some undertone I can't figure out.

Dylan and I stare at him until he looks between us and continues. "She should do whatever she wants. Go or stay or whatever." He glances at the house before leveling his steady gaze on me. "Don't let society dictate you."

Dylan's gaze hardens. "Don't let society dictate her? This isn't politics, Ian. It's my sister who's gotten sick with these powers, and we need to figure out a way to fix it. Don't be like your mom now."

Ian's eyes spark as his jaw clenches. "I'm just trying to help," he spits.

"Well it's not helping."

I hold out my hands. "Guys, please. Stop it."

Dylan softens as he turns to me, reaching for my arm. "Scarlett, we can—"

I shake my head, pulling my arm away and swallowing the stubborn lump in my throat. "You can't change my mind." Yes, he could. That's why I can't let him try.

"You promised you'd tell them," he says softly.

Ian looks away from us, shoving his hands in his pockets.

"You promised," Dylan says again. "You promised you'd tell Mom and Dad."

I swallow again and wrap my arms around myself. "I know," I say rasp. "I know, Dylan. But look at me."

His forehead wrinkles as he stares deeply at me. As if he's looking at me for the last time.

"I'm not...human."

Ian's head shoots up. "Don't say that."

"It's true."

"You're—"

"And don't say I'm fine because you both know I'm not." I barrel on before they can get any more words in. "We all thought these were just side effects from the attack and that they would pass, but they haven't. If anything, they've gotten worse."

"I thought you were feeling better today," Dylan says.

"I am. I mean, I'm not. Ugh!" I groan and rake a hand through my hair. "I don't know what to think. I don't feel sick anymore, but the fire hasn't gone away. It's...getting stronger."

"Are you sure you're not just imagining it's getting stronger?" Dylan asks, glancing back at the house at a burst of laughter.

"I'm sure."

"Well, I'm not." Dylan turns toward the house.

"Wait! Where are you going?" Ian and I both reach for him. Without thinking, I grab his arm. He hisses in pain and yanks away.

I freeze. "I—I'm sorry. I'm sorry. I didn't mean—"

"It's all right." He gingerly rubs his arm but hides it with a weak grin. Then he sobers, his voice hardening with resolve. "Scarlett. It's time to tell them."

My head drops as the breath leaves my lungs. "Do we have to?"

"Scarlett!" He steps closer, his eyes fierce. "You can't mean that you're going to run off and live in a government facility without a word to Mom and Dad!"

I wince and press a hand to my forehead. "I'm sorry. I didn't mean that." Exhaustion pulls at my muscles and I let my arms slump to my sides. "I'm just scared. I mean, I don't want them to be scared."

Despite already burning him twice, Dylan wraps his arms around me. I tense at first, but the fire inside me calms and I relax. My head rests on his shoulder.

"I know you're scared," he says into my hair. "But we need to tell them."

I take a deep breath before gently pulling away, keeping my eyes down. "Okay."

He studies me, still holding me at arms-length. "Tonight?"

"Tonight."

Little does he know, by the time the Henleys leave and he's ready to talk to Mom and Dad...

I'll be long gone.

CHAPTER FIVE

The air presses on me, weighing down my shoulders, thick and sticky and warm. Still, I shiver.

I scoot farther inside the shadows of the grocery store cloaked in darkness, watching an occasional car drive by. When I slipped out of the house, I just started running. I felt like I needed as much distance between me and my family as possible. For their safety.

I clutch my phone until I'm afraid it'll crack. *Just make the call.*

Every car that passes makes me freeze, wondering if it's my parents looking for me. Maybe they don't know I'm gone yet. At least, they didn't seem to notice when I slipped away while they were distracted by the board game Hannah was getting out.

The phone slips from my hand, slick with sweat, and clatters to the asphalt. I pick it up with shaking fingers and brush it off.

Just make the call.

I wipe my mind blank, emotionless, remove all second thoughts and doubts and fears and dial 911. My hands tremble as I lift the phone to my ear, listening to the warbling ring.

"This is 911. What's your emergency?" The woman's voice is quick and clipped.

Words scrape reluctantly past my throat. "M-my name is Scarlett Marley and I...I want to report a superhuman sighting."

"Where?"

My quivering hand knocks the phone against my jaw. I switch hands and press the device harder against my cheek. "I...it's me."

"I'm sorry, I can't hear you. Can you repeat that?"

I struggle to swallow. "*I'm* the superhuman. I'm turning myself in."

A pause. "You...where are you now?"

I look around myself, scraping a damp piece of old newspaper off my shoe. My voice comes out raspy and raw when I try to answer. I have to clear my throat before I tell her my location.

"I won't struggle," I add. "I mean, I won't resist."

A stretch of silence follows, long enough for me to think she hung up.

"Stay where you are." I blink at the sudden intensity in her voice. At my hesitation, she adds sharply, "Do you understand?"

I nod. "Yes."

After a soft crackling from the other end, a beep tells me she hung up. The phone slips from my fingers to the ground again. I don't bother to pick it up. In fact, I let the backpack I don't know why I packed fall from my shoulders too. I don't think they'll let me keep it where I'm going.

My ears strain, waiting for blaring sirens. I search for the glaring lights. I wait for it all to consume me, swallow me. The guilt finds me first. It wraps long fingers around my throat and squeezes. What will my family think when they find me gone?

A silent, black armored truck skids to a stop in front of me.

My feet twitch to run away, to go back home. I squeeze my eyes shut, keeping myself rooted. I slowly rise. My shoulders tremble as I try to keep my breathing even.

The back of the truck opens and a man jumps down. His black uniform and riot helmet blend with the night shadows. His dark visored gaze settles on me. "Scarlett Marley?"

I gulp and nod.

Arms grab me around the waist from behind, pinning my arms against my sides. The fire inside me, like sensing a threat, flares energy through my veins. I let out a strangled yelp before a sharp prick in my neck makes me stiffen. My vision blurs as my muscles release. My heart thuds in my ears. My mind spins and...

Everything...

Fades...

To black.

My mind is heavy, thickly blanketed by darkness. My head lolls side to side as my mind tries to grasp at half-formed thoughts and memories. My leg twitches, but when I try to move it, it doesn't budge. All my muscles feel hard as rock and just as heavy. A loud clang causes another muscle twitch. A cold, hard surface presses against my back and my legs. The darkness pulls at me to sleep. Why can't I open my eyes?

My body shifts without me telling it to. The cold surface falls away and I float through the darkness. I lower onto a soft surface, and my muscles release an ounce of tension. It's like a cloud cradles my body. Why won't my eyes open?

I try to wake my mind and gather my thoughts into coherent sentences. But the drowsiness is thick and relentless, like syrup dripping over my brain. Silence presses against my ears. Somehow, I get the feeling I'm being watched. It's a nagging itch on my conscience. Sleep gives a tug again, and I almost give in. A muffled voice keeps me conscious.

"Turned herself in." This voice is high and light, a little nasally. A woman. "Fire powers. The super who attacked Hermosa had fire powers." She pauses, leaving the suggestion hanging in the air. "Did they catch him?"

Soft footsteps pad closer to me. My neck won't obey my command to turn my face toward the sound.

"Yes. They found him on his way to Rapid." This second voice is smooth, detached, cold. I've heard it before. Somewhere.

The woman says something, but her voice is farther away, muffled under cottony clouds.

The man grunts. "Interesting."

My resolve breaks. Sleep wraps its gentle arms around me and pulls me under.

My ears ring a piercing note in my aching head. A spear of pain spreads through my skull and pulses behind my eyes. I keep them closed.

Where am I? What happened? Why do I feel so awful? My mind feels like it's stuffed with fluff as I try to get my muscles to move. A soft surface cradles my body. I wiggle my fingers and toes. Something thin and light presses down on me, stopping at my shoulders. A blanket. I shift my cheek muscles and lick my lips. Cold air numbs my skin.

I hear voices. Low murmuring. My eyes finally flutter open. The voices stop as sharp as a muted guitar string mid-note.

My vision opens to a glaringly white, high ceiling. I squint and tilt my head away from the light with a groan.

"How are you feeling?" The soft, female voice comes gently against my ears.

I turn my head to the other side, grimacing against the headache, and look up into a pair of green eyes.

A nurse in dark grey scrubs bends over me, fingertips on my blanket-covered arm. "How are you feeling?" she repeats, a little louder.

I look past her at a man in a lab coat standing near the iron door of the white-walled room. My vision blurs at that distance, obscuring his face. "I'm...I hurt."

"Where?"

I swallow and cough. I need water. "My head...eyes..." I try to clear my throat. That hurts too.

The nurse lifts my head and props another pillow behind it. I wince at the rush of pain attacking my temples. She proceeds to take my vitals and gives me a small cup of water and something for my headache. I watch her turn back to her computer, then scan the small room. The smooth concrete floor, three sprinklers on the high ceiling, the narrow bed beneath me, the chair bolted to the floor, a toilet hidden behind a half-wall of frosted glass, a small sink. And a mirror. I shudder at the thought of seeing my eyes glow again. The shudder turns into a shiver. This is the SCF?

My mind jumps to my family and my chest aches. What did they do when they found me gone?

I pop the pill in my mouth and take a gulp of water. The lab coat man just watches. Stares. It makes my skin crawl.

"Who are you?" I croak.

The nurse glances up at me, before looking at the man. She clears her throat and pulls out a pair of stainless steel bands, with a thick, round piece in the center. A small red light blinks in its middle.

I frown at it. It looks like some odd bracelet, but bulkier.

"It will alert us when your fire powers flare," she says.

My heart skips a beat at those words, but the panic doesn't quite reach my muddled mind.

She slips each bracelet over my fingers, resting the round piece in the center of my palm. She fidgets with it until it tightens uncomfortably around my hand, and the red light changes to blue.

The man steps forward, and I can finally focus on his face. It's that doctor, that scientist. Dr. Bailey.

"Hello, Miss Marley." His voice is smooth, almost monotone.

I lick my chapped lips. "Hello."

His sky blue blue eyes are even more intense in person. I shrink against the pillow.

Keeping his eyes on me, the doctor flicks a hand at the nurse. She quickly gathers her equipment and scurries out of the room. The door's locking system engages with a series of clicks and I'm left alone with the most famous scientist in superhuman research.

He folds his hands in front of his pristine coat. "How are you feeling?"

"The nurse just asked me—"

"And I'm asking now. How are you feeling?"

"I'm kind of just achy all over. My head hurts. And I'm thirsty." Those few sips of water did nothing.

He grunts. "That's to be expected." He takes a step closer and narrows his eyes at me. "Why don't you tell me about when you got your powers?"

I swallow and my parched throat scratches in protest. The memories flash through my mind in a split second. Burning eyes. Roaring flames. Skin unburned. I struggle to sit up, wincing. He doesn't help me.

"I was attacked. By a super." I lift my palm and stare at the blue light. "This came after that," I add softly. I clear my throat and give my head a shake before the memories resurface again. "So...this is the SCF." It's so cold. I rub my arms against the chill.

He strokes his chin. "You had no powers before that incident?"

I struggle to keep his piercing gaze."Right."

"No odd symptoms?"

"No, not before the attack."

"Hmm...interesting." He turns away, slowly pacing across the room, seeming to forget about me for several minutes.

I clear my throat. "What's...what's it like here?" My words are so soft, they almost die in the chilly air.

He barely glances at me, holding up a finger to shush me as he continues thinking and stroking his clean-shaven jaw.

I watch him pace until my eyes stray to the mirror. I don't want that. I don't want to see my eyes. The fiery glow—

"Scarlett."

I jolt and bring my attention back to the doctor.

He sits in the chair next to the bed and his face softens a little. "I need you to tell me exactly what you experienced during and after the attack."

His ice-blue gaze pierces me, making me squirm internally, but I force myself to hide it. I don't want to relive the fiery memories, but I spill everything. From that night behind the ice cream shop to the last time I talked with Dylan and Ian.

When I say their names, my voice dries up like a withered flower. I don't want to cry in front of this stranger, but hot tears sting my eyes anyway. I sniff hard and stare at the light blue blanket, blinking rapidly. Should I have left?

Dr. Bailey places a hand on my arm. I expect it to be cold and stiff, but it's warm, comforting even. "I know it's hard," he says. "I understand how powers can..." he pauses, jaw shifting, "tear a family apart."

I study him, but his gaze holds truth. I swallow back the tears and nod.

He stands and adjusts his lab coat. "I know this is a scary experience for you, but I'm going to need your cooperation."

I take a deep breath, stuffing down my homesickness before it swallows me whole. "With what?"

He turns toward the door and his voice bounces off the walls and echoes above us. "You'll need to stay rested and keep your strength up. We have specialists who know how to handle superhumans so," he glances back at me, "you don't have to worry."

I feel like an animal in a zoo. "Okay." The word trembles.

He offers a brief, purse-lipped smile. "Get some sleep. Tomorrow we will be conducting a series of tests."

I pull my legs up, wrapping my arms around them to get warmer. "T-tests? What kind of tests?" All the rumors about this place and what goes on its basements floods my mind. Needles, dark cells, isolation.

He just bows his head. "You'll see." He turns, polished shoes squeaking, and taps in a password on a touchscreen by the door, then swipes an ID card across it. It lets out a shrill beep before the door swings open.

Dr. Bailey looks at me once more. "Welcome to the SCF, 328."

He leaves, and the door closes right behind him. The thud of the door echoes through the room, reverberating in my chest. I listen to it before things go dead quiet.

A deep sigh drops my chin to my chest. For the first time I notice what I'm wearing. I squirm against the stiff, light grey jumpsuit with elastic drawing in the waist. Numbers stamped above my heart...

In bold, black: *328*.

I'm just a number.

I sleep because Dr. Bailey said so. I sleep because exhaustion pulls on my body. I sleep because I want to forget. Forget where I am, what I am, and what I left to get here.

I have no sense of time when I finally wake up. My brain is dull and lethargic as I sit up in bed. The lights in my room are out, but I don't remember turning them off. In fact, there's no light switch anywhere. When I stand, the bulbs flick on. I grimace and blink at the brightness until my eyes adjust.

My shoes whisper against the floor as I shuffle to the small sink, keeping my gaze away from the mirror. There's only a small stainless steel spout in the white sink, but when I lower my hands beneath it, the water runs. Lukewarm. I splash some on my face. The sensors don't seem to mind getting wet.

I glare at the restraints pinching my hands, wondering what would happen if it sensed a flare of my fire. When I try to adjust them on my hands, the band pinches my skin, and I wince. I clench my hands, resisting the urge to throw the devices across the room. Even if I dared yank them off, they're too tight and I don't know how to undo them.

I huff and drop my hands to my sides. My eyes trail to the mirror and linger there.

The jumpsuit hangs too baggy on my frame. They've slicked my hair back into a tight, low bun, parted in the middle. I move my eyebrows, but the hairstyle pulls on my face, limiting the movement.

I turn away from the reflection of shiny hair, red-rimmed eyes, and slumped shoulders to examine the screen by the door. I tap it and a clock lights up with glowing numbers. *10:34am*. I tap around some more, but it doesn't let me do anything else.

I turn to sit in the chair by my bed and lean my head back on the wall with a sigh, my muscles pinching in protest to my movements. The silence engulfs me. Reluctantly at first, I let in the images of my family. I savor their smiling faces and their laughter. Because I have nothing else in this silent cell.

A soft sound breaks the heavy silence, so quiet my ears barely catch it. My breathing pauses as I strain to catch the murmur again. It seems to come from beyond the wall I lean against. I tilt my ear toward the smooth surface.

Muffled sobs reach me, deep and gasping. The sound penetrates me to my very core. Suddenly the person on the other side of this wall is not just a superhuman, but a person. A person who's afraid like me.

It sounds like a girl. I imagine her my age, broken because her powers forced a wedge between her and her family, her dreams. My eyes sting and I sniff hard. I want to tell her that everything will be okay, tell her she'll get out of here soon. It's not all bad. We'll survive. Everything will be fine.

All lies.

I slide to the floor and tuck my knees under my chin. I wrap my arms around myself and squeeze, willing warmth into my body against the harsh chill of this room. I press my ear against the wall and listen to the girl cry. My tears fall with hers, dribbling off my chin and darkening the knees of my uniform. Will I ever see my family again? Were Mom and Dad ashamed when they found out the truth? Is Hannah afraid of me? I never even said goodbye to her.

That last thought makes angry heat pulse from my core and warm my palms. For a moment I worry that the sensors pinching my hands will go off, but her sobbing quiets. Mine does too. And with it my fire calms.

A beep makes me jolt and the iron door slowly swings open. The nurse hurries in, wheeling her computer stand after her. When she sees me on the floor, she stops dead in her tracks. "Are you—?"

"I'm fine." My voice is thick and trembles, betraying my words. I swallow and scramble to my feet, wiping my cheeks on my sleeves.

She blinks at me, obviously not sure what to do. She just goes about her job silently with tense shoulders. I slump onto my bed and barely notice her as she takes my vitals and checks my sensors. Then she leaves with nothing more than a pathetic pat on my shoulder. I scowl at my shoulder where she touched me. Is everything here so stiff and cold?

Only a few minutes after the nurse leaves, a quiet, persistent beeping pulls me from my thoughts. I frown at the blinking screen on the wall and walk over to it. The clock reads *11:45am*, but now there's a green notification bar at the top. *Meal time,* it reads.

"Prepare to exit your unit." A loud robotic voice makes me jump, the sound reverberating through the room and my head. I look up at the camera angled down at me above the door. Prepare...how?

The thought of going out into the rest of the SCF makes my heart quicken.

"Step behind the yellow line." The feminine computer voice makes me flinch again.

I jump back behind a painted yellow line in the middle of the room. After a harsh buzz, the door swings open. I wiggle my fingers against the sensor straps as the doorway reveals the hallway on the other side.

The hall isn't much different than my cell. White walls, cement floors. Guards dressed in black stand out in stark contrast against the glaring white, hands resting on weapons as they watch the grey-clad superhumans slipping out of cells and settle in a single file line. My feet won't budge.

"Proceed in line to the meal hall."

This time the computer voice doesn't surprise me. I force my heavy legs to move forward into the hall. The door closes behind me, and I resist the urge to beg to be let back in. A line of grey-jumpsuited supers lines the right wall of the hall. A nearby guard turns toward me, and I quickly step to the back of the line. My arms press against my sides as I stand stiff as a board. My muscles loosen enough to lean a fraction of an inch to look down the line. So many. Tall and short. Old and young.

I feel the watchful gazes of the guards, and I keep my eyes away from them, glueing my sight instead to the snowy-white hair of the pale boy in front of me. His stamped numbers stretch wide across his shoulders. I shift my shoulders, feeling the stiffness of my own numbers on the cloth across my back.

With how many supers line the hall, it's surprisingly silent. Barely a breath echoes down the corridor, everyone standing like stone sculptures, waiting for instruction.

The back of my neck tingles, sensing supers filing out of their units to line behind me. Alarms blare in my head, telling me to run, to get away from these superhumans. But I stand still like everyone else, kept in place by the guards' presence.

A loud scuffle breaks the silence, and a girl grunts behind me as she trips into my back. I suck in a breath when she touches me, clamping my arms tighter to my sides. My skin tingles at the thought of other supers being so near. I glance over my shoulder at the girl.

She meets my eyes for just a second. They're red and swollen. Her gaze darts to the nearest guard. "Sorry. I tripped," she says softly.

I study her tear-stained face and dark braids tumbling over her shoulders. The harsh lights above glow against her ebony skin. She sniffs. Was she the one crying?

"Better keep your eyes forward, friend."

The warning pulls me from my thoughts, and I lean over to glance past the girl. A boy behind her flashes an easy smile, mischievous eyes twinkling. He jerks his head toward the nearest guard, tousled brown hair draping over his forehead.

I look at the guard just as his head turns toward our part of the line. I jerk my head forward and straighten my shoulders.

Then the line inches forward. Silently, stiffly, we march down the hall as the guards prod us forward. The lights shine off their helmets and dark visors. Not being able to see their faces just makes them more intimidating. I keep my steps measured—I don't dare touch the super in front of me or behind. But it's hard, because the line is too cramped. A sharp coldness emanating from the boy in front of me makes me want to recoil. Maybe it's just my imagination, just this place. Our steps barely echo, like everyone walks on thin ice over a deep lake.

We enter through a wide doorway into a large room. Sunlight pours from the skylight soaring several stories above our heads. I slow for only a moment to gaze at the sky before a guard shoves me forward. I stumble and brush against the boy in front of me before I can catch my balance. I only come in contact with him for a split second, but an icy chill flares over my skin and I gasp.

He winces and arches his back.

"Sorry," I hiss hurriedly.

He doesn't turn around as he shifts his shoulders. "It's all right." The redness creeping up his neck slowly vanishes.

The line flows seamlessly into the long, grey tables in the hall. Plates of food sit at each place. I follow everyone else, trying to not look so clueless, so scared. The supers sit down as they reach their spot at the tables. The sequence places me at the end of a table halfway into the room, the ice-cold boy next to me. The girl with braids and the brown-haired boy sit across from us.

I scoot an inch or two away from the boy's coldness. Chills still creep across my skin on the side closest to him.

The supers bend over their food, forking the bland, colorless...*whatever* into their mouths. I poke at a mass that looks like mashed potatoes. My appetite flees like a scared rabbit.

I press my knees together and my arms against my sides. I scan the room without moving my head. So many supers. My heart quickens. This can't be safe. I can't believe I'm so close to superhumans. And a lot of them. My knee bounces nervously. My cell, albeit cold and lonely, would be safer than this.

Despite the number of supers in the room, there's only a faint murmur of conversation coupled with the clank of silverware on plates. I raise a smidgen out of my seat to try to see over the heads of the inmates to judge how many there are.

"There's more than that."

I plop back down. The boy with the mischievous eyes watches me.

"Huh?" Not only am I near supers, but I have to talk to them too?

He stabs his spoon in the glob on his plate. "There are more supers than what you see here."

My jaw goes slack. "More? But there's so many in here already."

"They cycle us. Another batch is probably on the outdoor grounds right now. Others waiting for their lunch."

I poke at my food again. "Oh." Sweat breaks out on my back as my heart beats out a nervous tempo. I press my arms closer to my body. So many supers in one place. They could—

Wait. I'm one of them.

"I'm Seth by the way."

I blink at him and try to smile. “Scarlett.” This conversation feels oddly normal.

“That seems to fit someone with fire powers.” The ice-boy barely glances at me, giving the faintest smile.

I raise an eyebrow. “How did you—”

“Well, he does speak after all,” Seth says with a wide grin. Too loud.

A nearby guard glances our way. I duck my head and shovel in a bite, then gag. Haven’t they heard of salt?

“That’s Ares, by the way,” Seth says.

I tilt my head. “Ares? I don’t think I’ve heard a name like that before.”

Seth snorts, smirking at Ares. “Yeah, neither have I.”

I don’t miss Ares’ subtle sigh.

“But it’s a nice name,” I say quickly. “Unique. That’s cool.” What am I doing? What do I care if his name was insulted?

He gives another small smile. “Thanks.”

The conversation falls silent, and some of the tension releases from my shoulders. I try not to think about what I’m putting into my stomach as I scoop in bite after bite.

A sniff draws my attention across the table. The girl with the braids sits almost motionless, blinking red-rimmed eyes at her untouched food. She must have been the one crying earlier. I know it.

Part of me wants to ask her if she’s okay. But that might embarrass her so I keep quiet. I chance another glance over the solemn supers eating their food. None of us are okay.

My stomach growls loudly, but not because of hunger. Like it’s about to reject the gloop I’ve been feeding it. A wave of nausea washes over me. I swallow and press my fingers hard against my lips. A few supers flick glances at me and my cheeks redden. The last thing I want is to empty my stomach in front of all these people. I pull my hand away and straighten my shoulders, but leave the rest of the food for the garbage can.

The clatter of a door opening echoes through the space,

turning heads. Out of the corner of my eye, I watch a guard approach our table from a side door. My gaze flicks to the weapons at his belt. Beads of sweat break out on my skin as his heavy boots thud across the floor in time with my heart.

He stops by me, and I shakily look up. He jerks his head behind him. "You have visitors."

CHAPTER SIX

My head spins as two guards escort me out of the meal hall and through the side door. My quick patter mixes with their thudding stomps and echoes down the narrow hall stretching ahead of us. Iron doors line the walls with numbers stamped on each. We stop at *12*.

The guards unlock the door and lead me inside. A lone, plastic chair sits bolted to the floor in the middle of the small room, facing a wall of thick glass with an intercom speaker in the center.

My parents sit on the other side.

My heart jolts. "Mom! Dad!"

They sit with their shoulders pressed together, hands gripping one another's, trying to smile. But it doesn't reach their raw, glistening eyes.

I lurch toward the glass, but a guard gives me a hard yank back. I barely notice the pain in my shoulders from his roughness when the guard finally lets go. I can only contain myself for a moment before lunging toward my parents again. My hands slap the glass, making my palms sting. The guards pull me back into the chair, then step back against the back wall, gripping their belts and watching.

I turn back to the glass, chest aching. Mom and Dad lean as far forward in their seats as they can, relief pouring in tears down their cheeks. Mom places a hand against the glass as Dad glances back at the guard on their side. Then he looks at me with red eyes, biting his lip as he shakes his head. "Scarlett..."

They hate me for this. I know it. I stare at my fingers knotted in my lap. Suddenly I can't bring myself to look at them. "I'm sorry," I rasp. But I'm not. I mean, I *had* to do it.

"Lettie, *why*?" Mom's choked question makes me look up. They both gaze at me, eyes shining with hurt.

"Why?" Dad repeats, more forcefully.

My jaw clenches. "Look at this!" I raise my hands. I turn them to stare at my palms. Faint red splotches I didn't notice before spread across my palms under the sensors. My voice weakens. "I'm not human. I'm...I need to be here."

They both shake their heads as more tears slide down their cheeks.

I blink back some of my own. My hands slowly drop back to my lap. "Did...did Dylan explain anything?"

Mom looks away and bites her lip, closing her eyes. Dad reaches over to squeeze her hand, keeping his eyes on me. "Yes. He told us everything he knew."

Then surely they see. Surely they understand. "Then why—"

"We could've figured things out, Lettie," Mom whispers. She glances at the guard then leans closer. "We could've...come up with something else."

I shake my head. "No, we couldn't have." My voice shakes. I clear my throat. "Mom...Dad...I have fire inside me. I can't..." I swallow the emotion clogging my throat. The next part comes out small, quiet, scared. "I can't leave." The images of the injured girl in the article are still seared into my memory. I can't let that happen to my family.

They stare at me, unblinking. Dad scoots forward, glancing again at the guard standing behind them like a shadow. "Don't worry, Lettie. We'll figure something out. We'll get them to let you go. Somehow."

I smile sadly and shake my head. "Thanks, Dad, but that's not going to work. I don't think supers ever leave."

Hope sparks in Mom's eyes and she leans closer. "On the news, they talked about a cure. What was that doctor's name?"

Dad nods eagerly. "Yes. Dr. Hiram Bailey."

She grabs his arm and nods. "Yes, him. He said something about a cure, didn't he?"

Hope tries to wiggle its way into my heart. I beat it back like it's a raging bear. I don't want to raise my hopes only to have them dashed to pieces. For now, I should just get used to being here. "That could be years away."

As I watch their hopeful eagerness fade, I almost regret my words. I press my hand to the glass, and the sensor clinks against the hard surface. Working up all the resolve and strength I have left, I plaster on the most genuine smile I can manage. "I'll be fine."

Silence passes between us as we share silent conversations through our gazes. They're hurt, but I understand they love me. And I love them. That's why I left. Whether they understand that or not, I can't read through their eyes.

"Time's up."

The guard on their side steps forward. He gestures toward the door behind him, and Mom and Dad stand reluctantly.

"Don't worry, Lettie," Mom says quickly. "We'll come back soon."

"We promise," Dad says.

I try to give them another smile, but my strength fades as they move farther away from me. "Goodbye."

I hold their gazes until they disappear behind the door.

"Time to go." The deep voice of my guard makes me jump. The guards take me by the elbows and lead me out of the room and back down the narrow hallway. We pass the meal hall, now empty. My stomach gives an odd gurgle at the memory of whatever I ate.

They leave me alone in my cell. The door clangs shut, and I listen, savoring the sound of it until the silence engulfs me again. I can't get the image of my parents' tear-stained faces out of my mind. It's seared there like a brand. Why did this all have to happen to me? My hands curl into trembling fists, and I kick the wall.

Toe throbbing, I hobble to the chair and sit. Was this all a mistake? Could something have been worked out like Mom said? I shake my head hard. This was the only option. The only way to keep my family safe from myself. Like Dr. Bailey said in the video, I was supposed to turn myself in. I did the right thing. But I still feel rotten inside.

My head falls back against the wall as tears stream silently down my face. They drop onto my chest, darkening my stiffly ironed uniform. Does the rest of my life just hold endless days in this cold, white and grey facility?

I barely notice the beep before the door opens. The quick, nervous steps and squeak of wheels tells me it's the nurse. I don't open my eyes until a second pair of footsteps piques my interest.

I lift my head to see Dr. Bailey watching me from behind the nurse as she quickly goes through her routine. I scrub the tears from my face with my sleeve and hold the doctor's gaze. Once the nurse finishes, she leaves without a word.

Silence hangs between me and the doctor. Suddenly I get self-conscious and wipe my sleeves over my face again to get any residual wetness. "M-more questions?" I ask, my voice hoarse.

"Are you all right, Scarlett?"

I'm a little surprised by this question, spoken gently. He still stands stiff as a board, but his eyes have softened.

I swallow and look down at the wet spots on my uniform. "My...parents came to visit me," I reply softly.

He doesn't say anything for a long moment. "Do you need anything?"

Nothing you can give me. Except... "I heard you say something on the news about a cure for superpowers. Is that true?"

He nods. "I said it. So it's true."

"So do you think... I mean, how long—"

"I don't think I can give you that kind of information."

My shoulders droop. "Oh."

I go silent, staring at my lap, feeling him watching me. He sighs and glances at the camera above the door before stepping closer.

"Listen, Scarlett," he whispers. "Some things we can't be sure of. A lot of things, actually. But..." He hesitates. "Yes, we are working on a cure. And we may be close. Very close." He pauses. "There's just one more hurdle we must overcome."

I blink at him, scrambling for a hold on the chair to push myself to my feet, gasping, "Really? You're close—"

He frowns and waves me back down in the chair. I sit, but my knee bounces violently as my mind spins with the possibilities. But why the secrecy? Why won't he tell me more?

Clearing his throat loudly, he slips a small tablet from his coat pocket. The glow of the screen illuminates his face as he taps the surface. "I'm going to ask a few more questions about your powers." His voice returns to normal volume. When I just stare at him, he looks at me and clears his throat.

"Okay." My fingers knot together again.

"So...your fire." He looks back down at the tablet. "How controllable is it?"

I blink. "It's not really."

He looks up.

"Well, I don't know how to control it." And I don't want to.

He just blinks. "So you've never tried to use it?"

"Well...yes." I forgot I'd told him everything.

"And?"

I squirm. "I guess I did manage to make a small flame."

"But you don't know how to control the output of fire?"

"No."

He grunts and continues to stare at the tablet screen, seeming to forget me for several minutes as he bends over the device just like he did last time.

I clear my throat. "Dr. Bailey?"

"Yes?" he mumbles, still not looking at me.

"How much do you know about powers?"

His forehead wrinkles as he continues to stare at the screen, and I realize it was a dumb question to ask of the leading scientist in superhuman studies. "Why do you ask?" he says.

"I just..." My voice fades to nothing. I just want to understand what's going on inside my body, about this fiery energy flowing through my veins and ruining my life. It's like I have a disease that I know nothing about. I take a deep breath and wrap my arms around myself. "Do you have a guess about when the cure might be finished?"

He sighs. "Be patient. You'll know soon enough."

But I want to know now. *Need* to know now. I swallow down demands I know are unrealistic. "Okay."

A small smile lifts the corner of his mouth as he slips the tablet back in his pocket. "You should get some fresh air and sunshine."

I smirk. "You sound like my mom." A sharp pang hits my gut. My smile drops.

I can feel him studying me for a moment before he turns toward the door. "This segment of units will be let out soon for outdoor time."

"Units?"

He looks over his shoulder, fingers hovering over the screen on the wall. "The cells."

Oh. I guess "units" does sound better.

But I don't want to go outside and be close to those superhumans again. I just want to stay away from them and sit alone in my...*unit*.

I look up to find him watching me. He lifts a tight-lipped

smile. "You need to take care of yourself, Miss Marley. Do as I say."

I nod. He leaves and the door cranks closed behind him. As the sound of the locking mechanism fades, the silence presses against my chest once again. I find myself breathing harder, just to hear the sound of life. Maybe I don't want to be alone after all.

Dr. Bailey was right. Only a few minutes after he left we're let outdoors. I keep every part of me as tight to my core as I can to avoid touching any of these supers. The knot in my stomach only grows as we get closer to the outdoor grounds. Isn't it dangerous to have supers in an unenclosed space? It's probably dangerous either way, no matter where you keep them.

The outdoor common ground is larger than I expected, easily the expanse of a football field. Numerous guards line the perimeter, standing just as strong and ominous as the building surrounding us on all sides. A dull wind tugs gently at the few wisps of my hair that have escaped the tight bun. My fingers itch to let it loose and feel the breeze through it properly. Grey clouds cloak the sky, casting the area in pale sunlight. A few clusters of trees dot the grounds and some supers sit under their branches or at rough picnic tables. Others sit in groups and talk, while some play basketball on a faded, cracked court. A circular flower garden draws my gaze, and even in the pale light the assortment of wildflowers seems bright. I almost move toward that direction, but most of the supers gather near it and my stomach knots tighter.

I hug myself and move away from the crowds to settle onto the grass under a tree and watch the basketball game. The boy I met at lunch, Seth, jokes with the others as he plays. His unruly brown hair and easy smile reminds me of Dylan and I smile a little. The girl with the long braids sits alone closer to the court, shoulders sagging as she shyly watches the players.

Seth catches sight of her. "Hey! Wanna play?"

She stiffens and shakes her head.

"Aw, come on. We have an uneven number."

She shakes her head again and looks away, tucking her knees under her chin.

Seth sighs, then his eyes fall on me. "How about you?"

Now it's my turn to stiffen. He doesn't realize I'd be no good on his team. I don't do physical activity. I'm a musician. Well, I *was.*

I glance over the other supers playing with Seth, all with the same kind of sensors around their palms. Even if I was good at basketball, I wouldn't play with *them.*

My face reddens under their gazes. "Uh, no thanks. Not this time." Not ever, probably.

He shrugs. "Okay." He snatches the ball from a girl with a long, dark braid and dribbles off. With the attention away from me, I relax a little and lean back against the rough tree bark. I satisfy myself with watching the rough basketball game and thinking about ukuleles and song lyrics.

A biting cold slithers over me. My muscles go tight and I wrap my arms around myself. *What is that?* Shivering, I look around, craning my neck to see around the other side of the tree.

The boy with snowy hair and pale skin sits against my tree, leaning his head back on the bark. He sits for a moment, then roughly shoves up his jumpsuit sleeves. His cheeks flush pink, and he swipes a hand across his forehead then jolts upright and turns around. His eyebrows raise. "Oh, sorry. I didn't mean to take your spot."

My teeth-chattering knocks my words as I respond. "No, you-you're okay."

He studies me. "No, I don't think so. We have opposite powers. They don't often react well being near to each other."

I try to stop my shivering but the chill is settling in my bones. "Um, yeah."

Ares stands. "Don't worry. I'll move." His skin returns to its frosty white complexion as he moves to a different tree.

He seems nice enough. I could've said something more than that, but I'm safer if I just stay away from them.

I tuck my knees under my chin, still hugging myself, until my warmth returns. It spreads through my body from my core and my skin tingles as if I'm sitting near a campfire. I take a deep breath and close my eyes.

A blaring alarm makes my eyes fly open. I bolt upright and frantically scan the grounds, heartbeat slamming my chest. My ears ache against the loud alarm pounding my eardrums. Light grey flashes past me, and I turn to watch a tall, thin super stumble toward the middle of the grounds. Supers close by scramble out of the way, watching wide-eyed as guards sprint after him and tackle him to the grass. He screams and writhes as they try to control him. His crazed eyes stare unseeing at the sky.

"Please let me out, please let me out," his cracking voice repeats over and over. "Please let me out!"

More guards rush from their stations on the perimeter, pointing guns at us and shoving us into lines. We scramble to obey. The alarm makes my heart stutter with every beat. I stand frozen and stiff, staring from the weapons pointed at us to the frantic super still struggling against the guards. The black uniforms crowd closer to him, blocking my view of his writhing body. One guard pulls a weapon from his belt and thrusts it at the man. After a sharp buzz, his body goes rigid, then slumps limply. Roughly, the guards pick him up and carry him away.

My arms shake at my sides. Was he so desperate to get away? I scan the buildings soaring above my head. Doesn't he know that this place is impenetrable?

My fingers tremble as I rub my temples and stare at the grass trampled from their struggle. Is this my future?

CHAPTER SEVEN

My hands won't stop shaking.

The blank, white wall of my unit only serves as a better screen to replay the event on the grounds. The man...his body trembling, eyes frantic. And his words...I shiver. How long has he been in the SCF?

No matter how hard I try to block the thoughts out, I can't help but think about how the rest of my life will go. Will I go crazy in this cold facility? So frantic to leave its thick walls that I lose my mind? My fingers tremble as I slide them over my hair, turning in a circle. With wide eyes I take in the room. White, white, white.

In a snap my fingers closed, clutching my hair, pulling it out of the pristine bun. Heat rushes through my veins and sparks in my palms. A frustrated scream builds in my throat.

A sharp beep makes me freeze. I lower my hands to see the sensors on my palms blinking rapidly. *Deep breaths, Scarlett, deep breaths.*

I stare at the camera above the door, angled at me. Slowly, controlled, I smooth back my hair and do my best to restore the bun. I roll my shoulders back and walk calmly to the bed to sit.

It's okay. Everything's fine. I'm not going crazy. Not yet.

The silence is deafening, threatening to crack my new resolve. I stand to pace, glancing between the iron door and the screen displaying the time. The camera's eye is always watchful, and knowing someone's watching my every move makes the back of my neck tingle.

As my heartbeat steadies and my breathing evens out, a numbness cloaks me. Bored, tired, exhausted numbness. Will I become like that crazed super? Will my family see me on the news as an insane super kept behind bars? What do they think of me now?

I let out a frustrated groan. My brows pinch in concentration as I try to keep thoughts of my old life out of my mind. Dwelling on that *will* make me go crazy.

The steady beat of my pacing footsteps reminds me of my metronome. An ache builds in my chest. An ache for music, my instruments. To just play and forget. I begin humming snatches of songs, closing my eyes until the melodies wipe my mind blank. Without thinking, my humming slips into the song Ian wrote, the one he tried to show me for his first gig. I wonder how that went. I'm sure he was a big hit.

I groan and grit my teeth as homesickness squeezes me again. I press my fists against my head. *Stop thinking about them.*

I lower my hands when the door opens and Dr. Bailey slips in. His gelled hair and silver tie clip catch the light as he steps over to me. He holds up a small, unlabeled jar in his hand.

"I've got something for you," he says with a slight grin.

I flop on the bed and scowl at it. "What is it?"

His smile falls away. "For your hands."

I huff. "What? Will it take away the fire powers?" I cross my arms and turn my scowl to the wall.

He raises a blond eyebrow and tilts his head, studying me. Then dismisses my bad mood with a chuckle, like a deep staccato note. "No, Scarlett, it won't." He sets the jar on the bed and bends over my sensors, fiddling with the clasps.

I watch him unlatch the bands, revealing the red splotches

on my palms. My jaw clenches as I stare at the discoloration. "So...what's the glop for?"

"Fire powers aren't an uncommon thing around here." He unlocks the other cuff. "We're not completely sure why yet, but this seems to create inflamed patches of skin on the person's hands."

My hands clench until my fingernails bite into my skin. Like I needed another reminder of what I am. "So that stuff will help?" I try to keep my voice even, but it still shakes.

"Yes." He picks it up and hands it to me. "Put a small amount of this on the red areas."

I take it from him and twist the lid off. A tingly, chemical smell pinches my nose as I stare at the pale, grey goop. Is everything around here a lifeless, dull color? I dip a finger in and suppress a grimace as I slather it onto my palms.

Dr. Bailey watches in silence, hands clasped behind his back. My frustration only sharpens as he continues to study me. In the silence that follows, thoughts of my family press again. I shove them away. Except one.

"Dr. Bailey?" I scoop some more of the mixture for my other hand. "My parents...they said they'd come back to visit." Eager to be rid of the greasy, slick feeling on my fingers, I hurry through the application and screw on the lid. "They, um...haven't come back yet." I wipe my fingers on my pants.

His forehead wrinkles faintly for a moment. "Are you sure they wanted to come back?"

I gape at him. "Of course they want to come back!"

"Now calm down." He holds out his hands as if soothing a nervous horse. "Some families...Well, they'd rather forget their superhuman relatives exist."

My teeth grind together. "They're not like that."

He smiles like I'm a naive little kid holding on to some vain hope. "I'm sure they're not."

My anger sparks, and it takes everything in me to make sure

my fire doesn't follow suit. "Don't look at me like that. I know my parents. They said they'd come back."

As he studies me, the patronizing look slowly fades. He nods. "Okay, I understand. But you see, Scarlett..." He steps closer, rubbing a finger along his nose in thought. "Sometimes we limit the visitation of family members. It helps them separate from their superhuman relatives. Helps them heal faster."

Words bottle in my throat, hot and stinging. I'm not sure which ones to let out first. The only sound I manage to make is a strangled grunt. Does my family need to heal from me? Learn to forget me? I remember again the incident of the crazed super on the outdoor grounds. Maybe they *should* just learn to forget me.

As I stare at the wall in silence, he takes the jar back and slips it into his pocket then secures the sensors back over my palms. "A nurse will bring this back tomorrow for another application." He turns back toward the door and punches in a password on the screen, blocking my view. "In the meantime, I want you to get some sleep."

As he shifts out of the way again I see the clock reads *4:15pm*. I frown. "Now?"

He turns back toward me as the door cranks open. "Yes. We will be running some tests later on, and I want you to be rested."

My heart gives a nervous flutter. "Tests? What kind of tests?"

"The cure, Scarlett," he says softly.

My eyes widen. They're going to use me to further progress on the cure? I think I should feel honored, but a smear of fear still clouds my thoughts. "What kind of tests?"

He must notice the worry in my voice or the fear in my eyes. "You don't have to worry."

But I do. Before I can ask anything more about these tests, Dr. Bailey slips through the door, and I'm left in solitary silence again.

When I look at the crumpled sheets on the bed, a wave of exhaustion washes over me. Sleep could mean forgetting nightmares or recalling them. I hope this time it'll just help me forget for a little while.

When I crawl into bed, the lights flick off. It feels weird to be sleeping at this time of day, but weariness seems to always pull at my muscles. Fear still wiggles in my gut at the thought of undergoing tests in this facility. Rumors fan the flames of panic as I wonder where they'll take me, what they'll do to me.

I shake my head to clear it and settle deeper under the covers, tucking them over my shoulders. I close my eyes and let sleep come, trying to ignore the growing itchiness on my palms.

I jolt awake, robbed of my deep sleep. My unit door's creaking echoes louder in the dark stillness of night. Wait, is it night?

My head spins as I sit up and squint against the white light pouring through the open door way. The clock screen reads *3:24am.* I've been asleep all this time?

The dark silhouettes of four guards march into my unit and stand in a line. One steps forward. "You'll be coming with us."

I swing my feet to the floor, glancing between their dark visors. "Where?"

He doesn't answer. Just looks down at me with feet spread and hand resting on his gun. I gulp and slide out of bed. They circle me and guide me out of my unit and down the silent halls, steps echoing off the walls. The steady, methodical rhythm of our march matches my thudding heartbeat. They must be taking me for the tests. My steps falter.

I try to keep my breaths even, but my heart pumps out of control. The guards take me through parts of the facility I haven't seen yet. One turn leads us down a hallway ending in shiny elevator doors. A guard punches in a code on the screen and swipes an ID card. The doors slide open, and I'm shoved inside. We slip down, down into the belly of the SCF. I'm sure in the silence the guards can hear my thudding heartbeat.

We finally stop and the guards prod me out and down more hallways. The ceiling is lower here and a new, stronger coldness seeps into my bones. I suppress a shiver.

The guards stop me at a pair of silver double doors. A guard enters another code on a pad on the wall and both doors swing open.

I gape at the confusing mix of screens, tables, gadgets, and shelves lined with bottles of who-knows-what. Dr. Bailey stands in the midst of it all, staring at the largest screen on the opposite wall. He turns and grins when he sees me.

"Ah, good!" He dodges cluttered desks toward a blue cushioned reclining chair on the left side of the room. Restraining straps hang down the sides of it like dead spider legs. "Come in, come in."

A guard has to shove me to get my feet working. My mouth goes dry and heat pulses in my hands as I force myself to move where I'm told.

"Calm down, Scarlett."

I tear my gaze from the chair to the doctor. "Huh?"

He nods toward my hands. I look down to see the light blinking rapidly, frantically. My fire coils underneath my skin, pulsing heat through my stiff muscles. As much as I crave the warmth in this cold room right now, I close my eyes and focus on calming myself until the fire goes away.

Dr. Bailey rests a hand on the back of the chair. "Have a seat."

I glance between the doctor and the chair before deciding it's probably best to do as he says. I cautiously climb in and settle into the squeaky leather. It's surprisingly comfortable.

"Good." Dr. Bailey stands at my side and looks intently at me. "How are you feeling?"

I'm going to get tired of that question real fast. "Sleepy. Why after three in the morning?"

He chuckles softly through his nose. "Secrecy." His cheerfulness dissolves as his gaze intensifies. "This must be kept a secret."

I blink at him.

"You are to say nothing of your visits here," he adds. "Understand?" The white light overhead casts eerie shadows over the doctor's features, making his cheekbones appear sharper and his eyes more sunken.

My mind doesn't even consider anything else before I nod. "Okay. I understand."

He nods, once and slow. "Good."

When he steps out of my line of sight, panic clutches my middle. Warmth bubbles in my core, and I take a deep breath. "Dr. Bailey?" I hate how my voice goes high and trembles like a child.

"Hmm?"

"You said there was one more hurdle."

A pause. "Hurdle?"

"Yeah, until the cure was ready?"

He pauses again, this time longer. "And your question is...?"

"What's the hurdle?"

He doesn't say anything for a long moment, and I wonder if he forgot about my question. Then he speaks, and if it wasn't for the echo in this room his words may have been lost, "You'll find out very soon, Scarlett."

There's a finality, a firmness in his tone that keeps my other questions at bay. I twist in the chair to try to see him. "What exactly are you going to do?"

"Now, now, don't be so alarmed." He comes back to the chair, snapping on a pair of latex gloves before turning his back to me again to busy himself with some junk on a small table.

I try to look around him. "You didn't answer the question."

He looks over his shoulder at me. "I guess I didn't." He turns back around with two black objects the shapes of small eggs. He nods to one of the guards, who steps forward to remove the sensors from my hands. I flex my fingers, happy to let my bones expand.

Dr. Bailey slips both egg-like objects into my palms and closes my fingers around them. "These are just more sensors." He opens a small box and takes out a handful of small, silver discs. He presses them on different parts of my head, neck and arms. The adhesive feels thick against my skin and I resist a grimace.

"More sensors," he explains.

I lick my lips and try not to panic, keeping my breaths even. He picks up a tablet and taps around on it, glancing between it and the sensors on my body. I wonder if he can see that my heart rate has skyrocketed. I take another deep breath and lean my head back.

"Calm down, Scarlett. No need to be so dramatic."

I look up to find him smiling reassuringly. I try to smile back, and some of the tension releases from my muscles.

My skin starts tingling under each of the sensors, but I wonder if it's just my imagination. I stay focused on taking even breaths and relaxing every muscle in my body.

Dr. Bailey steps closer to check the placement of the egg sensors in my hands. "Now, I want you to gently try to channel your fire into your hands."

"Wait, what? You want me to use my powers?"

"Yes."

"But I don't want—"

"It's for the test, Scarlett. It'll be fine."

My hands tremble. "S-so for the cure?"

He nods slowly. "In a way, yes." He looks sternly at me. "Now, channel your fire into your hands."

"That's where it always goes anyway."

He sighs and nods. "Go ahead."

I swallow and stare ahead, deciding Dr. Bailey's expression doesn't allow for more arguments or questions. His steady gaze on me threatens my focus, so I close my eyes to concentrate. I don't know how, but I coax the fire in my core to flow through my veins and pool into my palms. The smooth sensors warm and I open my eyes to see my veins faintly glowing. My heart skips a beat.

"Stop."

I flinch at Dr. Bailey's sharp order. The fire fizzles out instantly. I blink up at him, feeling the cold of the room overtake me again as he enters information on his tablet.

Breathing hard, I stare at my arms. The glowing is gone. How'd I even do that?

"I thought you said you couldn't control it." Dr. Bailey breaks into my thoughts.

I frown, still staring at my hands. "I didn't think I could," I say quickly. I can't. I don't want to.

"Hmm." He slowly turns away, still distracted by his tablet, to the nearest computer. I can't decipher any of the things on the screen's display.

I adjust in my seat to keep him in view. "So...is that it?"

"Hmm? What?" He looks at me like he forgot I'm in the room. "Oh, no. Definitely not. We have a lot more to do."

My stomach does a little nervous flip. This test was easy enough, but what more does this scientist have in mind?

The minutes tick by and blur into hours. At some point the sleep I didn't get to finish catches up with me, and I can't keep my eyes open. Dr. Bailey continues with his tests silently, like I'm not even here. I'm vaguely aware of him moving about the room and attaching different sensors against my skin. The soft cushion cradles my head as I drift in and out of sleep.

Rubbery fingers touch my arm. "Scarlett." Now a little shake. "Wake up."

I drag myself out of my sleep and for a moment I don't remember where I am. I blink against the white light above me and try to get Dr. Bailey's face into focus. "Huh?"

"It's time to go."

I try to sit up, then remember the restraints when they tug against my limbs. "Back to my unit?"

"No, we have one more test." He nods to the guards and they step forward.

I tense. "Where?"

Dr. Bailey's voice moves to the other side of the room. "You'll find out."

Drowsiness still clouds my brain as the guards unstrap me and half-drag me out of the room. They guide me by the elbows and I scramble to keep my feet under me as they march down the hall. They finally stop at a thick iron door and a guard breaks out of the group to unlatch it. They practically toss me in.

I trip over myself and collapse on my knees on the concrete floor. I wince and gingerly get back on my feet. I look up and gape at the enormous room. All sides are concrete; ceilings, walls, floor. Even though my shoes shuffle softly against the floor, the sound echoes off the walls and up to the ceiling, at least four stories high. There's a large viewing window almost as long as the wall, halfway up to the ceiling.

Behind it, Dr. Bailey looks down at me. The glint of the light off the glass blocks his face. "Hello again, Miss Marley."

The echo of his voice over the speakers makes me press my hands to my ears.

He doesn't waste any time with explanations. "See that target on the wall?"

A painted black circle as wide as my arm span covers the wall to my right. I look back up at the glass and nod.

"I want you to direct a fire output toward that target."

"You've got to be kidding." This place is so cold. "Just because I can get my veins to glow and maybe create a flame doesn't mean I can *shoot fire*." That sounds so ridiculous saying it out loud.

Dr. Bailey's sigh comes across loud and clear on the speaker. "*Try*, Scarlett."

My jaw clenches and I sigh, hoping he can hear mine too. I

turn toward the target and walk toward it, stopping ten feet from it.

"Anytime you're ready."

I'm not ready. I will never be ready. I'm not even supposed to be using my powers, and I don't want to. I don't need any reminders of what I've become.

I raise my hand, palm facing the center of the black dot. I press my lips together, trembling. This feels so wrong. So backward. I should be suppressing this fire raging inside me, not stoking it. Dylan's face flashes in my mind, the flash of fear in his eyes when I accidentally burned him. When I told him I belonged here.

I wish I had been wrong.

"Scarlett?"

I blink back to the present. "Yes?"

"Are you all right?"

The cold in this room makes my joints stiff and I flex my numb toes. "I'm fine."

"Why the hesitation?"

I clench my teeth. "This isn't the easiest thing in the world, you know."

"It should be. The fire is part of you."

I throw a glare at the window. "No, it's not," I snap. "I never wanted this. It was an accident." The fire is just a defect.

He pauses. "Relax. Take a deep breath and try once more."

I never tried in the first place, but I do as he says. The deep breath doesn't do anything to calm me, instead my frustration grows like a roaring forest fire. I clench my left hand against my leg until my fingers ache, and raise my other hand toward the target again. I wait. No fire.

"Concentrate."

"I'm trying!"

I close my eyes and block out his interruptions. It's like any heat inside me has curled up into my core, unwilling to emerge to the surface where the cold air will meet it. I frown in concentration, not even really sure what to focus on, and my hand trembles with the effort.

Slowly, like a gradual but steady crescendo, warmth spreads through my body. It scares me that I can make it obey, that I can make the fire in my body rise up. The odd mixture of fear and anger roiling in my stomach makes me nauseous.

"Harder, Scarlett."

I don't turn my attention to Dr. Bailey for fear of losing concentration, but his comment makes more anger flare up with my fire.

A flame shoots from my hand.

I stumble back from the force and almost lose my footing. The flame fizzles out with my break in focus. I gape at the black char marks streaking the wall. I've got terrible aim.

"Very good," Dr. Bailey mumbles. I imagine him typing on his tablet during the next stretch of silence.

I raise my hand to stare at my palm. Where the cream had been making the red splotches fade, they come back all the stronger now. My fingers tingle with residual warmth. My breath stills, and I swear I can feel the fire inside swirling around just under my skin, as if to ask if it did what I wanted before going back into hiding. It's like a pressure I didn't know had built up is released. My breath comes easier. I look again at the char marks just outside the black target.

It almost felt...good.

I grind my teeth and let my hand fall. No. Nothing about this is good. I look up to the viewing window. "Are we done?" Weariness clouds my voice.

Dr. Bailey steps into a part of the window that isn't hidden by the light glare on the glass, and studies me for a long moment. I stare right back, hoping the fire glow in my eyes will strike some small amount of fear in him.

He tucks his tablet under his arm. "Yes, Scarlett, you're done for now. You can get some sleep."

The fire surrounds me. But I'm not afraid. I'm not burned. The flames lick the night sky above me, outshining the stars. I stretch my hand forward and part the wall of fire like a curtain.

I see Dylan, Hannah and Ian. They cluster on the ground, huddling against each other, staring at me.

Charred skin covers almost the whole right side of Dylan's face.

My throat constricts. Did I do that?

They grasp each other, pull each other. Away from me. I take a step forward and reach toward them, opening my mouth to speak. But fear of the truth chokes my words. The three of them scramble to their feet. Ian scoops up Hannah and helps steady Dylan. They stumble off into the night, glancing over their shoulders at me.

The fear in their eyes cuts me to the core.

"How are you feeling?"

I clench my hands. Do these people have to ask that question so often? "I'm fine," I mutter.

The nurse eyes me as she takes my vitals and goes through her usual routine. "You sure?" she asks tentatively as she layers more cream on my splotchy palms.

I glare at the red marks instead of her. I guess I can't blame her. I've been scowling all morning. Scowling to hide the pain pulsing with every beat of my heart. Pain from the nightmare last night. I sigh and suddenly feel exhausted again. "I'm sure."

While the nurse closes the jar for the salve then clips my sensors back on, I study the fading splotches on my hands. I'm relieved that they're going away, but I don't like the itchiness that will follow. My fingers go limp as I stare at the pink skin.

Somehow I don't notice when the nurse leaves. I just sit on my bed, shoulders slumped, hands limp on my lap, staring. But I don't really see the pristine white wall. The memory of the nightmare replays over and over in my head, flashing by too fast for me to stop it. Suddenly all I see are three pairs of eyes. Three pairs of eyes for the three people that I care about most.

It was just a dream. But what if they really are afraid of me? Are they happy that I'm locked away? I want to scream at the skies that I'd never hurt them but...I look at my hands again, remembering the test last night and the fire that scarred ash stains across the wall.

Maybe I would hurt them. Maybe I can't help it.

I close my eyes and remind myself to breathe. That's why I came here. That's why I turned myself in. That's why I subjected myself to a bland future day after day in this cold facility. I need to remember that. And stop remembering them.

A cheery chime rudely interrupts me. I scowl, looking around the room until my eyes land on the screen by the door. A green phone icon pulses on it with *Dr. Hiram Bailey* in bold white letters above it. I can get calls on this thing?

I wipe away some tears I didn't know had fallen and walk over to the screen. My finger hesitates a moment over the surface before tapping the phone icon.

The doctor's face appears on the screen. I recoil at first. Wasn't expecting a video call.

"Hello, Miss Marley." He grins like the world is okay.

I'm in no mood for it. "If you're about to ask how I'm feeling, I'm fine."

He blinks. "Okay, then. Good."

I lean my hand on the wall by the screen. "What do you want?"

He raises an eyebrow and purses his lips. I guess I'm in no position to act like this—I'm the one locked in a cell—but I don't feel like talking to him. Or anybody. This whole place and the people in it remind me too much of what I've become.

He clears his throat. "I want you to get some sleep after your scheduled outdoor time today. And make sure you eat plenty."

"What are you, my personal trainer?"

He just shifts his jaw at my snappy sarcasm, giving a smile that doesn't reach his eyes. "I guess you could say that." His eyes pinch at the corners. "But do as I say."

I sigh, suppressing a groan. "Okay, but why?"

"You're not in a position to ask why."

Okay, yeah, I understand that already. Still, I want to argue, but Dr. Bailey ends the call and the screen goes black. I shove off the wall with a cross between a groan and a growl and collapse onto the chair. My stomach rumbles but I don't want to feed it. Because *he* told me to. I don't want to sleep either. I don't want to—

Okay, stop. I sigh and rub a hand along my face, despite the sensor. What am I thinking? Dr. Bailey's just trying to help. He's the expert here and I need to trust that. He knows more about what I am than I do. And this is all for the cure.

Hope lifts my heart a little as I stand and wait behind the yellow line. The clock blinks *10:26am.* Dr. Bailey must've ordered someone to let me miss breakfast and sleep after all the testing last night. My middle rumbles for food, but I'll have to wait for lunchtime. I try my best to keep my chin up, my shoulders erect, while I wait for the order to file out with the rest of the supers for our scheduled outdoor time.

CHAPTER EIGHT

I forgot how much I want to be alone in that tiny unit of mine until I get outside. The supers are more chatty today. Seth strides up to my spot underneath a tree.

He lifts the faded basketball. "Game?"

I shrink away from him. "Not this time."

He tucks the ball under his arm. "You said that last time I asked." He raises an eyebrow.

My jaw clenches, but I stamp down the flare of warmth trying to surface. "I said no. Just leave me alone please."

He pauses, then shrugs and turns back to the court where a few supers wait. I shift to rest my side against the tree trunk, crossing my arms and scowling at the grass. Maybe I shouldn't be angry at them for trying to talk to me. I guess I don't blame them for their cheerfulness; the sun's golden rays turn the grounds into an inviting field of warmth in comparison to the constant chill indoors. My gaze strays to the wildflower patch, but I still don't walk over to it; too many supers surround the blossoms. I try to block out the noise of the others and shift to lie on my back in the grass, arms outstretched, soaking up the warmth.

But I'm still relieved when I get back to my unit, despite the coldness that constantly plagues me here. My feet carry me in aimless, distracted circles before I remember Dr. Bailey's orders to rest. With a full stomach from lunch after outdoor time, I feel more drowsy now and crawl into bed. I lie on my side, tucking my hands under the pillow to protect my face from being scratched by the sensors. The lights flick off. I'll never get used to that.

I take a deep breath and close my eyes. I sigh at the darkness until, like a slow crescendo, the memory of my nightmares seeps into my mind. My eyes fly open.

I sit up, throat tightening, fingers trembling as I grip the blanket. *Turn the light on. Please turn the light on.* Darkness means remembering, remembering the nightmares. I don't want to remember again.

My heart already starts to beat faster as I try to force the memory of the fire, the fear in Dylan's, Ian's and Hannah's eyes from my mind. I even get up and do jumping jacks until I sweat. But my fire seems to build in the warmth from activity, so I stop and sit until it settles.

The lights finally turn back on. I let out a breath and glance at one of the cameras in the corner of the ceiling, mentally thanking whoever is watching. Then I just sit in the stillness, listening to my shaky panting and rejecting any temptation to sleep.

When a buzz sounds and the door starts to creak open, I'm almost thankful for the distraction. Still, I can't help but tense as Dr. Bailey strides in, his white, pressed lab coat contrasted in the midst of the black uniforms, tablet tucked under his arm.

I swing my feet to the floor and meet his cold stare. "More testing?"

His face doesn't soften. "You're supposed to be asleep."

I shift my jaw in annoyance. "Kinda hard with you here now, isn't it?"

He sighs. "I figured since you weren't obeying my orders to sleep, we'd get another test out of the way."

I look past him at the closed door. "Aren't we going downstairs?"

He shakes his head and slips out the tablet. "Not this time." He flips the tablet over to me. "Here."

I frown between the screen and him. "What for?"

He sets the tablet in my lap when I don't take it. "It's a written test. Should only take about five or ten minutes."

I look at the screen. It reminds me of a personality quiz. "What's this for?"

"To find out what kind of pizza you are."

I blink at him, then a laugh bubbles up. Didn't know he was capable of cracking a joke.

He huffs a chuckle and motions toward the screen. "Go on."

I bend over the tablet, fingers hovering over the screen, and frown as I skim over the questions.

How do you view superpowers?

What are your views on letting superhumans live the same as non-superhuman citizens?

What are your views on the Superhuman Containment Facility?

Do you think superhumans should be removed from society?

I take a moment to process my thoughts, then my fingers fly over the touch screen. My jaw slowly clenches tighter as my thoughts pour through my fingers. I release everything, every thought. Every bit of disgust and anger about superhumans stemming from the hate of my own situation. I don't leave out some biting words toward the government about their inability to handle the superhuman problem.

I can't help but think about Ian's mom as my fingers finally slow. What would she think about all this? Is she right about fighting for superhuman rights?

When I finish filling in the text boxes, I don't see anything like a submit button so I hand the tablet back to Dr. Bailey. "What does this have to do with my powers or the cure?"

He doesn't answer as he scans my answers.

"Dr. Bailey?"

He looks up. "Hmm?"

"Does this have anything to do with my powers or the cure?"

A slight pause. "Oh, yes, very much actually." He doesn't meet my eyes when he says it, returning his attention to the tablet screen. "Well!" he says finally, tucking the tablet back under his arm. "You get some sleep now." He smiles at me like I'm a toddler.

I frown and open my mouth to ask more questions. I need a better explanation about what this test has to do with the cure. But Dr. Bailey turns sharply toward the door, coat swishing.

I don't sleep.

A dull, nagging headache pulses in my temples as I fight to keep my eyes open during outdoor time the next day. I lean against the same tree I sat at when Seth tried to get me to play basketball. Again. I watch him now, playing with other supers that are obviously more skilled than he is. The ice boy—Ares?—plays too, though in a kind of hesitant way. The girl with braids, Nadia, timidly walks up to the edge of the court to sit in the grass and watches. The way she watches every movement tells me she wants to play, but she doesn't say anything.

I tuck my legs under me and try to enjoy basking in the warmth and letting the sun warm me to the core. The fire inside me meets the sun's rays, content. Happy. But I'm not.

I rub the back of my neck and look around. I'll never get used to being surrounded by superhumans in this free space. I prefer us all locked securely in our separate units. I scan the ground as I wrap my arms around myself. Even though the supers seem to be kind on the outside, I'm not fooled. I've seen the news stories enough times to know what their kind can do. And the photos in that article...

I suppress a shudder and hug myself tighter, then turn my focus back to the basketball game. Seth misses a shot—again.

The ball smacks off the backboard and bounces into the grass near Nadia. She stands to pick it up.

"I got it," Ares says. He picks up the ball off the grass and glances shyly at Nadia. She just stares at her shoes.

I endure the rest of the outdoor time observing the other supers, watching them talk with each other, play basketball, or just sit alone on the grass. I let out a sigh of relief when the guards escort us back into the building.

I march along with the rest of the grey-clad supers, staring silently ahead. Our regular routine through the hallways seems normal enough, until a few guards approach me. Fear clutches my throat as they grab my arms.

"Stay silent," one growls. They drag me out of line, branching off down a different hallway.

"Hey!"

I whip my head around to see Seth struggling against two other guards. They quickly wrestle him into submission. Four more guards surround both Ares and Nadia. They comply with nothing more than worried expressions. Fear flickers behind their eyes.

They drag us down the hallways, surprisingly silent and stealthy in their heavy boots. But my heart thuds violently against my ribcage, and a warm energy tickles my veins. I open my mouth to ask where we're going, but the only thing that passes my parched throat is a strangled croak. Sweat breaks out on my forehead and back as I clench my hands to stop the shaking. The three others trail behind me. I crane my neck to see them, but the guards jerk me forward.

We march on and on, my thoughts spinning and heart thumping. We don't stop until we've traveled down an elevator and reach the same large concrete room I was in when Dr. Bailey was performing his tests. The guards escort us inside, leave, and lock the door behind them.

We stand frozen, staring at the closed door. Slowly,

cautiously, we glance between each other. I take a small step away from them.

"Well, this is a fine party, isn't it?" Seth chuckles as he straightens his uniform sleeves.

No one returns his lop-sided grin.

I turn to look up at the viewing window. Dr. Bailey stands there, his white coat standing out in contrast to the black suits of three strangers with him.

"Welcome, supers," Dr. Bailey says, clasping his hands. "I'm sure you're all wondering why you're here."

The four of us glance at each other again. Seth crosses his arms. "Yeah, we are."

The doctor clears his throat. "These tests that you've been undergoing haven't been for nothing. They were for a purpose. A plan."

All of us? I thought I was the only one going through these tests. But I guess it makes sense; they'd need to test multiple supers for research for the cure. My chest swells with the thought of being close to the cure.

The silence hangs thick and we barely breathe, waiting for his next words.

The pause goes too long. I can't wait any more. "What plan?"

Dr. Bailey leans forward, voice gaining strength and force. "A plan to fix our country. No longer will superhumans ruin—"

The tallest stranger clears his throat. "Yes, of course. I'm... well, we'll keep my name confidential for now. To be more specific on what the doctor said...the government has chosen you."

Another pause. Seth tilts his head and narrows his gaze. "That's not much more specific."

My fingers knot against my stomach. The government chose us? Importance hangs heavily in his words and I struggle to take a deep breath as my thoughts spin. What does he mean?

The stranger chuckles. "No, I guess not," he continues. "You see, the government has been having some difficulty controlling the population of superhumans in our country. Especially in one area in particular. Rapid City, South Dakota. We just simply do not have the ability to combat that number of superhumans." He points at us. "But you do."

I almost laugh. What, they expect us four to go fight a whole army of superhumans?

Ares tilts his head, narrowing ice-blue eyes at the suited men. "So?"

"So..." The man leans forward, almost touching the glass. "You've passed the test."

Seth rubs his face. "You guys are being annoyingly vague."

He chuckles. "The government has chosen you to be a part of a mission to gain control of the superhuman criminals in Rapid City."

My heart lurches, and I rub my collarbone and stare at the floor. The pulse of my heartbeat vibrates through my fingertips. We'll leave the facility?

But isn't it dangerous to let us out? I frown up at the window. What do they expect us to do in Rapid with just us four teenagers? Those grainy helicopter shots I saw of the city come to my mind. The streets looked quiet, but who knows what lurks out of sight. I shudder.

Dr. Bailey gestures to us with his ever-present tablet. "You will all be going through more tests, much like you have already, and also combat training."

Nadia gasps. "Combat training?" She hugs her arms around herself.

My jaw goes slack as I glance between Dr. Bailey and the suited men. Combat training? I sneak sideways glances at the others and inch away. The last thing I want is to be around other supers who are *trained* in their powers. And I'm not particularly fond of the idea of facing criminal supers running free in a ruined city.

"You want us to fight them all?" I squeak.

Dr. Bailey dips his chin. "You must be prepared for any situation you might come across in Rapid."

I realize after a moment that he was answering Nadia's questions, not mine. Does that mean we *are* meant to fight the supers? My heartbeat quickens.

Ares crosses his arms. "What kind of combat training? I didn't think you people knew how to use powers."

Dr. Bailey clears his throat and adjusts his tie. "We will do as much as we can to get you all used to using your powers and gaining more control over them."

Ares' eyes narrow. "This doesn't make sense. You're going to let us out of here? How do you know we'll even do what you say?"

Even from here, I can see Dr. Bailey's face harden. "Because, Ares, if you do complete this mission successfully, all of you will be the first to receive the cure."

Energy zips through the silence and we all speak at once.

"So soon?" Nadia says quietly.

Ares jaw clenches. "That's our incentive?"

"Sounds good to me," Seth says, brown eyes eager..

"There is a cure," I whisper, not to anyone in particular. Will it feel odd to be out of the facility, even for a little while? A little bit of panic stirs my stomach. I'm here so the world will be protected from me...and now they're going to let us out? But the cure is finally within reach. I can grasp it, if we can just complete this mission.

One thought still tugs at me. "So you want the four of us to fight them all?"

The doctor shakes his head. "Not exactly. We will fill you in on details later."

I slide a hand over my hair and puff out my cheeks with a sigh. "You want to *train* us in our powers."

I didn't really address it to anyone, but Dr. Bailey answers, "Yes."

Nadia shrinks back, still hugging herself. My forehead wrinkles as I study her. Her eyes flick up to me, but only hold my gaze for a split second before falling back to the floor.

Ares takes a few steps away from us, staring at his shoes and thoughtfully stroking his chin. Slowly, his irritation melts away and is replaced by something else as his shoulders relax. I study him, but can't quite tell what's going on in his mind. Is that sadness that lurks behind his eyes?

He looks up at the viewing window, his chill demeanor in place again. "So what does that mean for us right now?"

Seth bounces on the balls of his feet. "Yeah, when do we get to go beat up the bad guys?"

Still, the thought of facing illegal supers makes my stomach clench painfully.

"Calm down, Mr. Calvin," Dr. Bailey says. "After two weeks of prepping, you will be sent—under cover, you could say—to Rapid City." He matches Ares' crossed arms. "For now, I want you all to rest as much as you can during the day in preparation for the nights you'll spend in training and briefing." He turns away. "That's all for now."

Dr. Bailey wasn't kidding about combat training. But it's nothing like I'd imagined combat training would be. Because we have superpowers.

It's obvious the SCF scientists, and even Dr. Bailey, don't know much about the powers within us. But they try their best, getting us in that enormous combat room every night and letting us take turns using our powers. My control grows and I feel like I'm learning to meld with the fire inside me.

I thought I had a chance of doing the *opposite* when I came here.

The thought that I'm getting better with my powers instead of suppressing them plagues my mind constantly. But then, there's the cure.

"Scarlett, let's concentrate, shall we?"

I know Dr. Bailey is irritated with how my mind keeps wandering. "Sorry." If only there was a way for me to stop my thoughts from spinning. Just focus on the goal, the cure. Maybe leaving here and going *home*.

Dr. Bailey nods down at us. "Okay...Ares," he mutters the name, then clears his throat. "Like we did yesterday."

Ares looks up at the viewing window, jaw clenched. He brushes past us to stand in front of the grumpy-faced dummy in front of the painted target on the wall. He looks at it for several long moments, his hands flexing and unflexing.

"Come on, Ares," Dr. Bailey says. "We don't have all day."

"Don't rush me," Ares snaps, glaring up at the doctor. He turns his attention back to the dummy. He raises his hand, and a spear of ice shoots from his palm. It pierces the dummy through the stomach and it falls on its side, the ice shattering like glass.

I gulp and scoot a half-step back. I don't think I'll ever get used to seeing that. Or being around someone who can do that as easily as sneezing.

"I didn't want you to do that," Dr. Bailey grumbles.

Ares glares at him again, then turns on his heel to stand by us again. "I don't care what you want," he mumbles.

Dr. Bailey clears his throat and two guards enter to take the dummy away while another two replace it with a new one. A few minutes pass as Dr. Bailey looks down at something and rubs his forehead. "Come on, Seth." His voice droops, like a weary father with misbehaving kids.

"Finally." Seth jumps forward. He doesn't wait for another cue. He takes a split second to crouch like a sprinter, then speeds around the dummy, faster, and faster until he's a blur. Wind whips my hair around my face and dries my eyes. I squint against it.

The wind increases as Seth goes faster. The dummy slowly lifts off the ground in the tornado, spinning and flipping. Then Seth slows for only a brief moment before he skids to a stop, shoes gliding a short distance across the concrete as he grins. "I needed that—" The airborne dummy crashes loudly to the floor just behind him and he jumps. He presses a hand to his chest and lets out a breath as he bends over to set the dummy back on its stand.

Dr. Bailey sighs. "All right, Scarlett. Your turn."

My face warms, not from my fire, as I shuffle forward. I can feel everyone's eyes on me and sweat breaks out on my forehead. I've done this numerous times, and it still makes my stomach tie in nervous knots.

"Are you all right, Scarlett?" Dr. Bailey asks.

I swallow and nod. "Yes, I'm fine." I don't want to be taken back to the lab just for nerves, so I try to push them away and lift my palm. The fire comes easier each time. Heat pulses in my hand and a ball of flames forms, growing bigger and churning inside its sphere. I thrust my hand forward, throwing the fireball at the dummy. It hits it with an odd thud and the figure tumbles backward. Dark char marks cover the face and chest.

"Good. You're getting better." Dr. Bailey types something on his tablet.

I scowl, keeping my back to the others. Better? Using superpowers was supposed to be illegal.

"Okay, so I'm going to have Seth, Scarlett, and Ares team up now," he says.

The three of us glance at each other as we step forward. Nadia shrinks back, staring at her shoes.

"What are we supposed to do?" I ask.

Dr. Bailey's voice sounds distant as he looks down at his tablet. "I want you all to direct your powers at the dummy at the same time." He looks up. "Ares, stay away from Scarlett."

Ares and I glance at each other and step farther away. I recall all the times I've had to move away from him. He's so cold and my fire can't stand it. I can't help but avoid it.

"Go ahead," Dr. Bailey says at our hesitation.

We stand in a wide semi-circle facing the dummy, Seth

between me and Ares. The three of us lift our hands toward it. Just as the fire builds in my hand, a gust of Seth's wind blows into my face and blinds me. I spread my feet for balance, squinting against fine debris stinging my eyes. I can't even see. I quickly swipe a hand across my eyes, but Seth's wind continues. I can hear Seth's and Ares' shoes against the floor as they attack the dummy, but I still stand blinded.

A shocking wave of cold washes over me from my left. I gasp as my body goes rigid and I fall to one knee.

"Scarlett!" Ares yells, and the cold ceases. "I-I'm sorry, I didn't realize I got so close—"

"It's okay." I say, trying to keep my teeth from chattering. I rub my hands over my arms to try to coax warmth back into my muscles.

"Ares!" Dr. Bailey's voice comes sharp and loud through the speaker.

Ares glances at the doctor, then back at me. He takes a step forward, but stops himself. "Scarlett?"

"I'm all right," I assure him. My muscles start to loosen, and I push myself to stand again.

"Ares, I told you to stay away from her. Your powers and hers are not compatible."

"Yeah, well whose genius idea was it to put us in the same room then, huh?" Ares turns back to me and softens. "Are you sure you're okay?"

Whether it's from the rubbing or my fire, warmth returns to my arms. "I'm okay. Really."

Does Dr. Bailey really know what he's doing?

Everyone goes silent—not sure what to do next—including the doctor. He rests his hands on the long table in front of the viewing window, staring down at us. I glance out of the corner of my eye at Ares. He glares back at the window. His gaze could freeze anything solid. Maybe literally. Why is he always so tense around the doctor? Any other time he's so chill. No pun intended.

"Let's move on, shall we?" Dr. Bailey says tiredly. "Miss Farlan..." He leans closer to the viewing window.

Nadia shrinks away from the doctor's gaze.

"It's your turn."

She bites her lip and stares at the thick concrete slab in the corner, set there just for her. She shakes her head.

"Nadia." Dr. Bailey groans and rubs his face. "Let's not go through this again."

Nadia wipes her trembling hands on her jumpsuit pants. "I can't..."

A little frustration leaks into me. I wrap my arms around myself as my fire continues to slowly warm me. We go through this every time. Dr. Bailey calls on her, she wants to back out, he presses until she gives in. I don't like using my powers either, but doesn't she realize the chance we have? My fingers tighten around my arms. I just hope she doesn't ruin this chance for me.

Dr. Bailey slams his fist on the table. "Nadia." He sucks in a deep breath and slowly lets it out through his teeth. Guards step into the room and we all stiffen. "Just do it. Now."

Nadia looks at the concrete slab again. "I-I can't, Dr. Bailey," she stammers. Moisture glistens in her eyes. Her hands shake violently, and she tucks them under her arms.

My annoyance melts away. What's wrong with her? The brief moment of concern flits away almost instantly and I huff. It's the same thing that's wrong with me. Superpowers. I'm not thrilled about using them either.

Dr. Bailey stiffens. Three guards advance closer to Nadia. She jumps away from them. "Fine," she rasps. "I'll do it."

"Good," the doctor says coolly. "We don't have all night."

Nadia looks away, but not before I notice her wipe at her eyes. She shuffles over to the concrete block and stares at it for a long moment, then takes a shaky breath and places her hands on the slab.

"Everyone else back up."

We're already cautiously moving backward before Dr. Bailey gets the words out.

At first nothing happens. Then Nadia's shoulder hunch, and a low rumble vibrates through the room. It intensifies, reverberating in my chest and making my feet tingle against the floor. My knees quake, and I stumble, trying to find balance.

Two cracks thread through the concrete slab under Nadia's hands. With an ear-splitting crack, it splits and crumbles. Dust rises from the rubble.

Nadia slowly straightens and backs away from the debris. Stiffly, she turns to face us, her gaze glued to her shoes.

I look past her at the remains of the concrete. It lies in ruin, crumbled like a stale cookie. She does that so effortlessly. Fear tickles my gut as I stare at the rubble. Could she make this whole room collapse too? The thought makes me shudder.

Sweat trickles down Nadia's forehead but I don't think it's from the effort.

"Good," Dr. Bailey finally breaks the silence. "Very good." He tucks his tablet under his arm and adjusts his striped tie. "The time has come."

CHAPTER NINE

The conference room is too small, too warm and too tense.

Seth, Ares, Nadia and I sit at the long, shiny wood table. My fingers knot together, pressed against my lap. The others shift uncomfortably in their own seats, leather chairs squeaking softly. Guards line the walls, watching us like hawks. Dr. Bailey and half a dozen government men fill the other chairs.

The same officer that talked to the four of us when we first came together in the training room stands at the head of the table. He smooths his suit jacket and leans forward to continue the briefing, palms pressed against the table. "We believe this superhuman named Rez is the leader of the gang of rebel supers in Rapid City. He is responsible for a number of attacks, robberies, looting, and kidnapping in the surrounding area. If we can capture him, other supers living outside the law may become more compliant." He lifts a finger. "You have to gain his trust. You will stay in contact with us the whole time you're away from the facility." He pauses to clear his throat and adjust the papers in front of him. "You'll play the part of four superhuman friends escaping Redfield, South Dakota to find a new life in Rapid."

Seth sighs and stares at the ceiling. "Sounds easy enough," he says, sarcasm lacing his words. "But I've been thinking about something." He leans forward and rests his elbows on the table, his face going hard. "What's stopping us from, say, running away?"

Running away? Doesn't he want the cure?

The man meets his stare flatly. "We will be tracking you, Mr. Calvin. And we have other means of keeping an eye on you as well." He leans back and some of his easy manner returns. "Besides, if you return successfully, you all will be the first human recipients of the experimental cure."

I lick my lips eagerly. For a moment, I allow hope to infiltrate my mind. Maybe the cure will work. Maybe I'll go back to normal. Maybe I can return home.

"It works?" Ares asks.

"Um, *'experimental'*?" Seth says, making air quotes.

Dr. Bailey pays no attention to Seth, instead tilting his head at Ares, a challenge in his eyes. "You doubt us?"

Ares' gaze sharpens. "Maybe just one of you."

The doctor matches Ares' narrowed eyes. "I know what I'm doing."

"Sure. You always do." Ares crosses his arms and stares at the table. "But I know different."

Dr. Bailey's face reddens and, after a moment of thick silence, he takes a deep breath. "Of course we're...not sure about *all* the details yet—"

"That doesn't give me warm and fuzzies," Seth interrupts, brows drawn together.

"This will work." Dr. Bailey directs his forceful words at Seth, but glances at Ares.

I lean forward, lips pursed. "But what if it doesn't?" Could an unsuccessful cure mess up my body even more?

Dr. Bailey looks at me, hesitating. "It will," he says. "If not now, then someday."

I swallow. "Will there be side effects?"

"We're not sure at this time."

We fall silent. Something could go seriously wrong. What if

it doesn't work and instead we're left worse off than we are now? What if it kills us?

Suddenly the thought of being the first to receive the cure doesn't sound as thrilling. My fingers knot together. "I don't know about this..."

The man at the head of the table frowns at Dr. Bailey, then back at us. "It's your only chance."

"For what?" Ares asks.

"To be normal again."

Unexpected, Ian's words from the night I left drift into my thoughts. *"Don't let society dictate you."* I blink hard and give my head a shake to erase the memory.

Ares leans forward, brows thunderous as he gathers his breath. I brace for a slew of angry words. Dr. Bailey lifts a hand, stalling him. His face softens a little as he slowly turns his gaze over each of us.

"Think of it." His voice takes on an almost wistful tone. "If the cure works, your powers would disappear. These powers that harm the people you love."

Nadia looks away, pressing a fist to her mouth.

"Without powers, you'd be able to live as you please. You won't have to be controlled by them anymore."

Seth bites his lip, staring with wrinkled forehead at Dr. Bailey.

The doctor's gaze lands on me. "You can go back to your normal lives. Your families."

A sharp pang hits my heart, squeezing the air from my lungs. I press my hands to my chest against the ache.

Dr. Bailey spares Ares only a brief glance. "You'll be free to go wherever you want," he says softly.

Some of the frustration leaks out of Ares' expression. His shoulders go limp, crossed arms unraveling. He stares distantly at the table, seeing something else.

I clench my hands into fists under the table, letting the heat fester in my palms. I could go back to my family like none of this ever happened. No one would need to be afraid of me anymore. We could go back to the way things were. I wouldn't be dangerous, a freak or some science experiment.

But this task is monumental, and there's just the four of us. I lift a finger. "One more question...What if we fail?"

The stranger at the head of the table and Dr. Bailey exchange a glance. The stranger's face darkens as he leans his elbows on the table. "If Rez finds you out, there's no telling what he could do."

I gulp, stomach clenching.

"But," he continues. "If you fail and somehow return to us..." He pauses to look at each of us in turn. "No cure for any of you. Maybe not ever."

My jaw goes slack. Not ever? Is this their way of motivating us? I study the stranger's hardened face, a threat glinting in his eyes. I lean back against the chair, narrowing my gaze. Is there some other punishment they'd have in mind beside withholding the cure? Some of those rumors about the SCF's basements filter back into my mind. I suppress a shudder.

"No cure for any of you. Maybe not ever." A slight tremble takes over my fingers as I rub my chin. No cure means never again normal. Never again free from this place. Never again will I be able to go home, see my family, or pursue my dreams.

Dr. Bailey rakes his gaze over us once more, then leans back in his chair, returning to his cold professionalism. "Still unsure?"

I meet his gaze, new resolve straightening my shoulders. "I'll do it." I may not even have a choice in the matter, but for some reason I need to say the words out loud. To show the fear and doubts swirling in my mind that I'm determined.

Nadia, Ares, and Seth stare at me. I meet their gazes, one by one, hoping my new determination will infuse into them.

Seth lifts his chin, eyes hardening. "Me too."

Nadia bites her lip. "Okay."

All eyes swivel to Ares. He still sits weakly in his chair, hands limp in his lap, still staring at the table. He works his jaw and looks at us, finally resting a chilly gaze on Dr. Bailey, who stares at his hands, jaw clenching. "Okay. I'm in too."

"Good!" The man at the head of the table claps his hands and smiles. "Now, some more details you must know..." The man next to him slides a beige folder across the table and he sits back in his chair and flips it open. "This leader, the man called Rez, has mind-manipulation powers. This will make things very difficult, so you have to be very careful."

I purse my lips. "How do we combat mind-control?" I squirm at the thought of someone controlling my brain. How powerful is it? What if he makes us attack people? I suck in a sharp breath at the possibilities.

He twists his mouth to one side, glancing at Dr. Bailey.

The doctor purses his lips. "We've found that superhumans with mind-manipulating powers tend to have one eye that is a different, more unnatural color. We believe that they use this eye for their powers. So avoid looking at it."

"Right." The man nods and looks back at the papers. "Once you've spent some time in Rapid and gained their trust, we will coordinate with you for the rest of the capture details. When the time is right, you will create diversions to separate the group into two or more. Our deployments will be better able to handle the smaller numbers. But..." He raises a finger. "Rez is the top priority. We know we won't be able to capture them all, but getting their leader would be very effective."

As he speaks, his voice grows in strength, projecting through the small conference room. It only makes my stomach knot tighter.

"And that's not all. We need information about their life and operations there. Nadia."

She jumps when he addresses her.

He doesn't seem to notice her tension. "You will be examining their food stores, how well they're supplied, where they get their supplies, and such things."

When he stares at her, she nods, biting her lip.

He nods, turning to Ares. "You will be taking note of their strength and numbers, if they're young or old, weak or strong, healthy or ill. This may very well affect how many men we send out." He doesn't wait for Ares' acknowledgment before turning to Seth. "You will be finding out what kind of weapons they have, if they are well-armed or not, and where they get their weapons."

Seth simply nods, face uncharacteristically solemn.

He turns to me and my chest tightens. "You will focus on keeping Rez distracted. We felt your quiet, unassuming demeanor best lent to this job. But based on your written test results we know you'll get the job done. Your task will allow the others to fulfill their part of the mission without arousing suspicion. You will be by his side as much as possible, as much as you can without making him suspect you. Keep an eye on where he goes and what his regular operations are."

My fingers tremble as I nod. This won't be so easy.

"And that also makes you the leader of your team," he adds.

My head jerks back as the others look at me. "M-me?" I sputter. Already my breath quickens at the thought. "Why me?"

He raises his hands. "Calm down, Miss Marley." Irritation edges his voice. "We chose you based on your written test results. This job means you will be in direct contact with Dr. Bailey during your time in Rapid."

My throat tightens and my stomach follows suit. I nod as my hands knot in my lap and I try to take even breaths. Leader? I don't know what they saw in me from my test answers, but surely I'm not the right one. Can I handle it?

My family's faces filter into my mind. My heartbeat steadies. I *have* to handle it.

As if reading my thoughts, the man goes on. "We have a contact in the city who will help you as much as possible. For the most part, without you even knowing it."

"Who?" Ares asks.

"Code name is 'Raven,' and they will reveal their identity when it is safe to do so."

Seth leans forward. "But how will *we* know who it is?" he demands, tapping his chest with a finger.

"You won't," he answers. "You will know when the contact decides it's best."

A short silence follows as we process our thoughts. I rest my elbows on the table. "One more question...Why us?"

Dr. Bailey steadily meets my gaze. "The written test you took...that was given to several supers in the SCF. Yours proved to be the most promising for the job." He flicks his glance toward Ares before nodding, as if satisfied with his own response.

The man at the head of the table leans back and flips the folder closed. "Dr. Bailey, are there any other tests that need to be run?"

The doctor folds his hands. "No. They're ready."

"Good." He stands again, all the other suited men with him. He takes a moment to look at each of us. "Then you leave in the morning."

We leave in the morning.

This thought and a flurry of others keeps me awake that night. I sit on my bed in the dark, wondering if Dr. Bailey is frowning at me from one of the cameras. He told us to sleep, but I can't.

I look over at the stack of normal clothes folded neatly on the chair. We're supposed to be up and dressed by the time guards come to get us close to our departure time at 5am. It'll feel good to get out of this stiff, scratchy uniform.

I sigh and look back at the wall. My stomach twists and flips in nervous knots as the last few weeks replay through my mind.

Training and tests, training and tests. The more time that passed the more tense I got. The more tense we all got.

For once, I welcome the dead silence in my unit. But as I blink at the dark, my mind threatens to spin out of control. Part of me lifts at the thought of leaving this facility with its pristine, white walls and the cold that seeps deep into me. I take a slow breath, longing for fresh air and open space. But a bigger part of me eats away the fragile new hope. My hands knot together so hard my knuckles pop. So many things could go wrong on this mission. The possibilities flip through my mind at a dizzying speed, making my heart beat faster.

The mission could go south. We could be hurt. Or worse. Then all of this would've been for nothing.

I repeat all the details of our mission under my breath. I try to mimic Dr. Bailey's detached, cold voice, as if that will break off the swirling emotions making my chest tight.

Go to Rapid, find Rez and his gang, gain their trust...Then betray them.

I bite my lip until it hurts too much. This shouldn't bother me. They're just a bunch of criminals, dangerous supers who are defying the government. They're probably responsible for Rapid being reduced to almost rubble. It shouldn't matter to me that we have to earn their trust only to break it. It's not like they're human.

I freeze. If I truly believe that, then I have to believe I'm not human either.

Maybe I'm not.

What will this superhuman gang leader be like? My mind pictures a man with sharp, hard features. Tall, broad, intimidating. An eye capable of controlling my mind. A shiver trickles down my spine.

I look down and realize my hands are shaking. My stomach clenches. I roll my shoulders back and take a deep breath. My body calms but my mind still whirls. I lie back on the bed, resting my hands under my head. The blank ceiling just makes it easier for my thoughts to overtake me. I see my nightmare on the ceiling, the fear in the eyes of those I love. Fear, burns, my glowing eyes—

A buzz cuts into my thoughts. I turn my head to see the door creak open and a tall silhouette in the white light through the doorway. I squint until the figure enters and the door closes. The lights turn on at half-brightness.

"Dr. Bailey." I swing my feet back to the floor.

He frowns at me, tucking his hands in his pockets. "You're supposed to be sleeping."

I glance at the camera. Guess he *was* watching me. I turn my gaze to the floor. "I can't sleep."

He steps forward, flops the stack of clothes onto the bed, and sits in the chair. He leans his elbows on his knees and stares at the floor. "Second thoughts?"

I wrap my arms around myself. "Not exactly." I pause. "Well, yes...I guess. Just a little."

He doesn't look at me, but he says gently, "Want to talk about it?"

I study him for a moment, gauging how much of my deep worries I want to share. "I just...this job, going into Rapid and..." I break off. I can't get my thoughts organized into words.

"You feel maybe it's wrong after all. The thought of turning in all those supers scares you."

I raise my gaze to meet his. I nod and shrug one shoulder. "Yes."

"Scarlett." He turns to face me more fully. "I want to tell you something. Many years ago, I lost a daughter because of superhumans." His hands knot together as he stares at the floor again. "My little girl was kidnapped. I was taking her with me to work that day. We were overtaken on the road by...by them."

I watch as a storm of memories battles in his distant gaze. Slowly, smoothly, cooly, he turns back to me. "That was near Rapid." He blinks several times. Swallows. "Scarlett, if you and the others succeed in this mission, you will be making this world safer. You will be helping purify our country from superpowers. These supers in Rapid have chosen to go against the law and as a result they are free to commit crimes and hurt people." His eyes spark. "They don't deserve to live. They're less than human."

I stare at him, trying to hold his gaze. "So...that goes for me too?"

He grimaces and rubs a hand along the side of his face. "That's not what I meant—"

"No, no." I lean my elbows on my knees too. "I think you're right."

He hesitates then places a hand on my arm. "Scarlett, by going along with this mission, you are different from them." He stands. "Besides, if the cure works, you won't need to call yourself a superhuman anymore." A small, hopeful smile lifts the corner of his mouth. "The world will know your name."

I can't bring myself to smile back. His words, *they're less than human,* keep ringing in my mind. I just nod.

His smile falters as he slowly transforms back to the stiff, professional doctor and scientist of the SCF. He clasps his hands behind his back. "You should get some sleep now."

I purse my lips and stare at his shiny shoes, nodding again.

He leaves and the lights flick off after a second, plunging me into the cool darkness with nothing but my memories, nightmares, worries, and long-ago dreams.

My new clothes feel like heaven. I sit in my chair as the moments pass by, enjoying the softness of the worn graphic tee and jeans. Even my toes are enjoying the socks and sneakers. I don't care if they look old, they're normal, and that's closer to home.

I shiver from the coldness on my bare arms and struggle on the navy hoodie. As I yank it over my head, the door opens and a nurse comes in, equipment in tow. She gives me a grin before going right to work with her usual routine.

Dr. Bailey follows her in. "How do you feel, Scarlett?" he asks, folding his hands in front of him.

Scared. Terrified. Sick to my stomach. "I feel okay."

He doesn't need to be a detective to see through that lie. "Everything will be fine," he says. "Beware of Rez and his manipulation. You can resist it if you try hard enough and are careful." He takes a step forward, gaze intensifying. "Do not listen to what any of them tell you. They're all just the lies of a criminal. They will try to convert you to their side, but you need to stay focused." He pauses, waiting for my response.

I nod. "Okay."

"And one more thing...don't trust anyone. Even the other three."

"Wait, why?" Aren't we supposed to be a team?

"Just remember what I say." He lifts a finger at me. "Monitor them and report to me any odd behavior."

"How do I communicate with you?"

"With this." He slips a black watch from his pants pocket. It looks normal enough. But he flips up the chunky digital face to reveal the sleek screen of a smartwatch underneath. He hands it to me and I buckle it around my left wrist.

Then he kneels in front of me and takes my wrist in his hands. He points to a few buttons on the side. "This watch functions like most smartwatches. You can receive and make calls and messages. Pay attention when we try to get in contact with you."

I hold the device close to my face to examine it. Dr. Bailey pulls it away again. "Look here." He points to a small, red button on the side of the watch. "Press this and the screen will display things like your heart rate, blood pressure, your hydration level, etcetera."

"Hydration?"

"Yes, you need to make sure you keep hydrated. One of the side effects of your type of power is dehydration."

I look at the small graphs showing on the screen face. "Okay."

"Listen to me."

I look at him and his icy eyes bore into me. For a fleeting moment they remind me of someone else, but I can't quite place who.

He sets his mouth in a hard line. "Do not trust anyone," he repeats slowly. "Keep an eye on the other three. If any of them are acting strangely or show signs of switching sides, tell us." He taps the watch.

It feels wrong spying on them. They're my teammates in this, right? I chew my lip. "Okay, Dr. Bailey."

He nods and stands. "Good luck."

He leaves the room and two guards replace him. They approach me, and I focus on taking deep, even breaths as they fasten handcuffs on my wrists. They escort me out, flanking me down the hallways. I feel like I'm only half present as we travel through the maze of the facility and down an elevator. We stop in front of a door in a short concrete hallway. A guard swipes his card over a scanner, and with a beep, the lock clicks and the guard swings both doors open.

We walk out into an enormous underground garage. The cold hits me with a gust of wind and I hug my arms close. Armored vehicles fill most of the parking spaces. Several guards stand stone still in front of a large armored truck with its back doors open. Seth, Nadia and Ares are already waiting.

As we approach, I study their faces, looking for a sign that I'm not alone in my worries. Seth stares at his hands, twiddling his thumbs. Nadia stands with tense shoulders and eyes wide with panic. Ares has his eyes closed, chin lifted slightly as he lets the chilly wind toss his snow-white hair.

As soon as I reach them, the guards usher us into the back of the truck, crowding in as many of them as they can with us.

Within minutes we rev along the road, stopping at the SCF gates and checkpoints to get clearance. Then we bump along in silence. I try not to focus on the pinch of the cuffs, the watchful gaze of the guards, or the stifling air of the truck.

I'm getting out. I'll be free...sort of. My gaze catches on the watch Dr. Bailey gave me. It must be how they're tracking me. They'll see wherever I go. This thought taints my fleeting dream of freedom. I take a deep breath and lean my head back against the truck wall. Just think of the big picture. The cure. I have a chance to go back to normal, to fix my...defects. And go back home.

Sitting on the hard bench in the back of this cold armored truck, I crave the warmth of the fire in my core. But I don't feel like stoking it. I glance at the others. They sit silently, staring at the floor.

Time passes, and with nothing else to do, I let thoughts of my family drift in, this time intentionally. I hope they think of me how I was before the accident, before I got powers. Before my fire, before the fear. I hope Dylan is still being the protective big brother for Hannah. I hope she's still giggling and that she played away the summer days before school started. I hope Ian's first gig was a big hit and he sang his original with pride. I hope he goes on to accomplish his big, crazy dreams in music. I hope maybe he'll even do some things for my sake, remembering me. I hope Mom and Dad are staying strong, focusing on Dylan and Hannah instead of me. Part of me feels guilty for trying not to even think about them these past few months.

The truck slows to a stop. My stomach clenches, chasing away the warm, soft feeling that my memories had brought.

The engine shuts off, and the doors swing open. The guards prod us and we hop out onto the dry grass. The truck rests on the side of a road in the middle of nowhere. So much space and room to breathe. I suck in a deep breath of crisp air.

We all congregate in a circle and one of the guards steps forward to face us. He grips his thick belt and rocks back on his heels. "This is where we leave you," he says. "You're about four and a half miles outside of Rapid City. We can't go any farther, so you'll have to walk there. It should only take about an hour and a half."

"Don't we get any supplies or anything?" Seth asks, glancing over his shoulder down the road where we came from.

"Food and water will probably be scarce," Ares adds, brow furrowed.

The guard shakes his head. "You'd look too prepared." He stares back at our blank faces. "You'll figure something out."

Seth snorts. "Yeah, thanks a lot."

I bite my lip and shift my wrists under the cuffs. "We'd better get going." It's still early—the sun has barely passed the horizon —but it's a four-mile walk and who knows how long it'll take to find food and water. My throat begs for water but my tight stomach would probably reject any food.

At a nod from the head guard, the others unlock our cuffs and step away. I rub my wrists, my finger scratching against the watch. I resist the urge to bolt, to just run until my legs give out and there's no one in sight. I lick my wind-dried lips and stare at my shoes instead.

The head guard looks us over. "Remember," he says, "we can track you. So don't try anything. Good luck."

Without another word, the guards load up into the truck and drive away.

We stand there in a circle, watching the truck disappear in the dim morning light, the sound of the engine dying in the distance. Then we're left in silence.

Seth looks down the road, toward Rapid City. "We'd better get going," he repeats my words.

We all nod and start our march toward the city. With every step my stomach twists and my hands shake even more. I can't keep the nightmares and memories at bay as the cold claws at the fire trying to warm my body. My muscles numb with the chill, making my movements stiff. I stumble over my own feet, willing myself to keep moving forward, to keep up with the others. Despite the fact that every step takes me closer and closer to a city run by criminals.

If only I hadn't been so stupid to go into the back alley that night at the ice cream shop. I was stupid to not run right away when I knew there was a threat. None of this would've happened. I wouldn't be here right now, walking into a danger zone.

Silence keeps its hold on us as we enter the city. Rapid is dusty and crumbly. Empty windows gape at us like dark eye sockets. Broken glass, pieces of building, and garbage litters the streets. A few shops are burned, goods stolen long ago. We walk in slow silence, looking over every inch. My senses tingle on high alert, waiting for a superhuman criminal to pop out and attack at any moment.

The sun climbs higher in the sky, finally warming me a bit. Weariness and hunger hangs on everyone's faces, especially Seth's. I just want water. I remember Dr. Bailey telling me to keep hydrated, but how are we meant to find fresh water in this place?

After more than an hour of walking around, we stop to rest in the middle of a street. I sit on the edge of the sidewalk with Nadia and Ares, while Seth paces. His fingers twitch with pent up energy.

Despite my exhaustion, I can't seem to relax. The back of my neck tingles and I look over my shoulder down a narrow alley behind me. Nothing. This time.

Instead of thinking about the city crawling with criminals, I turn my focus on our next step. "So, should we—"

"I think we need to keep going," Ares says, looking off down the street.

"Why?" Seth asks.

Ares glances at him. "To look for people."

"What about food? My stomach hasn't stopped growling this whole way."

"The important part of this mission is to find Rez."

"Well, we can't do that on an empty stomach."

Ares' eyes narrow. "If we find Rez first, he'll probably have water and food."

"Splendid idea, trusting the enemy to feed us."

"They don't know they're our enemy."

Seth crosses his arms. "Yeah, well, who put you in charge, anyway?"

"Just trying to help."

Seth rolls his eyes. "Sure you are. I don't remember us voting you for president."

I sigh. This is going great already.

"Scarlett," Nadia cuts through their argument, stopping it short. Her soft brown eyes bore into me. "What do you think we should do?"

"Me?" I squeak. I'm pretty sure I'm least qualified to lead us anywhere, but I remember what the government man said to me when he gave us our assignments. Apparently I am the leader.

She nods, and Seth glances between me and Nadia, frowning, but doesn't say anything. I swallow, then clear my throat. "I guess we should keep walking and look for someone to get information from."

"Okay." Ares hops up from his sidewalk. "Then let's go." He starts off down the street, tucking his hands into his pale jeans, not seemingly unbothered by a following gust of icy wind. The rest of us hurry after him.

The city remains quiet and empty. I had expected to be met by supers as soon as we entered their domain. We're newcomers, challengers. Shouldn't we be, like...attacked or something by now? I struggle to take a deep breath against the tension in my body as I scan every shadow and alley.

A crash behind me makes me jump. I gasp and whirl around.

Seth picks himself up from a tipped trash can, its contents sprawled out over the sidewalk. "Sorry," he mutters. He stumbles after us, leaving the mess behind.

I let out a breath and try to calm myself. I don't need to be so jumpy. My powers are stronger. I know how to use them. I shake my head. This is ridiculous.

I close my eyes for a moment. Just focus on the cure, getting rid of my powers, and going home.

"Are you okay?" Nadia's soft voice reaches through my thoughts.

I open my eyes, realizing that I'd stopped walking. I try to smile. "Yeah, I'm all right."

She continues to study me, brows furrowing over her soft, dark eyes.

"Well, what now?" Seth says, throwing his arms out.

Nadia and I jog to catch up with Seth and Ares.

"We've been walking and walking and not finding anyone, Mr. President," Seth continues, tapping his foot.

"We haven't been looking that long," Ares responds, looking up at the sky, white hair brushing his forehead in the breeze.

Seth runs a hand through his messy hair. "We need to find food and water. Now."

I groan and tip my head back. "Guys, come on. Stop arguing."

Seth looks at me. "What? We're just discussing."

"We're arguing," Ares states.

Their voices echo off the buildings and down the street. I slowly look around for movement anywhere. They need to keep their voices down or else—

I freeze.

Four men stand in a line down the street, feet spread and fists on their hips. One with shaggy blond hair and an athletic build steps forward. Even from here I can feel the challenge emanating from him. A gust of wind sweeps across the street, tossing his faded shirt. He lifts a long pipe in his hand, pointing it at us like a sword.

The wind dies, allowing his next words to reach us. "Boys. We've got company."

CHAPTER TEN

We stop dead in our tracks. My muscles turn to ice as if Ares infused them with his chilly touch. I struggle to swallow.

The man lowers his pipe, lifting his chin at us. "I don't think I've seen you guys before."

A tall, broad man with rippling muscles to his left cracks his knuckles, eyeing us and grinning, revealing a missing tooth. "Newcomers." He takes a heavy step forward, but the first man stops him with his pipe.

"Now hang on a minute, Davey," he says, turning his head toward his friend but keeping his eyes on us. "There doesn't have to be trouble."

Another man, his greasy blond hair standing in spikes all along his scalp, leans in close to the leader, his potbelly stretching against his ragged-hemmed shirt. "We could get a good price for 'em, Mikey," he whispers. A gust of wind carries his words toward us.

I glance at Seth to see his hands waving faintly, summoning the wind at his fingertips.

The fourth, a short man with a thick, crooked nose, crowds close too. "Yeah, Mikey," he hisses.

The man they call Mikey narrows his eyes at us. "Where do you come from?"

"None of your business," Seth snaps.

I frown at him and nudge his side with my elbow. He barely glances at me before fixing his glare at Mikey again.

Mikey huffs at Seth's words. "Look, buddy. This is my town. As long as you understand that, there won't be trouble. Not much, anyway."

His town? My eyebrows lift. Is this Rez?

I raise my hands. "Listen, we're not here to cause any trouble." Well, not yet anyway. "We've come from Redfield."

At this, the four huddle close again, discussing in whispers Seth's wind can't carry to us and casting wary glances at us.

After a few minutes pass, I huff and plant my hands on my hips, glancing at Nadia, who stands close behind my left shoulder. Her brow furrows as she watches the four men, fingers knotted against her stomach. She flicks a glance at me and barely shrugs.

Ares steps forward, weight balanced on the balls of his feet but his voice calm. "What do you want with us?" Frost slowly creeps over his fingers. He gestures toward me. "Like she said, we're not here to cause trouble. We'll just be on our way."

Mikey casually rests the pipe on his shoulder, but keeps a close eye on Seth even as he addresses Ares. I look over at Seth again. He half crouches, a scowl twisting his face. Wind swirls the street grit in a circle around his feet. I nudge him again, but this time he doesn't seem to notice. I purse my lips. No need to escalate things needlessly.

"Well, here's what's gonna happen." Mikey pauses to casually examine the end of his pipe, then he points it at us again. "You all are gonna come with me. Peacefully."

Now the swirling frost creeps up Ares' neck. "Why?"

"Not on your life," Seth growls. He launches forward in a blink.

I gape. "Seth, wait!"

Halfway toward Mikey, he stops and flings his arms forward. A gust of wind knocks all four back, tumbling and grunting down the street. Mikey is the first to get to his feet. The glare he sets on Seth makes me shudder.

Ares shakes his head and runs after Seth, mumbling something about being undiplomatic.

Should I help them fight? Try to reason with them? I glance at Nadia, but she stands board stiff, staring wide-eyed at the fight that's about to boil over. I can't wait for her to snap out of it. My shoes slap the asphalt as I hurry after Ares. My fire feeds off my energy, coming alive in my veins and heating my hands.

Mikey lurches at Seth before Ares can reach him. He swings his pipe and Seth narrowly ducks it. Just before he reaches them, Ares stretches out his hand and quickly creates his own stick of ice. As Mikey rounds another swing at Seth's head, Ares blocks it with his ice spear.

The broad muscled man picks himself off the ground. With a guttural yell he hurries to help Mikey, heavy feet pounding the ground. I grunt, forcing my legs to pump harder as spheres of fire the size of baseballs form in my palms. Before Davey can reach Mikey, I hurl the fire at his feet. Yelping, he skitters back before his shoes get burned. He settles a chilling glare at me, flexing his meaty hands.

I gulp and hold up my hands. "Hang on, can't we just talk about this?"

The man with the thick nose stands nearby. He just looks at me with disgust. Hands held calmly at his sides, he smoothly lifts into the air and circles the sky above my head. I back away from Davey, forming more fireballs in my hands and glancing between my two attackers as they get closer.

The flying man circles above me like a vulture, descending closer with each turn. My fire flickers, wavering as my hands shake.

Before I can decide what to do, the man in the sky descends like a hawk. I fling a fireball at him but miss. Half-blindly, I hurl another at the muscled man. The distraction costs me, because when I turn my head to see where the flying man is, all I catch is a blur of clothing before he collides with me. We tumble to the ground and before I can even stop rolling, he yanks me to my feet. I try to twist and yank myself away, but his grip is like iron on my upper arms.

He grunts under the effort of keeping me in his grip, but it doesn't loosen. "Carl!" he calls.

I struggle all the harder, trying to aim my heel at his shins. My foot collides with bone and he yelps in my ear.

"Carl!" he screeches again.

The man with spiky hair stumbles out of the dusty wind Seth makes. Dirt dots his face and he pants as he comes over to us.

"What?" He snaps. "Mikey needs help."

I still struggle and twist, trying to wrench in an angle that will let me attack the man holding me from behind. I wince against the pain of his nails digging into my arm.

"Davey!" he yells. "Help Mikey!"

Davey lumbers off into the wind storm, fists clenched. Even over the sound of rushing wind, I hear a heavy thump. Immediately, the wind vanishes, revealing Seth sprawled on the ground. Ares, breathing hard and blood leaking from a cut on his forehead, backs away from both Mikey and Davey. His ice spear lays in shattered ruins a few feet away from his feet.

"No," I growl, renewing my struggle even though my shoulders ache. Finally the grip loosens, but only to fling me forward at the man called Carl.

"Handle her," the flying man says.

Carl grabs me with new force, making me hiss in a breath. I lift my eyes to glare at him, twisting my wrist to shoot fire.

I still.

All I see is his pale purple eye.

My eyes widen at his mismatched purple and brown eyes. I forget about struggling. I get lost in the lilac color. It seems to grow larger, consuming my mind and thoughts, engulfing me in the mesmerizing swirl. Sounds dim as if underwater. A voice that sounds like mine but vaguely feels like it comes from elsewhere floats through my mind.

You will not resist.

I won't resist.

I stand quietly. The pressure on my arms releases and my fire quiets. My eyes refuse to blink, taking in the purple that has consumed my vision. It's so pretty. So—

"Scarlett!"

Nadia's scream pulls me out of my thoughts. Mind still foggy, I turn. She hasn't moved one inch from her spot. She clamps her hands over her mouth, eyes wide as she stares at something behind me.

I look over my shoulder, turning as if in slow motion. I blink and give my head a hard shake as my vision turns fuzzy. My breath is even and my heartbeat calms, but I clench my teeth in frustration. *Move faster!*

Davey flings a limp Seth onto his shoulder like he weighs nothing. Ares winces as Mikey bends his arm behind him with one hand, gripping his shoulder with the other.

No. I have to do something.

Be calm, my mind echoes.

No, they need my help! My muscles refuse my command to wake up as the mind-manipulator grabs my arms. Even my fire only gives a pathetic attempt to awaken. I squeeze my eyes shut until my temples ache. My mind slowly tries to pull out of the thick fog. But it's still too slow. It won't clear before it's too late. I have to think of something else.

My eyes fly open. Davey, Seth still bent over his shoulder, approaches Nadia. Hands still pressed over her mouth, she turns her panicked gaze on him, backing away. Her whole body shakes. Tiny cracks spread from under her shoes with each step.

My voice breaks free. "Nadia, do something!"

She looks at me, hands dropping to clamp tightly at her

sides. Davey continues to approach. She continues to scramble back. But she does nothing more.

Ares leans forward, pulling against Mikey's hold on him. "Do something, Nadia! Use your powers!"

She swivels her frightened gaze to him. Her mouth opens and closes, but no words come as she shakes her head. Ares and I look at each other. I clench my jaw until my teeth ache. All she has to do is use her powers. That would get us out of this. I know she can do it.

But she won't.

Without a bit of struggle from her, Davey grabs her by the arm. Smirking, he half-lifts her off her feet and drags her back toward us. Nadia clutches a hand over Davey's, grimacing against his iron grip. Ares and I glare at her, but she keeps her tearful eyes on the ground.

Mikey, still panting, looks over all of us. Sweat shines on his face and a bruise is already forming under his eye. "All right. Let's take 'em back to HQ."

My mind finally starts to clear, but not before I'm yanked by the arms and Carl zip ties my wrists. Ares stands deathly still, glaring at Nadia, as the flying one zip ties his wrists. She still stares at her shoes as they secure her. They tie Seth's wrists too as he stirs and groans on Davey's shoulder.

Mikey places one hand on his hip and the other tightly clamped on Ares' shoulder. He looks us over and nods. "They might fetch a good price."

Davey heaves a deep laugh. My stomach clenches. Price? For what, to whom?

"Back to HQ?" Carl asks.

Mikey nods. "Back to HQ."

They shove us down the street. My feet scrape against the ground, but with every step, some of my alertness returns. But it's too late now. Carl has a tight grip on my upper arm and my muscles quiver as adrenaline wears down.

As we trudge along, Ares doesn't take his glare off Nadia,

who still hasn't lifted her eyes from the ground. As Seth groans and comes to on Davey's shoulder, I can't help wanting to be mad at her too. She could've saved us. It would've been as simple as—

A tear slides down her cheek, dripping to the dusty asphalt.

I bite my tongue, biting back my anger at the same time.

We stop in front of a grocery store. The windows are knocked out, some half-boarded by strips of wood, and trash from food packages litters the sidewalk with the glass. They lead us through the propped-open sliding door. I trip over empty cracker boxes and crushed soda cans. Our shoes leave prints in the dust and grime on the yellowing tiled floor.

When we reach the back of the store, they order us to sit in front of the empty refrigerators. We do, sliding down onto fluttering candy wrappers and facing the aisles. I kick away an empty ice cream carton. Davey drops Seth like a sack of potatoes, and he bangs his back on the refrigerator door before sending Davey a sharp glare.

Chatting and laughing like old buddies, our captors shuffle away to a chipped card table farther down the aisle in front of us. They collapse into the chairs and Mikey picks up a torn backpack off a shelf and unzips it. The others lean forward hungrily.

"What'd you find today, Mikey?" Carl eagerly eyes the bag.

Mikey chuckles and holds him back. "Settle down, Carl. We all show what we found, remember?"

Immediately the others pull out backpacks and empty pockets, dumping them on the table. I sit straighter to try to see their hoard. Granola bars, a package of hotdogs, an assortment of candy bars, and an apple.

"Hey, where'd you find fresh fruit?" Carl asks, reaching for the apple.

Davey slaps his hand back and grins, showing off his missing tooth again. "That's for me to know and for you to never find out."

"Well, it doesn't matter anyway," Mikey cuts in as Carl begins to pout. "We'll split it." He slips a knife from the pocket of his faded jeans and carefully slices the apple into fourths. He gives himself a piece with a bruise and passes out the other three.

I expect them to gobble it down without a second thought, but they chew slowly, taking tiny bites. By the way they savor it, they must be starving.

I scan the dusty grocery store, trash littering the floor and piled on the empty shelves. I try to adjust my arms, but the zip ties pinch my wrists. I slump back against the refrigerator. This wasn't part of the plan. What do we do now? I look at Seth, who's fully conscious now, sitting on my right. He stares at our captors, his face blank. I turn to Nadia. She tears her eyes away from them to look back at me. Her dark brows furrow in uncertainty and when she looks at our captors again, something like compassion softens her face. Ares watches them finish off the last of their apple slices before sighing and staring at his sneakers.

Mikey stands and begins picking up the remaining food and piling it into his arms.

"Hey," Carl hisses—like we can't hear him—bumping Mikey with a sandaled foot. "What about them?" He jerks his head toward us.

Mikey looks at us and quirks his mouth to one side. "Hmm. I guess they need to keep up their strength." He pulls a granola bar from his load and walks over to us. He holds it out to Seth. "Here. Y'all can split it."

Seth doesn't move, eyes sparking. "What do you want with us?"

Mikey raises his dark eyebrows like he doesn't understand why Seth is angry.

The flying super spits an apple seed then smirks at us. "A particular someone will pay good money for you lot."

Seth rolls his eyes. "What does that even mean?"

Mikey drops the bar into Seth's lap. His face goes serious as he looks at him. "It means you're going to help us survive."

"You seem to be doing fine by yourselves," Seth says, sarcasm dripping from every word.

I cringe.

Mikey pauses, then he squats in front of Seth and leans his elbows on his knees. Even though he's not looking at me, I want to shrink away from his gaze. Seth licks his lips as a little of his confidence dims.

"I don't know where you come from," Mikey begins slowly, "but around here we have to do what we can to survive. Call us criminals if you want, but we're trying to make the best life for ourselves that we can without going to that fancy-schmancy facility over there." He pokes Seth's chest. "Even if that means turning in a few of our own."

Seth narrows his eyes and lifts his chin. "Yeah? And what if we resist?"

Mikey gives him a lop-sided grin and stands. He turns back to the others, gathers the rest of the food—leaving a candy bar—and disappears down another aisle.

Seth glares at Mikey until he disappears, then drops his head. I stare at his twisted face. What's come over him? He's usually in such a good mood.

Nadia leans close to me. "I'm hungry. You?" she whispers.

Part of me wants to ignore her. If it wasn't for her we wouldn't be here. But I'm supposed to be the leader so I try to smile, but just purse my lips. "Me too."

Ares' stomach grumbles. "Hey, how do you expect us to eat this with our hands tied?"

Davey and Carl blink at us. The third guy looks down his large nose at us. "Figure it out," he snaps in a nasally whine.

I catch Ares' gaze. If they untie us, then maybe we can get away somehow. "We can't eat with our wrists tied."

"Fire girl's right, Flint," Carl said, flipping the knife in the air. He points the tip at us. "Feed 'em."

Uh, wait. That's not what I meant.

Davey stops pouting at the unwrapped candy bar and slides

out of his seat. As he clomps over to us, we shrink back against the glass doors. He picks up the granola bar from Seth's lap and rips off the wrapper, then tears it into four pieces.

"There, there, there, and there," he says as he shoves a chunk of bar into each of our mouths. Then he crumbles the wrapper, tosses it over his shoulder, and wipes his hands on his stained t-shirt. "Done."

I almost choke trying to chew my chunk. It scratches down my throat and I cough, leaving my mouth dry. While I'm thinking about it, my throat feels dry too.

The watch pokes into my back. I can't get at it to check my hydration level. Or to tell Dr. Bailey the predicament we're in.

"Hey, can I have some water?" I ask, coughing again.

Carl stops twirling the knife and looks over. I look away from the purple eye. Davey grunts as he stands.

"Hey, what are you doing? Carl asks.

"Getting water."

"We don't have any extra."

Davey looks at us, contemplating. "I'll ask Mikey." He saunters off in the same direction Mikey disappeared to. After a couple minutes, they both return. Davey carries two water bottles and sets them both on the table. Mikey empties one into a can-turned-cup and brings it over to us. He sends a hard look at Seth before starting at the other end of the line—with Ares.

Ares slides a glance over to us before accepting the rim of the can. Mikey gives him a sip then moves down to the rest of us. He gives me two sips. When I raise an eyebrow at him, he just shrugs. "Fire powers. Need to keep hydrated."

I frown and manage a "thanks" as he gives the last bit to Seth.

After that, our four captors seem to forget we even exist. They sit around the table, drinking their water portions, dividing the candy bar "for dessert", and chatting like they're just normal friends. Not superhuman criminals.

I wince and try to adjust my position for my aching back.

The sun crawls at an achingly slow pace across the sky. My frustration grows as the light turns auburn, then grey. As the grocery store grows darker, Davey brings out an assortment of old flashlights and candle stubs. They light them and continue talking, discussing when and where they can find more food, what areas to avoid, safe spots, and people who are willing to help them.

"And don't get your stash snatched by Rez's kids this time, okay, Davey?" Flint says.

My breath stills as I tune in to their conversation.

Davey drops a large fist on the table and the flames flicker. "They jumped me."

Flint rolls his eyes. "They're kids."

He blinks. "They're fast...some of 'em."

Mikey pats Davey on the back. "It's all right, big fella. Rez trains 'em smart. We won't let him get our goods next time."

Davey shoots a glare at Flint. He just lifts his nose and looks away.

"What happened to you back there?" Nadia's low whisper startles me.

I tilt my head toward her without taking my eyes off the flickering flames, mesmerized by their movement. "What do you mean?" I whisper back.

She shifts to angle more toward me. "I mean when you froze."

I bite back an angry reply. *She* was the one who froze. "Oh. That."

She waits.

I try to shrug, but my shoulders just tense up by my ears. "I don't know, I just...looked too long."

"At what?"

I nod toward Carl, who pokes the knife tip into the wax of a candle. "Him. I think he has the same mind-manipulating powers we were warned about."

"You mean the same kind Rez is supposed to have?"

I nod.

"I think the important thing is why *you* froze, Nadia."

Nadia stiffens at Ares hard words, hunching her shoulders and staring at the floor. Her eyes go distant and glossy. When she opens her mouth, her lip quivers. "I'm sorry—"

"We needed you," Ares hisses. "You could've gotten us out of this mess."

Nadia hunches deeper, as if she's in pain.

Seth leans forward, looking between us three. "What happened?"

Ares' glare never leaves Nadia when he opens his mouth. I take one more glance at Nadia before quickly jumping in. "It's nothing."

Ares turns his chilly stare to me. "It's not nothing. This could be a problem for our miss—"

"She said she's sorry," I reply, flicking a glance at our captors. "It won't happen again." I soften my voice, leaning over to look Nadia in the face. "Right?"

She bites her lip, forehead wrinkled. All she whispers is another "I'm sorry."

Seth frowns at her. "Wait. What happened?"

Ares sighs loudly and leans his head back on the refrigerator glass. "What's done is done," he grumbles. "What we need to discuss now is what we're going to do next."

Nadia grimaces as she tries to adjust into a more comfortable position. I still study her, but address the group. "We're wasting time here."

Seth flops back against the refrigerator door with a sigh. "I don't know what we're supposed to do. It's obvious they can overpower us."

My legs begin to ache from sitting on my knees, and I groan as I stretch them out in front of me. "I guess we'll just have to wait and think."

A few moments pass. "My brain hurts," Seth states.

I chuckle a little and rest my head back on the refrigerator door. Darkness grows and a sleepy silence falls over the grocery store. The yellow glimmer of the candles flickers and moves across the surrounding aisle shelves. Davey falls asleep with his head on the table. Mikey sketches in a thin notebook with Flint looking over his shoulder. Carl stares at the empty shelves, as if dreaming they were filled with the junk food I'm sure he craves.

I yawn and pull my legs closer to save warmth. Before it can get too cold, I coax my fire to spread through my body to keep warm.

"That feels nice," Nadia whispers with a smile.

I smile back, though it's strained. "You're welcome."

The silence stretches on. Shadows lengthen and meld until darkness cloaks the city, and I purse my lips in frustration. We haven't even found Rez yet.

Soft, slow footsteps break the silence. We all stiffen. It echoes from the darkness at the front of the store, outside the circle of candlelight.

Mikey and Flint look into the dark. Carl kicks Davey under the table. He grunts and sputters awake. Then all four of them study the shadows, leaning forward, muscles tense. The four of us do the same.

The soft crunch of the footsteps echoes closer. They're slow, but deliberate and confident. Whoever it is doesn't care that someone hears.

The slim form of a woman steps into the circle of light. Her black clothes blend with the shadows. Candlelight dances in her emerald green eye. The other iris is the color of the darkest night. She smirks and tilts her head to the side, her raven black hair brushing her shoulder.

"H-hey, Crynn," Mikey says. He stands and takes a step forward in front of the table toward the woman. But his shoulders tense. None of them relax yet.

She puts a hand on her hip. "Mikey. Doing well, I presume?" She looks past him at us. The candlelight catches in her bright, green eye as it settles on me. I quickly look away.

She nods toward us, pale skin the color of moonlight. "Who've you got here this time?"

Mikey turns as if to look at us, but decides to keep an eye on the girl, Crynn. "Just some kids. We were gonna ask you if—"

"You know what I'm gonna have to do, don't ya, Mikey?" Crynn lifts her hand and examines her nails, then lifts her eyes to him, her smirk fading. "I've got orders to take those kids off your hands."

One more figure steps out of the shadows to her side. He's almost as big as Davey, but just as tall, muscles bulging through his dark grey shirt and bald head shining in the candle light. His stormy grey eyes scan over each of our captors, jaw muscles clenching under the stubble on his face. They shrink away from his gaze. Is *that* Rez?

Mikey gulps and clears his throat. His hand slips behind him and inches across the table toward the knife. "Nice to see you too, Ivon." His fingers grip the knife handle.

I gasp. "Look out!"

Mikey hurls the knife.

CHAPTER ELEVEN

Crynn slides to the side. The knife slips past her and clatters into the shadows. Ivon sprints toward Mikey, but Davey tackles him and they crash against the shelves. Crynn jumps over them like a cat, gaze fixed on Mikey.

He stumbles away from her, bumping into the table. He grabs for a flashlight and flings it at her.

She catches it and cracks it over his head. He staggers and slumps to the filthy floor.

Carl and Flint finally break out of their frozen state. Flint lunges for Crynn while Carl scrambles to help Davey.

After a solid thud, Ivon shoves off an unconscious Davey, heavy flashlight in hand. He grabs Carl before he can throw his punch and snatches Flint before he can reach Crynn. He tosses them both against the shelves like a couple of rag dolls.

Crynn hurries to us and pulls us to our feet. Without a word, she grabs my elbow and leads the way as we run out of the grocery store. I crane my neck to make sure the others are close. Seth follows just behind me, with Ivon helping Nadia and Ares with each hand.

As we slip into the night shadows, yells break out in the

grocery store. Mikey and his gang stumble out and trip after us, clutching their heads.

Running with my hands tied is harder than I expected. I try my best to match Crynn's pace, but I'm already panting. "Who are you?"

"Crynn Knox. I'm on your side. Follow." She lets go of my arm and I run on my own, following her steps as she slips into alleys, maneuvers through buildings and sprints around blocks until I think we're going in circles. She and Ivon are the only ones not gasping for air.

We stop in front of a large warehouse. Its high windows are dusty and broken and vines crawl up the bricks. It seems quiet.

Ivon scans the street behind us as Crynn opens a rusted metal door and motions inside. "Come on in." She grins. "Wipe your feet first."

I can't seem to catch my breath, and that two sips of water earlier wasn't nearly enough, but I force my shaky legs to carry me inside.

Immediately my eyes find the warm glow of a bonfire in the center of the large space. My shoes scratch against the gritty dust on the concrete floor as I move toward the blaze, my body craving the warmth. I can feel Nadia, Ares and Seth close behind me.

I finally tear my gaze from the warm blaze to take in the rest of the room. Figures drift around the fire, holding tin can cups and huddling in clusters, and some sleep in the corners. Their shadows dance on the walls in chilling, warped figures.

Supers. My spine stiffens. There are so many. Could this be Rez's place?

The door swings closed with an echoing clank and I flinch. Crynn pats my shoulder. "Come warm yourselves by the fire. Oh, Ivon." She waves a hand at our wrists. "If you don't mind."

Without a word—and keeping his steely gaze on us—he slips a knife from his pocket. I grimace as he slices through my zip ties, then sigh and rub my wrists. Silently, he moves to free the others.

Crynn plants her hands on her hips and gives that smirking grin again. "Better?"

I smile back. "Yeah, thank you."

She nods, then turns toward the fire.

I scan the faces lit by the firelight. A red-haired teen bites into a spotted banana, a couple kids whisper and giggle, sitting together on a wooden crate, and a middle-aged woman is lovingly taping a bandage over a young girl's elbow.

I scan the faces again, looking for someone who carries himself like a leader. Which one's Rez? I bite my lip and study the faces more closely. And who's our contact?

A shove from behind gets me moving. I glance over my shoulder at Ivon, who watches us as we approach the firepit. He slips back into the shadows and crosses his arms, observing.

I gulp and face toward the beckoning flames.

Crynn motions toward some crates and upturned buckets. "Have a seat and warm yourselves."

The four of us share glances as we lower ourselves onto the makeshift seats. Several heads turn our way. Some offer polite smiles and waves of greeting, but wariness clouds most gazes. I lean toward the fire, holding my arms close to my core, not acknowledging any of them.

Nadia leans closer to me. "Do you see him?" she whispers.

"I don't know if he's here," I hiss back.

Seth leans over from my other side. "Don't worry. I'm sure he'll be back from his burglary and vandalizing soon."

Ares scoots a couple feet farther away from the fire's warmth. "Just have patience." But his eyes dart around, lingering on every face, hands rubbing nervously on his jeans.

Seth doesn't say anything more, but his knee bounces rapidly. I find myself knotting my fingers in my lap. Nadia chews her lip.

"He's here." Crynn's voice, so close behind me, makes me jump. I turn in my seat to see where she's looking.

A tall man steps into the warehouse door. He looks about in his thirties, with broad shoulders, sun-tanned skin, rough stubble and chocolate brown hair. He hefts a large cardboard box on his shoulder and grins at the crowd. I realize everyone in the warehouse has turned their attention to him. This has to be Rez.

As he gets closer to the fire, the light catches in his one sapphire blue eye. I focus on his dark brown one instead.

Crynn crosses her arms. "It's about time."

His grin falters a bit when he sees her, but he quickly restores it. "Good to see you too, Crynn. Whatever happened to 'Glad you survived and came home all right'?"

Crynn huffs and reaches to take the box from him.

"No, no, I've got it." He looks around and squints into the shadows. "Oh, there you are, Ivon." He nears the fire and sets the box on a two-stack of crates. He notices us and raises his eyebrows then looks at Crynn. "New recruits?" He grins at us before turning his attention back to the box.

Crynn steps forward. "I found them with Mikey and—"

"Later, Crynn. Right now it's time for dinner."

She purses her lips and crosses her arms, waiting while Rez rifles through the box. At the word "dinner" everyone crowds closer to the bonfire. Children, all ages, shove to the front, grinning up at Rez.

There's got to be nearly forty people here. I slide a glance at Ares. He scans the crowd, discreetly tapping his fingers on his knee as he counts.

Rez gives most of the fresh fruit from the box to the youngest and oldest of the crowd. Others get an assortment of granola bars, candy bars, chocolate, canned beans, or crackers. Healthy.

Rez flips out a can of mandarin oranges and holds it up to the four of us. "Hungry?"

Seth's stomach grumbles loud enough to turn a few heads. My stomach pinches, about ready to copy Seth's.

Rez laughs, bright and deep, then pulls out another can of

oranges and two cans of beans. He crosses over to our side of the firepit to the only empty crate and sits down with a sigh. I stiffen when he slips out a knife from his boot and opens a can of oranges. He passes it to Seth, who eyes the glinting blade.

Rez opens the second can of oranges then holds it out to me. "You look hungry too."

I hesitate, then cautiously take the can. "Thanks." He nods and I study him a moment before lifting an orange slice from the sweet syrup. When it touches my tongue, it feels like the most refreshing thing I've ever eaten. I savor the juices, letting it coat my parched throat.

Rez opens a couple more cans of beans and hands them to Nadia and Ares. They nod their thanks then eat in silence. The warehouse falls silent as people either sit around the fire or go to their own corners to eat their food. Keeping my head bent over my oranges, I study their dirty, worn clothes and thin faces. Rez eats half a granola bar and hands the other half to a sticky-faced toddler. As the little boy's chubby fingers curl around it, the bar enlarges to double its size. Giggling happily, the boy waddles off, gnawing on the granola.

I gape, staring after him. When I look at Rez, he smirks.

Well, that's new.

"So," he says, wiping his hands on his jeans and looking up at Crynn. "Where did you find this bunch of kids?"

Seth bristles. "We're not ki—"

I nudge him with my elbow to shut him up.

Crynn steps forward from the shadows she disappeared into. Her carefree smile is missing as she tells Rez where and how she found us.

Rez just nods and rests his elbows on his knees. "So where are you all traveling from?"

I take a sip of the syrup. "East. Redfield."

He nods. "Traveling together?"

All of the sudden I sense Ivon's hulking presence behind me.

The back of my neck tingles and I swallow. "Yes." Under Rez's piercing gaze, my palms begin to sweat. I look away.

He looks up past us. "For goodness sakes, calm down, Ivon." When he looks back at us, I realize how mesmerizing his deep blue eye is. Like a jewel. He studies us for an uncomfortable amount of time. "They're our guests."

Ivon hesitates before stepping back into the shadows. I rub the back of my neck and try not to think about his stormy gaze on me.

Rez tilts his head as he continues to study us. "I'm sure you've figured out that I'm Rez. And you've met Crynn and Ivon." He motions to them both. "I would introduce everyone around here, but that'd take forever. All you need to know for now is that we're family." He smiles. "So what are your names?"

We hesitate a moment before Ares speaks up. "I'm Ares, sir," he says.

At the "sir" Seth snorts. I nudge him again. This is becoming a habit.

I clear my throat. "I'm Scarlett. And this is Seth and Nadia." I point to them both. Neither of them looked like they were going to volunteer that information.

Rez nods. "Nice to meet you. We're always happy to find new additions to our family." He stands and starts to turn, but pauses. "That is, if you intend to stay."

For a little while, at least. I nod.

"So how'd you get to Rapid? What's your story?" He turns away to pick up the box he brought in earlier. He takes out more food, handing it to Crynn—who seems to have taken to the shadows since Rez got here—and she puts it on the shelves.

I shift. "Well, um..." I flick a glance at the others. "I guess you could say we're just looking for a normal life."

I feel Nadia glance at me. Rez pauses and studies us. Just when I think he's going to ask more questions, he nods, as if understanding the meaning behind my answer. But I bet his guess is a bit off.

"So..." Rez hands another can of beans to Crynn. "What are your gifts, Scarlett?"

An orange slice goes down hard in my throat. I cover my mouth as I cough. "My what?"

"Your gifts. You know, your powers."

I swallow and wipe my hand on my jeans. I've never heard them called gifts. "Oh. I, uh..." I didn't expect this to be this awkward. "I have this fire... thing." Yeah, great job.

He just looks at me, waiting for more.

I sigh and lower my voice a little. "Fire comes out of my hands." I close my fingers over the red splotches on my palms. I wish I'd thought of taking the cream with me, but I'm sure Dr. Bailey wouldn't have let me.

He grins and glances at the healthy fire crackling in front of us. "That's fascinating. Fire powers always are." He strokes the stubble on his jaw. "So, if I understand your type of abilities, you can touch flames and not be burned."

I nod. "Yeah, I guess." I wish my skin could burn. Then I'd be human.

He brushes his hands on his zip-up hoodie and tosses the empty box away. Then he sits and rests his elbows on his knees. When he looks at me, firelight dances in his blue eye. "Would you care to demonstrate?"

I lick my lips and try to suppress the heat rising in my hands. I look at the popping fire, hoping he'll see how nervous I am and change his mind. I glance at him. He's still waiting.

I reach my hand toward the fire, feeling the others' gaze on me. My fingers slide through the bright flames. When I don't feel searing pain, I let out a breath. I flex my fingers, letting the warmth spread through my hand and all the way up my arm. I feel...energized.

When I feel the eyes of the whole warehouse on me, I pull my hand back and rub my thumb against my palm. Rez's gaze slides from the fire then back to me. "Fascinating," he repeats.

My cheeks flush. My eyes must be glowing again. I look away.

"You don't have to be embarrassed," he says. Even without looking at him, I can hear the smile in his voice. "What about your friends? What can the rest of you do?"

I'm thankful he dropped the subject of my powers. I don't care if I'm in a room full of superhumans, I don't like to advertise that I'm one of them.

Nadia hugs herself tightly and looks away. "I'd rather not talk about it."

Ares frowns at Nadia, then turns back to Rez. "I have ice powers," he says hurriedly, then scoots a smidgen closer, crate scraping across the cement floor. "Has someone with ice powers come here before?"

Rez nods. "Several."

"How old?"

Rez's brow furrows. "Varies. Why? Are you looking for someone?"

Ares opens his mouth, but catches us frowning at him. He swallows and shifts his jaw, then scoots away again, clasping his hands in his lap. "Maybe," he mumbles.

I watch Ares stare at his knees, white brows drawn together. *Is* he looking for someone? How would he know anyone who would pass through here?

Rez studies Ares a moment more before turning his attention to Seth, but he just stares at the fire, seeming to be mesmerized by the flames. Awkward silence passes before Rez decides Seth isn't going to answer. What's gotten into him?

Rez sits straight again and looks around the quieting warehouse. He pulls his sleeves over his hands, hunching his shoulders against a shiver. "Cold night, isn't it?"

Colder than you may think. At least for me. My fire curls into my core in protest.

In the silence that follows, sleepiness blankets us. Most of the supers find a spot of floor to fall asleep on, some under thin blankets. Through the broken windows above us, stars twinkle in the inky black sky. Dusty cobwebs cover the corners of the high ceiling soaring above our heads. A faint breeze trickles in through the windows, and I lean closer toward the fire's warmth. I watch the logs crackles and pop and the embers pulse with heat. I take a deep breath, watching the warping tongues of flame.

A sharp buzz on my wrist makes me jump. My eyes dart at Rez to make sure he's not watching before I look down at the watch. I resist flipping open the false face, instead glancing around the warehouse for spying eyes. I'll check it later.

I scan the room again, wondering if anyone saw. My gaze snags on a glint of deep green beyond the shelves. Half hidden in shadows, Crynn watches me. I turn my gaze back to the fire, resisting the urge to finger the watch.

"You all must be tired," Rez says, standing. "Especially if you've traveled far."

The thought of sleeping inside this building with dozens of criminal supers makes my shoulders tense. I wrap my arms around myself, glancing at the sleeping forms and the gritty dust covering the cement floor. Still, a yawn overtakes me.

Rez scans our faces again before nodding. "Let's get you all set up for the night."

The air chills me right to my bones. I cower against the brick wall outside the warehouse as a biting wind rakes over me, shivering as I try to get my stiff fingers to figure out Dr. Bailey's watch. It takes me a few minutes to find the message he sent me.

I tug my hoodie tighter around my neck and scan the darkness cloaking the city. A shudder shakes me as I wonder what the shadows could be holding. Hugging my elbows closer to my sides, I bend over the watch.

How are things? his message reads.

I click 'reply', and a microphone icon pops up, waiting for my voice. I bring the watch closer to my mouth. "Things are fine now," I whisper. "Send." The letters string together and the message sends off to the doctor.

Only a few moments pass before the watch vibrates with another reply. *Have you made contact with Rez?*

"Yes. After a slight delay," I whisper again.

Dr. Bailey: *Everyone is okay?*

He doesn't even want to know what happened? Me: *The first supers we encountered captured us, but we got out and everyone's fine.*

I can imagine the cool tone in his voice as he replies: *Good thing you had training.*

Another bout of frustration threatens as I think about Nadia, what she could've done to prevent it.

Me: *We had help.*

Dr. Bailey: *Okay. Good.*

Me: *From a girl named Crynn. Part of Rez's gang.*

There's a moment before he responds again: *Anything else to report?*

I shake my head, even though we're only having a text conversation and he can't see me: *Not much right now. Their HQ is a big warehouse, and there's gotta be about forty people in there. Not many weapons I can see as of yet, except for a knife Rez carries.*

The reply comes through instantly this time. *It's not your job to take note of numbers and weapons. The others have already told me.*

I blink. They did? When? How?

Another buzz. Dr. Bailey: *Anything on Rez?*

Me: *No. Nothing much has happened. People are settling down for the night.* I lift my head slightly to glance out into the still, darkness surrounding the warehouse.

Dr. Bailey: *All right. Get some rest. I'll be in contact tomorrow.*

After I decide his last message doesn't need a response, I remember the darkness and cold again as I snap the false watch over the screen. My arm drops limply to my side, the weight of the mission settling on my shoulders like a heavy, wet cloak. My chest aches for the warmth of home, just to see my family even for a few moments. My hands curl into fists. I'm doing this for them. Someday I'll see them again, when the cure has fixed me.

I turn toward the warehouse and step back into the den of criminal supers.

CHAPTER TWELVE

The concrete floor of the warehouse has already bruised my spine. The cold seeps into my bones, and I shiver. My fire feels too exhausted to warm my chilled body, and it lies dormant and calm in my core. I pull the thin fleece blanket over my shoulders, settling with leaving my feet uncovered. I slide my hand behind my head to give it some cushion and stare up at the ceiling. My eyes blink lazily as I watch the stars twinkling in the dark sky through the broken windows. Suddenly it occurs to me that it's the first time I've seen the stars in several months. They don't exactly let you go stargazing in the SCF.

It reminds me of when Dylan, Hannah and I used to sit outside on warm summer nights, talking and hoping to see a shooting star. We never saw one, but those were the nights we were most vulnerable with each other, sharing hopes and dreams and thoughts and fears. Even Hannah could come up with some pretty deep things sometimes. The memory brings a smile to my face. I hope they're still stargazing and waiting for their shooting star, maybe thinking of me.

Blankets rustle next to me. "You still awake?" Nadia whispers.

I sigh. "Yeah." Too much to think about.

She pauses. "Thinking about Rez?"

I hesitate, not knowing how to respond, suddenly aware of the pinch of the watch around my wrist as I wonder what Nadia thinks about Rez. And if what she thinks is wrong, should I tell Dr. Bailey?

"Not exactly...I don't know what to think about him yet, I guess." Safe answer. I turn my head toward her, even though I can't see her. "What do you think about him?"

Blankets rustle again, and her soft voice projects upward. "I don't know yet either. He seems so..."

"What?"

A deep breath. "I don't know."

I can guess at what she's thinking. Rez just doesn't seem like the destructive, hardened, superhuman criminal I thought he was. He actually seems...kind.

I shake my head to clear my thoughts. I need to stay focused, focused on the mission and the cure. Rez could just be putting on an act. A trick to get us to trust him. Still, he baffles me.

Maybe I shouldn't share my thoughts about Rez or any of my doubts about this with the others at all. I know they have means of contacting the doctor. Would they report me if I said something wrong? Would I report *them* if *they* did?

Nadia goes quiet, so I assume she's fallen back to sleep. I stare at the shadowed ceiling, and my stomach squeezes. How many supers are contained under this roof? And how many of them have used their powers to hurt people, maybe even to kill? I squirm under my blanket, shoving down the urge to sleep outside. Who knows what dangers lurk out there too. But isn't it dangerous to have so many of us in one building? The SCF always made sure we were separated into much smaller groups. And we weren't allowed to use our powers there, obviously.

I wriggle to my side, resting my head on my arm and curling myself into a ball to keep warm. Even though thoughts are a swimming buzz in my head, my eyelids droop and I slip into sleep.

Sunlight stirs me from my sleep as children's cheery voices reach my ears. Grogginess clouds my brain as I try to process the sounds.

I bolt upright. "Dylan? Hannah?"

They're not here. I'm not home. I'm sitting on the cold, hard floor in the corner of a dusty warehouse under an old blanket. The children's voices are from no one that I know.

I throw off my blanket. Nadia is gone, her blanket in a neat folded pile next to the brick wall. I leave mine in a heap and stumble toward the hub of activity around the firepit. The chatter of the supers gathered there echoes up to the high ceiling, where the dusty cobwebs clinging to the corners sway in the breeze streaming in from the windows.

Rez looks up from his same spot by the bonfire as yesterday. The sunlight filtering through the high windows makes patchy shadows through the stocked shelves behind him. Children crowd around him, all hungry smiles and frizzy bed hair.

He turns his smile to me when I approach. "Good morning, Scarlett."

I blink the sleepiness from my eyes and suppress a yawn. "Morning." I stop several feet from the circle of people. The brightness of morning light illuminates their worn, stained clothes. Holes in the sleeves, frayed jeans, and some children don't have shoes, bare toes catching the dirt of the city.

Rez grunts as he slides a crate off the nearest shelf, steps a few feet to the bonfire and puts the box on top of another, then proceeds to pass out some bruised apples from a crate to the waiting kids. "We're just getting breakfast. Care to join us?"

All the other supers crowd closer to the fire, pressing in to get their meal. I hug my arms close to my sides and take a half-step away. But my stomach rumbles. "Sure."

There's a tap on my shoulder, and I turn to find Nadia standing next to me. "Where were you?" I whisper.

"Just looking around." She glances around this end of the warehouse where the shelves and firepit are clustered, while the rest of the space is left free for sleeping and living.

I lean closer, lowering my voice even more. "Find anything interesting?"

She chuckles a little through her nose. "They really like to keep organized with their food stores." She sobers. "With what little they have."

Seth and Ares come shuffling into our group. Ares looks a bit more bright-eyed than Seth, whose hair defies gravity and sticks out at odd angles.

"Good, good! Come and join us." Rez beckons to us when he sees the boys.

The four of us shyly crowd closer to the firepit, warming ourselves while waiting our turn for the fruit. Stretching my fingers toward the flames' warmth, I spot Ivon in his same post as last night. He leans against the wall, muscular arms crossed and dark eyes watching our every move. I shift uncomfortably.

With all the Rapid supers here around the fire, I scan their faces again in the light of morning. I wish they'd given us more info on our contact. What if things go wrong and we need help? We won't know who to go to. I wonder who it is...

My gaze lands on Ivon, still watching us with those steel-grey eyes. He narrows his eyes at me. I shudder. Nope. Can't be him. I gulp and return my attention to the fire.

People get their share of breakfast fruit, and the crowd around the firepit thins as the supers retreat into corners or outside to enjoy their food. The four of us claim seats on the empty crates, same as last night. Rez tosses each of us an apple. I bite into the glossy skin and savor the sweet juice coating my mouth, not even caring there's a squishy bruise on one side. For several minutes, no one speaks and the warehouse fills with sounds of crunching and chewing.

Rez polishes off his apple—including most of the core—before us and tosses the remnants into the fire, then wipes his hands on his pants. "Well, who wants to join me today? Get a feel of how we operate."

The four of us glance at each other.

"Where?" Ares asks around his apple bite.

Rez smirks. "On a mission, of sorts."

Seth spits a seed into the fire, glowering at Rez. "To do what? Rob and loot?"

Rez matches his gaze. "You'll see if you come."

Seth drops his apple core in the firepit. "Not interested."

"I'll just stick around here," Ares adds, picking at his apple's skin and glancing at the supers clustered throughout the warehouse.

Nadia avoids looking at Rez, twirling the stem of her half-eaten apple between her fingers. "I think I'd rather stick around here too."

Rez's smile falters at their refusals. He turns to me. I frown at the others. Don't they want to find out what he's up to? Oh, right—their assignments. And this one is mine. I turn back to Rez and clear my throat. "I'll go." Maybe I'll have something to report to Dr. Bailey.

"Great!" Rez stands and walks over to the shelves to grab two beat-up backpacks. As he passes me toward the door, he tosses the smaller bag to me and jerks his head for me to follow. "Come on."

I scramble after him, jogging to catch up with his long strides. He swings open the same door we came in last night and steps out into the morning sunlight. I hurry close behind.

Crynn stands on the grass-infested, gravel parking space outside the warehouse, her hands stuffed in her back pockets. She looks our way at our crunching footsteps.

"We'll be back soon," Rez says without looking at her.

She watches me, green eye glowing in the sunlight, and I keep my eyes to the ground. As I pass her, she leans toward me. "Stay sharp," she whispers.

I frown at her over my shoulder, but she goes back to scanning her surroundings. I trip over an empty plastic bottle and decide to watch where I step instead. A light wind tumbles through the street, smelling dusty with a tinge of smoke. I step over a pile of bricks spilling over the sidewalk and scan the quiet upper floors of the buildings. I can't help but feel like I'm being watched. It's too quiet here.

Rez whistles with the beat of his easy stride. I take almost two steps to his one. He maneuvers easily around the trash, garbage, and rubble littering the streets. He even tosses a few wrappers and crushed plastic bottles into a nearby trash can, but I don't see the point.

We cut straight through the city into the quiet countryside. Tall grasses whisper eerie melodies in the wind coupled with our crunching steps. I slow to look back at the city behind us, then jog to catch up with him, panting from the brisk walk. "Where are we going exactly?"

He keeps his eyes on the horizon, barely squinting against the head wind. "Ashland Heights."

"Where?"

He chuckles. "It's a small town. We should reach it in about two hours." He flicks a glance at me. "Where are you from anyway?"

"Hermosa." As soon as the word escapes, I bite my tongue. Rez raises an eyebrow at me and I scramble for words. "I mean, I-I used to live there," I stammer. "Then Redfield. That's where I, uh, met the others."

"Hmm, we've had some supers from Hermosa drift through here."

"Really?" From my town? There were more?

"Yup, not a lot of them stayed long though. Most were heading farther east, probably because they wanted to get as far away from old memories as they could." He pauses and some of the spring leaves his step. "Some are traveling west."

I tilt my head. "What do you mean?"

He takes a deep breath and looks up at the sky. A few birds

flit across the cloud-streaked expanse. He falls silent for so long that I think he won't answer. I focus on the road ahead.

"You've heard of the SCF, right?" he says softly.

My throat goes dry. "Yeah. Who hasn't?"

"Well..." He sighs again. "Some supers—especially when they just discover they have powers—think it's a better idea to turn themselves in there instead of trying to make a better life for themselves."

"A better life?" I blurt before thinking. "You're calling this" — I gesture back to where we came from— "a better life?" I know the SCF feels like a prison, but this place... It's a city reduced to bones and ash and rubble. How desperate does someone have to be to live here? You can't make a place like this a home.

Instead of getting angry at my outburst, he just smiles sadly at me, like I'm a child who doesn't understand yet. That sparks more frustration in my gut. He's the one who doesn't get it.

"Yes, I call it a better life." He slips his hands into his pockets. "Better to live freely and have a chance to make a difference in the world—especially for supers—than rotting away in that prison with their needles and scientists and—" He breaks off as his voice escalates, then takes a slow breath. "They make you feel like a science experiment, Scarlett. They make you feel like you don't belong on this earth." His voice is tainted with pain and memories. For the first time, I really study his eyes, not thinking about the possibility of his mind-control. What kind of backstory would a superhuman like Rez have?

He clears his throat roughly and shakes his shoulders, bringing back that easy smile. "Enough of that dreary mood now, am I right?"

I give him a small smile. Despite his forced cheerfulness, not a word passes between us until the first building of Ashland Heights comes into view. As we get closer, Rez makes some futile attempts to clean himself up. He brushes some dirt and dust off his clothes, straightens his jacket, and knocks some mud off his boots. I look down at my fairly clean clothes. Softly worn, but not dirty, stained or torn like most of the supers in Rapid.

We slip quietly into the city. It's smaller than Hermosa, which makes me nervous. It'll be harder to blend in here. Do we need to blend in?

I tug Rez's sleeve. He doesn't slow, but leans his ear closer to me.

"What are we doing here exactly?" I ask.

"Getting supplies," he says immediately, like I should've guessed that.

I keep my voice low. "Is it...safe for us to be here?" Won't people know his face?

He still doesn't look at me, keeping his nonchalant manner. But I see his eyes carefully scanning the surroundings and every person we pass.

"No, it's not," he mutters, barely audible. "But it's got to be done."

"But you're a wanted criminal."

"*Shh*, not so loud." He turns toward a small grocery store. "Are you trying to get me arrested?"

I swallow. "I whispered," I reply, tripping on a thick clump of grass in the asphalt.

I follow him into the store. The gush of air conditioning makes a shiver run down my spine. A redheaded cashier at the checkout counter to our right barely lifts her head from her phone. "Hello. Welcome."

I grimace at her air-quotes-worthy "enthusiastic" greeting as Rez lifts his hand in a responding half wave. She doesn't look up, so I hurry to keep up with him, eager to be out of her line of sight. Rez's boots leave clods of dirt on the shiny tile. We slip into the canned goods aisle, and I kick the dirt Rez left under the lowest shelf, where dust bunnies gather in droves. I hug myself and rub my arms against the chill as he starts examining the cans, glancing once or twice at the ceiling. Looking for cameras?

"Keep watch," he mutters.

I blink. "What?"

He takes a can of green beans off the shelf and shoves it into my backpack before I can protest.

"What are you doing?" I hiss, yanking the can back out.

Rez grabs the can from me, glancing up and down the aisle. "I said, keep watch."

My jaw goes slack. "You're stealing?" My hands curl into fists. *That's* what he brought me here to do?

He sets his jaw. "I'm not Mr. Moneybags, Lettie."

I clench my jaw. "Don't call me that. Not ever." That's only for my family. And he's far from it. I blink back a hot, angry tear.

He leans back, blinking. "Sorry. Just a nickname."

I hook my thumbs through the backpack straps. "Let's just go."

He puts the can in my bag again and zips it closed. "We need to get food. I'm not leaving here until I get some." He turns back to the shelf. "Go back if you want to. Good luck not getting lost. But if you stay, you help."

My legs won't move, even though I want to slam the can back on the shelf and march right out of there. But I don't know how to get back. What if Rez gets caught and in trouble and won't have help because I left?

I rake a hand through my hair. Why do I care what happens to him? My feet still won't move.

Rez picks up two cans of baked beans and glances at me. "Decided to stay?"

I cross my arms and scowl at the shelf.

He nods. "Good." He slips off his backpack to put cans in it. "Then get some cans and make it quick. No more than four total. Any more than that will be hard to hide." He slings the bag back on his shoulders.

I look at the cans of mandarin oranges next to me. My mouth goes dry and sweat breaks out on my forehead. My heart thuds in my ears. I swipe my sleeves over my face and glance down the aisle once. Twice. No one's in sight.

My hand shakes as I reach for the can. Then pull back. Reach again. Back and forth, back and forth. Finally, I close my eyes and snatch it off the shelf. In an agonizing moment, I have the can tucked in my backpack. That's all I'll take.

I feel hot and cold at the same time. Sweat slicks my skin and my muscles freeze like Ares is too close. I watch Rez as he continues down the aisle.

That's all I'll take. No more. He can't make me.

Standing rigid on the yellowing tile, my thoughts won't stop whirling: *I'm stealing food, I'm stealing food, I'm a criminal, I'm stealing food.* My fingers tremble as Rez casually saunters down the aisle, scanning the shelves like a normal shopper. The bag on my shoulder weighs like a ton of bricks.

I'm stealing food.

He disappears around the shelves, and I don't follow. I wait until he comes back, carrying a bag of apples and a box of crackers.

He doesn't look at me when he nods for me to follow. "Let's go."

To my confusion, he stops at the cash register. He digs some crumpled bills from his pocket and pays for the apples and crackers. I try to control my shaking, nervously glancing at the girl ringing us out. Frizzy red curls covering half her drooping, freckled face, she barely even looks at us.

My heart doesn't stop its frantic beat until we're out on the street again. I let out a breath, but I want to get out of here, out of this town. Rez's pace is painfully slow.

"Can't we speed it up a little?" I don't try to mask the anger in my voice.

"Relax," he says. "I know what I'm doing."

"Obviously," I mutter. I wonder how many times he's done this. Probably a lot.

Not a word passes between us as we reach the countryside

again on our way back to Rapid. With the walk, my muscles finally loosen up and my breathing evens out. But I won't look at him. I didn't know that he meant we were going to steal when he invited me on this little "mission" with him.

I stole food.

The thought won't leave me. Suddenly my mind jerks to my parents. What would they think if they saw me now? Will I tell them if I see them again? I feel like a criminal. Am I?

"I have a feeling you're not happy with me." Rez breaks the silence, his tone a little lighter now that we've left the town.

"I am," I spit, fists clenched. A cold wind yanks my hair, dampening the fire that's stirring in my gut. I tuck my fists under my arms for warmth.

He slips his hands into his pockets and gazes at the trees lining the road. "It's what we have to do around here, Scarlett. It's not like the supers of Rapid can go out and get regular jobs."

"You should be in jail."

"And you should be in the SCF because you're less than human."

I glare at him, clenching my jaw. "No, I'm not." But I'm not sure I believe my own words. My jaw loosens as I lift my hands to glance at my palms. How can I be human with this fire inside me?

He finally looks at me, his gaze softer than I expected. "Exactly. That's why I do what I do, because I don't like how the world treats supers in that government facility. We're not a science experiment." He looks ahead again. "People need to realize that supers can do good or bad just like any other person. Our powers can even be useful to society."

I turn my glare to my shoes instead. He's wrong. That's not what Dr. Bailey says. We're too dangerous to be left free. With the cure they're working on, we have hope to be cured.

I glance up at Rez again, wondering how he ever thought he could go against the government and form this band of criminal supers in Rapid. There are children there. Doesn't he know they'd have a better life in the SCF rather than starving in this abandoned city?

The cans clank against my back as Rez finally quickens his pace. The backpack of stolen food isn't the only thing weighing heavily on me.

CHAPTER THIRTEEN

My thoughts spin too fast. I don't say any more the rest of the way back to Rapid. Rez tries to start a conversation a couple times, but I don't respond. I don't know if I'm angry with him still or just confused.

We don't go back to the warehouse like I expected. Rez turns down a silent street with cookie-cutter houses, overgrown lawns, patchy roofs, and broken fences. I study each boarded window, my breath hitching with the slightest movement. Did supers take over this street after the regular citizens had to evacuate? How many are hiding behind those locked doors right now? A shudder races up my spine as a chilly wind tickles the back of my neck. I rub it and scan the street behind us.

My toe catches on a thick clump of grass pushing through a crack in the street, and I stumble. Rez steps up to a house with faded pink curtains covering the front windows in layers of lace. I wait behind him, hands tucked in my pockets. A pile of full trash bags leans haphazardly against the wall by the door, spilling several empty plastic wrappers onto the porch.

Rez steps over these and knocks on the chipped green door.

"What are we doing here?" I whisper, scanning the street again.

The door opens a crack, and a pale, wrinkled face peeks through the opening. The elderly lady smiles, revealing a missing molar, and throws the storm door open wide. Rez skips back, narrowly missing a door to the face. "Rez, dear! Good to see you!"

Rez smiles back. "Good to see you too, Rachel."

"Well, don't just stand there in the cold. Come in, come in." The wind whipping through the door flutters her dusty pink, floor-length robe, dotted with coffee stains. She steps into the house, beckoning with her wrinkled hand.

I hesitate at the door, eyeing the old woman. Is she a super? What are we doing here? I scan the low, yellowed ceiling. My breath quickens with the familiar panic of being in an enclosed space with a super. I watch as Rachel shuffles weakly. I guess she can't do much harm. I swallow and step inside, then close the door behind me.

Rachel leads us through a small, dimly lit living room with stained blue carpet and into a small kitchen. Specks of dust float in the beams of grey afternoon light streaming through the window above the sink, resting in square patches on the yellowed, tiled floor. I nearly trip on a piece of vinyl curling away from the edge of the doorway.

Rez sets his load of food, including the backpack, on the kitchen island with a relieved sigh. Rachel stoops into her fridge and pulls out two juice boxes. Besides a couple water bottles, one more bent juice box, and a half-empty tub of applesauce, the fridge is bare. When she turns around, her gaze freezes on me, her hazel eyes wide and blinking behind thick-lensed glasses. "Oh. Who's your friend?" She gets the third juice box.

I cross my arms. I'm not his friend.

"This is Scarlett," Rez responds.

I hold my breath, dreading any more questions. I don't want to write *lying to a sweet old lady* next to *stealing* on my list of accomplishments today. I glance over my shoulder at the door, itching to leave. What are we doing here?

Rachel smiles at me and slides a juice box across the counter. "Nice to meet you."

I force a grin and take the juice box. "Thanks. Nice to meet you too, Mrs..."

She waves a hand. "Oh, just call me Rachel. No need for formality around here."

My gaze narrows. "Are you...a super?"

She blinks at me, then bursts out laughing, a single clear note. "Oh, dear me, no." She squints at her juice box as she struggles to stab the straw through the top. "Had a nephew who was though."

Rez opens the bag of apples and empties half of it into Rachel's fridge. He takes a sleeve of crackers from the box and slips out a can of baked beans and puts them in the cabinet.

I stab the flimsy plastic straw into my juice box with a frown, watching Rez. Are there more normal people in Rapid? Does he deliver groceries to them all? I take a small sip of the apple juice, but grimace at its coldness in my stomach. I discreetly set the box on the island counter.

Rez zips up the backpack and places his hands on his hips. "Anything else you need from me before we go?"

She taps her chin with a thin finger. "Oh, yes! The lightbulb went out in the living room, but it's so high and I'm afraid to stand on anything to change it..."

Rez holds up a hand. "No need to worry. I'll have it done in a few moments." He disappears down a hall and emerges a few moments later with a new lightbulb. Rachel and I follow him into the living room and watch while he pulls a rickety wooden chair under the light fixture and changes the bulb. He hops down, puts the chair back, and tosses the old bulb into a nearby plastic trash can. "All done. Anything else?"

"No, I think that's it." Rachel hobbles over to him, robe swishing around her thin frame, and pats his arm. "Thank you, dear. I appreciate it."

Rez smiles. "My pleasure. You know who to call when you need anything."

She nods, still smiling.

He turns to me. "I guess we should be going." He adjusts the backpack on his shoulders.

After final goodbyes, I follow Rez out the door and back onto the street. I frown at my sneakers scuffing against the side-walk concrete. This was part of the mission? To deliver groceries to some old lady? Why is she even still living in Rapid? And what happened to destroying cities and breaking into houses and kidnapping for ransom money? I didn't know supers did...*this.*

Rez slows his steps to fall back next to me. He glances at me. "You're confused."

It's not a question. Like he knows my thoughts. I look away toward the broken skyline of Rapid City. "I just thought..."

He follows my gaze and looks on the broken and crumbling buildings. His eyes soften. "We're all still people, Scarlett, no different from those without powers. We can do good or do wrong."

I rub my palm and bite my lip, remembering how Mrs. Henley told Mom I could've been attacked just as easily by a non-super.

"Don't you agree?'

"I..." I want to say "no." We're criminals because we have powers and we're not locked up in the SCF, but he dares to think differently. Doesn't he realize that supers are attacking people and cities across the country?

Dr. Bailey's voice cuts through my thoughts. *"Trust no one."* I step faster, pulling my hoodie sleeves over my hands. "We'd better be getting back."

He pauses, then matches my stride. "Sure."

Wind whips me, beating back the fire that's trying to warm my insides. I let the backpack slip from my shoulders and hold it limply in one hand. It bumps against my leg with every stride, the weight of the stolen cans wearing a bruise into my calf as well as my mind. I tuck my chin against the head wind fighting us.

"You know, this really is a pretty cool place," Rez says softly, breaking our silence.

I look at him. "Here?"

He chuckles and scuffs his boot against a rock. "I guess that does sound pretty crazy. But yeah." He looks back up at the buildings with fondness. "I've come to love it. The good in it."

"What can possibly be good here?" The question leaks out before I can stop it. I bite my cheek.

Rez looks at me, wind tossing his chocolate brown hair across his forehead. The sun glints in his sapphire blue eye and I look away from it. "A lot of things. We're trying to bring healing to the people whose lives have been changed by their powers. We teach them how to use their gifts for good, to help others." He waits a moment, as if wanting that to sink in.

I don't meet his eyes.

He looks straight ahead again. "It's a rough life, but it is a life. Better than what we'd have at that government facility they're running." He smiles a little. "You know, Ivon even started a garden."

I raise an eyebrow. "A garden? Ivon?" Somehow I can't imagine that much muscle caring for fragile plants.

He chuckles, nodding and rubbing his stubble. "He really is a nice guy once you get to know him. A lot of the kids like to help him tend the vegetable garden. Some of them even have powers that help the process. They really enjoy it, and it'll help provide some fresh food for all of us, which can be hard to come by."

"Rez." I shake my head. "Why do you do all of this? Don't you know the government is after you? Everyone thinks you're just a criminal."

He nods slowly. "Yes. But that doesn't have to stop me from doing what I should. We're not mistakes. And we don't have to be the blight on society that people think we are." Excitement lights up his face. "Just think of all the possibilities for supers if they were taught how to use their powers in the right way."

My face warms and I stare at my shoes. I've never heard anyone say anything like that before, not even Mrs. Henley. I shift my wrist under my watch's tight band. No wonder he's a criminal. His views are dangerous.

Rez doesn't press me for any more conversation and I don't ask any more questions.

Crynn's not at her post when we cross the gravel to enter the warehouse. As soon as we step inside, I give the backpack to Rez, glad to be free of the guilt it reminds me of, and head toward the fire. My stiff body aches for heat again. There aren't many supers around right now, just a few kids playing a dice game in the corner and a pre-teen girl sitting in a corner with a tattered book. I scan the dusty warehouse as a shiver shakes me. Where are the others? Do they go food-hunting too?

It doesn't look like Ares, Nadia and Seth have moved away from the fire, but I know they were probably looking around while we were gone. Ares sits a couple feet back from the others. He probably finds the heat just as repulsive as I find the cold unbearable. Seth pokes the logs with a long, thick stick, staring at the flames with a faraway look in his eyes.

Nadia is the first to see me when I stride up to the bonfire. She stands and watches me as I stretch my hands toward the fire. Ares and Seth look up at me too.

"What happened?" Seth asks.

I look over my shoulder for Rez. He's already gone to organize the new supplies on the shelves. A toddler waddles up and tugs on his pant leg. He hoists the little girl onto his hip and continues with his work.

I jerk my head toward the door. "Outside."

I don't wait for them, just march back out into the cold. Away from Rez and the stolen food and the fire I crave. But I can feel the others close behind me.

As Seth closes the door, I scan the grassy gravel lot and frown. "Where's Crynn?"

Seth shrugs. "She came in soon after you left, talked to Ivon, then we haven't seen her since." He waves his hand. "But that doesn't matter." He steps closer and lowers his voice. "What happened?"

I sigh and rub my arms. "We went to a nearby city and...got some food."

Ares tilts his head. "That's all?"

I bite my lip and stare at the sky as another sigh escapes. "Well...we didn't exactly....*pay* for it all."

Seth's eagerness breaks and he chuckles. "Pfft, that's not a surprise. I mean, what did you expect?"

I rub the back of my head, grimacing. "I know, but...I just didn't think *I* would have to steal."

Seth looks at me like it's not a big deal, but Nadia cuts in before he can speak.

She places her hand on my arm. "I'm sorry he made you do that."

I give her a grateful glance, but shrug, digging my toe in the gravel. "I could've refused."

Before Nadia can say anything more, Seth interrupts, "Doesn't he have minions to run his errands for him?"

A burst of wind hits my back and I rub my arms against the chill. "I dunno. He just said it had to be done."

Ares strokes his chin in thought, then he narrows his icy eyes at me. "Was that all you two did?"

Another gust of wind seeps down into my skin from the neck of my hoodie. Now I wish we'd stayed by the fire. "No, we delivered some of the food."

"Delivered it?" Seth squeaks.

I nod. "To an old lady named Rachel on the edge of the city."

"A super?" Ares asks.

I shake my head. We fall into thoughtful silence. I replay the day's events in my mind, trying to make sense of it all.

Seth glares at the ground, stuffing his hands in his pockets. "It's probably just a trick," he mutters. "Trying to get us to think he's the good guy."

"Trust no one." Those words seem to follow me wherever I go. I tuck some hair behind my ear. "Yeah, maybe. But—" I break off, but they all stare at me, waiting for me to go on. "That lady, Rachel...she just had so little. It's like Rez is the only one keeping her alive."

Ares still strokes his chin. "Why doesn't she just leave?"

Seth rolls his eyes. "Not everyone has that kind of money, Ares."

Nadia frowns and tilts her head. "Didn't the government help the ordinary citizens get out of Rapid when things got bad?"

I shrug and we fall silent again. Nadia's soft voice slips into the quietness, almost lost in the faint breeze. "Maybe we're not doing the right thing."

Ares raises his eyebrows at her. My jaw goes slack, surprised to hear the words that I hadn't let enter my mind.

Seth glares at her. "Are you kidding me?" he snaps. "These are criminals we're talking about. One kind act toward an old lady doesn't erase all the other crimes he's done." Redness creeps up his neck and face as his voice lowers. "What about those families affected by super attacks, huh?" His voice cracks. "What about all those children left without parents because supers—" His voice catches again and he swallows hard. But instead of going on, he just stares at her, waiting.

Nadia bites her lip and stares at her shoes, hands knotting in front of her. "I-I didn't mean—"

Seth huffs. "Didn't ever think about that, did you?" He shakes his head and looks away. "Don't be so naive."

I gape at Seth, then glance quickly at Nadia. What's up with him now? Ever since we left the SCF, he's been so angry and different from that mischievous boy I first met.

Nadia opens her mouth, but all that comes out is a strangled squeak. She sniffs, then turns on her heel. "I'm going for a walk."

The three of us watch as Nadia strides away until she disappears around a corner.

Ares sighs, rubbing the bridge of his nose. "Was that really necessary?"

Seth points a finger in Ares' face and a wind lifts his white hair. "Don't get started with me."

"We're supposed to be a team," I say. "Ares is right."

Anger glints in Seth's gaze as he turns toward me. Fire suddenly flares up inside me. Energy tickles my veins and I know my eyes spark. Literally. I hold up a hand. "Don't, Seth. Let's just all calm down. What's wrong with you anyway?"

He clenches his jaw, but bites back whatever words he was about to hurl. I hold his gaze. Like a dying ember, his anger slowly seeps out of him.

"I'm just—" He breaks off, staring at his shoes as he shakes his head. "It's nothing." He looks off toward where Nadia disappeared, then drops his gaze to his shoes again. He scuffs a foot against a clump of weeds, grimacing and rubbing the back of his neck. "Sorry, guys," he mumbles. "I don't know what..." He sighs, shoulders slumping.

I soften and let my fire calm. "We're not the ones who need the apology."

Seth looks sheepishly at me then back at the ground. He shrugs one shoulder, but nods.

I look off again toward Nadia's disappearance. I hope he does actually apologize.

"Whatcha up to?"

Our heads snap to the open warehouse door. Crynn leans out, wind tossing her short, black hair.

Ares smoothly slips his hands in his pockets. "We're just talking."

Crynn studies us with a raised eyebrow. "Better come inside. We gotta put you kids to work."

"Work?" I squeak.

She smirks and lifts her chin. "Yup. Everyone has chores around here."

"Yay," Seth says flatly.

Crynn chuckles, then looks around. "Where's that other girl?"

I look toward the city. "I'll go find her."

"Want help?" Ares asks.

"No, that's okay. Thanks." I jog in the direction Nadia took. I press against the wind, imagining the breeze whipping the muddled thoughts from my mind and leaving them tumbling across the street with the rest of the trash.

"Nadia?" The city's eerie quiet and stillness in the early evening light makes me shiver as I study the sky. There's still plenty of light, but I don't like the thought of walking back to the warehouse in the dark. I quicken my steps.

A sharp sniff reaches my ears from a nearby alley. I stop in my tracks, then creep forward.

My fingers grab the rough brick corner and I peek my head around it. Nadia sits on the damp ground in the alley, knees drawn up and face in her hands. Her black braids tumble over her shoulder, and she's trembling.

"Nadia?" I hurry down the alley, stepping over shards of glass and crumbled asphalt. I crouch by her side and touch her shoulder lightly. "Hey, you okay?" I glance around at the shadows, uneasiness creeping into my gut.

Nadia sucks in a breath. "I can't do this," she says, her voice catching. Her shoulder quivers beneath my hand. She's more upset about what Seth said than I thought. Or is something else wrong?

"Can't do what?"

She takes a few shaking breaths and her hands drop from her face. "This is all just so—" She breaks off and shakes her head. "I can't...use it again. I've already broken my promise."

"Nadia..." I shake my head. "What are you talking about? What promise?"

Her hands curl into fists and she stares at them as she raises them in front of me. I swallow, blinking between her clenched hands and her glistening eyes.

She grits her teeth. "My promise to never use my power again. Ever." Her fists loosen and she drops her hands to the ground, ignoring the glass and pebbles that must be digging into her skin.

My hand slides from her shoulder. "Why?"

She closes her eyes and tips her head back to rest against the brick wall behind her. She's silent for several moments and I squirm, wondering if I should leave her alone or say something.

Then she finally speaks, words fragile. "Because...because I killed someone once. With my powers."

She says it so low that I barely catch the words. But I hear. It's like a punch to my gut, and my stomach heaves. I want to ask how, when and why. I want to know if I should even be here, sitting so close to someone who has taken someone else's life. Chills creep up my spine and down my arms.

She looks at me with red eyes. I just look back, my heart thumping hard in my chest. Then her eyes widen, and she clamps a hand over her mouth. "No, no, no." The words are muffled against her hand. Before I can figure out what to do, she scrambles to her feet and hurries out of the alley. Leaving me alone in the growing shadows, wondering what in the world to do next.

I lift my wrist to look at the watch, fingers trembling. Does Dr. Bailey know about this? I look after where Nadia disappeared around the corner. The shadows stretch farther, like dark fingers reaching for my neck. I gulp and scramble out of the alley.

I hurry through the city and back to the warehouse. Now that evening is approaching, the space is filling up with people, milling around the firepit. But no Nadia. Did she make it back okay, or is she still out there somewhere?

A few kids run up to me and grab my hands, hair wild and

eyes bright. A little boy hops on his toes, gripping my pinkie. "Can you help us?" he asks.

I blink, hoping he won't pull my finger out of its socket. "Uh..."

"With the fire," a girl with frizzy ringlets explains.

I shake my head. "Oh, um, I don't know if—"

They don't let me finish, dragging me by the arms toward the firepit. Rez looks up at us when they stop me in front of the pile of cold ash and dry sticks and leaves. I look over the big, pleading eyes of the children.

Rez chuckles at me. "We like to use our gifts for chores around here when we can. It proves to be pretty efficient." He smiles at the kids. "We haven't had someone pass through with fire powers in a long time. It's quite a show for them."

Suddenly I feel the pressure of the attention of the crowd. My fingers tremble at my sides, and I swipe a wrist across my forehead. Suddenly I feel like I'm back in the SCF's concrete training room with Dr. Bailey watching my every move. My feet itch to leave this place, but I scan the young, eager faces.

I hesitate at first, then take a deep breath and bend over, stretching one hand toward the pile of wood. Half the hum of conversation stops and I frown, trying to focus. The back of my neck prickles beneath their gazes.

I lick my lips and concentrate, but no warmth comes at first. Finally, a pathetic sputter of sparks shoots from my palm. I purse my lips and rub my hands together before trying again. This time the flames burst, bright and healthy, catching the dry wood on fire. The flames turn into a blaze in only a few moments, and the warmth dispels the growing chill.

The kids squeal and clap their hands, hopping onto crates and overturned buckets to scoot closer to my fire. They stretch their hands toward it and wiggle their fingers, basking in the warmth.

I smile and sit on one of the wooden crates. Something other than my fire sits warm and comfortable in my chest. I've never used my powers for something useful before. With Dr. Bailey's testing and experimenting, I felt more like a weapon. A hazard. But right now I feel useful. Helpful. I feel...different.

Crynn squats down beside me and tucks some of her hair behind her ear. "You don't have to do what he says, you know," she says, her voice low under the crackling of the fire.

I frown and look at her, but she stares across the fire at Rez, eyes narrowing a fraction as her jaw shifts.

"I know..." I look at my hands. "I wanted to."

Crynn tears her gaze from Rez and fixes it upon me instead. Her eyes narrow again and a furrow lines the space between her brows. Abruptly, she stands and leaves, slipping into a shadow between the lines of storage shelves.

The evening progresses, the fire glowing brighter against the darkness created by the sun's descent. Nadia silently slips into the warehouse a little later, and I watch her as she hesitates outside the circle of firelight, studying me. I try to offer a smile, but can't tell if my apprehension shows through. What she said still makes my stomach twist.

After a moment's hesitation she takes her spot beside me, though stiffly, and Rez and Crynn pass food around for a meager dinner. Once they finish their canned beans, Seth, Nadia, and Ares stand from the fire to go to bed. I stay, enjoying the flames and warmth. Warmth that I gave for everyone.

Nadia passes by me to go to her sleeping corner. I flick my gaze up at her, but she keeps her eyes away from me. I wonder if she regrets telling me what she did. Remembering her words makes my insides go cold again.

More supers drift away to go to their respective sleeping spots, and quiet blankets the warehouse. I stretch my hands over the fire and flex my fingers over the blaze. Somehow the quiet of this night reminds me of the stillness of that evening I told Dylan and Ian I had to leave. Some of the joy from starting the fire dissipates and a sigh escapes me. What are they doing now? Maybe Dylan's helping clean up after dinner, Hannah helping him wipe countertops. And Ian? Probably songwriting. He's in his last year of high school now. Has he picked out a college yet? A sharp pang stabs my heart. Will I ever get a chance to do that?

I didn't notice my hands had fallen to my lap. I lift them toward the fire again to savor the warmth of the blaze. The firelight glints off the face of the watch. I should contact Dr. Bailey, give him an update.

I stand and stretch with a yawn, scanning the warehouse. Only a small cluster of adults remain by the fire, talking softly. Without a word, I step quietly to my sleeping spot. I curl up on the ground, wincing at the way the floor cuts into my bones.

I blink at the darkness, pinching my hand to stay awake until everyone is asleep. Hours pass, and when everyone, even Rez, has gone to sleep, I silently stand from my blanket and slip out of the warehouse.

The night envelopes me in its cold embrace, and I hold my arms tighter to my body. I lift the watch close to my face, trying to see the buttons in the dark. There's no message from the doctor, even though he said he'd be in touch. I guess I'll start the conversation.

Me: *Hello. I figured you'd want me to contact you before I went to bed.*

I wait a few minutes, hopping on my numb toes and blowing on my stinging fingers. Finally, the watch buzzes.

Dr. Bailey: *You should've contacted me sooner.*

I roll my eyes. *You said* you *would contact* me.

Dr. Bailey: *What information have you gathered on Rez?*

I blow out a frustrated breath. *I went with him on one of his missions today.*

His reply comes immediately. Dr. Bailey: *And what did you do?*

I bite my lip. *We...stole food.*

Dr. Bailey: *From where?*

Me: *Ashland Heights.*

Dr. Bailey: *Does he go there often?*

Me: *I got the impression that he does.*

Dr. Bailey: *I'll notify the local authorities.*

I don't know why, but my stomach clenches.

Dr. Bailey: *Anything else?*

Me: *Not really. We just delivered some of the food to an elderly lady.*

A longer pause this time. Dr. Bailey: *Really?*

Me: *Yes. It seems Rez is the only one taking care of her.* I pause, thinking about Rachel's joy when she saw Rez at the door.

A long moment stretches before Dr. Bailey's reply comes: *It's a trick. He's just trying to get you to trust him so you'll be on his side. It's an act.*

Of course. Me: *Okay.*

Dr. Bailey: *Stay focused.*

Me: *Right.*

Dr. Bailey: *What about the others?*

Me: *The others?*

Dr. Bailey: *Yes. The others.*

Me: *They're fine.* I frown, contemplating my next words. *Nadia seems...upset by all this.*

Dr. Bailey: *Okay. Get some rest.*

Just '*okay*'? Does he not care? Me: *All right.*

Dr. Bailey: *Remember the cure.*

I take a deep breath. Me: *I know.*

Despite my drooping eyes and my stiff muscles craving even the meager warmth of my thin blanket, Dr. Bailey goes on: *Stay sharp.*

I nod, even though he can't see me, and leave it at that. Fingers trembling from the cold and teeth chattering, I snap the false watch face closed.

Fingers grab my shoulder. I yelp and twist away, throwing my hand out to ward off the attack. Flames burst from my palm and a dark-haired figure dodges and grabs my other shoulder, giving me a shake. "Hey, calm down!"

I freeze, breath heaving in my throat. "Crynn!" How long has she been there? Did she hear me whispering into the watch?

The moonlight illuminates her pale skin and emerald eye.

She drops her hands from my arm, annoyance wrinkling her forehead. "You shouldn't ever be out at night. Not around here."

"Oh. Okay." My voice is surprisingly even despite my rapid heartbeat.

She nods, turns and heads back into the warehouse. I take a slow breath to calm myself. Maybe she didn't hear. She would've said something. I wait several moments—maybe minutes—shoulders tense, before I follow her inside. The hinges creak a complaint as I slowly pull the door shut behind me.

"What were you doing outside at this time of night?" Rez's sharp whisper stops me cold. I freeze in the shadows. Is he talking to me? My fingers tremble as they pick at the watch face.

I turn slowly to face him, but he's standing over by the fire. The dying embers cast dancing shadows on the wall behind him.

Crynn stands opposite him, arms crossed over her black t-shirt. "Why?"

Rez rolls his eyes. "Come on. Where were you? You know it's not safe to be out at night." His voice is missing his usual lightness. It's low and deep. Irritated, even.

Crynn is silent as she stares at him with a lifted chin.

"Cry—"

"You're my brother, not my dad," she snaps.

"I may as well be, with how much I had to fill the role. It's not like there was anyone else to." His outburst bounces off the walls of the warehouse. He lowers his voice, "I'm trying to protect you."

I gape at the two of them, unnoticed in the shadows. Rez is Crynn's *brother*?

She uncrosses her arms and whirls away from him, jaw clenched. "I don't need your protection."

I wait, still as stone, until Crynn disappears into the shadows behind the shelves. Is that where she sleeps?

Rez stands at the diminishing fire, staring into its glow for a few minutes. Finally, he rakes his hand roughly through his hair and retreats deeper into the warehouse in the opposite direction of Crynn.

I wait, struggling to keep my breathing noiseless in the quiet of the night. Soft snores whisper from one corner, and the wind hisses through the crack beneath the door, but there's no sound of Crynn or Rez. I creep through the shadows to my sleeping corner. Blind in the dark, I adjust my blankets and settle onto my back, staring at the darkness overhead.

Rez and Crynn are siblings. But why the secrecy?

CHAPTER FOURTEEN

The morning sunlight is still faint and grey when I wake, and sleep flees like a scared rabbit. No matter how much I toss and turn and try to get comfortable on the hard floor, I can't get back to sleep.

I sit up and rub my bleary eyes. Nadia is still asleep, her deep breathing calm. She actually looks peaceful, which is a change from her usually knotted brow. At least she can find some rest. I fold my blanket neatly this time and flop it against the wall. Then I stand, pondering for a moment in the early morning silence of the warehouse.

I guess I might as well look around to get more familiar with the city's layout for the capture plan. A sick feeling twists my gut.

I slip out of the warehouse and take a big breath of the nippy air. A few birds streak across the sky, black dots against the grey clouds. A shiver shakes me and I stuff my hands in my pockets, following along the warehouse wall. Voices draw me around the corner to the other side.

Ivon squats in the small patch of grass, a little boy and girl huddled next to him. His big hulking form towers over their small ones as they bend over a rectangle of upturned dirt, grey-brown and dry. I stay tucked behind by the wall, watching them.

"Here. Go ahead and try it," Ivon says to the girl.

The gentle breeze tousles her wispy blonde hair as she stares at the dirt. She looks back up at Ivon with uncertainty.

"Go on," he gently prods.

She stretches both hands forward and digs her fingertips into the soil. After a short moment, tiny pale-green plants wiggle up through the dirt, leaning and twisting toward the girl's hands.

She giggles and jumps back, her messy braid swinging. "It worked!"

Ivon smiles. "Yes, I told you it would. Let's just hope what you planted is edible." He tousles her hair, and she beams from him to the new plants.

"Can I water them?" the little boy asks, bouncing on his toes as he stares at the new life.

"Of course. Go ahead."

The boy stands and holds his hands over the dirt, fingers pointing down. Water trickles from his fingertips and patters on the soil like a soft rain. He moves his hands around until the soil is sufficiently soaked.

"Good job!" Ivon smiles at him and gives him a playful nudge. The boy puts his hands on his hips and stares at his water work with pride in his eyes. I can't help but smile at them.

"Good morning, Scarlett."

I jump, my head snapping up to meet Ivon's steel-grey eyes. I swallow. "Good morning."

"Why don't you join us?"

I eye him, wondering if he's mad at me for spying. But his thick brows aren't as knotted as they were when we first arrived. There's still a glint of wariness in his eyes, but his posture is relaxed, thick arms draped over his knees.

I fidget with my hoodie drawstring as I hesitate, then shuffle forward and kneel on the cold, hard ground next to the garden.

Only Ivon would've been strong enough to churn up this hard-packed dirt.

"See?" The little girl smiles at me. "I did it." She tenderly fingers a leaf of one of the plants.

"And I watered it," the boy adds, jabbing his chest with his thumb. "And now we'll have more food for everyone."

Ivon chuckles, thick and deep. "All right now, you two go play. But stay close."

They sprint off, skipping and laughing, before Ivon can change his mind.

He shakes his head at them, a grin softening his sharp features as he pulls a crumpled seed packet from his pocket. "We really don't know what she planted here. I need to be sure we have something edible," he explains.

I nod. "Oh."

I watch him out of the corner of my eye as he moves the dirt into soft, round rows and nestles the seeds in, covering them with more soil. I didn't know he could be so gentle. The deep rumble of his voice somehow makes me more calm, even though he could crush me like an ant with his superhuman strength.

He pauses to finger the stem of one of the girl's plants. "Fascinating, isn't it? Powers can be used for useful things."

All the news stories and articles I've seen about demolished cities, kidnappings, killings, and looting done by superhumans flip through my mind. So does my attack behind the ice cream shop. I scowl and yank up a fistful of dead grass. "They can be used for a lot else, too," I mutter. Fire is destructive. It attacks and eats up everything like a ravenous dragon.

He glances at me, eyebrows raised. "Well, you proved my point last night when you started the fire for us." He grins again, an expression I hadn't thought possible for his hard, chiseled face before.

"Ivon!"

Ivon shoots up at the call and runs toward the warehouse

door. I follow close behind him. A boy of about fourteen stands in the doorway, waving his arm at us. "Hurry!"

We burst through the door after the boy, scanning for trouble.

A crowd chokes the space, all facing the center of the warehouse. I trail behind Ivon as he shoulders his way through. I lean past his broad frame to see Seth and Rez stand facing each other like feral dogs coiled for a fight. The pressing crowd circles them like the boundaries of a boxing ring.

My throat constricts, staring wide-eyed at Seth's clenched jaw and shaking fists, while Rez stands controlled. Did Seth challenge him to a fight? That's not like him, but he hasn't been acting himself since we got here.

"Stop trying to tell me how to think!" Seth yells.

The muscles in Rez's jaw flex. "I'm not. I'm just trying to help."

A flare of cold washes over my neck. I look to my right to find Ares and Nadia next to me, eyes wide as they glance back and forth from Seth to Rez.

"What happened?" I hiss. "Did you see how it started?"

Ares tilts his head toward me without looking away from Seth and Rez. "Rez was just trying to talk to Seth, but something rubbed him the wrong way. Like, really bad."

"I don't need your help!" Seth yells, pointing a finger at Rez like a knife. "Just leave me alone."

Rez looks around him at the crowd of spectators. He settles a calm gaze back on Seth. "Seth. You need to calm down."

"Don't tell me what to do." Wind kicks up dust into swirls on the floor, flowing out from where Seth stands.

Rez quickly flicks a glance over the crowd again, gaze lingering on the children nearby. He takes a step closer. Only a couple feet separate them now. "Just calm down, and we can talk about this."

Seth opens his mouth to spit out another response. But his face smooths, and his muscles relax. He stares almost unseeing at

Rez for a moment, then he growls and grabs his hair with both hands. "Get out of my head!" Still clutching his head, he storms past Rez, bumping his shoulder on the way. He doesn't stop, leaving the warehouse and slamming the door behind him.

Silence covers the crowd, tension lingering in the air as everyone turns to Rez. He takes a deep breath and stares at the dusty floor. So that's what it looks like for him to use his powers?

Could he be manipulating my mind to make me trust him?

Crynn stalks up behind Rez. "Starting to use our powers now, are we?

Rez closes his eyes and tips his head back with a sigh. "Crynn...I don't have to explain anything to you."

She just stares at the back of his head like a lioness ready to pounce.

One of the younger kids shuffles tentatively up to Rez's side. He gives her a weary smile and brushes the top of her head before turning to face his sister. "You'd better get back to stocking the shelves."

Crynn tosses her hands up and laughs, sharp and bitter. "You're not my boss, Rez. Let someone else stock those shelves. What's the point, anyway? None of this matters. We're all going to die eventually. Or end up in the SCF." She turns on her heel and storms away from him.

She's about to pass me when she stops by my shoulder. She leans closer, her green eye almost glowing. "You coming?"

I blink and glance at Ares and Nadia. I don't need to look at him to see that Rez is watching us too. "W-where?"

Crynn looks behind her shoulder at Rez. She lifts her chin and shrugs one shoulder. But when she looks back at me, I see the challenge in her eyes. "Just to have some fun." Her gaze hardens as she stares a few moments more at her brother. Then she turns toward the door, all eyes in the warehouse on her. "We never have any fun around here. Come on."

When she slips out of the door, all eyes shift to the three of us. I glance at the other two, avoiding Rez, before reluctantly following after Crynn. I don't want her as an enemy so perhaps humoring her is the best choice. I'm relieved when I hear Ares' and Nadia's footsteps following close behind.

We jog to catch up with her and follow her onto the streets. Away from the warehouse and her brother, Crynn calms. She slides her hands into her black jean pockets and looks up at the sky as clouds scuttle across.

I walk beside her with Ares and Nadia behind us. I glance over my shoulder, regretting leaving the warehouse. My mission was to stay near Rez. Should I go back?

Crynn nudges me with her elbow. "So, when did you find out you had powers?"

I raise my eyebrows at her, surprised at her light tone compared to a few minutes ago. I don't think I'll ever get used to how these people talk openly about powers. I clear my throat. "In May." I finger a loose thread on my hoodie sleeve.

She nods. "I bet you miss your family."

When I look at her, she shrugs. "Most of the supers around here had to leave some family behind because of their powers." She pauses, eyes growing distant. "Or had family leave them."

I swallow and stare at my shoes. "Yeah, I do miss them."

She stares ahead as wind tosses her hair. "I bet you'd do anything to get back to them, wouldn't you?"

My jaw clenches. "I can't go back. Not with my powers."

She waves a hand. "I know. I mean, you'd do anything to get rid of your powers, wouldn't you?"

My fingers curl into fists. "Of course." I hesitate. "But there's no way to do that." Not quite yet anyway. But very soon.

She looks at me out of the corner of her eye and smirks. "No. Not yet."

"Where are we going?" Ares interrupts our conversation with a question we're all thinking.

Crynn grins and turns, walking backwards. "You know that bunch of bozos we rescued you from?"

Nadia frowns. "You mean Mikey and all of them?"

Crynn's grin widens. "Yup." She pivots to walk forward again. "Rez thinks he's the only one who can get supplies..."

I glance at Nadia and Ares, then back at Crynn. "What exactly do you have in mind?"

She pulls her hands out of her pockets and scans our surroundings. "What those guys lack in brains they make up for in good finds. We're going to, shall we say, free them of some of their burden."

I frown. Stealing again? Does it count if we're stealing food from these guys who already stole it? It still doesn't feel right.

"You're not chickening out, are you?" Crynn breaks into my thoughts, a challenge edging her voice.

I slip my hands into my hoodie pockets, trying to match her attitude. "No."

She nods. "Good. Let's pick up the pace."

We match her quickened strides, and my apprehension grows with each step. I'm not totally fond of the idea of going back to those guys.

Ares jogs to get closer to Crynn. "I'm not sure this is a good idea."

She doesn't look at him. "Loosen up, Ice Man."

Ares purses his lips, but doesn't say anything more.

We reach the corner of the grocery store. Crynn holds out her arm to stop us, and we line up against the brick wall.

She waits, listening and watching. The wind tosses a crushed water bottle across the street. It scrapes along the asphalt as a lone bird sings an eerie song from a glassless window.

"Okay, come on," she whispers, beckoning us to follow. "I don't think they're home right now. If they were, we'd hear them."

We follow her, stepping over the trash and bricks littering the ground in front of the store. Our shoes crunch over shards of glass and dirt as we squeeze through the doors.

She heads straight for the back of the store. "Come on. I happen to know where they keep all of their most valuable stuff."

I don't ask how. I can feel Ares' cold presence and Nadia's nervous one just behind me. Crynn leads us to the back of the store to an "authorized personnel only" door, where she pauses.

She presses her ear against the door for a moment before swinging it open. "Jackpot."

The room is smaller than I expected. Nothing more than a large closet. But the floor-to-ceiling shelves are filled with cool finds. Not just food and drinks, but other useful things like flashlights, batteries, bags, ropes, tools, cracked cell phones, and even a CD player.

I step inside and my breath catches as my gaze settles on a scratched ukulele. Where'd they even find this? Softly, my fingers glide across the string. The sound that hums from it is way out of tune, but it brings a smile to my face anyway. My hands itch to pick it up, tune it, and make it sing again. I smile sadly instead, fingering the curve of the body. An ache overtakes my chest at this reminder of home. Of my dreams.

"See what I mean?" Crynn jars me from my thoughts, grinning as she looks over the stash.

"Yeah, I guess," I mumble, still lingering on the instrument.

She grabs a flashlight and a handful of batteries. "Come on, you guys. They could get back here any minute."

Biting my lip, I look at Ares and Nadia, then reach for a dented box of cookies. Maybe the kids will like them. Ares and Nadia just start to pile more batteries and flashlights into one of the bags when a clatter makes us all freeze.

Crynn pulls us all farther into the room and closes the door until all she can see is a sliver of the grocery store. She crouches, peering through the crack. We wait, the sound of our breathing seeming too loud.

Crynn stiffens. I lean over her head, shifting back and forth to try to see. "What? Who is it?" I hiss.

She clenches the flashlight until the plastic cracks. She turns, hair whipping, snatches the bag from Nadia, and throws the battery and flashlight she's holding into it. "Time to go," she says, zipping it closed and throwing it over her shoulder.

"Who is it?" I ask again.

She ignores me, peering through the crack again. Slowly, she lets the door swing open. Without turning around, she grabs my shoulder and hurries out of the closet. "This way."

Ares and Nadia step softly but quickly after us.

In the quiet, empty store, our steps echo too loud. Papers crunch under our feet and our toes skim crushed cans. We crouch and hurry down the farthest aisle against the wall of the store. I keep my eyes glued to Crynn as she rounds the corner of the shelf.

She collides with something, or someone, and stumbles back with a yelp. I skid to a stop and all of us squish together with the sudden change of pace.

We look up into Ivon's frowning face.

Crynn shifts. "Hey, Ivon. Fancy meeting you here."

He lifts an eyebrow as another figure steps out from behind him. Rez glares at Crynn, then shifts his gaze to the rest of us. I look away, clutching the box of cookies.

He turns his attention to Crynn again. "What are you doing?" It doesn't sound quite like a question; more like he already knows and wants to hear her say it.

She fingers the bag straps and lifts her chin. "Just getting supplies."

He clenches his jaw and looks around. "That's not how we do things, Crynn. You know that."

"That doesn't make any sense, Rez. You steal from a grocery store in town and won't steal from other criminals—"

"It's not like that—"

"Then explain it."

Rez's eyes flick to the box of cookies in my hand. He points to the supply closet door. "Go put it back."

Crynn grabs my wrist as I turn, though her eyes remain glued to her brother. "Don't go anywhere." She crosses her arms. "He's about to explain."

Rez sighs and drags a hand over his face. "You've heard me say this a thousand times."

She waits.

And I wait. I want to know what the difference is too.

He finally relents and steps forward, looking intently between me, Ares, and Nadia instead of Crynn. "The other supers in this city are having just as much of a hard time surviving, maybe even harder. I can get food from those who can afford a few missing cans, but I'm not going to steal another super's meals for the next three days because it's more convenient." He pauses, glancing between us. When his eyes settle on me, I shrivel inside. "They would've stretched that box of cookies over a week between the four of them. We can find that elsewhere. The only way we can be better than what the world sees us as is if we help build each other up."

I look down at the box, unable to bear Rez's gaze anymore. Shame pokes at my gut, and I rub the back of my neck and grimace. His words make sense. What am I doing? Stealing food from a few guys who are starving? Shame keeps my head bent as I wonder why I even care. I'm not supposed to care. What would Dr. Bailey say?

Crynn uncrosses her arms, but she still has fire in her eyes.

Rez still doesn't look at her. "Please put the stuff back."

When Crynn doesn't move, Ares surprises me by taking the backpack from her shoulders. She stares at us as we go back to the closet and put every item back the way we found it.

When we come back, Rez and Crynn still aren't looking at each other. Ivon steadily watches us as we walk up like scolded children. His face is nothing like how it was when I talked with him by the garden. Hard. Cold. Irritated. Maybe disappointed?

Rez grimaces as he rubs the back of his neck. "Crynn—"

She brushes past Ivon, marching out of the store and disappearing into the city.

Rez stares after her, regret wrinkling his forehead. He draws out a long, deep breath and rakes a hand through his hair. When he turns his attention back to us, he doesn't show any signs of softening. I look away from his piercing gaze. Is he mad at me? Or the real question is, *how* mad is he?

"Let's go back," he says. He turns toward the door.

Ivon waits until we follow before taking up the rear.

When we're out of the protection of the store, the wind whips my ponytail into my face and numbs my cheeks and nose. I slide my hands in my pockets, walking behind all the others—except for Ivon—and watch Rez in the lead. He walks with long, powerful strides, but his shoulders sag a little, weighed down by some invisible burden.

My shoulders slump as a sigh escapes me. I've disappointed him. I huff, kicking a can into oblivion. Why do I care?

My wrist watch vibrates, and I slap a hand over it and look up at the others. They walk on, not seeming to notice my furtive surprise. Tucking my hands in my hoodie pouch, I slow my steps so Ivon can pass me, but he stops at my side and raises an eyebrow.

I move my gaze up to meet his, but as soon as I see the hardness there, I look at my shoes again. "I-I'm just gonna take a walk."

He studies me for a long moment while I sweat, then steps ahead of me, boots beating the asphalt.

I watch the group ahead of me, letting the distance stretch between us. As they round a corner of a building, I stop and check the message.

Dr. Bailey: *How are things?*

I glance at Rez again. Me: *They're fine now.*

Dr. Bailey: *Now? Did something happen?*

Me: *No, not really.*

Dr. Bailey: *Were you attacked? Are you compromised?* His urgency and near-panic project even from his message.

Me: *Everything's under control. Still going according to plan.*

I imagine him sighing with relief. Dr. Bailey: *Okay. Anything else to report?*

For a split second I contemplate telling the doctor what really happened. But if he knew, he'd probably laugh. At me. He'd think it's ridiculous that I care that the leader of this criminal gang is disappointed with me. Me: *Nope.*

There's no reply, so I click the watch closed and tuck my hands in my pocket again to warm them. Then I jog, pressing against the wind, to catch up with the others again.

When we reach the warehouse, Ares, Nadia and I hang back while Rez steps inside without a word. Ivon gives us another hard look before following.

Ares scuffs a shoe on the gravel. "I don't think I've seen him that mad before."

Nadia nods, rubbing her arms. "We should've refused to do it," she says softly.

I bite my lip. "You're right."

She looks at me. "You think we could make it up to him?"

Ares frowns contemplatively at the warehouse over his shoulder. "Maybe it's not really us he's mad at."

I huff. "He's mad at us at least a little. I think that much is obvious."

I jolt like I've been shaken to my senses. Why are we talking like this? We shouldn't care whether or not he's mad at us, or worry about making things up to him. He's a superhuman criminal and we were sent here for one thing:

To help the government capture him.

Dr. Bailey's words drift into my mind. *Not fit to live...less than human.*

My stomach clenches and I rub it, looking around. "Has Seth come back yet?"

Ares looks at the warehouse door, hesitates, then walks over to peek his head in. After a few moments, he comes back. "I guess not. I don't see him."

"He was pretty upset when he left," Nadia says.

I rub my chin, looking into the city. "We'd better go find him." I don't know what's come over him since we got to Rapid, but he shouldn't be alone. Not in a place like this. And I don't want him getting into anymore fights and complicating the mission.

They follow me into the city, and we split up to cover more ground. I don't like wandering around here by myself, but I try to focus on finding Seth. I call his name up and down the streets, into alleys and empty storefronts, quickening my pace with every yell of his name.

The shifting clink of glass nearby halts my feet. I scan the street and my gaze catches on a corner antique shop. The glass has been knocked out of the windows and it lies in shards on the sidewalk. Part of the brick underneath the front windowsill has crumbled away from the building. I take a step closer to the shop. Seth stands inside, facing the back wall. A soft wind tosses dust in a circle around him as he stares at something out of my sight.

CHAPTER FIFTEEN

"Seth!" I sprint across the asphalt to the shop. "We've been looking all over for you." I slow to carefully navigate the broken glass and brick. The splintering wooden door is broken off its hinges and sits at an angle against the doorframe. I kick aside a couple bricks from the front steps and squeeze inside.

Seth shows no sign of hearing me. He just continues to stare, his wind brushing my cheeks. I blink against the dust in the air and follow his gaze.

Above a smashed glass counter, a realistic painting hangs in a dull gold frame, on a faded backdrop of the floral wallpaper. Under a fine layer of dust, it shows a small farmhouse with chipped white paint and green shutters on the windows, surrounded by a swaying field of grass. The sky above it is covered in grey clouds, and a few dark birds hover suspended just above the chimney of the house. I can almost smell the threat of rain in the air. Despite the gloomy weather, it feels peaceful.

Seth stares at this painting, still showing no sign of noticing my presence. None of his usual cheerfulness lights his eyes. They're distant and glossy as he gazes at the art.

I reach for him, but stop, not sure what to do. "Seth?" I say softly.

He sucks in a slow breath, as if he's been barely breathing. He takes a step forward, shoes crunching on bits of glass and old jewelry littering the thick rug. "This..." He raises a hand and swipes his fingers across the glass covering the painting, revealing four streaks of clarity. "Reminds me of home."

Now I can see the faint texture of the paint where Seth's fingers cleared the dust. He swallows hard, and for the first time I notice a trail of wetness down his cheeks.

I touch him lightly on the shoulder. "Are you okay?"

He blinks and finally looks at me, eyebrows slightly raised like he didn't realize I'd been standing next to him. His wind fades away as he quickly scrubs his face with his sleeves, forcing a chuckle. "Yeah, I'm okay." He shrugs. "Always." He forces his signature grin, but it doesn't reach his eyes.

I glance at the painting again. "You sure?"

He shrugs again, but avoids my gaze. "Yeah, sure." He gestures to the painting. "Just reminiscing."

I'm not convinced, but he steps past me and out of the shop. I take one more look at the painting before following him. When I step beside him, he turns his face in the direction of the warehouse.

"You guys have been looking all over for me, you said?" Some of that mischievous glint returns to his brown eyes. "Were you guys worried about me?"

I shift my jaw as I study him. "Yeah. We'd better get back."

He nods and starts down the street. As I walk beside him, several questions try to roll off my tongue, but I hold them back, not sure which ones would be best. I cast a glance at him, then back at the old antique shop before we make a turn and it vanishes out of sight. Do his memories have something to do with how he's changed since coming to Rapid?

What happened to him before he came to the SCF?

The grey clouds thicken, reminding me of the painting. The farther we walk, the stronger the wind whipping down the street beats back the fire in me. I wrap my arms around myself, wondering how such a strong wind could come on so fast.

Seth kicks a can, sending it skittering across the street. "I hate them," he mutters, words low and dripping with a bitter tang.

I frown at him. His face has morphed from the haunted quietness in the shop or even the forced cheerfulness when we left the store. The muscles in his jaw bulge as he grinds his teeth, brows drawn sharply as he glares ahead.

Another gust of wind hits me, and I brace myself to keep my balance. "You hate who?" I know he's not particularly fond of Rez, but he said *them*.

He stares forward, face hard against the wind he creates. His jaw clenches harder. "All of them. Supers."

"But...we're one of them."

He stops and whirls to face me. Wind slaps my face and I struggle to keep my eyes open. "No, I'm not," he spits. "I never wanted this." His eyes spark, but something else lingers behind the redness.

I swallow.

"I'm not one of them," he continues weakly. "It's their fault. They—" He breaks off. He still stares at me, but his eyes go out of focus, seeing something else. Memories? Nightmares?

"They what?" I ask quietly.

He hesitates, then swallows and straightens his shoulders. The wind finally dies off. "We'd better get back." He sets off at a quicker pace.

I half-run to keep up with him. Halfway back, Ares and Nadia join us from a side street.

Ares raises a hand. "Oh, good you found—" He breaks off, frowning at Seth then sharing a glance with me and Nadia. After that we fall into heavy silence.

Once we're back at the warehouse, we all go inside. Immediately, I go to the fire to warm myself. The others seem to handle the cold just fine, while I shiver from head to toe. I wish my fire wasn't so sensitive to the cold. It curls up in my core at any threat of chill.

I stretch my hands toward the roaring blaze, keeping my head down while I glance around the room. Supers mill about, talking, children playing games, some stocking shelves. Rez is among them, walking between the racks, organizing and putting items on the shelves from wooden crates and boxes.

My gaze lands on Seth, who sits on an overturned bucket. His shoulders slump weakly as he rests his elbows on his knees. He stares unseeing at the flames, occasionally half-heartedly glowering at supers who get too close. Those eyes that usually have his spark of playfulness are dull and tired. What is he carrying inside him? My mind goes to the painting in the shop. What happened to land this boy in the SCF?

Just when I feel like the warmth is returning to my body, Ivon bursts into the warehouse. He looks frantically around.

Rez leans out from behind a shelf, frowning. "Over here, Ivon."

Ivon strides over to him. "Mikey and his gang are heading out of town."

Rez sets the boxes down. "That can't be good."

Ivon shakes his head, still breathing hard.

Rez walks around the shelf, steps quick and sure. "Scarlett."

I look up, a little surprised he's talking to me. "Yes?"

"Get your friends. We have to stop them."

Why us? My heartbeat quickens. "Okay."

My hands are already shaking when I stand and turn toward the others. A strong hand on my shoulder stops me.

I turn and meet Rez's two-toned eyes. The blue almost engulfs me. I swallow and focus on his chocolate-brown eye.

"Now's your chance to prove yourself, Scarlett," he says quietly. "Don't make me regret welcoming you and your friends into our family."

Warmth creeps over my face as I resist squirming. I swallow. "Okay, Rez."

He nods, then turns toward Ivon.

I suck in a breath and turn toward the others. "Did you hear?"

Ares nods. "We heard."

"They need our help."

Seth huffs and crosses his arms over his grey sweatshirt. "You won't catch me helping him."

"Come on, Seth," I plead. "Don't think of it that way. We're going to stop the bad guys. Do something really *good* with our powers."

Seth stares at me a long moment, then sighs. "Fine. We'd better hurry," he mumbles.

I smile and pat him on the back. "Let's go."

We find Rez and Ivon standing outside, talking in rushed, low tones.

"Come on!" Rez grips a metal pipe and waves it at us, then takes off running. We follow close on his heels, pumping our legs harder to keep up with Rez and Ivon's strides. Seth is the only one easily keeping pace with them without breaking a sweat.

We follow the same road Rez and I took to Ashland Heights. We run until we're panting and sweating and my fire flares and writhes inside me, relishing in the movement.

Finally, as we round a bend in the road, we spot Mikey, Davey, Carl and Flint. They shove each other and chat loudly, unaware of our approach, like they're just going to town for a normal grocery run. But I have a feeling nothing about what they're planning to do is normal. All the news stories and coverage of superhuman attacks flash through my mind like a nightmare at blinding speed.

Including the image of the pair of fiery glowing eyes, bright against the darkness behind the ice cream shop. Engulfing flames, consuming fire. I run faster.

Rez doesn't say anything until we're nearly twenty feet from them. Their own loud voices cloak our footsteps.

"Mikey!" The sharpness in Rez's voice even makes me jump.

Mikey flinches and skids to a stop. They all fall silent and turn to face us. Muscles twitch. Eyes dart between us. My fire coils, ready.

We stop ten feet from them, panting. Ivon clenches his huge fists, muscles bulging underneath his shirt. Rez draws his shoulders up, settling his glare on Mikey. He slowly turns the pipe in his palm.

I take a deep breath and straighten my shoulders, trying to infuse the same confidence into my stance. My fire senses my anticipation and flows energy through my veins. My palms grow warm, making my chilled fingers tingle.

Rez narrows his eyes. "What are you up to, Mikey?"

Mikey lifts his chin. "You're not the king of Rapid, you know."

Rez points the pipe at him. "You know it's dangerous to go into other cities. If you're just going to find food, then there won't be a problem between us." He takes a step forward. "But if you're going to cause trouble and further smear the reputation of superhumans, then I'm going to have to stop you."

Mikey huffs. "Smear our reputation? The people hate us, and there's nothing we can do about it."

Rez takes another step forward. "Yes, there is, Mikey. We can show the world how we can make it a better place. But what you're about to do will feed the lies they believe. Lies that tell them all supers are dangerous."

Mikey hesitates, staring at his faded sneakers. His comrades glance between him and Rez, shifting uncomfortably.

When Mikey lifts his eyes to Rez again, some of the confidence is missing from his gaze. "You can't change the mind of the whole world, Rez." His words almost get carried away by the wind.

Rez steps forward again. "We can't change everyone's mind, no. But if we can change just a handful of people, that could spread. It would change life for all supers."

Mikey rubs the side of his face and his shoulders slump,

stance no longer resting on the balls of his feet, ready for a fight. I relax a little. My fire still surges energy through me, begging to be released, but I keep my hands closed.

Mikey straightens his shoulders again, resolve and something else hardening his face. "Sorry, Rez. There's no use anymore." He turns back toward the road. Davey, Carl and Flint follow him.

Rez clenches his jaw, clutching the pipe harder. He sprints after them. The rest of us are only a split-second behind.

Rez is the first to reach them. He grabs Mikey's shoulder just as he begins to turn around. Davey growls and reaches for Rez. Ivon slams a thick fist into his gut. With a grunt, Davey doubles over.

I peel my gaze away from their fight. Flint has his pale green eyes set on me, baring his crooked teeth. He bends his knees slightly. Balanced. Ready.

When I get within six feet of him, he flings out a hand. A string of blue lightning whips from his finger. I gasp and stumble to the side. It passes over my right shoulder. But as the string of electricity flicks back to Flint, the tip catches my upper arm. I wince and clutch the searing sting.

Okay, then. Didn't know he could do that too. I'm in trouble.

Seth zooms past me. A sharp wind follows him and swirls around his body like a protective bubble. He throws out his hands toward Flint, and a gust of wind sends him tumbling back on the road.

Seth stands over him, hands clenched, shoulders rising and falling with his heaving breaths.

"Seth!"

Ares' yell gets my mind back on task. Still clutching my arm, I look over to see Carl sprinting toward Seth from behind. Ares runs after him, ice crackling around his hands. But he'll be too late. I glance around, looking for...

Nadia stands rooted to ground, arms pressed against her sides and spine rigid. She stares wide-eyed at the tousle, jaw slack.

My jaw clenches, and my fists follow suit. "Nadia!"

All she does is flinch.

Carl is almost to Seth now. Flint stares at Seth, a little shine of panic in his eyes at the speed of his approach. He shifts his glance past Seth to Carl, pressing his hands against the ground to push himself up. By the time Seth sees Carl, it will be too late.

"No!" I thrust out my good arm. Fire blasts from my palm, so powerful I have to set one foot back for balance.

The force hits Carl square on the back. He shrieks and flies forward from the impact, colliding with Seth. They go rolling on the ground, grunting.

Flint finally scrambles to his feet, dirt from Seth's wind streaking his face. He turns to help Carl, forgetting about me.

His mistake.

I sprint, forgetting about the searing pain in my arm. I jump over Seth and Carl. Mid-air, I turn my palm toward Flint.

Time slows to a crawl. Flint's eyes slowly raise to meet me. I close my eyes, feeling the fire channeling through me. It surges through my veins like a dragon hungry for battle. I must control it. Heat and fire puddle in my palm. Flames swirl together and form a sphere, taut like a balloon ready to pop. My fingers tremble with the force building up. In the last moment, I dial down the ferocity of the ball of flames. I hurl it at Flint.

It slams him in his bony chest. He yelps as he flies backward, tumbling across the road. Then he lies still, grimacing and clutching his chest.

I freeze, staring down at him. Flint rolls over. Part of his shirt is singed away, revealing reddened, blistered skin peeking out from under his hand. His face twists in a grimace as he groans.

My hand creeps over my mouth as my stomach twists with nausea. I raise my other hand, staring at the red splotches on my palm and the soft flames flickering around my fingers.

I didn't want to hurt him. Not really.

A thud jerks me back to the fight. Rez struggles in Davey's firm grip before Ivon slams a fist into his skull. Davey goes limp and his broad frame falls to the ground with a ground-shaking thud. Mikey's already leaning against a fence pole, wincing and cradling his head. A small wound on his forehead trickles blood down his cheek.

Nadia finally moves to gently examine a bruise already blossoming on Ares' arm, even though he glares at her. I can't help but let my gaze sharpen as I watch her face. She did nothing. Again. I know she dislikes using her powers, but she needs to do her part just like everyone else. For the cure.

I turn away from her to see Seth on top of Carl, pinned against the gravel. He lifts his fist and pounds it into Carl's face

Over

and over

and over again.

"Seth, stop it!" I lurch forward and grab Seth's wrist before he can land another blow.

Blood, dirt and sweat darkens his face as he glares knives at Carl, making him look ten years older. Fiercer. His jaw clenches tight and his nostrils flare with each breath he heaves in. He doesn't even seem to notice I'm here.

I clutch his wrist harder and drag him off Carl's limp body. "Seth, stop!"

He finally sees me. Whatever is going on in his stormy gaze, it makes me want to shrink away. He yanks his arm out of my grip. "Leave me alone," he snaps.

I reach for him, but he twists away. My fire coils, ready, but I force it to soften.

There's some sort of hurt in this boy's eyes. Deep and painful. Though he cloaks it with his hardened face and bloody knuckles.

I reach for him. "Seth, just calm down. It's over." I can't keep my outstretched fingers from trembling as he glares at me.

His breathing finally starts to steady as he glances past me at Carl, who groans as he tries to lift his head. Slowly, Seth's face falls, shoulders slump, eyes dim.

Ivon steps in front of him, tense and ready to keep Seth from beating in Carl's face again. But Seth still stares blankly past him, even though Ivon's blocked his view of the mind-manipulator.

Rez steps next to Ivon, breathing heavily. He studies Seth with a frown before kneeling over Carl.

"He'll be okay," he says after a minute. He stands and places a hand on his hip, the other resting the pipe on his shoulder as he turns to Mikey. "Get you and your friends back to Rapid." His voice carries authority. Confidence. I wish I had some.

Mikey glares up at Rez, dabbing a sleeve over his cut. "Okay, Rez. Okay."

Rez nods and turns back to us, glancing once more at Carl. He sets his hard gaze on Seth, who doesn't lift his gaze from the ground. Rez lets out a long breath. "Let's just...go home."

Ivon and Rez turn back toward Rapid. Nadia and Ares follow close behind.

When Seth doesn't move, I wait. "You coming?" I say softly.

At first he does nothing, says nothing. His shoulders slump like the weight of the world is on him. Or just old memories.

"Seth?"

"I'm coming," he mumbles. He turns toward the others and shuffles down the road. I match his pace, looking at him out of the corner of my eye. He stares at the ground, not really seeing it. He's somewhere else, remembering something else.

I gently touch his arm. "Are you okay?"

He shrugs and slips his hands in his pockets. A little of his old cheerfulness comes back again. But just like when we came out of the antique shop, it feels like a mask. Maybe it always was. "I'm fine." He offers a small grin, then quickens his pace.

I slow for a moment, watching him jogging to catch up with the others. I study the figures in front of me...What kind of memories do Ares, Nadia, and Seth hold trapped inside them? What families did they have to leave because of their powers? I'm not the only one with fears and doubts and dreams cut short. What are they hiding behind their masks?

CHAPTER SIXTEEN

Walking alone behind the others, I wrap my arms around myself. And not just because of the nippy air. Something about the lonely road with the bare trees creaking in the cold wind that stirs the stiff grasses makes me long for home. How long have I been away? I mentally count the months from that summer night I left.

I turn eighteen today.

The thought, unbidden and unexpected, tears through my mind like a tackle from behind. My steps slow until I drift farther away from the group. The sound of their voices and footsteps as they head back to the warehouse are drowned out by that one thought... It's my birthday.

A churning wave of homesickness washes over me, twisting my stomach and squeezing my heart. I don't know how I forgot, the day I become an adult—

"Something bothering you, Scarlett?"

I jolt at Rez's voice, not realizing he'd dropped back beside me. "Oh, um, it's nothing."

His gaze bores into me, but I keep my eyes fixed on my shoes. "You miss something...or someone, maybe?"

I gnaw the inside of my cheek and cast him a glance. Can I

tell him about my family? Would that make everything else pour out, ruining our mission? My chance for the cure?

I look down at my hands, the skin still red from the fight. The image of Flint's burned skin flashes in my mind, and I clench my hands into tight fists. Balls of fire. "I just wish this never happened."

Rez hesitates, taking a slow breath. "What do you mean?"

"I got attacked by a super and...I got my powers from it somehow, I don't know..." My gaze falls to my shoes again.

"Scarlett." Rez leans forward to catch my gaze. "Why do you see that as a bad thing?"

I gape at him. "How could I not? It's changed my life. For the worse."

He doesn't blink. "How?"

Is he joking? I clench my jaw. "I had to leave my family." The words seep out through my teeth.

Rez looks away for a long moment. "But that doesn't have to be the end."

I pull my gaze from the broken city rising before me. I can't help the frustration seeping into my voice. "No. It is the end." I'm destined for a life in the SCF, living out the rest of my days as a science experiment in a government facility. Keeping the world safe from me. Keeping my family safe from me.

Unless the cure works. Which is why I have to go through with this, so I can at least have that chance.

Rez puts a hand on my arm to stop me, but I slip away and keep walking. He hesitates, then keeps pace with me again.

"That's the thing with a lot of supers, Scarlett," he says, seeming unfazed by my coldness. "They think their life is over when they get powers. They think they'll waste away in the SCF."

I scowl at the grass on the side of the road. It's like he's reading my thoughts. Can he do that with mind-manipulation powers?

He studies me a moment before letting out a breath. His

voice quiets. "God can use bad for good, Scarlett. That's what we believe around here. We want...*I* want to help supers do the good that they are called to do."

I scoff. "What does God have to do with this?"

He grins, a brightness shining in his eyes. "Everything." He looks ahead again. "Someday you'll see. I believe that. ."

I slip my hands in my pockets, brows pinched. The blog post I read that night back home comes to my mind, the blogger's words "God made supers too." But for what? I glance at Rez out of the corner of my eye. He's a rebel, and a liar. Does he just pretend not to see the danger that supers are to the world? What about those family members who've been killed by their loved ones because of these powers?

But a traitorous whisper stirs in my heart. What if...what if he *is*, somehow, right? What if I could believe my powers were meant for good, and I could accept them as who I am? Is that even possible? To embrace this fire that could hurt everyone around me? My insides quake. I'm not strong enough to do that. I'd make a mistake and risk everyone's lives.

I stuff down the doubts warring in my mind. Burn them to ashes. I'm not special, and these powers aren't good. I'm a freak. We all are.

And I have a chance to fix it. If I can complete this mission, I'll save so many lives with this cure. I straighten my shoulders, lifting my chin, as if my posture will reflect the resolve I'm trying to conjure. The cure offers me a chance and it's a chance I'm going to take. The faces of my family, the sound of their laughter, fills my mind and presses against my heart. It's a chance I *have* to take.

I wait outside while the others file into the warehouse. Rez gives me one last glance before closing the door behind him. A sigh escapes me as I lean against the brick wall and let my legs lower me down to the gravel. Exhaustion tugs at my muscles and drooping eyelids as I prop my arms on my knees and lean my head on them.

A sharp buzz on my wrist draws my attention to the watch. I purse my lips and flip the false clock face over with more force than I need to.

It's Dr. Bailey. Of course.

Dr. Bailey: *How are things?*

Tears I didn't expect and don't want sting my eyes. I roughly swipe them away on my sleeve. What's wrong with me? I scan the area before pulling the watch close to my mouth.

Me: *Fine.*

A short pause. Dr. Bailey: *You sure?*

Me: *I said everything's fine.*

I imagine him narrowing his eyes at the tone that probably comes through my message. Dr. Bailey: *Anything to report?*

I lean my head back on the wall, closing my eyes, simultaneously thinking about my answer and letting my mind calm down.

"Scarlett?"

I jolt, slap the watch closed and yank my wrist behind my back.

Ares steps out of the warehouse and slips his hands into his pockets, studying me with those piercing ice-blue eyes. The wind tosses his snow-white hair across his forehead.

I swallow and try to steady my voice, despite my slamming heart. "Hey, what's up?"

He shrugs one shoulder and digs a toe of his sneaker into a thick weed. "Just thinking."

I adjust to sit straighter against the wall. "About what?"

He takes a step forward, then stops himself. I can already feel the cold emanating from him, an even sharper chill piercing the cold air. He takes a half step back then lowers himself to sit cross-legged and rests his chin in his palm.

"What are you thinking about?" I repeat, still keeping my wrist hidden. I don't know why I feel like I have to hide it. I don't want him to think I was spying on them and reporting to the doctor. Do they spy on me?

He lifts his eyes to me again. Studying. Searching. I hold his gaze. For a moment, his calm persona flickers, revealing something behind it. Something not unlike the doubt that's been consuming my thoughts. His white brows draw together as he bites his lip. Is he as unsure as I am?

He opens his mouth, closes it, repeat. He remains silent for a long moment, picking at a loose thread on his sleeve. "What... what do you think about Rez?"

Right now, I don't want to be around him. I don't want him to be nice to me. Most of all, I don't want to have a face to put to the betrayal we're about to go through with. "What do you mean?"

He shrugs again. "I mean he's...different."

"Yeah."

He looks up. "You agree?"

I adjust the watch on my wrist. "Um...yeah, I guess."

He falls back into thought, biting at a fingernail. Then he stands and turns back to the warehouse, in a thoughtful daze. "Yeah...different."

I blink, wide awake, at the ceiling as I lie on the unforgiving floor, waiting until the only sounds in the warehouse are deep breaths and soft snores.

My thoughts won't allow me to fall asleep. Despite my resistance, Rez's words replay through my mind. I shove them back, but they appear again and again. Dr. Bailey slips in to battle Rez. *"Trust no one."* Especially the leader of this criminal gang. He's just trying to win me over, like the doctor said.

I clutch a fistful of blanket. Rez is wrong. I'm not special. I'm a weapon that has to be controlled. Fixed, if possible.

The watch vibrates. I push off the floor and slip outside into the cool night. As soon as I'm several feet away from the warehouse, I flick open the watch. I blink at the green and red phone icons bouncing on the screen. A call? I tap the green one.

"Dr. Bailey?" I whisper.

"Yes. Scarlett, it's time."

I blink again. "Time for what?" I breathe. But I know exactly what he's talking about. My stomach clenches.

"To finish the mission. From what the others tell me, you seem to have gained their trust. And faster than we expected, I might add."

I nod slowly. So the others did have contact with Dr. Bailey. I wonder what they told him.

"Scarlett? Are you there?"

"Yes, I'm here."

"Did you hear what I said?"

"Yes, but I..."

"Yes?"

"I don't think it's time."

Dr. Bailey's sigh comes through clearly. "Why not?"

I bite my lip and look around in the consuming darkness, as if I'll find the right words there. "It's just...too soon. We need more time."

His silence unnerves me.

I close my eyes. "Just a little more." What could convince him? "In order to make this work right, we need more time."

"Okay, Scarlett," he says. "But just remember, succeeding means getting the cure. And that means going back to your family."

I clench my hands and grit my teeth together. I know, I know. I know.

"And you're playing a part in purging the country of superhuman criminals. It's about time these freaks got what they deserve." His last sentence slithers through clenched teeth, words uncoated in their usual smooth control.

I grimace and swallow the bitter taste in my mouth. I want to retort with some of the same words Rez has said. But anything I say could reveal my true feelings. My true feelings? No, my mixed feelings. My doubts. Whatever they are, he can't know those.

I end the call and stare into the thick darkness of the shadows, arms limp by my sides. Tears coat my eyes, but none fall. What do I do? It's like my family and Rez are battling for my attention, my favor.

I'd choose my family every time. But is this the right way to do it? Is there any other way to get the cure without going through with this? If I back out, will they still let me have the cure?

A slim figure slips out of the inky shadows.

My throat tightens and I step back. "Crynn."

The corner of her mouth lifts in a smirking grin. "Scarlett."

She heard. I know she did. I clench my hand until my nails bite into my flesh, wishing Dr. Bailey had just messaged me instead of calling, like before.

She tilts her head. "You should call Dr. Bailey back soon."

I try to swallow. "Who?"

Crynn chuckles softly and steps closer to me. She glances over her shoulder at the warehouse door before leaning closer. The sparse moonlight dances in her green eye, glinting like a jewel in the light. It's so deep, so mesmerizing. But I force myself to focus on her brown eye, an endless dark abyss.

"I'm Raven."

My heart skips a beat. My throat constricts as I stare at Crynn. My mind swims with her words. "You're who?" I croak.

She huffs a one-beat chuckle. "Yes. I'm the contact."

I manage to swallow.

She ignores my stunned silence. "You really should contact the doctor soon. We don't want to wait much longer to carry this plan through."

I just blink at her.

"You know the plan? How it needs to go?" She stares at me, waiting.

Words jumble in my throat and won't make it past my tongue. She raises her eyebrows. I clear my throat. "Yeah." I rasp.

She purses her lips, apparently annoyed at my half-hearted response. "The soldiers they send in won't be able to handle all of them at the same time," she continues, taking my uncertainty for ignorance of the plan. "We'll have to split them up."

A hint of panic clenches my insides. Wait, I need more time. I need more time to think and decide if...

If I even want to go through with this.

"We should split them up into at least two groups. That will make it easier to capture as many as possible. Rez being the priority. We'll work out more details later."

My head still spins and I shake it. "Um, okay."

She gives a sharp nod, then turns to go back inside.

"Crynn?"

She stops and looks over her shoulder.

I shift from one foot to the other, fingers knotting together. "How do you do it? I mean, isn't it hard doing this...being so close to Rez?"

She pauses. "I manage just fine."

"Yeah, I mean...with you two being siblings and all..."

A shadow passes over her face. "That's none of your business."

She would do this to her brother? "Sorry. I-I understand."

Without another word, she slips back into the warehouse.

I stand in the dark, my feet like blocks of cement. The watch pinches my wrist, reminding me of Crynn's words to call the doctor back. To finish this. But I don't want to call him now. I still need time to think about things.

But now Crynn's getting things going while I want to slow it down. And if I decide not to go through with it, what will Dr. Bailey do? What will happen to me?

My legs finally obey my command to move. I step back into the musty, cold warehouse and make my way silently back to my sleeping corner.

The biting cold, achingly hard floor, and my battling thoughts keep me from falling asleep.

I go through the day jumpy and dazed. My mind still swims with all my thoughts and worries. I keep glancing at Crynn, who goes about her day as the reluctant assistant to her superhuman leader brother, as usual.

I keep seeing things I want to block out. The little children giggling and running around, using their powers freely and openly. Ivon managing the garden with tenderness I didn't know he was capable of. Rez bandaging up a wound on a reckless teen who decided to challenge someone in a fight. People helping each other, loving each other, creating the best life they can in this broken, ruined city.

Going through with the plan and capturing all these people seems so cruel. I'd be betraying Rez, and he's been nothing but kind to me. I feel different here, in this warehouse full of supers like me.

I don't feel like a freak. I feel almost...normal. Like I belong.

I scowl and shake my head, glad Dr. Bailey doesn't have a direct line to my thoughts. The overturned bucket I sit on squeaks as I lean closer to the firepit, listening to the crackling and basking in the comforting warmth. My eyes get lost in the blaze, and it pulls me in, trying to get me to forget about anything else. But I glance at Crynn again, who's helping Rez with some inventory.

This time she notices me, but her face is blank. Cold. Scheming. Ready.

And I feel like mush. I stand to see where Nadia, Ares, and Seth are. I find Nadia sitting in a corner of the warehouse with children surrounding her. She tenderly tapes a bandaid on a little boy's skinned knee, then lifts a crumpled tissue to a little girl's nose and hands her a steaming cup. The little girl says something too low for me to hear and Nadia laughs.

A smile tugs at the corner of my mouth seeing Nadia laughing, happy. *Focus, Scarlett.* I shake myself and stride over to her, then grab her arm and lead her to where the boys huddle by the warehouse door, talking in low tones and glancing at Rez.

"I need you guys to come here a second," I say, brushing past them and stepping outside.

They follow slower than I want, and I can feel their gazes on me as we gather in a close circle on the gravel.

I take a deep breath. "Might as well cut to the chase." I glance around to make sure no one's near, then take a step closer to them. "Crynn is Raven."

Eyebrows raise as they stare at me. Nadia picks at the end of one of her braids. "Really?" she breathes.

I nod. "She told me last night."

"At least we know now," Seth says, forehead wrinkled as he stares at the ground and slides his hands into his jogger pockets.

Ares tilts his head, narrowing his eyes. "What else did she say?"

I swallow and clench my jaw. "She wants us to hurry up and finish what we started." I watch their faces for any sign that they have the same battle raging in them that's in me. They're silent.

I sigh a little. "We'll have to create diversions to split them up." My voice trembles. Saying it out loud makes it too real. Like we're going through with it. Right here, right now. My throat constricts. I guess we are. "They'll have more luck with smaller numbers."

Nadia stares at her sneakers, scuffing the toe of one against a clump of grass overtaking the gravel lot. Ares slowly crosses his arms over his white t-shirt, working his jaw back and forth.

A small, hidden part of me lifts. They're not sure either.

Seth claps his hands. "Well, we have a plan, so let's get a move on."

And then there's Seth.

"But is this..." Nadia begins, taking a slow breath. "Is this the right thing to do?" Her voice is hushed and quiet, and she doesn't hold anyone's gaze.

Wind whistles against my ears in the moment of tense silence.

Shakily, tentatively, I say, "I was wondering the same thing."

We look at Ares.

His pale brows furrow in concentration as he studies us. "Maybe it'd be wise to think about this more."

I suppress a relieved sigh.

Seth huffs a one-beat laugh and looks at us, incredulous. "You've got to be kidding me!" He throws his arms out. "This is what we came here for. What's wrong with you guys?" He casts a challenging look at all of us. "What about the cure?"

We look away, fiddling with shirt hems, scuffing shoes on the ground.

"We're just trying to do the right thing," Ares says quietly.

"Oh, come on." Seth whirls on him. "Don't make me the bad guy here."

Ares still doesn't look at him. "That's not what I said—"

"I heard what you said. Why can't we go ahead with this? We're so close!" He pauses, observing all of us standing in silence. "Don't you remember what we get when we accomplish this?"

"Seth." Ares finally looks at him, uncertainty in his clear eyes. "We're just trying to do the right thing, make the right decision. What we've been sent here to do...it may not be the right thing."

Seth jabs a finger at his own chest. "I'm trying to do the right thing here too! They're about to get what they deserve."

"What do you mean, Seth?" I say, stiffening against the glare he turns to me. "A lot of these people haven't attacked anyone or committed any crimes. Is this just about revenge for you for something?" As soon as the question leaves I wish I could snatch it back. I bite my tongue.

Seth's expression goes grim as he turns to face me square on. He steps closer until his face is inches from mine. The muscles of his temple bulge as he clenches his jaw. "You want to know what they did to deserve it?" He squeezes the low words through clenched teeth. "Well, I'll tell you. I lost my parents because of them, because of supers. We thought we were safe from them, but we weren't. They broke into our house, even out in the middle of nowhere. When we tried to stop them, they—"

He breaks off. The muscles in his neck strain as his face turns red. Moisture shines in his eyes. A sporadic wind brushes my cheek and circles around us. I gulp, trying to keep myself from stepping away from him, trying to keep my fire calm.

"I survived," Seth continues. "But not without scars." He finally takes a step back.

Breath seeps out of my lungs as I gape at him, heart beating against my ribs. Nadia and Ares stare at him, too, unblinking. I remember again the painting in the antique shop. I imagine Seth and his parents living there, laughing together. Then...it was all shattered.

Seth takes a moment to study each of us. He finally rests his eyes on me. "I hope I can trust you to do the right thing."

CHAPTER SEVENTEEN

Chewing on the last bite of a stiff granola bar, I brush the crumbs off my pants. My stomach still rumbles after that measly dinner, but I'll have to settle with it. Everyone else does.

Evening has already begun its takeover of Rapid City, cloaking it in soft darkness. The farther the sun sets, the more supers return to the warehouse for the night. Once everyone's had some form of dinner, they gather around the fire, drowsy from the warmth and food. Including me, Nadia and Ares. I'm not sure where Seth is. Again. But even in his absence his words plague me.

Nadia and I huddle against the night chill, leaning toward the fire. Ares sits slightly behind us. Numerous supers crowd around the warm blaze and the firelight casts dancing shadows on the brick walls. The darkness of night and the drowsy children sitting nearby keep the conversations to a low murmur. Rez is talking to the group of supers closer to the fire, but I try to block out his voice. I want to imagine I can't hear or see these people I'm supposed to turn in to the SCF.

The firelight glints off something green in the shadows at the edge of the fire's flickering circle of light. Crynn watches me from the warped patches of darkness. I pale under her intense gaze and look back to the fire.

"Here, Scarlett."

I stiffen at Rez's voice and look up. He offers me another granola bar. "B-but I've already had one," I stutter.

He shrugs. "I'm not very hungry."

I know that's not true. I would hate to take food from him when I know he's still hungry. I would hate to make him go hungry through the night until tomorrow morning. I hate that he's being nice to me.

I reluctantly take the bar. "Thanks."

He nods and sits back down.

I rip the wrapper off the granola bar and bite into it. It's stiff on my tongue from the cold and scratches down my throat. I wince. Picking off a chunk of almond from the bar, I chance another glance at Rez. He smiles at a little girl bounding up to him, holding up a frail little flower. She doesn't speak, but holds up the drooping plant with a smile. Rez chuckles and takes the blossom to tuck it behind his ear. The girl giggles, wrinkling her freckled nose, then skips away.

My appetite flees and I stuff the granola bar into my jacket pocket.

"So how was your day, Scarlett?" Rez asks as he pulls out his knife to sharpen it. Which is a pretty weird sight considering the yellow flower still in his hair.

I swallow, throat dry from the granola bar. "Could I have some water?"

"Sure." He stands and takes a few strides to the nearest shelf to pull a bottle of water out of a box, then tosses it to me.

The loose label crinkles as I catch it, and I take my time twisting off the cap and taking several gulps.

"So, your day?" Rez prompts.

"What?" I say, feigning forgetfulness.

He chuckles a little. "How was your day, Scarlett?"

"Oh. It was fine." Another lie. It was filled with churning

thoughts and indecision and scheming and betraying the people that made me feel welcome for the first time since I got my powers.

Rez slides his knife back into a sheath in his boot. "You seem to be getting more confident in your gifts," he says.

I glance down at my hands. Funny how I've barely thought about the red splotches on my palms. The firelight flickers around my fingers. I shrug.

He shrugs too. "Just seemed that way to me. It doesn't seem to scare you as much."

Still staring at my palms, I frown. Being around other supers has almost numbed me to my powers. Sometimes I forget about being different or weird. I remember our first night here when Rez asked me to put my hand in the fire. I wasn't scared of burning. I was scared of *not* burning. I was scared to see more evidence of how I wasn't normal. But things are different here. They don't make me feel like a science experiment. They make me feel...whole with my fire.

Rez leans his elbows on his knees and studies me. "Are you okay?"

I realize I haven't said a word in response. I tuck my trembling fingers under my armpits and look up. He shows genuine concern in his two-colored eyes, brows furrowed as he waits for an answer.

My chest tightens. "I'm okay," I rasp.

His frown doesn't leave. "You sure?"

I squeeze my eyes shut. "I just need some air." I stand and my bucket clatters back on the cement floor. I don't stop until I get outside, then suck in several deep, long breaths, the cold air chilling my lungs and biting at any bit of bare skin. I rub my hands together and blow on my fingers to warm them, then try to pull my sleeves over my hands. The bulky watch on my wrist makes that difficult.

The watch...

I scan the silent darkness. A clatter of a tin can to my right makes my heart jump to my throat. A raspy meow makes me let out a breath, but takes me back to that night behind the ice cream shop. Before the memory of consuming fire can take over, I give my head a sharp shake.

My gaze rakes over the area once more, lingering on the door for several moments, ears straining. My numb fingers flip the cover, then hover over the glossy screen reflecting the silver moonlight. I bite my lip, fingertip over the call button next to the doctor's name. Should I just message him instead of call? It might be safer, quieter.

Still, my finger lowers closer to the phone icon. Maybe hearing his confident voice will help solidify the resolve I'm trying to grab onto. Resolve that eludes me. I tap the call icon and bring the device close to my mouth, scanning my surroundings again.

"Scarlett?" His voice sounds concerned, confused. Maybe he thinks it's odd that I'm calling him and not him calling me.

"Hi, Dr. Bailey." My jaw shifts as words suddenly leave me. How do I tell him that I need him to re-convince me that this mission is a good idea? Will that make him doubt that I can do it and keep the cure from me?

"Is something wrong?"

"No, I just..."

"Yes?" His impatience makes me want to end the call right then and there.

"I just...don't know about all this, Dr. Bailey."

He pauses, his soft breathing crackling through the tiny speaker "I know it must be hard, Scarlett. Doing the right thing usually is."

I close my eyes and take a deep breath.

"But remember," he continues, "you're making this a safer country. For everyone. For your family." He pauses, as if letting that last bit sink into my mind, my heart. "Keep your eyes on the prize. The cure. Imagine what it'd be like to be normal again."

Still, I can't find the right words to say. Suddenly, having powers isn't as scary as it used to be. Here in Rapid City, I feel like I belong. Like I could contribute and help people.

"Don't you want to go back to your family?" His question, crackly over the watch's small speaker, echoes softly into the silent night and through my heart.

I press a fist against my chest and take a deep breath. "Yes," I breathe. "More than anything."

"Good."

We both go silent for a moment as the night chill seeps into my bones. I can feel the fire inside me retreating into the deep corners of my body. It takes some doing, but I coax it to flow into my hands to warm my stiff fingers. Suddenly I remember what Rez said about me getting powers. Bad can be used for good. Can I do good with my powers?

I squeeze my eyes shut and shake my head. I'm not anything special. I have to be fixed. And there's only one way to do it.

Dr. Bailey cuts into my thoughts. "Hello? Are you still there?"

"Yes, I'm here."

"Okay. Let's finalize the rest of the details now."

"Right now?"

"Yes."

A weight settles on my chest. My fingers rub my collarbone as an ache spreads to my heart. I'm not ready. And yet I am. I want the cure, but...Does the end justify the means?

"Okay, are there suitable locations to separate their numbers?"

Words come like thick honey, reluctant. "Um...yeah."

"And?"

"There's a warehouse—that's their main base—and another large grocery store building that should work." Mikey and his gang will probably get caught in between this. I don't know why they came to mind or why I care.

"Okay, good. We'll set it up for tomorrow."

My stomach drops like I'm falling off a cliff. "Tomorrow?"

"Yes. You're going to create diversions to separate the group into two smaller ones, correct?"

I hesitate. "Yes."

"Okay. Time it so that the groups are in their respective buildings at noon tomorrow."

This is too real. It's worse than debating and worrying and going back and forth. We've got a time, date and place. "Okay."

"We'll send out a deployment of armored trucks. They'll wait outside of the city until the correct time. Meanwhile you will have to contact them to coordinate. I'll add the commander to your contact list."

Queasiness rolls in my stomach. "All right."

"Then at noon tomorrow, they'll take it from there." He pauses. "That's all you have to do, Scarlett."

I huff. Like it's that easy. Doesn't he understand how I feel? Yet how could he?

The speaker crackles slightly. "Relay the information to the others. Make sure they understand."

I swallow and chew my lip. "Okay."

"Do you have any questions?"

Thousands. Like, why am I doing this? Am I so desperate to be normal that I will turn Rez and the others over to be locked up in a prison for supers? There's no other way to get the cure that doesn't involve doing this to them?

Am I doing this to be with my family again, or just because I want to be normal?

"Scarlett." A hint of irritation edges Dr. Bailey's voice.

"No questions."

"Good. Contact me if there's any change of plan or if anything goes wrong. Okay?"

I nod. "Okay."

"All right. Try to get some sleep."

When the call ends, my arms drop lifelessly to my sides. Numbly, I slip back into the warehouse and shuffle to my sleeping corner, barely noticing that no one's around the fire anymore. I lie down and throw the blanket over me, covering my head. I tell myself to feel nothing, think nothing, remember nothing. *Just do what you need to do to get what you want.*

I close my eyes. Hours tick by. Sleep never comes.

As soon as morning light fills the warehouse, my eyes fly open. They're gritty and sting from lack of sleep. My muscles resist as I sit up, stiff from the icy floor. I need warmth. I need fire, and mine is reluctant to surface.

I stumble from my tangled nest of blankets to the firepit to find no one there yet. Half-burned logs sit in the pit's bottom on top of dusty ashes. I glance around before tossing a few more sticks over the logs from a pile by the wall nearby, then hold my palm near the wood. Flames pour from my skin and over the logs. They ignite and soon the comforting crackling, popping and sizzling echoes softly through the quiet space.

Waiting for the chill to leave me, I sit on one of the crates scattered haphazardly around the firepit and wrap my arms around myself. Today's the day.

The fire finally draws my own flames from my core to warm my body. I lift my wrist to check the time. *6am*. Now I regret getting up so early. Even though I can't sleep, I could've pretended. I wouldn't have to interact with anybody. I wouldn't have to see the faces of those I was turning over to the government. Now I have a six-hour wait.

I look over my shoulder and scan the sleeping bodies, chests rising and falling with even breaths and soft snores murmuring through the quiet morning. I catch Ares' shock of white hair. A snort draws my attention to the other side of the warehouse, where Seth groans in his sleep as he turns on his side. I chew the inside of my cheek as my gaze sweeps back over to Nadia, dark braids spilling over her shoulders.

I still haven't told them the plan yet. I bite my cheek harder.

And I'm not going to. The thought of going against Dr. Bailey's order to relay the information to them makes my stomach stir, but Nadia and Ares...It's like they've adjusted here, gotten attached. Would they try to stop me? I glance at Seth again, who has his arm draped over his face. I guess maybe I could tell Seth. But can I keep him from telling Ares and Nadia? He doesn't strike me as someone who can keep a secret. I don't want to take that chance.

Guess it's on me then. When it's all over and done with, I'll explain to Dr. Bailey why I had to do it this way. I take a deep breath, but it does nothing to dispel the tightness in my middle.

I hug myself tighter and scoot closer to the fire's warmth. The heat softens my muscles, but doesn't touch the cold that's settled into my bones since last night.

Rez is the first to join me by the fire. He shuffles up, his jacket crooked, hair spiked in all directions. He stretches his hands toward the fire, rolling his shoulders and blinking the sleepiness from his eyes.

I barely breathe, keeping my gaze on the firepit.

"G'morning, Scarlett," he says over a yawn.

"Morning," I squeeze out. In a blinding flash, my mind flips through the plan for capture. My throat tightens and I swallow to loosen it, and flick a glance at Rez. "Going on another food run today?" My weak voice almost gets lost in the expanse of the room.

He stretches his arms above his head with a groan. "Not today. I like everyone to stay near the warehouse when they can. No food run means everyone hangs around here." He grins. "Hungry?" Before I can answer, he turns to inspect the shelves.

So they'll stick around the warehouse today. They'll all be together by noon. A wave of nausea hits me, and I press a hand against my stomach. Just nerves? I glance at Seth, who still snores. I guess he can trust me to do the right thing. I am doing the right thing...right? My gaze catches on a few of the children curled together for warmth in the corner. I look away.

As Rez scans the lines of shelves on the back wall, he runs his fingers through his hair to make it lie flatter. His gaze freezes on something on the ground, and he stills before squatting to peek under the shelves. "Those crazy kids," he mutters before disappearing behind a shelf.

I leave the fire to follow, hoping for anything to distract me. "What's wrong?"

We round a shelf toward the back to find a cardboard box turned over and a variety of candy scattered across the dusty floor. I raise an eyebrow. "Candy?"

Rez sighs and squats down to turn the box right side up. "Yeah. It's hard to find, so we rarely give it out. Sometimes the kids get into it when I'm not around."

I kneel next to him to help scoop the candy back into the box, trying to brush some of the dirt off the wrappers. I lean over to get a piece of candy under the shelf and my eyes catches on a glint of gold in the sunlight.

I sit up, forgetting about the candy. Books line the shelf at my eye-level. I can't help the faint smile that tugs at my mouth. I finger the dirty, worn pages. "Where did you get these?"

Rez kneels next to me and swipes some dust off the spines. "We found most of them in the abandoned houses."

My fingers brush a black leather-bound book with shiny gold page edging and the words *Holy Bible* stamped in gold letters on the front. Rez reaches across me to slide it off the shelf. He flips the pages with his thumb and the sun catches the gold edging, sending it glittering through the air. "This one's my personal favorite." He glances up at me. "Ever read it?"

I shake my head, watching the gold reflection dance on the brick wall.

He grunts again, letting the book flop closed in his hand. "I learned a lot of great things from this. A lot about my powers."

I blink. "Your powers?" I don't know much of anything about the Bible, but I didn't know there was anything about superpowers in it.

Rez chuckles. "Well, not powers specifically, I guess. Just learning that my powers weren't a mistake, that I have purpose." He looks me dead in the eye. "God doesn't make mistakes, Scarlett."

The way he says this for the second time, makes it stick to my mind. I hold his gaze a moment before letting my eyes drift away. God doesn't make mistakes? Then why do I have powers? What are they for? Why would God give people powers? I look up again to find him still staring at me, sincerity in his eyes.

"There's this verse," he says. "1 Peter 4:10 that says, 'As each one has received a special gift, employ it in serving one another as good stewards of the manifold grace of God.' For us, our gift is our powers. And some people are using them as they were intended: for good. There are superheroes out there. Real ones. It's not just something from those old movies."

I blink at him, fidgeting with my sleeve as he steadily holds my gaze. I imagine him as a little boy pouring over beat-up old comic books, reading about superheroes saving the day and aspiring to be like them. He must truly believe this. I look back at the Bible resting in his palm. But is he right? Can that possibly be true? Dr. Bailey's voice cuts through my thoughts yet again in his neverending mantra. "*Trust no one.*" Still, my mind doesn't quite let go of Rez's words.

"Here." He holds the book out to me. "You might like it."

I slowly take it from him, not really knowing what to say. I just stare at the wide, fading letters on the cover. "I don't know if..." If I'll understand? If I'm the type to read it?

He chuckles softly, as if sensing my discomfort. "Start with the book of Mark. It's my personal favorite."

I clear my throat and lift my hand to slide over the other books on the shelf. My fingertips brush the worn edges of some superhero comic books. "I thought these were banned." Subject change.

Rez pauses, then slips the Bible out of my limp hand to put it back in its place on the shelf. "They are," he says with too much lightness.

I smile. "Dylan would like these." He never could resist learning a bit about the superhuman's point of view.

"Dylan?"

I nod, not looking at him. "Yeah. He's my brother."

His eyebrows lift with interest. "Oh. How old is he?"

"Fifteen."

"Does he have powers too?"

"No, he doesn't." Thank goodness.

"He's a superhero fan then I assume?"

My brows furrow. "I don't know if I'd say that. But he didn't think they were all bad, anyway." He never really said that much out loud, but I knew.

"Well, he's right," Rez says quietly.

I shrug. "I guess so." I glance down at my watch again. *6:28am.*

"You all right?"

I nod, not meeting his eyes.

"Are you sure?"

"I said yes!" I snap. My face reddens, and I bite my tongue. Why did I do that?

Rez blinks at me as I hurriedly toss the remaining dumped candy into the box. "I'm sorry," he says. "I was just checking."

"It's okay," I blurt without looking at him. "It's not you. I just feel...off today."

"That's all right." He takes the filled candy box and slides it onto a high shelf. We both stand and brush the dust off our pants.

"Well," he says, resting his hands on his hips. His voice is light again, like I didn't just yell at him out of the blue. "I have garden duty this morning. Want to give me a hand?"

I twist my fingers together. As much as I'd like to avoid him, the thought of being outside and digging my hands in the dirt sounds good. Maybe it'll be a distraction. Temporarily. I nod.

"Awesome. Let's go." He turns, then pauses. "Oh, would your friends want to join us?"

I grimace inside, recalling Dr. Bailey's order to fill them in on the plan. What will they think when they find out? Will they be upset with me? Except maybe for Seth. I steel myself inside. He said he hoped I'd do the right thing. That's what I'm doing.

I shake my head. "No, probably not."

"Okay. Let's head out then." He leads the way out the door and around the warehouse.

We round the corner of the brick wall and kneel beside the upturned plot of soil. I poke a clod of dirt. It's hard from the cold. Stiff and unforgiving and uncaring. I feel like that. I feel like dirt.

"Scarlett?"

"Hmm?" I look up.

"Let's just start with the weeds. Get the stuff you don't want to do out of the way first, I always say."

"Makes sense," I reply, reaching for the nearest weed. I lean close to examine each plant before I pull it. I'd hate to pull out a useful plant.

Why do I care? I won't be here much longer. None of us will be.

We pull weeds in silence. As I pull up the last few, Rez disappears into the warehouse and comes back with a couple bottles of water. He pours these evenly over the plants, the water darkening the dirt and making it soften.

"Messing with my garden again?"

I jump at the deep, rumbly voice behind me. I look up to see Ivon's broad form silhouetted by the morning sun.

Rez chuckles and continues watering while Ivon kneels down to examine the small garden. The cluster of plants on one end, where I saw the girl use her powers to plant them, is at least an inch taller than the others.

"So, you mentioned you have a brother," Rez says. "Do you have any other siblings?"

My throat constricts. Does he have to ask? "Yes. A little sister."

"What's her name?"

"Hannah. She's six."

He nods, still examining the garden. "Must be nice having siblings."

I nod and study him. "It is." I hesitate. "Do you have siblings?" Why does he keep that a secret? Crynn never said either.

Rez crushes one of the empty water bottles in his fist. He takes a deep breath through his nose before answering. "One."

Ivon's gaze flicks to him. Rez doesn't go on, and I decide not to press it. We sit in silence for a few long moments, staring at the garden but not really seeing it.

I discreetly glance down at my watch. Almost *8am.* I push myself out of the grass and brush a few dirt specks from my pants. "I'm going for a walk." Maybe I can clear my head, get my mind to focus.

Rez and Ivon both look at me, but say nothing as I stride off. I tug my hoodie closer against my neck and stuff my balled hands into its pocket. Biting wind rakes over me, and I tip my head against it as I stroll through the city. Occasionally I look up, squinting up at the towering buildings against the breeze drying my eyes.

I take a deep breath and let it out through my teeth. I'm really doing this. Really going through with it. Will Nadia, Ares, and Seth be mad at me because I didn't tell them? I should've told them like Dr. Bailey told me to. But I'm afraid Nadia or Ares might try to stop me. Then it would all be ruined. No cure. No going back to normal.

The walk finally warms my muscles, and I eventually stop in the middle of a street. I glance up and down the road. Somehow, my mindless wandering brought me in front of Mikey's grocery store, but they don't seem to be home right now. The trash littering the ground in front of and in the store looks even worse in the light of day. The wind kicks a ripped newspaper across the sidewalk like a tumbleweed, knocking it into a crinkling pile of empty chip bags.

I'll have to bring some of the supers here soon. I stare at the store, going through the rest of the mission in my mind. But instead of the detached resolve that I thought would come, my mind conjures up a different image...

Rapid supers, some Rez's, some of Mikey's, screaming and scrambling away from the guns of the SCF soldiers. Some fight back with their powers and escape. Some don't. A lot don't. Bruised and bloody, the soldiers cuff them and shove them into trucks.

A sick feeling twists my stomach, and I press my fist to my forehead. *No, no.* Why'd I think about that? Why'd I let my mind play that out? I'm standing plotting the demise of the only people who've made me feel at home since I got my powers. Now they'll be locked up in that prison forever.

Unless the cure works. Then maybe they can go back to normal too. Then they'd understand why all this had to happen.

My watch buzzes, and I flinch. I clench my jaw in frustration, angry that the vibration still makes me nervous. But I welcome the distraction and flip it open before tapping the bobbing phone icon and bringing the device near my mouth. "Hello? Dr. Bailey?"

"Yes. What's going on? Are you all right?"

"Everything's fine. Why?"

"Your heart rate is going up."

He can see my heart rate? I press my right hand over my heart to find it beating at a frantic pace. I take a deep breath and close my eyes. "Just nervous, I guess."

"Everything will turn out fine. The trucks are already waiting outside of town. You should contact them now."

"Okay."

"And Scarlett?"

"Yes?"

"Stay sharp. You've come this far, don't let those people change your mind."

I swallow and nod, staring at my shoes. "All right. I understand."

"Good." After a faint rustle in the speaker, the doctor ends the call.

My arm drops limp to my side, like the device is too heavy for my muscles to carry. I angle my wrist just enough to see the time. *9am.* I lift the watch again to check the contact list, seeing the second person Dr. Bailey added. The name field simply says *Callaghan.* I tap it and start my message.

Me: *This is Scarlett Marley.* I don't know what else to say, so I just send that and wait. I squeeze my numb toes in my shoes and shake my chilled fingers. I wish my fire would emerge to warm me instead of retreating from the chill.

The watch buzzes with a message. Callaghan: *Callaghan here. What are the locations for the capture? We can use your watch's tracking feature to locate each spot.*

I sniff against a tickle in my nose, trying to ignore another sick squirm in my middle. Me: *Okay, good. Where I'm currently at is one of the locations, a grocery store. The second is the warehouse, their HQ where the other three still are. Do you see it?* I imagine Callaghan looking at a map on a tablet with an aerial view of the city, four blinking red dots marking our locations.

There's a long pause before his response. Callaghan: *I see it. Still on schedule?*

Me: *Yeah, so far.*

Callaghan: *Good.*

I nod and flip the watch closed and turn back toward the warehouse. My entire body feels cold and stiff again by the time I get there. Not just from the chill wind. I hurry inside and make a beeline for the firepit, which still holds my blazing fire. Nadia and Ares sit on one side, while Seth sits on the other side of the fire staring moodily into the flames. They all look up at me when I stop by the firepit, avoiding their gazes.

"Where have you been all morning?" Seth asks.

I keep my eyes on the crackling blaze as I stretch my hands in front of it. My icy fingers sting from the heat. "Out."

"Out where?"

"Just walking, okay?" He's the one who disappears all the time, why is he grilling me?

He stares at me a moment longer before turning back to the fire. The only sounds echoing through the warehouse are the crackling and popping of the fire and the soft murmur of conversation from the clusters of supers scattered around. Rez was right. They are sticking around the warehouse. The atmosphere is almost cozy, with the fire casting a warm glow on smiling faces, children sitting on blankets, playing games and eating picnic-style. In another corner an elderly super sits with two toddlers on his knees, telling a story in hushed tones while they hang on his every word.

I groan inwardly and force myself to look away, to just focus on the fire. Still, my chest aches. I close my eyes and take a deep breath, trying to will some of the same surety Crynn has about this plan. Dr. Bailey said the right thing is often hard to do. I just have to stay focused.

The fire warms and energizes me, and my muscles relax. But my insides are still stiff, twisted and fluttery. Noon will be here before I know it. Before then, I'll have to create the distractions to separate the gang into two groups. How can I handle them both?

There's a soft touch on my shoulder and I flinch. Crynn leans close by my ear, her hair brushing my cheek.

"It's almost time," she whispers. "Stay calm, stay focused. I'll distract Rez while you keep Ivon here."

My shoulder stiffens under her touch, imagining her emerald green eye. Is she using mind manipulating powers on me? But no, it feels nothing like when Mikey's friend, Carl, manipulated me. I'm doing this of my own free will.

She gives my shoulder a squeeze. "Got it?"

I gulp and nod. She nods too, and her hand slips off my shoulder. I suppress a shiver.

Crynn disappears, and I shrink a little away from the circle of firelight to check my watch Time passes at a sluggish crawl. Rez and Ivon come inside, laughing and jostling each other as they make their way toward the fire to warm themselves. Ivon smiles more and more each day as he gets more comfortable with us newcomers. They look content. Happy. I look away from them.

Before anyone can talk to me, I slip away and step back outside into the nippy cold. I miss the fire's warmth, but it hurts too much to watch them. But the images are branded into my mind...Nadia kneeling in front of a little girl, who shyly watches Nadia examining a small cut on the girl's pinkie. Ares frowning in concentration as some of the older kids try to teach him one of their dice games. Seth standing close by, watching with a faint scowl wrinkling his brow.

And they still don't know what I'm about to do.

My thudding heart beats against my chest and a touch of lightheadedness washes over me. My teeth grind together. *Get it together, Scarlett. Do this, and you might be able to go home.* A few tears well up in my eyes just thinking about going home. Seeing my family again. Even going to college for music. Getting back on track with my life.

I don't know how long I've been standing outside when Crynn appears beside me. Her presence seems to always make me tense. I look at the watch. *11:50am.*

"It's time," she says. "I hope you're a good actress." She pauses with her hand on the doorknob. After a deep breath, she flings it open and runs inside. I stay planted for a moment, as she yells Rez's name.

I blink, gaping after her. Wait. Not yet. Too fast. My heart beats wildly in my chest. I clutch a hand over it, feeling my lungs heave in breath after breath. I force my feet to follow her, feigning confusion and concern with the rest of the supers.

Crynn stops in front of Rez, hands on her knees and panting.

Rez's shoulders tense. "What is it? What's wrong?"

She doesn't look up at him, just gulps in unneeded breaths. "There's a big fight... in the grocery store." She throws her arm out in the general direction.

I slip behind the cover of a well-stocked shelf.

"Are you sure?"

She throws a sharp glare at him.

He shakes his head, waving his hand. "Sorry. Never mind."

Crynn throws her arm behind her toward the door. "I think someone may have followed me. They may attack here next."

Ivon steps forward, placing a hand on the shoulder of a young boy with a nest of wild curls. "I'll stay here with the kids," he says.

Perfect.

Rez nods. A group of adult supers gather around him, faces focused and ready.

Ares stands from the dice game and hurries to the circle. "We'll help too."

Nadia stands with him. Seth just sends a hard look at them both.

I close my hand into a fist and press it against my mouth. No. They weren't supposed to do that. Surely they'll realize what's going on and back out. This wasn't part of the plan.

Unless...they've already decided to not go through with the mission.

I angle myself to make sure the shelf stays between me and Rez as he and his group of supers run out the door. Ivon stares at the door several moments after they've left, worry etched in his thick brow. He doesn't even notice as a toddler stuffs dry leaves and twigs in his cargo pants pocket.

Crynn finally straightens, breathing more normally. "I'll go see if I can help," she says quietly. She casts a brief glance my way before slipping out the door.

I stand frozen to the spot for a long while, my senses on high alert, palms sweaty, ears ringing. My fire pulses through my body with each heartbeat, adding to the swirl of nerves flipping my stomach. I peek between the shelved boxes to keep an eye on Ivon, who's bending to comfort a little girl. If he leaves, I don't know what I'll do to keep him here without arousing suspicion.

Glass shatters above me and I yelp, covering my head with my arms as shards rain down. A silver object flies past me and clatters to the floor. The cylinder rolls against my shoe, shiny exterior reflecting my wide eyes. What is this? I bend to touch it, but jerk back as more shatters and clattering echoes through the warehouse. Cries fill the space as Ivon gathers the children toward him, his gaze darting between the rolling silver objects.

White mist hisses from one end of the cylinder at my feet.

Commotion envelopes the warehouse as the mist creeps across the floor. Worried, confused chatter. Children screaming and crying. Panic is so thick, I can taste it. I swallow and grimace. Ivon's deep, rumbling voice cuts through it all as he tries to gain control, keep them calm. He says something about getting outside. But they don't listen, drowning out his voice with their own.

The room tilts and my vision blurs. I cough, glancing down at the object still hissing mist. I pull my hoodie over my mouth and nose and slip out the door under the cover of the panic and noise.

I freeze, staring down a line of guns pointed at my chest. I can't breathe, I can't think. Fear closes my throat.

"She's with us!" a shout calls from the end of the line, and the guns lower.

Bile rises in my throat. I stumble out of the way as two guards step forward to drop a blockade in front of the door. I watch them, blinking rapidly. There are other entrances, but I keep my mouth clamped shut. Maybe they have more soldiers there anyway.

The guards back away, guns still trained on the door. One man growls in frustration as he tips his gun down to grab me by the elbow and drag me out of the way.

The door knob jiggles. Then harder. A fist pounds from the other side. Another pound, and another, until it beats with the same frantic tempo of my heart. Children's screams and shouting scrape my eardrums. The pounding grows softer, weaker, then stops all together.

I press a fist to my mouth. Please let Ivon be gathering the children to leave through another exit. Please let the gas have not taken them all out.

After a stretch of silence, the two dozen guards step forward. Two step forward again and remove the blockade, grunting. Once they get back in position, another one flings the door open and they rush in. I hold my breath, straining for any sound.

Ivon's yell splits my ears.

I can't move, even as shoes scuffle against the floor, guards yell, fists thud against flesh. Two gunshots echo through the warehouse and I flinch backward, my hand over my mouth. Who was that? Then all goes silent.

Words tangle in my throat, but don't make it past the lump. I move closer to the open warehouse door, but pull back again when guards shuffle through, grunting under Ivon's weight. Two carry his legs, and two under the arms. His head lolls back, even as his jaw sets in a grimace. Like he wants to keep fighting, keep protecting, but the gas's effects have taken him over. His cloudy gaze sweeps toward me. I look away before his eyes can meet mine. I don't want to see what I know is lurking there.

A black SCF armored truck drives up just in time to relieve the guards of their load. A guard bumps into my shoulder from behind as he passes me. I step out of the way, watching as he carries the limp form of a little girl to the truck, as they're fastening thick cuffs on Ivon's wrists.

I bite my lip, harder, harder, until it bleeds. I wince at the pain and clamp a hand over my mouth. Guards glance at me, and I blink rapidly to hold back the tide of tears.

Why am I crying? I shouldn't be crying. It's all for the greater good. For the cure. They'll all understand some day. Then they'll thank me. They'll thank me for...

A guard shoves a scrawny teen as he stumbles across the gravel, head bent and a bruise on his temple.

They'll thank me for...

Slung over a guard's shoulder, a little boy whimpers, tears staining his cheeks, as he weakly pummels the man's back. His chubby hands curl up to wipe over his eyes.

They'll thank me for...

Ruining their family?

A strangled cry escapes my throat before I clamp my lips shut. I turn my back on the scene as guard after guard carries, pushes, drags the Rapid superhuman children from their only home, half-drowsy from the gas, some unconscious. I press the heels of my hands against my ears until my head aches.

It'll be over soon. I just need to remember the cure. Home. Returning to my family. It's for everyone's good. Mine, my family's, the Rapid supers, the country, Nadia, Seth, Ares...

Seth said it was the right thing. Dr. Bailey said it was the right thing. Crynn said it was the right thing. Does that make it the right thing?

I stand there, still as stone except for my pounding heart and heaving breaths. My hands slowly drop away from my head.

The silence from the warehouse is deafening. Soldiers slam truck doors closed and climb into drivers' seats. One who I assume is Callaghan, supervising the proceedings, checks something on his tablet, then looks at me. "We're leaving."

My hands shake as I stuff them in my hoodie pocket. My fingers knot together as I nod. I take one step when a hand claps my shoulder. I gasp and twist away, turning around to see who's behind me.

Most of the slim figure is hidden by the shadow the building casts against the sunlight. Only one side of a delicate face is exposed to the light. Pale skin, raven black hair. And one emerald green eye.

I shrink back.

Crynn steps closer and nods her chin toward the trucks. "Nice work, Marley."

My throat suddenly goes dry. I try to swallow.

She raises an eyebrow. "What's wrong with you?"

I turn my back toward her. "Leave me alone."

She grabs my shoulder to turn me back around. "What's wrong?" When I don't answer, a vein in her temple bulges as her jaw clenches. "I don't like to ask twice."

My teeth grind together as pain from what I just witnessed squeezes my lungs. My pain looks for someone to blame. Someone other than me. "And *I* don't like to talk to people like you."

She barks a laugh. "People like me? Are you serious?" She leans in closer, dropping her voice. "We're the same."

I take a step back. "No, we're not."

She raises an eyebrow, then straightens, chuckling. "Oh, I see. Seeing the error of your ways, huh?"

"Well...I..."

She smirks. "You don't sound so sure."

My mind scrambles, thoughts tripping over each other and words refusing to form on my tongue. Is her manipulating power messing with my head?

She pokes my shoulder. "Even if you did decide to stay, change sides, everyone's gone—"

"It's your fault!" I smack her hand away.

She pauses and tilts her head. "*My* fault?"

My hands tremble. "Y-yes. You...you tricked me." I gulp. Yes, that's right. She tricked me. It's not my fault. I didn't want this. "Your powers."

She pauses for a long moment. Then she erupts in a laugh, leaning back with hands on her hips. The sound bounces through the empty street. "Powers?" she says between chuckles. "*My* powers?" She lets out another bout of laughter.

I grind my teeth. What's so funny?

Crynn finally gets a hold of herself and dabs a finger to the corner of her eye. "Silly girl. I have no powers."

My mind trips. I blink at her, throat tight, my eyes darting from her brown eye to her green one. No powers? But her eyes...

Crynn's lips twist in a disgusted grimace. She narrows her eyes. "Unfortunately, I wasn't *blessed* with power like my brother."

I search her eyes as I shrink away from her. Jealousy and bitterness drip from her gaze. She *wants* powers? No, she wants *power*.

Confusion wraps my mind. Her eyes are two different colors, like her brother's. "H-how...?"

She shrugs, tucking her hands in her pockets casually. But the sharpness hasn't left her face or her eyes as she glares at me. "They just never came. Green eye but no powers."

Suddenly her gaze grows distant. She looks past me at the warehouse, dark brows knit together. "I just wanted..." Her face hardens again and she shakes her head. "My mission is complete," she mutters, turning.

"W-where are you going?" I don't know why I feel like someone should remain here. To take care of the place?

She looks over her shoulder at me, then glances at the warehouse. She sniffs and lifts her chin. "Away from this place."

She disappears around the corner, leaving me alone. I stand, panting shallow breaths beneath the building pressure in my chest. I don't turn when I hear Callaghan's crunching footsteps approach me.

"We're leaving," he says again.

I try to swallow down my parched throat. "I—I'll follow in a minute."

He hesitates. "Meet us outside of town." Then his footsteps crunch across asphalt again. After one last door slams, the trucks roar to life. Their rumble fades as they head to the edge of the city.

Silence cloaks me. I can't stay here. Fire flickers in my gut, and I run. Not daring to look back at the warehouse that somehow became so like a home in such a short time, I take off down the street toward the edge of the city like a rabid dog nips at my heels. Wind whips my eyes, streaking a few hot tears across my cheeks.

The horde of armored trucks line up just outside of town, their back doors open wide and gaping like a lions' mouths. Soldiers load up the last of the half-unconscious supers, adults that would've been with Rez at the grocery store. Some unconscious are carried in. They're all cuffed, some with the same sensors over their palms that I had in the SCF. But they all have one thing in common: slumped shoulders, eyes to the ground, sniffing and wiping their cheeks with their sleeves.

I suck in lungfuls of air as two soldiers carry Seth, unconscious, out of the back of a truck. They must've realized he was with us. With a sick twist of my stomach, I remember that he stayed behind at the warehouse.

I watch silently. A cold, numb feeling slithers over me, sounds muffle, blood rushing through my ears, lurching with the pound of my heart. The energy of my fire is limp, weak, dormant. My gaze falls to the dead grass, and my shoulders sag beneath the weight.

"Move it." At the guard's barked order, I look up. Nadia and Ares shuffle groggily into the back of a truck.

I gasp and sprint to Callaghan. "Wait!" I stumble to a stop next to him. "Why are they in there?"

He doesn't look at me, just narrows his steely eyes as he watches Nadia and Ares. "They resisted."

I pause to swallow. "But can't you let them out of the truck?" I don't have a reason. Just maybe my guilt.

"They resisted us. So they get the same treatment as the others."

I shake my head and grab fistfuls of hair. No. That wasn't supposed to happen. We were supposed to all get the cure. Have I ruined it for Nadia and Ares by not telling them the plan? If I had told them about the plan from the start, maybe I could've convinced them and everything would've gone according to plan. My heart beats a fast, painful tempo against my ribcage. Nadia is the last to climb into the truck. Just before the soldiers close the door, her gaze sweeps over to me. Blood trickles from a cut near her eyebrow. Her face is just...blank. The warmth that usually fills her soft brown eyes is gone as she looks at me.

I turn away, sliding my fingers into my hair and squeezing. The guard points to a truck a little distance away from the others. "Wait in there. We'll be leaving soon."

I shuffle over to the truck, the dead, dry grass crunching beneath my shoes. Trembling, I open the passenger side door and climb in. The sound of my breathing is magnified by the small space as the vapor from my breath clouds the window. I lean my head against the cold glass, my hair falling over my face. Guilt crushes my chest, pressing the air from my lungs. I squeeze my eyes shut until pain stings behind them and pulses through my temples.

This isn't right. This isn't right. I should never have done this.

I bolt upright, heart lurching against my ribs. Wait. I never saw Rez. Of all the supers I saw loaded into the truck, I never saw Rez among them. Could he be...?

I jump out of the truck and run toward the city, as fast as my legs will carry me. My lungs burn and my muscles ache, but I keep going. My sneakers slap the asphalt with more intensity and I jump over piles of garbage and crumbled bricks. I don't stop, don't slow. Barely breathing until I reach the warehouse door.

I hope there's someone left.

I freeze in front of the old rusty door, my breaths puffing out in thick mist. No sounds come from the other side. I close my eyes and lean my forehead against the cold metal and fight the stinging tears springing to my eyes. I have to face it, though, whatever lies within.

I throw open the door and walk in.

Rez stands in the middle of the warehouse, hand pressed

against his ribs, with a dozen kids surrounding him. His soft, comforting words don't seem to be calming their frantic whimpers. He winces and grips his side tighter as he tries to usher the kids toward the back of the warehouse.

Then he sees me.

He draws himself straighter, grimacing and favoring his right leg. He stands there; legs spread, one hand wrapped around one of the kids'. His jaw clenches and his breathing echoes through the entire space. Blood dribbles from a cut on his stubbly chin.

I slowly bring my gaze up to his glare. My heart drops and my stomach twists at what I see in his eyes. Disappointment. Hurt.

"It was you, wasn't it?" he says, voice shaking as he blinks. His eyes glisten.

My mouth moves, but no words come.

"Well?" Rez snaps, his voice cracking. "Are you going to finish the job and tell your government friends that they missed a spot?" The muscles in his jaw bulge. The children crowd closer together behind him, staring at me like I'm a monster.

I take a step back, shaking my head. Hot tears threaten to spill out of my eyes and my jaw works, but no words come. Finally, I say, "No, I...Rez." I sniff and swallow. "You don't understand. I...had to."

"Sure." It's like a hard shell has covered him, but still his eyes glisten.

I can't help the tears that start sliding down my cheeks. Saying that I could explain seems so petty, like a band-aid on a bullet wound. "I had to," I repeat, my voice low and raspy.

Rez pauses a moment to draw a breath, then slowly shakes his head. "No. No, you didn't."

My hands tremble at my side. I clench them and squeeze my eyes shut. I can't look at him anymore, remembering what he'd done for me while I was here, a stranger. And I just made him watch soldiers take away his family.

"Freeze!"

The order from behind makes me jolt and I watch in terror

as soldiers pour in through the door, guns pointed at Rez. Still more file in from a back door, weapons ready. Rez, anger and fear flashing in his wide eyes, gathers the children closer to him as he looks around for an escape. There is none.

One of the soldiers lifts a watch to his mouth. "We got him."

The fight slowly seeps out of Rez. His gaze sweeps the guards again. Then those eyes land on me.

I can't hold his gaze for even an instant. I spin and stumble through the open door. Back to the waiting trucks full of the once-hopeful supers I betrayed.

CHAPTER EIGHTEEN

I barely feel the prick of the needle as it slips into my vein. I barely notice as the blood flows from the underside of my arm into the vial. I barely notice anything.

"Feeling okay?" Dr. Bailey mumbles as he pulls the needle out and presses a cotton ball to the puncture wound.

I know he's only asking to make sure I'm not feeling queasy from the blood work, but it's not that that's making me uneasy.

Without lifting my head, I scan the room. This lab is neater, more pristine, and not as bone-chilling cold as the one I'm used to, the one hidden away in the underbelly of this facility. The floor is still concrete but the walls are a soft, dusty blue. Nurses hover around, scurrying at Dr. Bailey's orders and bending over me, watching me like hawks, like I'm going to jump up and escape. They throw nervous glances at the viewing window in front of me, spanning almost the whole wall. News reporters nearly press their faces to the glass, talking excitedly into microphones and pointing fingers at me. I squirm, turning my head away from them.

The way they stare, with wide eyes and jaws slack, pointing and beckoning for cameras to get closer...I feel like I'm at the zoo. And I'm the one in the cage.

I glare at my knees and flex my bicep against the tightly rolled up sleeve of my jumpsuit. "Why are they here?"

Dr. Bailey pauses as he pulls the familiar black, egg-shaped sensors from a box. "Hmm?" His gaze is lowered to his work, barely paying attention to me.

I shift my glare to him. "Why are they here? The reporters."

He glances toward the window. "Oh. Them." He sniffs and places the sensors in my palms.

I squeeze them under my fingers, willing them to crack. They don't budge.

He presses his fingers onto my arm firmly until I relax my muscles. I open my mouth to repeat the question, when he finally answers.

"This is a big event," he says quietly. "We publicly announced the testing of the serum."

That was fast. We just got back from Rapid this afternoon. Did they announce this before we even finished the mission? I nod my chin toward the glass. "So they know I'm one of the guinea pigs."

A frown flashes across his face. "Guinea pig? You're a hero in their eyes."

My gaze flicks to the reporters again. A woman with perfectly curled honey-gold hair locks eyes with me, then quickly looks away to say something to the camera. My gaze rolls over the other reporters. They either meet my eyes for a split second and look away, or they divert their gaze before I can look at them.

Hero might be a stretch. More like...well, superhuman. Irregular. A science experiment.

I can't hear a word they're saying through the thick glass. And I want to keep it that way. Still, my stomach churns thinking of the things they might be saying. Is this live? Is my family watching? What do they think of me now? Bile rises to my throat.

I shift in the cushioned chair as my foot falls asleep, noting the nervous glances that poke me from everyone but Dr. Bailey. I fix my eyes on my jumpsuit pants instead. "Do they know about Rapid?" I rasp.

At first the doctor shows no sign of hearing me, but then he purses his lips and sighs. He bends, pretending to adjust the straps securing my upper arm. "Would it be a problem if they did?" he mutters.

I flick a glance at the reporters. Still staring. Still babbling. My jaw shifts as I study the doctor's face. His gaze doesn't meet mine as he fiddles with the black strap. I narrow my eyes. "So they do know."

He still doesn't look at me. "Like I said, you're a hero in their eyes. You accomplished something big out there." He straightens and sighs again. I realize I'm glaring at him, and now his ice-blue eyes pierce me. His hands clench into fists in his lab coat pockets as he turns away to a computer on a desk nearby.

Words coil on my tongue, but I bite them back and scan the room again. The reporters shrink from my gaze and the nurses avoid it. The guards behind the reporters and cameramen stand in a perfect line, clutching their belts and surveying the crowd. They're not like the usual guards, who dress in all black and wear protective helmets. These look more like mall security. I guess they didn't want to scare the reporters.

Dr. Bailey turns from the computer and takes a deep breath, rubbing his hands together. He gives a brief smile and nod to the reporters before turning to the guards lining the wall behind me.

"Okay, we're done here for now," he says. "Take her away."

I can barely hear my own breathing, even in the dead silence. The shoulder seam of my jumpsuit sticks into my skin and I shift with a wince. I rub my fingers together to warm them, trying to ignore the pinch of the sensors strapped over my palms. Sighing, I stretch my arms across the smooth table and rest my cheek on the cool surface, staring at the bland cream-colored wall of the empty conference room.

Silence. Dead silence.

Not unlike the silence blanketing Rapid city after the soldiers swept through.

I groan, closing my eyes. My fingers slide across the table, then I tap my nails on the wood. Thumb to pinkie, thumb to pinkie. Even and steady, like a piano scale. I listen to soft tapping, latch on to it, try to make it distract me from the images that are seared into my brain. The tears streaming down the children's faces. Ivon's limp form. Nadia's cold gaze. And fear in all their eyes.

The door opens and I sit up. Silent and solemn, Dr. Bailey leads a line of government men into the room. They circle the table and settle into the cushioned chairs with barely a squeak of a wheel. A guard accompanies Seth, ushering him into the empty chair across from me. A deep bruise shadows his jaw, but he throws me a grin.

I look back at the door as it swings closed with a click, then turn to Dr. Bailey. "Where's Nadia and Ares? Are they okay?"

Dr. Bailey doesn't meet my eyes as he adjusts his dark grey suit coat. "They're fine."

I frown. "Where are they?"

The muscle in his temple bulges as he shifts his jaw, staring hard at the center of the table. "They resisted our soldiers, fought on the wrong side." He lifts his gaze to me. "They require more security now. Isolation."

My frown deepens as I imagine them sitting in some cold, small cell in the basement of the facility. Alone. "Will they...?"

The doctor huffs sharply at the ceiling. "Yes, Scarlett. I was *informed* that all of you will still get the serum."

The same anonymous government man that seems to be in charge sits at the head of the table. He grins and leans forward, greased hair catching the lights overhead. He glances at Dr. Bailey before looking at me. "You've accomplished a great feat, and we're thankful." He leans back, turning his head slightly, still grinning. "And as thanks we're giving all your friends the serum instead of..." he pauses as his grin falters, replaced with something darker, "giving them what they deserve."

The subtle threat makes me wish I could command sparks to my eyes. But any thought of summoning my fire makes my stomach clench.

"Besides," the man continues. "More test subjects for the serum would be beneficial." He raises his eyebrows at Dr. Bailey, who nods in agreement but still stares at the table.

Seth collapses back into his chair with a dramatic sigh. "Well, that's a relief. I thought that Nadia and Ares messed things up for me."

I swivel my glare to Seth. I wonder if the fire-glow really does appear in my eyes because his lop-sided grin fades instantly when he sees me.

His eyebrows raise, then draw together in confusion. He turns to Dr. Bailey. "When do we get the cure?" he says, leaning forward eagerly.

Irritation still wrinkles the doctor's forehead as he looks over Seth and me. "Soon."

Seth sighs. "You guys really enjoy being vague, don't you? *How* soon?"

Dr. Bailey rests his tightly folded hands on the table and clenches his jaw. "You're in no position to make demands. You will get it soon and that is all you need to know." He glances between us, as if expecting a challenge, an argument.

I lean back in my seat, limp hands in my lap.

Dr. Bailey clears his throat and adjusts his tie. "Before you go to your units, we'll need some answers."

I frown. "Answers?"

He nods. "We have a lot of questions about Rapid, Rez, and what their operations were there."

My head falls back against the chair as a sigh escapes me, deflating me and making my shoulders slump.

They hurl question after question at us. Seth is more willing with the answers than I am, which draws more frustration from Dr. Bailey toward me. I don't care. I just want to put this whole thing out of my mind and go back to my unit. I want the silence, the isolation, the cold. I want to just curl up and forget everything, waiting for the cure, going back to normal. I want to go home.

That is, if the cure works. Surely it will. It has to. Then the Rapid supers, *everyone*, will understand. They'll understand why I did what I did and it'll all make sense to them.

Maybe it'll make sense to me, too.

Finally, the guards march Seth and me out of the conference room, up an elevator, and through the facility toward our units. Exhaustion drags on me, making my feet slap weakly against the floor. Soon I'll be alone. Then there'll be quiet. Maybe I can rest...

The guards turn us a different way.

Seth and I glance at each other as the guards take an unfamiliar path through the maze of hallways. Soon there are no more iron unit doors lining the walls. My stomach twists as a drop of sweat slips down my temple. Where are we going? I'm tired of being in the dark, never really knowing all of what's going on. Can't they just tell me everything? Didn't I do enough dirty work for them to deserve that at least?

I glance at the guard at my left, guiding me by the elbow. "Where are we going?"

"Yeah," Seth says, tripping as he tries to look at a guard behind him. "This isn't the way."

They stay silent as they march and prod us down the hall. We finally stop at four lone doors. I frown, glancing up and down the hall. Only these four doors?

A guard reaches past me to punch in a password on the screen by the far left door and swipes his ID card. After a buzz, the door swings open.

Where I expect to see the familiar small unit with glaring

white lights, white walls, and bed and chair bolted to the floor, I'm met with something else entirely. The unit is about the same size, but the wall opposite the door is clear, thick glass. Reporters and cameras buzz behind it like bees near a flower. My feet root to the floor. I'm not going in there.

The guard gives me a hard shove and I stumble inside. Still gaping at the staring reporters, I barely notice as the guard removes my handcuffs and leaves me alone in the unit.

Well, not really alone. I glare at the reporters, the cameras, hands clenching against my legs. Then I tear my attention away from them long enough to survey the room.

Everything's different, so different. I stand stiff beside the bed in the center of the room. I finger the woven fabric of the blanket draped over it. It's more like a hospital bed than the narrow one I had before. It's wider, the mattress deeper and softer. A TV screen hangs in the upper corner beside the glass wall. I round the bed, eyes set on the small bookshelf against the wall to the left of the glass. I bend over and run my fingers over the spines. Classics, mostly.

A sigh escaped my clenched teeth. What is this?

I turn to face the glass walls—with circular silver intercoms in the centers—separating the next three units following mine. Identical. Seth gapes at me from beside his bed in his unit on the far end, then turns his wide-eyed gaze over the unit, stopping at the glass wall where reporters watch him. Glass, glass, glass. So many watching eyes, pointing fingers, cameras.

I turn my back to the glass walls, fists clenched against my legs. I frown at the armchair sitting in the corner. What's with all the luxury now? I look over my shoulder at the reporters milling around. Is this all because we're the first to try the cure?

Trying to ignore the pressing presence of the people leaning in close against the glass, I sit in the armchair. The soft cushions hug my body and I let my head lean back against the top with a sigh. I close my eyes, pretend I'm alone, still and quiet, like this is my old unit where there was no one but me and the camera in the wall. Inhale. Exhale. Mind blank, silent, still...

Faint voices reach my ears, and I scowl at the interruption. My eyes fly open and I sit up, scanning the room.

A tall reporter stands with his back to the wall, mic to his chin and he talks to the camera trained on him. He angles slightly toward me, gesturing in my direction. My breath stills as my ears strain. I can hear him, just barely...

"The superhumans are getting settled now, preparing for the first injection to come soon," he says. "These four are the same superhumans that had a big hand in the victory in Rapid City, South Dakota, where the SCF captured many of the rebel supers there, finally gaining control of the area."

I slide my sweaty palms on my legs, then grip my knees. I can't help but stare into the camera, at the millions that must be watching. Watching *me.* Sweat breaks out on my forehead.

"You can see here," he continues, angling himself more and gesturing at the glass, "one of the superhumans already in her unit, preparing to receive the cure injection. Scarlett Marley turned herself in several months ago when she contracted superpowers after an attack in her hometown of Hermosa, South Dakota—"

I slap my hands over my ears, and hunch down over myself, trying to disappear into the armchair. I don't want them talking about me, telling the world about my life, my struggles. I can almost feel the ravenous eagerness of the people watching this live, leaning in, pointing, shoving to get a better look at the superhuman girl in her cage. I'm not an animal or some alien to gawk at. I'm real. I'm human.

My heart thunders in my ears. Those desperate thoughts sound like someone else I know. They sound like something I've heard before. Isn't that what Rez was trying to tell me all along?

CHAPTER NINETEEN

When Dr. Bailey enters my unit hours later, my arms ache from holding my hands to my ears. I lie curled up on the bed, wishing the reporters, the voices, the watching eyes would just go away.

Dr. Bailey taps my shoulder. When I don't respond, he tugs on my arm. "Sit up."

I twist my neck to look at him over my shoulder before slipping my hands from my head. Cold air brushes against my sore ears as I press my hands against the mattress to push myself up.

Dr. Bailey glances at the glass wall, then clasps his hands in front of him. "Getting settled in okay?"

I narrow my gaze at him. His frustration seems to have melted away. The cameras catch my eye again and I press my lips together. Or maybe it's just hidden for now.

I don't bother to conceal the irritation in my tone when I look up at him. "Why the glass walls?"

A frown barely flickers across his features. "They have to be able to—"

"Can we have no privacy?"

A muscle in his jaw jumps. He rolls his shoulders back and takes a deep breath, as if composing himself before answering. "The reporters need to see so the world can see," he says simply.

His gaze bores into me, studies me, as if digging for my feelings. "You do want the world to see, don't you?"

He asks almost sweetly, as if daring me to say the wrong answer. I lift my chin, covering my quivering insides with a confident posture. "Why wouldn't I?" I want to add that I want the country to be part of this historical event with the cure. But my confidence is flimsy, weak enough to be knocked away by a lie.

His eyes narrow for a split second. "I don't know. Why wouldn't you?"

As he eyes me, my confidence quickly fades. I swallow and clear my throat. "Of course I want them to see. This is...history."

Dr. Bailey rocks back on his heels with a nod. "Do you need anything? Are you comfortable?"

I frown at him and the questions, spoken too loud for the distance between us. Like he wants someone to hear. I glance out of the corner of my eyes at the cameras. Maybe he does. So now they're all about treating us right?

My chin lifts again. Dr. Bailey raises an eyebrow. "I'm not quite comfortable, doctor," I say.

He blinks, hands shifting. "Okay, what do you need?"

I jerk my head at the reporters. "For them to leave. Then I'll be comfortable." I smile sweetly, relishing as redness creeps over his face and his lips purse.

His eyes dart to the right, toward the viewing window. He forces a chuckle through his nose. "Enough with the jokes. If there's nothing else you need, then—"

The clank and echo of a unit door opening silences us both. We turn our attention to the unit next to mine as the door swings open. Two guards escort Nadia into the room. My stomach twists at the sight of her wrists in cuffs. Don't they know she wouldn't hurt anybody?

At least, not on purpose.

Her gaze stays on the ground until the guards take the cuffs off and leave the unit. Then she lifts her eyes. As soon as she sees the glass walls and all the people and cameras, she stiffens, eyes wide. Hands trembling, she slowly backs up until her shoulders hit the wall, and she flinches at the touch.

I turn my gaze to the reporters. They press against the glass like children watching an exotic fish in a tank. Cameras leaning closer, reporters talking faster. Nadia shrinks further and further into herself, curling into the corner. I want to scream at them to stop.

Nadia's frantic eyes dart around the room, snagging on Seth for only a second before flicking to me. She freezes. Some of the panic leaves her gaze, replaced by something else. Her brows draw together and her lips purse slightly as her hands unfold from their clenched form. They still tremble, and she tucks them under her armpits. Still staring at me, her frown deepens even more before she turns away, leaning her back on the glass wall that separates us.

I turn away, scrubbing my hand over my face. That familiar aching weight presses on my chest again. I rub my sternum and avoid looking at Nadia again.

Dr. Bailey clears his throat and adjusts his tie as if he didn't just witness Nadia's reaction to the reporters. To me.

"Well, as I was saying," he says. "If there's nothing else you need right now, then I'll be going."

He turns toward the door, but before he can go another step, the door to the only empty unit swings open. Ares trips through the doorway, colliding with the bed. He whips around to throw a glare at the first guard that approaches to remove his handcuffs. The second guard stands near, tense and balanced on the balls of his feet. Ares switches his icy gaze between them both. A large patch of skin on his cheek glows red, as if he's been slapped. Hard.

Cuffs off, the guards cautiously back away and out of the unit. The door clangs closed behind them. Ares stares at the door as his anger dies away and his breathing evens out. His shoulders droop and he brings a hand to the mark on his cheek.

Then he freezes. Slowly, he turns around and meets the eager eyes of the reporters standing behind the glass. His eyes widen a fraction, heel skidding back a half step.

His gaze swivels over to my unit, locking on to Dr. Bailey. As quickly as he'd entered, a cool indifference settles over Ares. Eyes boring into the doctor, he smooths a hand over his white hair that had fallen over his face when he stumbled in. He shakes his head slowly, as if saying he's not surprised by any of this, before turning away.

This time Dr. Bailey doesn't brush it off with his calm voice. He continues to stare at the ice boy, even though his back is to us.

"Dr. Bailey?" I say.

He flinches, then turns back to me. "What?" he spits. His sky blue eyes turn stormy.

I dare to meet his gaze. "You were leaving, weren't you?" At least that'd be one less person watching me.

His usual composure melts back over him. Spine straightens, hands clasp, forehead smooths, eyes cold and indifferent.

I cross my arms, matching his expression. He's not the only one that can wear a mask.

Movement catches my eye and I glance past the doctor's shoulder. Ares, still angled away, stares at me over his shoulder. The look in his eyes makes me turn cold. My mask falls away and I chew my lip.

Dr. Bailey turns to leave. I reach out. "Wait."

He stops, sighing, then turns back around. "What?"

I look again at the others. Nadia's back to me, Ares eyes like shards of ice stabbing me. I drop my voice low. "They still get the cure. Right?"

Dr. Bailey's composure maintains. Barely. "Yes. I already told you that."

I let out a breath. Maybe then they'll understand. Maybe then they won't be mad at me. When all of this is over and we're back to normal. My spine loses its hold and my shoulders slump. I stare at my hands, limp in my lap. "When do we get it?"

"Soon."

"How soon?"

He sighs again, almost groaning. "I said soon. That's all you need to know."

Heat sparks through my veins, pulsing in my hands as they snap into fists. "*When?*" My voice comes out hard and trembling, surprising me. I swallow the tightness in my throat, and wilt again. I press my hand to my face. "I just...want this to be over."

Dr. Bailey says nothing for a long moment, just standing still while I try to keep it together. The last thing I want is to break down in front of the whole country.

Letting out a breath, Dr. Bailey lowers to one knee, coming a little lower than eye-level to me. He waits until I look at him. His eyes still bore into me, but something different swirls in the icy blue, brows knotting faintly. Hurt. Grief, maybe. Is that what's behind his mask?

He takes a deep breath before speaking, voice surprisingly soft. "Scarlett, do you remember me telling you about my daughter? How I lost her thirteen years ago?" He swallows and blinks a few times.

The fire inside me fizzles out as I stare at him.

"I lost her to a gang of superhuman rebels. These criminals are hurting our country and its people, and deserve to be behind bars, here at the SCF. What you accomplished, it..." He pauses to swallow again. "Some of the same supers who kidnapped my daughter could be among the numbers that we captured from Rapid City."

My chin drops to my chest and I stare at my palms.

"What you did was a big step to a safer country. You should be proud. Everyone will look to you as a hero. Maybe they already do. Maybe someday the world will be rid of the blight of superpowers forever. Maybe everyone will be normal again. We can fix this."

Tears sting my eyes. I clench my jaw, swallow, blink. Anything to keep them at bay. One slides free and I quickly swipe it away. "You're sure?" I ask softly, voice cracking.

He hesitates, only a moment. Then nods, a small smile crossing his face. "Yes. I'm sure. We'll fix you. Everything will be fine."

I sniff and nod, eyes falling back to my hands. He gives my arm a pat before standing, then leaves my unit.

I wipe more tears I didn't realize had fallen on my sleeve, curling up again on the mattress, my back to the other units. I blink through blurry vision at the wall, absently rubbing a thumb on my right palm.

Dr. Bailey said he'd fix me. Everything will be fine. It'll all make sense in the end. I hope.

In contrast to the constant hum of chatter from the reporters on the other side of the glass, in the units on this side, it's dead silent. The back of my neck tingles as I imagine Ares and Nadia sending glares my way. They know what I did. But they'll see too. They'll understand someday.

I nestle down in the bed, covering my eyes against the light with my hand. But before sleep can dull my mind, nurses come in with trays of food. My stomach gives an odd twist at the sight of roasted potatoes, veggies, and sliced meat. But it's not so much the nauseating thought of food right now that churns my middle, but the fact that it's not the same glop from the meal hall. I glance at the cameras still eyeing us. Things are different when the world is watching.

We eat in silence. Seth digs heartily into his food while Ares and Nadia poke at it and nibble here and there. Despite not feeling like eating, my middle pinches with hunger. I lift my fork and stab at a chunk of potato. Swallowing down my reluctance I lift tiny bites of each into my mouth. My tongue welcomes the rich flavors. So they finally found the salt.

I surprise myself by finishing all my food, despite the continued watchfulness of the reporters. After nurses take away our dishes, including Nadia's and Ares' nearly full plates, guards step into our units. I stiffen at first, then slowly release the tension coiling my muscles as they escort the four of us out, through the echoey halls, and to the outdoor grounds.

I expect to see grey jumpsuits clustered around the common grounds, coupled with the hum of soft conversation. But it's empty and silent. Grey clouds roll overhead, making the early evening seem darker, denser, with the slight tang of rain on the breeze. A lone bird streaks across the sky with a mournful cry. I shiver as a cold wind slithers down my collar.

The guards silently leave us, stepping back to line the perimeter of the grounds, like immoveable pillars. I hug myself against the cold, risking a glance toward the others. Nadia and Ares move away to sit under the nearest tree without looking my way. I watch them, how they angle away from me. Crossed arms, furrowed brows, eyes staring but not really seeing. Maybe they're thinking about something else, something like...Rapid.

A sigh escapes me as I turn my back on them, hugging myself tighter.

"Hey, Scarlett."

I blink and turn around. I'd completely forgotten that Seth was still standing beside me. I swallow. "Hi."

He stares at the sky, sliding his hands on the jumpsuit pants as if looking for pockets. Finding none, he just crosses his arms. "Crazy times, huh?"

I pause. "You could say that." I stare at the ground while he continues to scan the clouds.

Then he turns toward me. "You okay?"

I flick a glance up at him. "I'm fine," I mutter.

"Good." He grabs my wrist and tugs me toward Nadia and Ares. "Then let's join them, shall we?"

"Wait." I give a pathetic resistance before letting him pull me under the sparse tree where the two barely acknowledge our presence.

"Nice day today," Seth says, looking around and rocking back and forth on his heels, cheerful tone in stark contrast to the thick mood hanging over everyone else. "I like windy days."

Ares shrugs, the breeze lifting his mop of white hair. Nadia just sighs.

I raise an eyebrow at Seth, simultaneously wondering why I let him drag me over here and why he wanted to. Is he gloating about the mission's success?

Nothing but silence passes between us for the next several minutes. I stare at the grass and clutch my hands together in front of me, tension knotting my shoulders as my thoughts run faster. If only I could explain to them why I did it, maybe they wouldn't be mad. Maybe they'd understand. Don't they have families they want to return to?

A pat on my back jolts me out of my thoughts.

"Congrats, by the way," Seth says.

I clench my jaw, throwing a glance at Nadia and Ares as they look up at him. "For what?"

He pauses at the tension in my voice. "For completing the mission. The criminals are being detained here like they should be. Justice is being done."

"I don't think it's justice to count someone a criminal just because they have special gifts," Ares says, staring at the ground again.

Nadia rips a dry blade of grass in two. The expression on her face says enough. Maybe too much.

"Not everyone uses their powers for wrong," Ares says, tucking his hands behind his head and staring at the sky. "There are a lot of good people with superpowers, Seth."

Seth crosses his arms and frowns at both of them. "You just don't get it, do you?" he mutters, before turning and striding away.

I watch him leave, head bent and hair tossed by the wind, wishing he'd come back. *Don't leave me alone with these two.* They just...remind me of everything.

Ares avoids my gaze, keeping his blank stare on the spindly

tree limbs. Nadia glances at me, but as soon as I look at her, she looks away again. I heave in a breath, wrapping my arms around myself again and turn away. I head toward the door, hoping there's some way I can get back to my unit.

Loud, rapid *thwumps* overhead made me jerk away from the door. I tense, half-crouching, scanning the sky. A helicopter flies over the grounds, pausing to hover over us. A news channel logo is painted on the side.

I scowl. Always watching. Will I ever be alone again?

Something in my gut twists at the idea. Do I *want* to be alone with my thoughts?

When the guards escort us back to our units later that evening, I sigh with relief when I get there. No reporters. No cameras. No watching eyes, pointing fingers, mouths open in shock. I shake my head and crawl into bed. I allow myself to enjoy the softness of the mattress and the press of the blankets on my body, pulling me toward sleep.

Sheets rustle as I turn on my side, back to the other units. I try to block out Ares and Nadia and the haunting faces of Rez and the other supers. The lights flick off as I pull the blanket over my head. I blink at the darkness, struggling to wipe my mind clean of everything. Every face, every look of hurt and disappointment and...Rez's face takes over it all, despite my efforts, his words echoing in my mind.

He said I was special. He said I wasn't a mistake. I think I believed him, or maybe I was beginning too. But I betrayed him. Now his family is torn apart. Torn *away.* Sitting alone in some cold unit, he probably regrets every nice thing he said or did for me.

As much as I try to erase his words from my memory, they echo through my mind over and over. During my time in Rapid,

I felt valuable. Not *except* for my powers, but *because* of them. I meant something. Surrounded by others like me, I felt normal.

But that wasn't real, was it? It'll be better this way, in the end. I have to believe that.

An image of the last time I saw Rez flashes through my mind like glinting light off a knife blade. I bite my tongue, squeezing my eyes shut as if that will block out the memory. I hurt him, after all he'd done for me and for supers everywhere. That was the thanks I gave him for trying to help me.

I reject the comfort of sleep. I don't deserve it.

I curl tighter up under the warmth of the blanket, clutching a hand to my chest against the aching want for my family.

CHAPTER TWENTY

Light prods me awake, but not like the gentle glow of sunrise through the warehouse's broken windows. It's bright and harsh and sudden. Coupled with a low hum of conversation. My eyes struggle open and I blink against the blur in my vision.

A headache pulses in my temples as I sit up and rub my eyes. My mind tips with dizziness and I sit still until it steadies. Still, the low hum. What...?

I look up and suck in a breath. Half a dozen pairs of eyes meet mine, reporters and cameras reflecting the eyes of the rest of the world.

Right. Glass walls. History being made, and all that.

I press a hand over my heart, focusing on taking deep breaths until my heartbeat steadies. But the pressure of people's gazes watching my every move makes my palms sweat. I wipe them against the blankets, considering crawling under them again.

A buzz sounds behind me, and I turn in the bed to see my unit door swing open and Dr. Bailey stride in. Before looking at me, he gives a polite smile and nod to the cameras. A nurse follows close at his heels, wheeling in her equipment to check my vitals and whatever else she does.

Dr. Bailey presses a button on the side railing and the bed

cranks to an upright position. "How are you doing?" His forehead wrinkles faintly, breaking his placid expression as he glances over my face.

I lift my fingers to my cheeks, then scrub my sleeves over the skin. Dried tears.

He stares at me, still waiting.

"Fine," I croak. "The cure...when—?"

"Scarlett," he says firmly, face hardening. Then in a split second his expression smooths again, almost pleasant. "Patience. Okay?" His tone takes on a more fatherly note. But I'm not so fooled by this act that I don't notice the irritation beneath.

I nod. His chin dips, then he steps back to let the nurse finish her work. Then she and the doctor leave my unit to move down to Nadia's. She stares wide-eyed at the reporters as they hover close, following Dr. Bailey's every action. She's barely moved a muscle by the time the pair leaves to step into Ares' unit.

When the nurse nears Ares to do her job, he waves her away.

"Ares," Dr. Bailey says sharply.

The nurse glances nervously at the doctor before resuming. Ares swats her away again. "Leave me alone."

Dr. Bailey angles his back toward the cameras, leaning stiffly toward Ares, face dark. "Stop making a scene," he mutters. "Let the nurse do her job." He beckons to the nurse, but she stays put, staring nervously at Ares' sour expression.

"Ares," Dr. Bailey says again, louder, sharper. When Ares doesn't respond, the doctor grabs his wrist.

Ares wrenches away, white hair swinging. "I don't want it!"

Silence stretches for only a second. Dr. Bailey's hand falls away as his chin lifts. "You what?"

Ares snaps his knife-sharp glare to the doctor, fists clenched. "I said I don't want it."

My jaw goes slack as I stare at the silent battle warring in their eyes, their faces. I glance at the reporters crowding closer, frowning. Low murmurs skipping through them as they glance between each other.

Ares acts like the world isn't watching his every move. "I don't want it," he repeats, jaw clenched. "The cure. I don't want the cure."

Beneath his pristine lab coat, Dr. Bailey's chest lifts and falls with heaving breaths. He jerks his hands in his pockets to hide clenched fists, glaring at Ares as if that alone will make him take back his words.

"I don't either."

Through the glass, the soft-spoken words are almost lost, but the intercoms pick them up. Eyes swivel to Nadia, who stares at her blanket, hands knotted in her lap.

Dr. Bailey turns on her and after a stretch of silence, she lifts her eyes to him. "I don't want it either," she says again, voice firmer, stronger.

I gape at her, flicking another glance at the cameras.

Then the doctor glances at the viewing window and pales. He whips out a sleek phone from his pocket, taps the screen, and lifts it to his ear. After a moment, he speaks to the person on the other end, keeping his eyes on Ares. "Yes. Clear the cameras."

The security guards in the room with the reporters move into action, escorting the crowd out of the room, despite many objections. The nurse slips away too.

Silence follows, tension thick and anger dripping from the doctor's and Ares' gazes.

With a sharp growl, the doctor turns away from Ares, pacing toward the viewing window. For a long moment he stares at his reflection in the glass, shoulders lifting with his breaths, hands flexing and unflexing at his sides.

He whirls around, face and neck red. "You have no choice!"

I flinch at how his voice carries through the glass. My shoulders stiffen at the anger rolling off him. His gaze sweeps us, starting with Seth. When he reaches me, I look away.

He steps closer to Ares' bed, voice lowered but still carrying intensity, authority. "What makes you think you have any rights? You're superhumans. You have no rights, no choice. This decision is not yours to make." His eyes lock on Ares, who stares back unblinking, icy frost crawling up his neck from under his collar and creeping over his fists.

I frown at them. The tension roiling off them is so intense it clutches my gut even from this distance.

"Whether you like it or not," the doctor continues as beads of sweat slide down his forehead, "you are getting the serum. I don't know what kind of garbage you had put in you in Rapid City, but you're not there anymore. You're not special. You're a mistake we're trying to fix—"

"Does that go for her too?"

I'm surprised by the calmness, almost sadness in Ares' voice, in stark contrast to Dr. Bailey's yelling. Her? I glance at Nadia, who stares at Ares with confusion knitting her brow. Seth frowns at Ares too.

A shudder passes through Dr Bailey, and just for an instant the anger is gone, replaced by...I don't know what. It's gone in an instant and he snaps upright again. Dr. Hiram Bailey. In control of everything.

He takes a deep breath, slowly meeting each of our gazes again. Then he stares at the unit door behind Ares, face relaxed. When he speaks again, his voice sounds almost weary, deadened.

"Don't let fear control you," he says evenly. "Once you get the cure, you will see." His eyes go distant for a split second. "You'll see. You'll understand. This will fix everything."

A long moment passes as his words hang in the air, then the doctor shakes his head. He strides toward the door, stopping besides Ares' bed for a last moment. Ares stares at the blankets, working his jaw, blinking rapidly.

Dr. Bailey barely tilts his head, looking at him from the corner of his eye. "This will fix everything," he repeats. Then he leaves, leaving silence in his wake.

The nurse slips back in, finishes her job in a hurry, and slips out without a word.

The three of us stare at Ares. He draws his knees up and rests his arms on them, then his head sags to his forearms. Nadia wraps her arms around herself, still studying him. Seth frowns at him for a moment longer before pacing around his unit, arms crossed.

In the quiet, my heartbeat throbs wildly in my chest. I look down to find my hand clenched around a chunk of blanket. I glance at Ares and Nadia again. How could they? How could they not want the cure? Dr. Bailey's right. It'll fix everything. It all can go back to normal. Don't they want that?

Cloaked in the deafening silence, my chest aches with my cravings of home, security, warmth, familiar faces. Just to be held by my mom like a little girl. To hear Hannah's giggle or tease Dylan. Listen to Ian's songs and tell him he's going to be a big star. I'm weary of this uncertainty, weary of...just all of it. My tight fingers uncurl and I stare at my hands, the red splotches on my palms. Are these powers part of me, or a defect that should be removed?

"God doesn't make mistakes." Rez's words slip into my mind without warning. I clench my hands and press my fists against my thighs. If what he said was true, then *why* do I have powers? What's the purpose, if the world is going to look at me like I'm a circus animal?

I remember Rez changing Rachel's lightbulb and filling her fridge, and giving me his granola bar when he was still hungry. And Ivon's thick brow furrowing as he carefully tended the garden so they could have more food. Always trying to do good things in the sparse, broken community of Rapid City. Rez protected the supers, gave them a home with other people like them and used his powers to protect others. He did *good.* He was a superhuman and a wanted man, but he did good for others.

I look again at Ares, head still bent, and Nadia, shoulders

still tense as she stares at the glass walls. I need to know why they want to refuse the cure. Why they—

A sharp buzz cuts through my thoughts as the unit doors swing open. Guards come into our units, roughly escorting us out, down the maze of halls, and to the outdoor grounds. Once we're outside, they leave us clustered on the dead grass as they take up their posts on the perimeter.

Immediately, Ares and Nadia shuffle to their same tree to sit under the branches.

Seth glowers at them, then turns to me. "What's up with them?" He huffs and shakes his head. "Refusing the cure? Are they crazy?"

He looks at me, waiting for some sort of response. I shrug and scuff my shoes on the brown grass. "I dunno. I don't..." I lift my gaze to Ares and Nadia. "I don't understand it either."

Seth's jaw clenches slightly. "Well I'm going to get some answers." He strides off toward the tree.

I sigh at my shoes, replaying the scene in my mind. Ares refusing the cure, Nadia following suit. Dr. Bailey's anger and tension so thick between him and Ares that you could taste it. Warmth tickles the back of my neck, and I turn to look up at the sky. Morning sunlight breaks through the thick clouds in golden beams, glowing on my face. I close my eyes and soak in the warmth, my fire flowing like adrenaline through my veins at the heat. I hope the clouds will roll back for the sun to shine through. Everything seems better when the sun shines.

A cloud passes over the warm light as a chilly wind rakes over me. I shudder, wrapping my arms around myself, and turn toward the tree where the others are gathered. Seth stands in front of Ares and Nadia, fists on his hips as he says something I can't quite hear. I need answers too. From the moment I heard the rumors, I believed the cure was the best thing that could happen to our country. But they refused it. I need to know why.

My feet feel like cement, but I force them to trudge across the grass toward the others.

When I reach them, Seth turns to me and throws his arms out. "You try to talk sense into them, Scarlett." He drops to the ground and runs a hand through his unruly hair, shaking his head. "I sure can't."

Both Nadia and Ares flick glances at me, then stare at the ground, ripping dry blades of grass from their roots.

I swallow. "I need to talk to you guys." I hate how shaky my voice is. Weak. Pathetic.

They stay silent. Seth nods, already in apparent agreement. But he doesn't quite know what I'm about to say.

I look to Nadia, but she looks away, rubbing her arm. My shoulders slump as I turn to Ares. "Ares?"

He sighs, but looks at me, holding my pleading gaze.

I take a step closer. "Ares...why?" I say quietly. "The cure...it's a chance to...well..."

Ares glances down, then lifts his gaze to mine again, ice-blue eyes penetrating me. "He can't change me. I won't let him." A frown darkens his pale features as he looks away, no doubt thinking about the doctor's words. We don't have a choice. Ares voice is softer when he speaks again. "He has no right."

I blink. "Dr. Bailey? He's trying to help us."

He flicks a glance at me before looking away again toward the rooftop of the building surrounding us on all sides. His face darkens, twisting for a split second. Then it smooths back to calm when he looks back at me. "His shame of me won't change who I am or how I was born." He says it like that's enough explanation.

I frown. "What are you talking about? Shame? Why in the world would he be ashamed of you? You barely know each other."

He purses his lips, shaking his head. "We know each other." He shifts his jaw as he stares at me, as if contemplating his next words. "He's my father, Scarlett. Dr. Hiram Bailey is my father."

My heart skips a beat. Nadia and Seth lean forward, sharing a glance, brows knotted. My breath stills as I stare at Ares. "He's... your *dad?* But your last name—"

He shrugs. "So he changed my last name on the records here. He doesn't want people to know. How would it look for the leading scientist in superhuman studies to have two super children of his own?"

My mind spins even more, making me dizzy. "Hold on. *Two?*"

Ares looks down at his shoes, blinking rapidly. "Yes. My twin sister." He sighs. "That's why he chose me to be on that mission. He knew I wanted to find her. He thought he'd be rid of me if I struck off on my own to look for her." His jaw clenches.

I blink, mind turning as the pieces come together. The same girl Dr. Bailey talked about losing is Ares' sister? "What happened to her?" I ask quietly. Something tells me Ares' story may be different than the one Dr. Bailey told me.

He shifts, crossing his arms, then uncrossing and crossing them again. All the while blinking repeatedly and chewing his lip. I almost wish I hadn't asked. Maybe what Dr. Bailey already told me was true. Maybe I should just drop it.

"I guess I don't really care if people know now." He slides his hands along his jumpsuit, forgetting they don't have pockets. He drops his arms to his sides and sighs deeply. "Like I said, it was an embarrassment when my dad found out he had two superhuman children. He took my sister to the SCF but on the way, a band of supers kidnapped her."

"Why didn't he take you?" I ask.

"I don't know...Maybe Mom stopped him, or convinced him..." He grimaces and rubs the back of his neck. "But now I need to find her. I had a chance, but..." He trails off, gaze turning cold.

Realizing, I look away. He was going to look for her if we stayed in Rapid. And I ruined that chance. What more could I mess up? When I say nothing more, Ares stands and strides away.

I turn away from the others, hugging myself again against the cold. I wander toward the center of the grounds, thoughts tugging on my mind as I reach the small flower garden. I stiffen against a gust of wind and lower myself to the ground. My knees sink softly at the edge of the soft dirt and the wildflowers gently bend in the breeze. I finger a delicate petal and the faint scent of upturned soil reaches my nose, reminding me of Ivon. Guilt rams me in the stomach, leaving me breathless.

Dr. Bailey isn't who I thought he was. I messed up Ares' chances of finding his sister. I tore Rez's family apart. Why does it seem I always find out the truth when it's too late, when I've already made my decision? When it's too late to go back and change things?

I pull my knees up to my chest and rest my forehead on them. The capture of the Rapid supers replays in my mind, gut clenching at each new flashback. The tangible feeling of fear. The cries echoing in the warehouse. The row of guns covering the door. The children being carried into the armored trucks.

My eyes squeeze closed as I press the heel of my palm to my forehead. My teeth grind together. I'm *so selfish*.

Ares and Nadia wanted to refuse the serum. Should I? Why do I still want it? Do I believe powers are a gift or a curse? Do I believe that there are good supers and bad supers, just like any other normal person? What will happen if I don't get the cure? Will I be locked up here forever?

I press both hands to my head, wanting to quiet the questions hurling through my brain. Will I ever be sure about anything ever again?

A sniff draws my attention over my shoulder. Nadia sits alone under the tree now that Ares is wandering around and Seth is jogging the perimeter of the grounds. She sits cross-legged next to the trunk, picking at the dry grass. I bite my lip, wondering if she'll talk to me. I can at least try. It's worth the chance of her ignoring me, if I can distract the storm inside me. I shove off the ground and stride toward her.

My steps lose their surety as I get closer. When I stop in front of her, she looks up.

Her gaze narrows a fraction. "What do you want?" she asks, voice low.

I swallow, focusing on the numbers stamped on her uniform, avoiding the subtle chill in her gaze. "I just..." Words jumble, and I'm not sure which ones to let out first. I growl in frustration, grabbing a fistful of my hair, then lower to my knees. "Why?"

It's just a whispered word, but Nadia seems to know what I'm talking about. Her shell cracks as she studies me, face softening. I welcome some of that familiar warmth returning to her chocolate-brown eyes.

She looks away for a moment, dark brow furrowed. "Scarlett..." She takes a deep breath. "It just doesn't feel right anymore."

"But...why?" What about her promise never to use her powers again? Doesn't she want the possibility of accidentally hurting someone erased?

Her gaze grows distant as she speaks, as if she's talking to herself and not to me. "Who's to say that powers are wrong? There are plenty of people without powers that are doing harm. I just feel like..." She pauses to shrug. "Like someone's trying to play God here."

My brows pinch together as I sit in silence for several moments, thoughts mixing and swirling. Sitting here next to Nadia reminds me of when I found her in that alley. When she told me her secret. She shared a deep part of her then—even if she regretted it later—and it makes me want to do the same with her.

"Nadia." I scoot a little closer. "I don't know what to do. With the cure injection...A part of me *does* feel like it's wrong to change myself." Saying those words out loud makes me glance at the nearest guards. "But my powers have messed up my life. I miss my family. I just...want to be normal again."

Nadia places a hand over mine and gently squeezes. "I know. But remember what Rez said."

I sigh wearily. "Which part?"

"He said powers are a gift that can be used for good. Good supers are the only ones that can fight against the bad ones. Just think of the old comic books and superhero movies of supers saving people and protecting people. That can be true. Real."

I stare into her deep brown eyes. Her quiet conviction slithers into my heart and beats through my blood along with my fire. Ares' words echo through my mind too... *"I won't let him change me."*

Nadia rests her hands on my shoulders. "Be yourself, Scarlett. *All* of yourself."

CHAPTER TWENTY-ONE

All of yourself.

The three words ring in my head like a suspended chord, echoing in my skull. I didn't even know my fire was a part of myself until after the attack. Does that still mean that it's part of me, even though it entered my body by accident? Like a scar after a wound. One that won't go away.

After we were taken back to our units, I expected the hordes of reporters and cameras to return, always watching, always pointing. Hints of fear in their eyes. Wonder in some. But the room beyond the glass is empty.

As I settle onto the still-upright bed, I blow out a slow breath, welcoming the silence from the crowd's absence. But another sound cuts through the quiet I crave, bouncing between the glass walls. A familiar voice...

I scowl at the screen in the corner. Who turned the news on?

I search the room, finding a thin black remote tucked in the bookshelf. The voices from the news are too loud, too normal. My thumb touches the power button, but Dr. Bailey's face on the screen makes me freeze.

"Yes, things are going very well," he says to a young reporter with jet black curls who holds a mic toward him. The doctor stands in a small room with blank, light grey walls, reporters and cameras surrounding him in a semicircle, and two guards flank him.

The reporter brings the mic to his own mouth to speak, but Dr. Bailey leans forward. The mic quickly flips back to his chin.

"Yes, very well," he continues. "We've been preparing the test subjects, making sure they're strong, in good health." He pauses, flicking a glance at the camera. "The first injection will be tomorrow morning."

I choke, covering my mouth with my fist. Tomorrow morning? So soon. My stomach twists.

Sliding back onto the bed, I look at the others. Their eyes are fixed to their own screens. I study them, not sure what I'm looking for. Seth leans forward eagerly, something like hope in his eyes as he bites his lip, hanging on the doctor's every word. Ares, stiff and cold as ice, narrows his eyes at the screen. His face goes hard, but I can see the trembling in his hands, even from here.

As I shift to Nadia, she swivels her gaze to me and we lock eyes. Her chest heaves in uneven breaths, shoulders tight and panic in her dark eyes. Biting her lip hard, she looks away to stare at her palms instead. Fingers trembling as she turns the remote over in her hand. Her eyes slide closed as she gulps.

"And do you foresee any difficulties at this time?" The reporter's question brings me back to the screen.

Dr. Bailey bends toward the mic, hands clasped behind him. Everything clean lines, perfectly pressed suit, controlled. Unlike his reaction to Ares' and Nadia's attempts to refuse the cure.

He pauses. I can almost feel the reporters, cameras, and viewers leaning in, ears straining, waiting on his every word. I lean back on the bed with a huff, but my breathing quiets as I wait for what he's going to say.

"Of course there are always concerns with something like this," he says calmly.

My stomach twists with a wave of nausea and I swallow again.

He clears his throat before continuing. "We're not always sure how a body can react to a new substance, but we have every hope that this will be successful."

The collective TV noise lowers a notch, followed by a clatter. I look over to see Ares crossing his arms, glaring at his dark screen. The remote lies on the floor. Nadia slowly lifts her remote to turn off her screen. Seth turns up the volume on his.

I grip the remote until the plastic threatens to crack. Not from anger, I don't think. Just a boiling mixture of thoughts and emotions going back and forth in my head, pushing me to decide, taunting me: *Which side are you on, anyway?* My gaze fixes on the doctor's face again. So calm, collected, controlled.

He couldn't have told us about tomorrow's injection himself? We had to hear it from the news?

A snap makes me jump. I look down. A thin crack slithers between the buttons on the casing of the remote. I toss it onto the blankets.

A sigh draws my attention to the neighboring unit. Nadia settles into her armchair, set near the glass wall separating us. Her braids fall over her shoulder as she dips her head to rub her fingertips along her forehead.

I slide out of bed and approach the glass. "Nadia?"

She looks over her shoulder. I steel myself, expecting to see the coldness in her gaze again. But it's softer, wearier.

She adjusts in the seat, tucking a leg under her, to face me more squarely. I crouch, pressing a hand against the cold glass. I'm not sure what to say. I'm not even sure why I came over. Maybe I'm just afraid of being alone with my loud thoughts again.

"Are you scared?" she says softly. Even though fear shines in her eyes and clenches in her muscles, she's asking *me.* Checking on *me.* I didn't even think about asking her. I guess I really am selfish.

I nod, swallowing, throat parched. "I've been…thinking about what you said."

Some of the panic leaves her gaze as she takes a deep breath. "I meant it."

"I know." I manage a weak smile. "Thank you."

She returns the smile and nods.

My smile fades just as quickly as it came. "But…"

Her smile drops as she tilts her head.

I press the heel of my hand to my forehead. "I just…I don't know. If what Rez said was true, I…I still don't know *why* I have powers. Why it had to ruin my life…"

She presses her fingers to the glass, as if wanting to reach for my hand. "Things don't always make sense. But Rez was right." Her smile returns. "You are special. Here for a reason."

I try to smile back, but fail. Kindness replaces the fear in Nadia's eyes. I think she shoved it aside for me, because I was scared, to comfort me. I feel like a child.

I study her face, skin the color of cocoa and dark braids draping over her shoulder. The way her brow always seems to be faintly knotted. My mind flashes to the scene in the alley when she told me her secret. Does she struggle coming to grips with her powers too?

I attempt a smile again, this one more genuine. "That's true for you too, you know."

Her expression darkens and her fingertips slip from the glass to knot in her lap. She shrugs one shoulder. "Don't know about that."

I bite my lip, watching her hands tremble as she stares at the floor. I wonder if she believes for herself the same words she speaks to me. I wonder what exactly happened in her past that holds her back, makes her so afraid of everything, afraid of herself…

Her bent form in the alley flashes through my mind again, and her words that hit me like a train. I was afraid then of what she could do. We knew she was powerful when she used her powers, though rarely. Only when forced. After she hurt—killed —someone however it happened...you'd think that'd make her excited for the cure. Yet she wanted to refuse it. Still, her hands shake.

I tap my fingernail softly on the glass, drawing her attention back to me. Her eyes glisten.

I offer her a grin, hoping some of the same kindness she shows me projects back to her again. "You scared?"

A soft, one-beat laugh escapes, almost a hiccup. "Yeah. You?"

"Thought that was obvious."

Another chuckle. Even though her fingers still tremble, her shoulders relax.

"Nadia..." I shift to sit on the cold floor, leaning my shoulder against the glass. "After the cure...if it works..."

She curls up in the seat cushions with a sigh, leaning her head against the back and staring blankly at the glass wall. "Then I'll still be me, I guess. What's left. Even if they tried to change that."

The silence of night lets the patter of my pacing footsteps echo softly through the units. Darkness cloaks the room, except for a thin strip of light under the thick glass walls. The others sleep peacefully, Seth's snores the only sound joining my footsteps.

Warm energy sparks through my veins. Heat pulses in my hands, clenched at my sides. I don't stop it, don't suppress it. Not this time.

The clip of Dr. Bailey announcing our first serum injection on the news replays in my mind over and over. He was supposed to be the man that would save my life, return things to normal, fix my problem.

Why do I always call it a problem? Just because I'm different, I'm wrong? Something to be changed or fixed? I lift my fists in front of my face and feel my fire flowing through my veins, just below my skin. Pulsing, writhing, alive. I walk over to the small square mirror above the bookshelf and press my hands on both sides against the cool wall. It does nothing for the warmth in my palms. I stare at my reflection. A pair of fiery eyes stare back. The fire-like glow flickers around my pupils, brightening my irises.

This is me. Scarlett Marley, fire in my core and flames flowing through my veins. I'm this way for a reason. A feeling in my gut I can't explain tells me I was born for *something.* I have to be. All this can't be for nothing. I can't let it be for nothing, after all this has ended. Maybe with my powers I can accomplish so much more. I was born for this fire. Made for this.

Because God doesn't make mistakes.

My fingers curls, hands still pressed against the wall. I lift my chin, jaw set.

As much as it goes against what I'd hoped for for so long...*No.* I can't let them change me. They have no right to take this part of me away. I'm not sick or deformed. I'm just different...for a reason. I can do good with my gifts, and I can't believe I'm just fully realizing that now.

I get lost in the reflection of my own eyes, the depths of fire and fury. My nails dig into my palms. Did I really let my desire to be normal impede my conscience? I betrayed the very people that had made me feel more welcome than I ever had since my powers came. I'll never forget the hurt in their eyes. Hurt that I caused for a reward that isn't even guaranteed to work. I'll never let that happen again.

I press a fist against the wall until my knuckles crack, staring myself down. No more. I'm going to fight for myself, how I was made, and those like me. I'm going to make it up to Rez, my friends, the supers locked up in this cold facility. I'm...

I'm going to save them.

A smile curls the corner of my mouth as I slowly back away from the mirror. My fist leaves a faint charred mark on the wall. My mark of rebellion against this place. I pull my hair out of its sleek ponytail and throw it up in a messy bun. That's more like me. I roll my shoulders back, coaxing my fire to calm. For now. Reluctantly, it cools and dims back to my core. But energy still zips through my muscles.

Heaving in a deep breath, I look up at the small white camera in the corner. The first injection looms on the horizon, just tomorrow morning. So close. How will I save the supers and help them return to Rapid before losing my own powers? These things take time. Maybe I can fake it, substitute the serum for something else, something harmless. I groan and shake my head. I don't even know what it looks like yet. I can't figure all this out on my own...

I turn toward the glass walls separating our units, watching the sleeping forms. Even in the dim light I can see Nadia's dark braids spilling over her pillow and the shock of Ares' snow-white hair against the dark.

I'll need help. Their help.

CHAPTER TWENTY-TWO

Energy from my fire still lingers from last night, making my hand tremble as I fork scrambled eggs into my mouth. I glance for the millionth time through the glass walls at the others. They eat their breakfast in silence. Clinking silverware would be the only sound if it wasn't for Seth having his TV on.

And the reporters, of course. They slowly trickled in soon after we woke, fixing the cameras' ever-watchful gazes on us.

I swallow a sip of orange juice, shifting nervously in the armchair. My knee bounces under the tray, making the dishes rattle. I take a deep breath. *Be patient.* Even though my knee stops bouncing, my fire still senses my excitement, warming my body, sparking more energy through my veins. I relish the feeling, the warmth pulsing through my muscles.

Out of the corner of my eye, I look at Nadia again. She sets her fork down over her half-finished breakfast and pushes the tray away. Twirling a braid around her finger, she leans back in the chair and stares at the floor, occasionally glancing toward Seth's TV. Ares sits cross-legged on his bed, spine straight, angled toward Seth's screen, even though he could turn on his own. But he stiffens every time Dr. Bailey comes on screen or his name is mentioned.

Not a word has passed between us all morning.

I don't blame them for being quiet, considering the coming events. With a scowl, I spear another chunk of eggs on my fork. But the fork falls out of my limp hand.

Out of the corner of my eye, I can see the charred mark on the wall from my fist last night. Will Dr. Bailey ask about it? It probably won't matter to him. He's about to get rid of my powers anyway.

I slide the tray away and stand, feeling eyes swivel toward me at the movement. I refuse to look at the reporters, instead circling my unit, pacing, to let some of the energy out. My eyes stay fixed on the floor to avoid seeing the cameras.

Despite my shuffling steps and the hum of the reporters' conversations, the news on Seth's TV carries over it all. And from the words I catch through the intercoms on our walls, they're talking about us right now. About the cure. About this historic event.

I rub a thumb along my right palm, tracing the lines, feeling the warmth pulsing in the center and spreading to my fingertips. If only there was a way. If only there was a way to stop this. When I round my bed, facing the glass wall separating me and Nadia, I catch her watching me.

A flicker of an uncertain frown crosses her face. Thoughts churn behind her eyes.

I bite my lip. Maybe she can see it on my face. Something's different. I press my fist into my palm. But I can't tell her here, not now. I glance at Seth, who hasn't looked away from the screen all morning. I wish I could trust him, I wish I could tell him my new plan, but...he's made his standing on this clear. He could jeopardize my plan to save the Rapid supers. And if this doesn't work...I don't know what I'd do.

Ares still sits rigid on the bed, pretending not to be watching Seth's screen, but clearly listening anyway. Now seeing him reminds me of Dr. Bailey. And his twin sister. I try to imagine what she looks like. White, flawless skin like her brother. Long, flowing hair the color of milk, and ice-blue eyes. I clench my fists. I have to help him find her. I owe it to him.

My eyes shift over the reporters, gaze narrowing. I'll just have to wait until we get outside. That'll be my best chance to talk to Ares and Nadia.

The restless wind slithers through the bare tree limbs, making the branches clatter together ominously. I crave the warmth of sunlight, but instead thick clouds cloak the sky again. As usual, Ares and Nadia head straight to the nearest tree and sit on the crunchy grass. Seth meanders toward the basketball court after tossing a glowering glance at Ares and Nadia, scanning the grounds for the ball.

Keeping my eye on Seth, I hurry toward Ares and Nadia. Catching the gaze of the nearest guard, I force myself to slow my pace and take my time to settle onto the ground near the other two. Act natural. My heart thumps in my chest and I press my hands against my legs to keep from shaking.

Ares and Nadia stare at me, confusion wrinkling their foreheads.

I shift my glance toward the guards again, then to Seth. He's found the ball now, tossing it toward the basket. It bounces on the rim, and he jumps to fetch it again. He's distracted for now.

I lean forward, launching into my spiel before I lose momentum. "Look," I begin. I swallow to steady my voice. "I know what I did was wrong. I realize that now."

Nadia softens into an encouraging smile, but Ares just blinks at me, his brow creased into fierce lines.

"I...I want to fix everything," I say.

Nadia's eyes light up and she gives an eager nod. Ares tilts his head, arms crossed, listening.

I take a deep breath, scooting closer toward them. "You tried to refuse the serum. I didn't get it before, but..." Another deep breath. "I understand now." The memory of last night, my realization, pulses new resolve through my chest. "I want to fix my mistake. I want..." I glance toward the nearest guards, their black uniforms stark against the light grey cinder block building as they scan the grounds. One sweeps his gaze toward me and I turn back to the others and lower my voice to a whisper. "I want to get the Rapid City supers back home." An image of Rez sitting in a cold, hard cell flashes through my mind, and a sharp stab of guilt spears my gut. "Get Rez's family back together."

The wind almost tears away my words. But they heard, I can tell. They blink at me, jaws slack. Even Nadia's eyebrows raise.

I can't stand their silence. "Well?" Maybe they think I'm crazy. Maybe after what I did in Rapid they won't want to help me. My stomach sinks at the thought.

A smile breaks out on Nadia's face as she leans closer. "That's a great idea," she whispers. I smile back, then we look to Ares.

He leans back against the tree, arms still crossed. After a stretch of silence, him squinting at the ground, a faint smile lifts a side of his mouth. It might be just my imagination, but a spark of mischief glints in his eyes. "I think that's a good idea too."

I beam at him, hope surging through me.

"But..." His eyes narrow again. "It sounds impossible."

My hope deflates.

"I mean," he strokes his chin, "this is the SCF. How are we going to break out dozens of supers without getting caught? Or worse."

I draw my shoulders back and set my jaw. "We'll figure something out. We'll be...superheroes."

Ares raises an eyebrow, and Nadia gives a small grin.

"But it's going to take more than a little motivational speech," Ares says, not unkindly. He studies me for a long moment, and I let his icy gaze search my fiery one. "But I'm in. What's the plan?"

I blink. "Well, there...isn't much of one right now. The first injection is today...I had a thought of switching the serum somehow with something harmless. Then we'd still have our powers."

We fall into thoughtful silence.

"I don't know if that's a good idea," Ares says finally. "We don't know what the serum looks like, so the first injection is inevitable."

I chew my lip. "Maybe just one injection won't affect our powers too much."

"I hope not," Nadia says softly. "Anyone hear what time the injection is supposed to be?"

Ares and I shake our heads.

"Hey! Wanna play a game?"

Seth's voice makes me jump and I turn to see him striding toward us, basketball tucked under his arm. A grin lifts the corner of his mouth, but it doesn't quite reach his eyes. What happened to the carefree boy from before the Rapid mission? His gaze flicks toward Ares and Nadia and something I can't read flashes in his eyes. Confusion? He opens his mouth to speak, then frowns as he looks past us.

I twist back to find guards approaching. The closest guard gestures toward the door. "It's time."

He doesn't have to tell us what for.

My heart slams against my chest. Throat dry, I try to swallow.

When we return to our units, the hospital beds have been replaced by the reclining chairs from the lab. The ones with restraining straps. Nurses hustle around the units between the equipment scattered through the rooms, a blur of dark grey scrubs. Their tense chatter adds to the nervous hum of the reporters beyond the glass.

There are so many reporters now you couldn't fit another body or camera into that room. Security guards line the back wall, watching the crowd.

Nurses guide me into the chair, then secure the straps on my legs and arms. My breath quickens as the straps tighten over my muscles. I give them a discreet tug. They don't budge. Sweat breaks out over my body. I look to my right, where Nadia, Ares and Seth are going through the same routine. Even though Seth is the only one looking forward to the cure, he still looks nervous. Scared. Maybe even terrified.

Light glints off a stainless steel tray near my chair. A large syringe sits on the shining surface, filled with an unnaturally blue liquid.

Heat flares over the back of my neck, and my vision blurs. I lean my head back on the headrest, trying to calm the nauseating twist of my gut.

A light touch on my arm makes my eyes open. Dr. Bailey gives me a purse-lipped grin, gaze always darting toward the viewing window. "Hello, Miss Marley. Sorry we're running a little late. How are you feeling?"

Like I'm going to throw up. I just swallow and nod.

He studies my face, then gestures to someone behind me. A small cup of water is passed over my head and Dr. Bailey brings it to my mouth. "Just a sip."

I lean toward the cup as the doctor tips it. The cool water is refreshing as it washes over my tongue and throat, cooling the nervous fire pulsing through me.

He takes the cup away and hands it to a nurse, then turns to the tray with the syringe. He picks it up with gloved hands, lifting it toward the light, turning it.

"We'll begin shortly," he says. "Are you ready?"

I don't answer, knowing my voice will shake. I just swallow again.

He studies me again with those ice-blue eyes. Eyes, I realize, that are so much like Ares'. He waits for my answer.

I lick my dry lips. "I...well, I'm not sure if—"

He presses a cold hand to my arm, simultaneously setting the syringe back on the tray. "It's all right, Scarlett. Everything will be fine." His words should be comforting, but the firm edge to his voice just makes me tense even more. My neck and shoulders begin to ache.

He looks over his shoulder at the reporters, then turns back to me. "This will fix everything," he says quietly. "Remember?"

A drop of sweat glides down my temple. My arm involuntarily tugs against the restraints, wanting to wipe the sleeve across my forehead. "I" —A nurse mops up the sweat on my face and neck; I nod my thanks— "remember."

This *will* fix everything. But I think Dr Bailey and I are thinking of a different "this."

The doctor opens his mouth to say something else, but instead his gaze flicks up past me and he frowns.

I turn to look where he stares. At the black smudges on the wall from my fiery hand.

His gaze sharpens as he looks at me again, raising an eyebrow.

I swallow, then shrug. "Happened in my sleep?"

His penetrating stare doesn't relent for a long moment before he turns toward the tray with the syringe again.

Nurses bustling back and forth block most of my view, but I lean forward in the seat, trying to see the others. The nurses hovering over them make it hard to see their faces. I get a flash of Nadia's wide eyes, a glimpse of Ares' clenched fist. Their panic just makes mine rise stronger, constricting my throat.

Dr. Bailey's light chuckle turns my attention back to him. The lights cast hard shadows over his face. I press back against the cushions.

He pats my exposed arm with his fingers. "Nervous?"

I nod.

"That's normal. But don't worry. The discomfort won't last long."

I pale, head going light, dizzy. "Discomfort? It'll hurt?" My heart thumps painfully against my ribs, sending blood rushing through my ears. I tip my head to keep from hyperventilating.

But my hands begin to glow red. I jolt when a spark escapes from my clenched fist.

A cold, wet cloth slaps over my forehead. I suck in a sharp breath. Dr. Bailey covers my hand with his. Cold and clammy. The fire-glow in my hands fades, but my heart still beats like a drum. When he's convinced that I've calmed down, he removes his hand. A nurse hands him a new pair of latex gloves before ripping open a small packet, removing a thin wipe, and swiping it over the inside of my right elbow. The coldness of it sends a chill down my spine, making my fire retreat.

"Dr. Bailey, please." My voice comes out raspy, trembling. I clear my throat. "Just...a little more time."

He looks at the cameras again, then leans closer. "Don't let them down, Scarlett. The country is watching." He turns away to examine the syringe again.

My eyes fix to the nearest camera. I stare into the lens, meeting the eyes of millions across the country. Maybe even my family. Ian, the Henleys. What if they're watching? I have a feeling they are. Glued to the screen, eyes wide and mouths hanging open as they watch me get pumped full of this blue liquid. Watch me get stripped of my powers. They'll probably think it's a good thing. Maybe someday I can explain everything to them, get them to understand. But still...as they watch their screens, watch *me*...I hope they're not ashamed.

My gaze softens as I continue to look into the camera, hoping my family knows I'm looking at them alone, not the whole country.

A touch on my arm makes me stiffen again. Dr. Bailey's eyes bore into me, stirring the uneasiness in my gut. I lean past him, trying to see the others again, grasp onto something familiar.

I barely catch Nadia's gaze before he steps into my line of sight. "They're fine. They'll get theirs soon enough."

Fingers curled around the syringe, he bends over my arm, bringing the needle tip closer to the soft inner skin. My arm tenses.

He gives my arm a tap. "Relax."

I take a deep breath and force my arm to go limp. He brings the needle closer, closer. So slow. I wince at the sharp prick as the tip slides into my vein. The doctor slowly pushes the serum into my bloodstream. The muscles in my arm begin to ache as cold slithers through my veins. The feeling deepens, spreading through the rest of my body as my heart pumps the blue liquid through me. I imagine the blue invader attacking the fire living in me. Choking it. Killing it.

Dr. Bailey removes the needle and presses a piece of gauze on the puncture while he reaches for a bandage. He hands the empty syringe to a nurse then tapes the bandage over the gauze.

The room tilts as my vision clouds. My head spins, feeling light, as if it's floating above my shoulders. Dr. Bailey says something, but his voice slurs like he's underwater, and he fades to a faceless shadow leaning over me. All I hear is the frantic beating of my heart in my ears. The ache seizes my muscles as the coolness spreads through my insides. My head lolls back against the headrest. I close my eyes against the bright lights. A headache throbs in my temples, piercing. I groan.

An arctic chill claims my body.

CHAPTER TWENTY-THREE

Pain throbbing in my skull prods me awake. I groan, grimacing, and turn my head against the pulsing ache. But that only brings on a fresh rush of intensity. I try to wiggle my fingers, then my toes. My muscles resist, cold and stiff and numb. I try to lift my arm again, but something stops it. I twitch my fingertips, feeling for a restraint. The soft weave of a blanket meets my touch.

My eyelids flutter as I try to open them. Sleep tugs heavily, but I finally squint out into my room. I welcome the darkness of night, considering the pain pulsing in my head. A soft, white light glows from my right, where the glass wall is illuminated. I blink through the blurriness and sleep still pulling on me. For a moment I can't remember what happened. I give my head a gentle shake, trying to clear the fogginess.

Slowly, it comes back. The needle. The blue liquid. And the cold. Aching cold.

With a grunt, I prop myself on one elbow. I squint toward the door, looking for a small screen that displayed the time, like in my old room.

There. Numbers glow on the screen embedded into the wall. *4:23am.*

I groan, rubbing a hand over my face. Why did I wake? I

push my numb body into a sitting position and close my eyes against the wave of dizziness that spins the room. My headache still pounds my skull like a hammer, but when the dizziness subsides enough, I shakily get to my feet, hoping stretching my legs a bit will help the ache that lingers in my joints. My knees threaten to buckle under the sudden weight, and I grab the bed railing to steady myself.

I stand there for a moment, panting breaths echoing through the small room. Carefully, I feel for the fire in my core. Is it still there? Has one injection made it disappear? I lift my hand to my face. The white glow of the glass wall silhouettes my trembling fingers. Why am I shaking so much? From fear? Weakness? The cold that has encased me? I close my fingers into a weak fist and press it against my heart. It still trembles against my sternum.

It's fear. Fear that my fire has been stolen from me.

Gingerly, I lower myself to the floor and lean against the glass wall, tilting my hand closer to the light. Dimly, I can see the faint, red splotches still covering my palms. I let out a shuddering breath. How odd that I've come so far from the terrified girl who discovered her powers one summer evening to this—glad to have the mark on my hands that reminds me of the fire in my being.

I take a deep breath, curling my hand into a weak fist. Closing my eyes, I lean my head against the glass. Maybe my fire is still there. Buried deep under the ice encrusting my body. A shiver racks my shoulders.

I focus my energy and try to channel fire into my trembling palm. Nothing happens. My heart flutters. Is it too late? But then warmth begins to collect underneath my skin. Faint, wispy flames swirl above my cupped palm. Weak, timid, but there.

I drop my hand as a breath whooshes out of my lungs. Why do I feel like I just ran a marathon? Is it really this hard now to summon my fire? Still, hope lingers in my heart. The fire is still there, hanging on.

My legs shake as I stand, leaning heavily against the glass.

Dizziness tilts the room again and I grip the edge of the bed for support before I fall. My stomach knots with nausea. If this is the result of only one injection...I sigh. I'm still me, I still have my fire. But not for long. I look over my shoulder at the other units, though I can't see more than vague shadows in the darkness. Another sigh. Can we figure out how to get the Rapid supers back home before our powers are gone for good?

I try to lower myself gently back into bed, but my weak muscles plop me down like a hot potato. I wince at the persistent throb in my temples and lie back against the pillow. Shivering, I pull the blankets over me, then wrap my arms around myself against the cold that seems to have settled into my bones.

I'll have to do all this again. Bustling, nervous activity before the serum is injected into my bloodstream. Aching muscles, persistent cold. So many eyes watching. How many times can I endure before my fire gives in?

I glance at the dark viewing window. The quietness seems odd compared to the crowds it usually holds. Did my family watch? Did they see me staring into the cameras, forgetting that the country was watching, and only looking at *them*?

I nestle deeper against the mattress, pulling the blanket closer around my neck. Will I ever see them again? Saving the Rapid supers could mean I'll never be able to return to normal. No, I'm certain it *will* mean that. It's like jumping off a cliff without knowing where I'll land. The sick twist of my stomach as I plummet through the unknown, knowing wherever I land, nothing will ever be the same. I clutch a fistful of my blanket and swallow, blinking against the tears leaking out of the corners of my eyes, picturing the faces of my family, their smiles...

They'd understand. Surely, they'd understand. Mom and Dad would never call me a mistake, and some deep part of me tells me that they'd understand what I'm doing, why I have to save the Rapid supers from their fate in this facility.

But, man, does it scare me. It's not every day one decides to defy the government and break out a horde of superhumans.

I sigh and roll over to my side to stare at the wall. My future is as blurry as my vision is as I lose the battle against my exhaustion. My aching head is tired of thinking, so I close my eyes, ignoring how they sting.

———

A low hum, a sound becoming more and more familiar each day, gently prods me awake. I groan before I even open my eyes, knowing what I'll see—crowds of reporters and cameras shoving to get nearer to the glass. To get a better look. To point, to stare.

A warm hand presses against my forehead and my eyes flutter open. A nurse smiles as she bends over me, blonde ponytail nearly brushing my nose.

"How are you feeling?" she asks quietly.

I swallow against the roughness in my parched throat and she helps me wiggle to a sitting position, adjusting the bed's angle. I lean back against the pillows, closing my eyes and waiting for the dizziness to pass. It doesn't.

I lick my chapped lips. "I'm..." A shiver racks me. "Dizzy, headache, blurry vision." Another shiver. "And I'm cold. Very, very cold." Is my fire still there, lurking somewhere I can't feel it?

The nurse tugs the covers up closer to me, tucking them around my waist. "I'll get you another blanket." She smiles again. "Glad to see you're doing well."

I find myself smiling back, though I don't know why. But it fades as I scan over the reporters lining the wall. Staring at me with open mouths like I was in a coma for twenty years and I just woke up. I glance at the nurse, who turns her back to me to type things on a computer. She glances several times at the cameras. I huff. She's probably just glad to see me well because it means the serum isn't killing me on live TV. So far.

The room still tilts and warps from the dizziness. I shift to my side to face the other units, tucking my knees under my chin.

Seth still sleeps, his blankets a tangled mess and his head half-hanging off the bed. Ares' bed is in the upright position and he sits straight and composed, ankles crossed, head bent over a book. But when I watch him closer, I see his hands tremble as he weakly turns the pages. And his skin...it doesn't seem as pale. For a normal person this would be good, but not for him.

A motion draws my attention closer to Nadia's unit. I'm surprised to see her tentative smile as she waves her fingers in hello. I try my best to smile back, returning the wave. But dark circles accent her eyes and her shoulders droop weakly. I frown, giving her a thumbs up, hoping she'll understand my silent question: *You okay?*

Her weak smile disappears altogether. She shrugs one shoulder, then points to me, tilting her head.

I force a smile, copying her one-shoulder shrug.

An increase of the conversation hum draws my attention back to the viewing window. Reporters practically press their noses to the glass, cameras shifting from me to Nadia. I scowl, pursing my lips. They probably saw that whole exchange. How difficult would it be to give us some time without the country watching our every move? Even just an hour of quiet would be heavenly.

Nadia must've noticed too, because she pulls her knees to her chin and wraps her arms around her legs, angling her gaze away from the crowd.

I grimace, rubbing my fingers against my temple where a headache still lingers. Resting my head against the pillow, my gaze bounces between the cameras as I try not to think about how many people are watching. I wonder again if my family is among those numbers. I wonder what they're thinking as they watch me, on display like a science experiment for the world to see. I feel for my fire. It pulses weakly in my core and my stomach knots tighter.

A sharp pang stabs my chest as Dr. Bailey's words all those weeks ago about limiting—he really meant *banning*—family visits rush back. I clench my hands under the blanket. I would give anything to see them again. Just once. The Henleys too. Even though we had our differences, we were still good friends. Like leafing through a scrapbook, memories of good times flip through my mind. Getting ice cream, Ian and I swapping sheet music and writing songs, family trips to the park and even vacationing together once. A deep ache burns my chest. I shake my head, rubbing my collarbone. Faint warmth touches my fingertips, reminding me that I can't go back to that. Not ever. I blink back a hot tear.

A touch on my shoulder brings me out of the memories. The nurse gives another smile. "Dr. Bailey will be in to see you all shortly. Do you need anything?"

Yeah. Let me keep my powers and leave. "Just the blanket."

She nods. "Of course."

Only a few minutes pass after she leaves before Dr. Bailey comes in. As usual, he offers a smile and nod to the reporters before looking at me.

When he finally does turn his gaze to me, his eyes narrow as they study my face. "How are you feeling?"

I'm not looking forward to having to repeat the same information several times every day. "Dizzy and cold. Headache too."

He slips a tablet out from his coat pocket, frowning in concentration as he types. Then he gestures behind me, and two nurses I didn't realize had come in with him step forward. One places the black egg-shaped sensors in my palms while the other sticks flat disc sensors to my head and arms.

Still staring at the tablet screen, Dr. Bailey places his fingers on my arm. He glances at the cameras again before looking at me. "Okay, Scarlett. I want you to try to use your powers. Just gently."

I swallow against my parched throat, shifting to a more comfortable position. I bite my lip as I try to coax my fire from my core, prod it awake. Nothing happens. My heart skips a beat. No, it can't be gone now. Please, no.

I squeeze my eyes closed, trying to block out the noise and the feeling of people watching. My heartbeat quickens and my breaths heave in my chest. What if I can't do this? What if the fire last night was the last of it and now it's gone?

Then slowly, warmth seeps through my veins and pools in my hands. The more it flows, the stronger it becomes. A smile tugs at my mouth as I relish the warmth increasing—

A firm touch on my forearm makes me open my eyes again.

"That'll do," Dr. Bailey says, looking at his tablet again. Then he gestures for the nurses and they remove the sensors and leave to Nadia's unit.

The doctor tucks the tablet under his arm and clasps his hands in front of him. Smiling, he leans closer. "See? I told you everything would be okay."

Again, the fatherly voice, as if he's talking to a toddler. Even as my teeth want to grind, I force a grin and nod.

He returns my nod. "As soon as we're done with these tests, you four are going to get some fresh air. Sound good?"

The best opportunity for us to figure out this escape plan would be on the outdoor grounds. I nod again. "Yup."

"Good." With another glance at the cameras, he leaves my unit and joins the nurses in Nadia's.

I try not to show my impatience as the trio of doctor and nurses test the other three. Still, my foot bobs under the blanket. Then my finger taps on my leg. I take a deep breath and blow it out in a slow gust. I have to keep calm. Don't arouse suspicion. My stomach twists nervously. Can I even do this? Get the Rapid supers home before I lose my powers for good? The size of this task, the weight of it...it threatens to crush me.

I shut my eyes for a moment, stilling my thoughts. Nadia and Ares are with me too. I'm not in this alone. We can do it together. A little of that crushing weight lifts again.

I realize my hands are trembling and I tuck them under my blanket. Finally, Dr. Bailey leaves with the nurses, and guards come in to escort us outside. It takes all my strength to measure my steps, not let my pace show my impatience to get outside.

I breathe a sigh of relief when we step into the outdoors. Cold wind slithers over me and my muscles tense, but despite that, I feel like I can breathe again. No countless reporters and cameras. I'm sure they're watching somehow, but at least I can't see them.

Seth makes a beeline for the basketball court. Ares follows to watch him from the sidelines. At a strong gust of nippy wind, he tenses. Does he feel the cold's bite more now? Nadia goes to our usual tree and gingerly lowers herself to the ground and leans against the trunk. As I follow her, I glance around at the black-clad guards lining the perimeter. My gaze catches on a stark white contrast and my steps falter.

A doctor stands near the entrance door, tablet in hand. Watching us. Monitoring us. I'm sure he's just here to monitor our health, but still...the back of my neck tingles.

Grass crunches under me as I sit cross-legged opposite Nadia. My muscles tremble, barely wanting to hold me up. I shift to lean against the tree trunk and rough bark pokes my back through my jumpsuit. Sunlight breaks through a gap in the clouds and winks through the bare branches and warms patches on my face, and I close my eyes to take a deep breath as a soft wind tickles my cheeks. If I keep my eyes closed, I can almost imagine myself back home, sitting under one of the oak trees in our backyard, talking with Dylan as we watch Hannah play. A smile tugs at the corners of my mouth. But it doesn't last long.

Will I ever see them again?

No, I *will* see them again. I promise—

"Scarlett?"

I open my eyes to find Nadia frowning at me. "What's wrong?" she asks.

I manage a smile. "It's nothing."

She studies me a moment longer, then leans back against the tree again. Nothing but silence passes between us as we watch

Seth coax Ares onto the basketball court. Despite them being weak—and lacking skill—they seem to have fun. At least, Seth is. Ares keeps glancing over at us. Without moving my head, I glance at the doctor watching us. Somehow, we have to talk about the escape without him suspecting anything. My eyes scan over the guards. Without *any* of them suspecting. My knee starts to bounce.

"We won't ever see our families again, will we?"

Nadia's soft-spoken words spark that familiar deep ache in my chest, pressing a sigh from my lungs. Hearing those words out loud makes it more scary. The uncertainty of our future casts a dark shadow on me.

Nadia stares at the grass, brows drawn together, and doesn't look up as I turn to her. I pull up a fistful of dead grass and let it trickle through my fingers. "We will. Someday." The answer comes quicker than I'd expected, with more confidence than I feel. The words feel dead and meaningless on my tongue. Because I don't know what will happen.

I study her as she stares at her hands, fiddling with the grey fabric of her jumpsuit.

"Do you...have family somewhere?" I say quietly.

She offers a tight smile and slowly nods. "My mom and two aunts. We lived together." Her voice is thin and shaky, like paper in the wind, but a slight smile brightens her face. "We had a good life. Until..." Her face twists and she looks away.

Her words bring back my own memories. Will I ever be able to remember my family without feeling pain? I lean forward, blinking away the sting in my eyes. I reach out and give her hand a squeeze. I'm surprised to find it warmer than mine. I still feel so cold. "You want to talk about it?"

Something tragic happened to this girl, and she's been carrying that alone. I suddenly wonder how she's endured this cold facility, alone in her room with her thoughts, memories, nightmares.

At first she doesn't say anything. Doesn't move. Barely

breathes. A single tear slips down her dark-skinned cheek. She wipes it away, still not looking at me. Then, a slight nod. She angles toward me again and I tuck my legs under me.

She wipes another hand across her face, even though no more tears have fallen. "I just realized I've never talked about it. Never said it out loud—" A strangled sob cuts her short. She presses a fist to her mouth, eyes squeezed shut.

I bite my lip. "You don't have to—"

"No. It's okay." She drops her hand, takes a deep breath, and swallows. "I want to."

I go silent, wanting to give her every opportunity to say what she wants to say.

For a long moment, she doesn't move, just stares at her hands. Working up the courage? When she finally speaks, she keeps her eyes down. "I discovered I had powers when I was about seven years old." With a sad chuckle, she looks up at the sky. "Seems so long ago now. So much has happened." Her face twists again but she sucks in a breath and lets it seep out slowly, calmly. "I was...amazed. At the power. The intensity. The ease of how the quakes came from my hands." She lifts them to her face, almost glaring at them. "I didn't have enough sense to respect it then. I treated it like a toy."

She falls silent for a long minute. I bite the inside of my cheek to keep from urging her to go on. Let her speak in her own time.

"One night, I was playing in the street with my cousins. We lived in a kind of run-down part of the city and we liked to use abandoned, boarded-up houses as our playgrounds." Another deep breath. "I...wanted to tell them about my powers. It was the first time I told anyone about it. I thought they would think it was cool, but they didn't believe me." Her jaw clenches, straining her next words. "So I had to prove it to them. I showed them what I could do. I don't know if my hurt pride made my power stronger or..." When her voice shakes, she pauses to swallow again. Her words become a harsh whisper. "Things went wrong. I lost control. One of my cousins...the building..." She buries her face in her hands.

She's trying not to cry, to not let out the sobs, because her shoulders tremble, her whole body tensed. Still, tears seep through her fingers.

I swallow the dryness in my throat and scoot closer to wrap and an arm around her shoulders. Several times I open my mouth, but each time I close it without saying anything. I don't know what the right words are. This girl...she lived with this since she was *seven*? It haunted her, tormented her as she spent years in this facility. And despite all that, she's still so kind, so gentle. Asking me if I'm okay while she has *this* tearing her apart inside.

I squeeze her tighter, taking deep breaths to keep my own tears at bay. It doesn't work. Some slip past, dripping into her hair.

"I didn't know what to do with myself," she says, words muffled against her hands. "When SCF forces arrived I just...let them take me."

I rub her arm, still not sure what to say that will make her feel better. Maybe I don't need to say anything. Just listen. Listen, and be present.

"What's wrong?"

We look up to see Ares standing over us, brows pinched as he glances between us.

Nadia sits up and quickly wipes her cheeks on her sleeves and swallows several times. Still, she gives Ares a weak smile. "Everything's okay."

Ares doesn't look convinced as he slowly lowers himself to the ground. As I wipe my own face, he opens his mouth to say something, then closes it again. He clears his throat as he scans the grounds and leans his hands back on the grass. "So...what's our plan?" he whispers.

I wipe my cheeks one more time as my stomach tightens. "Where's Seth?"

"Jogging. Had energy to work off, he said."

Just as he says that, Seth comes into view around the tree. He glances at us, then focuses on the track again. I frown as I watch his feet drag. He's slower. Much slower. Still faster than the average teenage boy, but he seems to struggle. I wonder if he's tried to use his wind powers since the injection.

"Should we tell him?" Nadia whispers.

Ares immediately shakes his head. "I don't think so."

Nadia frowns. "Shouldn't we at least give him a chance?"

Ares huffs. "I think it's pretty obvious why we can't."

Nadia quirks her mouth to one side, frown deepening. She has to know it's true.

"He's made himself quite clear on this," Ares mutters, shifting to lean back on his elbows.

"Yes, but..." Nadia twirls one of her braids around her finger. "Shouldn't we give him a second chance? Maybe he's changed after coming back from Rapid."

I shake my head. "I doubt it. He's as stubborn as a mule."

As I say that, Nadia's and Ares' eyebrows raise as they look up past me. I turn to see Seth striding toward us, panting. Sweat darkens his hair and sticks it to his forehead and darkens his uniform on his chest and underarms. He shouldn't be this tired. Not a boy with super speed.

When he reaches us, he catches our gazes and smirks. "Whatcha talking about? Not me, I hope."

Did he hear? Nadia, Ares and I share a look. I force a chuckle, trying to brush off the tension that came with Seth's presence. "Yeah, we were talking about you. How you're as stubborn as a mule."

Seth groans and rolls his eyes dramatically. "All of my good qualities and you have to pick that one to talk about."

I laugh nervously, fingers knotting as silence follows. I stare at my hands but I can feel Seth shifting his gaze between each of us.

He takes a step closer into our circle. "So what are you really talking about?"

When no one responds, Seth narrows his gaze at Nadia. Perceiving a weak spot? She blinks at him, shrinking back against the tree. "We're just talking..." She shrugs timidly.

Seth studies each of us again. When his eyes reach me, I look away, fidgeting with my sleeve. He grunts and nods slowly. "The way you're all whispering tells me you don't want to be overheard, hmm? Which probably means you're up to no good."

More silence. My fingers twitch as they pick at a loose string on my sleeve. Maybe Nadia is right. Should we tell him? Give him a chance to change his mind? His twisted expression when he told me what happened to his parents comes to my mind from when we were in Rapid. I bite my lip. He may be too far gone to help us now.

Seth's face hardens as he crosses his arms. "All right. What's going on here?"

Ares looks away, biting his lip. Nadia looks at me, eyes pleading. I purse my lips and give a subtle shake of my head.

She swings her gaze up to Seth. "We're going to save everyone."

CHAPTER TWENTY-FOUR

"Nadia!" I hiss.

She blinks at me as if confused and I press my lips together and pinch the bridge of my nose. Surely she didn't take my headshake as a go-ahead. My gaze bounces to the guards, then up at Seth, whose face has gone blank. I tense, expecting him to run off and tell the nearest guard our secret.

He shifts his jaw to the side. "And by 'everyone' you mean the Rapid supers?" he says slowly, flatly.

Nadia nods eagerly. "And whoever else we can save." She raises her eyebrows at me. "Right?"

"I...uh..." I gulp. "Yeah, the more the merrier." I eye Seth, waiting for any movement that'll tell me he's about to bolt and ruin everything.

Ares sits up, pale brows furrowed over stormy eyes. When he turns to Nadia and opens his mouth, I jump in to interrupt.

"We need to do this, Seth." He knows now. Might as well go all the way. I stand, meeting his blank stare. "I need to do this. Make things right."

His eyes flick to the nearest guard. My fingers twitch to grab his arm to keep him from running off and telling them about our plan, but I force my hands to stay at my sides. "You didn't see what I saw...The children and the gas and the trucks." My voice thickens and I clear my throat. "It just needs to be done. The Rapid supers need to go home."

He studies me for several moments, eyes narrowed, jaw working. "I don't suppose I'll be able to convince you not to go through with it."

I steadily hold his gaze and shake my head. "Seth, the supers are being held here just because they're different." Suddenly Seth's story about what happened to his parents flashes through my mind. "Listen, I know a lot of supers are doing wrong with their powers" —He breaks my gaze to stare at his shoes, arms uncrossing— "But other supers are suffering for it. They branded us all criminals. The only way we can show the world that we're still human and keep the true criminal supers from hurting people is to get out of here."

He looks away, brow furrowing and chewing his lip as he slides a hand through his sweat-dampened hair. Nadia and Ares watch him, barely breathing.

"We can stop supers from hurting any more families," I add softly.

I resist looking at the guards again, forcing myself to relax my posture. I lean against the tree and cross my arms casually, but keep my gaze trained on Seth. A breeze gently toys with my hair and a few strands tickle my cheeks. I don't bother to brush them away, silence holding me as we watch him.

He angles away from us, staring hard at the ground, rubbing his chin. Finally, after heaving in a deep breath, he turns to face us. "Okay. Where do I sign up?"

I blink. "Really?"

He shrugs. "I'm in."

"Hang on," Ares stands, cocking his head at Seth. "Why?"

Seth shrugs again, sliding his hands along his jumpsuit as if looking for pockets. His gaze jumps between us. His shoulders slump a little when he stares at his shoes instead. "Just...trying to do the right thing," he mumbles. He lifts his gaze to mine. "I want to keep them from ruining any more families."

I nod and a slight smile lifts my mouth. But I still eye him carefully, trying to figure out if he's being genuine.

Seth rubs the back of his neck, still not looking at us. "What more do you want? I said I want to do the right thing here."

Yeah, you told me the same thing in Rapid City.

Nadia stands, leaning a hand against the tree for support. She smiles at Seth. "Good. Now we're a team again. But for the right thing this time."

When she shifts her smile to me, I can't help but return it, although weakly. My focus turns back to Seth as Nadia brings her smile to Ares, who doesn't see it because he's staring at Seth too.

Is Seth genuine? Or is he setting us up for a betrayal, one that could ruin my chance to fix my mistake? My stomach twists at the thought of the Rapid supers never being together again.

Seth meets my eyes for a split second, then he clears his throat as he glances at the guards. "Better sit down, folks. I assume you don't want them to know, right?"

We lower back down to the dead grass and silence engulfs us as we sit in thought.

I poke my finger into the hard ground. How can we do this while being monitored almost 24/7? "Maybe we need someone on the inside to pull this off."

Ares raises an eyebrow. "You expect to find someone who works for the SCF that will help us?"

I wave a hand. "No, that's not what I mean." I almost say Rez's name to suggest we get in contact with him somehow, but guilt presses my gut. He probably wants nothing to do with me. I clear my throat. "Ivon's here. I saw him get loaded up into one of the trucks. Maybe we could find him, contact him somehow."

Nadia leans forward. "Get him a message?"

I nod. "We could tell him what we're planning."

Ares scratches his head, grimacing. "How would we do that? We're isolated."

I chew my lip in thought, finger tapping on my knee. "A note..." Paper. Somehow I need to get paper. Or any surface that will take ink. My thoughts drift to my unit, and the small bookshelf in the corner.

I snap my fingers, making everyone jump. I wince. "Sorry. But listen...I could use a blank page from the back of one of the books in my unit."

Nadia's eyebrows raise. "That could work."

I scan the grounds, noting clusters of trees and rough picnic tables. "I could hide it somewhere..."

"Yeah but what are the odds he'd see it? He'd have to know to look."

I look over the grounds again and my gaze stops at the wildflower garden in the center. I think of Ivon bending over the small plot of upturned soil in Rapid. It wouldn't surprise me if Ivon frequents the garden here too.

I rub my fingertips along my jawline. "Maybe the garden."

Nadia tilts her head. "Hmm?"

I point my thumb over my shoulder toward the garden while I frown at the ground in thought. "Remember the garden Ivon had in Rapid? He might hang around this garden too."

Nadia nods. "You hide it in the dirt. The guards wouldn't see it."

Seth chews his lip. "You'd have to put it there without the guards seeing." He hands knot together. "Maybe this isn't a good idea."

Ares rakes a hand through his snowy hair, not seeming to notice what Seth said. "That's taking another big risk. There could be some supers here who don't want trouble just as much as the SCF. They could tell someone about the note."

I shrug, hiding the swirl of thoughts his words stir. I hadn't thought about that. I assumed every super would want a chance to get out. I bite my lip and pick at my fingernails. "I'm out of ideas, Ares. It's a big risk, yes, but it could work. It's *got* to work. What else do we have?"

Ares sighs and scrubs a hand over his face. "All right. Let's try it then."

Seth leans forward. "And what if it doesn't work?"

I stare at him, chewing the inside of my cheek as my fingers drum a rapid pattern on my knee. Suddenly this all sounds so crazy, so impossible. Busting superhumans out of a government facility. What if this doesn't work out? What if all my plans fail and Rez will never get out, never get his family back?

I do my best to square my shoulders. "Then at least we know we tried."

Seth shakes his head, rubbing the side of his neck. "I'm not sure this is a good idea anymore." He says it softly, as if to himself rather than us.

I eye him, wondering if he's going to stick with us. Was his decision to join us genuine? Could he be planning to betray us? I chew my lip, hoping it wasn't a bad choice to give him a chance.

At the sound of voices, we turn to see the doctor monitoring us gesturing toward the guards. I stiffen as they approach. They heard. They suspect something. I know it. They—

"Time to go back to your units." The closest guard waves toward the exit door.

A breath seeps out of my lungs. I stand, knees wobbly from my wave of panic. I use the tree to steady myself and offer Nadia a hand to help her up. She nods her thanks and the four of us calmly line up to march back to our units.

When we get there, Dr. Bailey is already waiting in my unit. He looks up from his tablet with a smile as the guards leave and I settle onto the hospital bed.

"How are you feeling?" he asks.

I can't help but stare at the reporters, longing for the quiet of the outdoor grounds again. "A little weak, but okay." I tuck my trembling hands under the blanket. An extra one sits folded at the foot of the mattress.

He nods, typing on his tablet. "Good, good."

As he falls silent in his tapping, I glance at the book shelf, then at the crowd of reporters again. I purse my lips. It'll be hard to get a page from one of the books without someone noticing.

Dr. Bailey is still typing when he says, "This is just a quick check-in, then I have to leave for an interview. After that I'll come check on you guys again, okay?"

That's one less person I have to worry about watching. "Another interview? You must be famous or something."

He looks up from the screen, then must decide I'm joking because he huffs a chuckle. Without another word, he leaves to check on Nadia. A nurse takes his place, going through her usual routine with me. I try to ignore her, but my eyes catch on the pen tucked in the pocket of her scrubs shirt.

A pen, of course. I'll need that too. My eyes scan over the reporters again. Somehow...

I clear my throat loudly. "Dr. Bailey?"

He looks up from his tablet, standing beside Nadia's bed. Irritation skitters across his features. "Yes?"

"Can we be let outside again in a bit, since we're feeling so good?"

He frowns, and when he looks at the others, they all nod. The doctor rubs his chin, still frowning as he studies me. "Okay. I guess that'd be fine."

I smile. "Thanks."

He gives a purse-lipped smile and nods before leaving Nadia's unit to step into Ares'. It only takes him a few minutes to check on the boys before leaving for his interview. The reporters trickle out of the room, I assume for the interview.

The nurse picks up the blanket to unfold it and drape it over top of my covers. "Need anything?"

I glance at the armchair sitting beside the bookshelf. "Um, yeah. I want to sit over there. Would you help me? My legs are still weak."

She smiles and bobs her head. "Sure."

As I scoot to the edge of the bed, she offers her hands. I take them, leaning heavily on her support. My knees shake when my feet rest on the floor. Of course, a little exaggerated.

When I lift my foot to take a step, I let my leg buckle under me. The nurse gasps and grabs me around the waist. "Easy there."

"Sorry." Still feigning hopeless weakness, I slip the pen from her pocket and tuck it into my sleeve. She still focuses on getting me balanced.

Pen poking my arm, I settle my balance back on my feet and give her a sheepish grin. "Sorry about that."

She guides me toward the chair. "Don't worry about it." Once I settle into the cushions, she lets out a breath and plants her hands on her hips. "Anything else?"

I grin. "Nope, I'm good. Thanks."

She returns my grin with a nod, then leaves to check on the others. I lean back in the chair, resting my arm on the armrests, the cool pen pressing against my skin. I look over at Nadia's unit. The nurse is already with Ares. A frown crosses Nadia's face as she watches me. Checking to make sure all the reporters and news cameras have left, I lift my hand in a wave, hoping she'll see the bulge of the pen in my sleeve.

Her frown deepens for a moment before realization smooths it back. She nods subtly and takes a deep breath as she settles back against the upright bed.

Just as the nurse leaves Seth's unit, my trembling fingers reach for the nearest book. I pay no attention to the title or the words strung across the pages. My right hand slips to the back of the book, fingers latching onto the very last page. As I pretend to read, hand covered by the bulk of the pages, my fingers tug at the paper.

I force myself not to look at the small cameras in the units, or consume the tension radiating from the others as they cast glances at me. My heart thuds wildly in my chest as my fingers rip the last bit of the page from the binding. Still hiding my hand behind the book, I crumple the page into a tight ball and close my fist around it.

Faking a yawn, I slide the book back to its place then crawl back into bed and pull the blankets over my shoulders. It takes every bit of my strength and concentration to carefully smooth out the paper and pull out the pen under the blankets without moving my arms too much or changing my facial expression.

I close my eyes with a sigh. I never was very good at pretending I was asleep, Mom told me that plenty of times. But I focus on taking deep, even breaths as I press the pen tip to the paper. I'll have to write without looking. I just hope my words will be legible. Remembering Dr. Bailey's approval for more outdoor time and realizing guards might come any minute to get us, I write quickly:

Ivon, I can't explain much, other than that we're trying to get you back home. We're forming a plan to get the supers out of here. If I can, I'll write more of the plan here when we come up with it. Just be ready. Tell anyone you can trust. Write back if you get this message. -Scarlett

After scribbling my name, I realize I didn't include any apology about what happened in Rapid. The page isn't big enough for that, so I settle to tell him about it in person. Hopefully.

I click the pen closed and slip it back into my sleeve. Blanket still tucked over my shoulder and hiding my hands, I fold the note into a small square and tuck it into my jumpsuit collar.

I ditch trying to pretend I'm sleeping and slip out of bed. My feet itch to pace and I satisfy them. The paper cuts into my skin and I try not to wince.

When my legs grow weak, I lean back against the wall by the door with a sigh. I lift my hand and trace the lines on my skin, searching through my body to feel the fire that should be around somewhere. Cupping my hand so I almost form a fist, hiding my palm from the camera facing me on the opposite wall, I dig deep for the flames that have been hiding in my body after the cold invasion of the serum. My hand warms and soft, whisper-thin flames bloom from my palm, caressing my fingers. I snap my hand closed and a couple sparks fly.

I press my fist to my chest. It's still there.

The unit doors buzz open.

I jolt and jump away from the door. I finger the small bulge on my collar as the guards step in, then force my hand to my side.

One of my guards gestures toward the door. "More outdoor time."

I nod and step through the doorway, and they fall into step beside me. Followed by Nadia, Ares and Seth and their escorts, we march back outside. This time the sunshine peeks through the thick clouds in patches, relieving some of my tension. A bird bounces in the bare branches of our normal tree, whistling a choppy tune. I take a deep breath, relishing in the warm sunlight on my neck. The note pokes my collarbone.

The guards leave us to take up their usual positions. Again, a doctor stands near the door to monitor us. We head toward our usual tree and the other three sit while I lean past them to get a look at the patch of wildflowers.

I could tuck the note in the soft dirt, like Nadia suggested. "I'm going gardening."

They look up at me. Seth's face twists. "Huh?" Then his eyebrows raise. "Oh. Right," he whispers, then hops to his feet and runs his hands through his hair to disguise a discreet glance at the guards. "I'll help you."

I catch Ares looking at Seth with narrowed gaze as the two of us stride toward the garden. When we reach it, I kneel at the edge of the upturned dirt, a line of guards at my back and the line in front of me half-hidden behind the tall grasses growing with the flowers. My fingers brush over the hardy plants, standing strong against the chilly wind.

I take a deep breath before bending over the garden patch, reaching my fingers into the dirt to rearrange it around the flowers, packing it in here and fluffing it up there. I brush against a patch of browning plants, petals drooping and shaking in the breeze. Here. I can see Ivon bending over this spot specifically, to care for it to try to bring it back to life, even though there aren't any garden supplies available.

Seth grabs my wrist. "Stop."

I freeze, breath stilling. "What? What is it?" I glance over my shoulder, but the guards haven't moved.

"Are you sure this is a good idea?"

Did he stop me just to try to convince me of that? I pull my wrist away. "You're drawing attention." I go back to my fake gardening, bending a fraction of an inch lower behind the grasses to slip the note out from my jumpsuit.

Seth reaches for my hand again and I hold the note away from his grip. "What are you doing?" I hiss, trying my best to keep my body language neutral. I scoop some dirt to form a hole by the dying plants and stuff the note in.

"Scarlett, I came over here to try to convince you not to do this."

My jaw clenches as I slip the pen from my sleeve and drop it into the hole with the note. "What are you talking about? You said you were with us."

His breath quickens slightly and I nudge him. "Relax," I say. "Everything will be fine."

He takes a deep breath, but his hands tremble as he fingers a fuzzy leaf. "You don't know that."

He watches while I pat dirt over the note and pen then pull some weeds and pile them by me in the grass.

"You guys..." Seth glances where Nadia and Ares still sit, then drops his voice, staring at his hands in his lap. "You're the closest thing to friends I've had in—"

He breaks off and I look at him, a weed dangling from my fingers. Seth meets my gaze, jaw set. "I just don't want anything bad to happen. Not again."

I chew my lip. His words make me think of the consequences of this whole escape plan. People will get hurt. Killed? My stomach lurches. I swallow hard and go back to weeding, but soften my voice. "It's okay, Seth. Everything will be okay."

I wonder if Rez ever had to calm someone down like this, tell them that everything's going to be all right. Did he leave out details, like my thought about people getting hurt or worse? Is that what a leader does?

Seth holds my gaze for a long moment, then breaks it to glance at the guards. A couple of them look our way for too long.

"Well," I say loudly, pushing to my feet. "I'm done getting my hands dirty, so do you wanna join the others now?"

My forced cheerfulness seems to calm Seth. He draws in a deep breath and nods, forcing a smile. "Yeah, let's go."

As we walk back toward our tree, the back of my neck tickles, as if the guards' gazes follow us. I resist looking at them and instead dig the dirt out from under my fingernails as I lower myself back to the grass next to Nadia to lean against the rough tree bark.

Seth's brow furrows faintly as he joins our circle. He bites his lip as he stares at the garden, eyes distant. I study him, wondering if my words helped. Is he going to stick with us?

When he continues to stare at the flowers, I shift uncomfortably, hoping the guards aren't following his gaze. I kick Seth's foot with mine. "Talk or something," I hiss.

Seth breaks out of his daze and blinks at me. "Huh?"

I purse my lips. "Stop staring at the garden and talk about something."

Ares nods, glancing at the doctor watching us from the door. "Right." He pauses, grin lighting his eyes. "So, uh...nice weather we're having?"

I roll my eyes and groan. Nadia chuckles.

"That's not suspicious at all," Seth mumbles.

Ares shrugs, scratching the top of his head. "I don't know. Think of something better then."

Seth frowns and rubs his middle. "I'm hungry."

Nadia raises an eyebrow. "Aren't you always?"

Seth grins and shrugs. "If you could eat anything in the world right now, what would it be?"

I pick more dirt out from under my pinkie nail. "Anything, huh?"

"Anything in the world."

Ares rests his elbows on his knees. "I dunno, maybe some of the simply marvelous food they have in the meal hall. Glob a la SCF, ya know? Good eats."

Seth fakes gagging. "Please, don't make me sick. I'd go for a cheeseburger. With bacon. Three of them."

"Three?" Nadia sputters, then clutches her stomach like she's already sick from eating three burgers. She shakes her head in disapproval. "A good salad maybe?"

I groan. "Oh, stop, my mouth's watering."

Seth gags again. "You're both such girls."

Nadia laughs, then nudges me with her elbow. "What'd you pick?"

My fingers still for a moment as I think. "Chocolate. Any shape, size or form, just give me chocolate." I can't even imagine what a candy bar would taste like right now. Probably like heaven.

Seth stretches his legs out to cross his ankles, then nods his chin at Ares. "You? That first answer doesn't count considering it made all of us sick."

Ares licks his lips. "Milkshake. Strawberry."

Seth rolls his eyes. "Of course. I should've known."

Ares raises his eyebrows.

Huffing, Seth swipes a hand over Ares' white hair. "It's a cold drink. Of course you'd pick something cold."

Ares smooths down his hair with a frown. "What? I can't help it."

We share a chuckle, and the sound warms my insides. That small lift of happiness only sparks another ache in my chest for my family. I'd give anything to hear their laughter again.

Nadia stretches her arms above her head with a groan. "Is the note hidden?" she breathes.

I nod subtly, flicking a glance at the doctor typing on his tablet. The guards continue their routine scan of the grounds. Back and forth, back and forth. It doesn't look like anyone suspects us. For now.

"What now?" Nadia whispers.

I grimace at the stubborn dirt still clinging to my fingers. "What do you mean?"

"Well, it could take some time for Ivon to see the note." She fingers the shoulder seam of her jumpsuit. "We have more injections coming. What are we going to do about that?"

I dig the dirt out of my nails harder, channeling my frustration through the motion. "I don't know. I had thought about—"

"Wait." Ares gestures toward the basketball court, eyes darting toward the doctor. He stands and clears his throat loudly. "Let's play a game."

I want to look at the doctor monitoring us, but I keep my gaze on Ares. A basketball game might be a good plan to avoid looking suspicious.

Seth springs to his feet in half a second. "A game? Basketball?"

Ares steps back at his enthusiasm. "I think I may regret this—"

"Ha! Ice boy, you read my mind." Seth grabs his arm and drags him toward the court. "And we have even numbers!"

"I don't think *anyone* can read your mind," Ares mumbles.

I grimace and follow after them, Nadia close behind me. "I'm warning you. I'm no good at this."

When I get closer, Ares leans in. "You don't have to be good. You just have to look like you're playing instead of planning a breakout."

Seth picks up the ball and joins our cluster in the middle of the faded court. "All right, two on two. Who's captain?"

Ares reaches for the ball, but Seth pulls away, grinning. Ares raises an eyebrow. "We only have four people," he says.

"Boys against girls then?"

Ares shrugs. "Fine."

Seth tosses the ball to Ares. "Your enthusiasm is overwhelming."

Nadia turns to me. "What were you about to say before?"

I blink, biting my lip. "I had thought about creating a harmless substitute for the serum. But I don't know how that would work, and I'm not good at science-y stuff."

Nadia nods. "That might be a good idea though."

"I don't think so," Ares states, frowning. "That's not safe. What would we substitute it with that would be safe? I mean, we're injecting something into our bloodstream here."

Hearing that out loud makes it sound even more dangerous than I thought. We all nod in agreement, and I erase that option from my mind.

Nadia bends to pick a weed from a crack in the court and twirls it between her fingers. "Is there anything we can do to avoid getting our powers taken away?" she says softly. "What if... there's nothing we can do about it?"

I watch the plant spin between her fingertips. "What if we faked it? I mean, pretend our powers are disappearing faster than they really are? Then they might stop the injections early, thinking our powers are gone."

Ares bounces the ball a couple times by his side. "I don't think that would work. Their tech has the ability to read the level of our powers in our bodies without us using them." His brow furrows with that thought as he takes a few steps closer to the hoop and shoots. It bounces off the backboard and zips against the rusting chain net.

Seth retrieves the ball, raising his eyebrows at Ares. "I think you have a hidden talent."

Ares stares at the hoop. "That's the first time that's ever happened."

Nadia and Seth chuckle, while I angle away from them, rubbing the tension in the back of my neck as I work my brain. Ares' words replay in my mind. What if there's nothing we can do? What if we have to endure possibly losing our powers while we form the escape plan?

I turn back to the others with a sigh just as Seth goes in for a layup, misses, and mutters, "Disgusting."

"We're just going to have to risk it," I say quietly.

Nadia and Ares look at me, and Seth dribbles for a few moments before he finally turns his attention our way. I shrug and sigh again, sliding a hand over my hair. "In the time we need to plan this escape, we may lose our powers. That is, if the serum is as successful as it has been so far."

I feel for my fire briefly. A faint pulse of warmth in my core reminds me it's not defeated yet.

Seth turns away to try another layup, while Nadia and Ares exchange a glance, then stare at their shoes.

"I guess it's a risk we'll have to take," Nadia says softly. Then she joins Seth under the hoop and he gives her the ball so she can try to shoot.

Ares nods, then looks at the sky. The wind lifts his hair, brushing it across his forehead. He pushes it out of his face, then gives me a faint, sad smile. "Guess it is." He moves to stand beside Nadia and watch her shoot.

I watch as Nadia's shot cleanly plummets through the hoop. Ares claps while Seth mutters something about life not being fair. I guess they're right. Losing our powers is a risk we'll have to take. And it's worth it to be able to plan this breakout and get the Rapid supers—all the SCF supers, even—back home. To have them free once again and reverse my mistake. Rez's family can be whole again.

I cross the cracked court to join the others. I just hope Ivon sees the message sooner rather than later.

Seth looks up at my approach and grins. "Ready for our game?"

I can't help but grin. "Girls against guys, you said?"

Seth lifts his chin and props his elbow on Ares' shoulder. "Yeah. You think you can take us?"

My smile widens and I sling my arm around Nadia's shoulder, matching Seth's posture. "Of course. I have Nadia." No matter her skill level, it's got to be better than mine.

Ares blinks at Seth. "Can we take *them*?"

Seth drops his arm to frown disappointedly at Ares, then bounces the ball against his shoulder. "Of course we can."

CHAPTER TWENTY-FIVE

My heart beats like a drum. You'd think after going through this once already I wouldn't be as nervous the second time, but my gut churns just the same. What if this time my powers are taken completely? Would that change things for the escape plan?

Dr. Bailey presses a gloved hand to my arm. "Just relax, Scarlett."

I take a deep breath and rest my head back against the head-rest, trying not to think about the restraints securing me to the chair. "I'm trying."

The doctor turns to examine the serum syringe while the nurse sanitizes the injection site. My foot bobs nervously as I scan over the crowd of reporters and cameras. I close my eyes again and suck in several deep breaths. If my family's watching, I don't want them to see me nervous and undone. I don't want them to worry.

My mind strays to the note I tucked in the garden yesterday and doubts begin to squeeze me. What if Ivon didn't see it? What if he never sees it? Would we have to forget about our plan?

A sharp prick pierces my inner arm and I flinch. My eyes fly open to see Dr. Bailey already injecting the serum through my vein. The nurse holds a calming—or restraining?—hand on my shoulder.

As the blue liquid flows into my veins, the ache sharpens and spreads through my arm and the rest of my body. I clench my teeth against the pain, waiting for the numbing cold to follow. I feel for my fire, and in that split second, I feel nothing. Like the cold has overtaken me. Like there isn't some living power inside me anymore. My heart lurches against my ribs.

"See? It was quick." Dr. Bailey gives me a brief smile as he pulls away the empty syringe. The nurse presses a round piece of gauze to the puncture wound and secures it with a strip of tape.

I shift, trying to get comfortable in the tight restraining straps. "That's the easy part," I mutter. A wave of pain washes over my body, and I groan, shivering against the chill seeping through me. All I get is a pat on the arm.

While nurses still hover over me, Dr Bailey moves on to Nadia's unit. I blink back the reflex tears from the pain and watch as the doctor works. Unlike me, Nadia seems more in control of her nerves this time while the serum is injected into her bloodstream. Then on to Ares, who keeps his chilly gaze glued to the viewing window while the doctor goes through the routine. Only when he leaves does Ares let his head tip back against the headrest, grimacing as a rosy hue blooms over his cheeks.

Seth gives the doctor a tight grin when he enters. I watch, trying to distract myself from the ache and cold, though unrelenting shivers seize me. He clenches his jaw as Dr. Bailey injects the serum into his bloodstream. As the doctor sets the syringe back down, Seth hisses, eyes flying wide and his back arching against his bonds.

I lean forward in the restraints, trying to see clearer. What's happening to him? I twist to the nurses at my side, eyes wide. "What's wrong with him?" Something must be wrong. The ache in my limbs hurts, but never like that.

The nurse glances over her shoulder, only looking for a moment. "He's fine. Don't worry."

I stare at her, open mouthed but wordless. He's *fine?* That doesn't look fine to me! I look back at Seth, struggling to see through the three layers of glass between us and the nurses bustling around.

Dr. Bailey leans close to Seth, studying him with a deep frown. The reporters crowd closer. "Mr. Calvin?" he says. "Can you hear me?"

Seth's head twists to the side, sweat dripping down his forehead, darkening his hair. His skin pales, body trembling. Then he falls limp against the chair. Still.

My pulse quickens. "What's wrong with him?" I ask again, louder.

The nurse steps to the side, blocking my view of him. She glances nervously over her shoulder, then at the reporters crowding closer to Seth's unit. "Everything's fine." Her voice shakes.

My arms tug against the straps as I fight helplessly to get free, to go to Seth. "No, it's not. That didn't happen last time."

"Some people may respond to the serum differently—"

"He didn't do that last time!"

A few reporters glance my way. The nurse grabs my forearm, her fingers digging into my flesh. I suck in a breath and blink up at her.

Her face is still calm, composed, almost kind. But a warning lights her green eyes. "Everything is fine. Stay calm."

I try to yank my arm free of her grip, but the straps stop me. She removes her hand, exchanging a nervous glance over my head at the other nurse.

I press against the cushion, trying to lean back to see Seth past the nurse. I can only see the top of his head, sweat-dampened hair sprawled over the headrest.

Another wave of aching pain washes over me. I clench my jaw, curling my hands and toes against the onslaught. A shiver shakes my body. A nurse tosses a thin blanket over me, but I feel like I'm losing the fight against this devouring cold.

The reporters set all their focus on Seth. Dr. Bailey angles his back toward them, hiding his stiff shoulders and worried expression. He checks over Seth for a few minutes before straightening and wiping a wrist across his forehead.

"It's all right, everyone," he says, mostly to the reporters. "He's just unconscious. He'll be fine."

A wave of drowsiness presses against me, despite all my effort to keep my eyes open, to see what's wrong with Seth. Sleep tugs at my muscles, making them go limp. My eyes slide closed. *No, I need to know...need to know what's wrong...*My head falls back against the chair as sleep snags me from reality.

That familiar hum of anxious chatter pulls me awake. I groan, twisting my head side to side against the pain throbbing in my temples. My eyes flutter open to meet the stares of reporters and cameras. I close my eyes again and roll onto my side, not ready to face so many gazes and lenses this morning.

The note.

The thought pokes my brain, chasing away drowsiness. I sit up too fast, then hold a hand to my head until the dizziness passes. I swing my legs over the edge of the bed, but as soon as my feet leave the blanket, icy air chills them and sweeps up my whole body. I shiver and pull my legs back in to curl into a ball, pulling the covers over me again. But from that brief moment, cold air already settles into my bones.

I look across through the glass walls into the other units. Nadia's already come to. She paces back and forth beside her bed, tossing frequent glances toward Seth. A nurse stands over him and worry stirs my stomach. Was he watched all night?

Ares stirs in his bed, rubbing a hand over his face as he wakes up. It doesn't take him long to join Nadia's worried watch over Seth.

I reach to the button panel on the bed's railing and crank it to an upright position, straightening to get a better view of Seth.

Nadia glances over her shoulder and sees me. With one more look at Seth, she crosses her unit to the wall separating us.

"He's still asleep," she whispers.

I move to get out of the bed, but then decide to stay under the warmth. "Unconscious or asleep?"

She bites her lip. "I don't know."

I jerk my chin toward the nurse. "She been there all night?"

She shakes her head. "I think she's been there the whole time we were asleep, but it's still the same day."

"What?"

"The injection was earlier today. We slept less this time. It's late, but still the same day."

I bite the inside of my cheek, casting a glance at the reporters. Their attention is zeroed in on Seth. "The message," I faintly mouth.

Nadia's eyes widen a fraction, then she nods subtly. We both jump when my unit door cranks open.

Dr. Bailey strides in, a smile plastered on his face. He stops beside my bed. "Well, how are you—"

"What happened to Seth?"

His smile falters. "He'll be fine."

"That didn't answer my question."

He leans closer, smile disappearing fully as he angles his back toward the viewing window, expression going dark. "Do I need to remind you again? You have no right to ask questions."

"He's my friend," I bite out, fisting my hands in the blankets.

"I said he'll be fine." He straightens, smile returning, although more strained. "So how are you feeling?"

I don't try to resist giving him the glare that he should receive. "Cold."

He raises an eyebrow. "That's it?"

"A little dizzy. Headache."

"But better than last time."

I pause. "Yes."

"Good." He pulls out his tablet again to enter information. As he does, the door opens again and a nurse comes in to take my vitals.

When she finishes, both of them leave for Nadia's unit. They don't spend much time there, or at Ares' either. They bend over Seth, talking in low tones for a long while. As they study him, he stirs. Everything goes silent as all eyes turn to him.

He groans slightly, shifting under the tangle of blanket. His eyes flutter open, then widen when he sees all the gazes on him. He snaps upright, then grimaces and presses a hand to his head.

"What's going on?" he says, looking over the four of us, Dr. Bailey, the reporters.

"How are you feeling, Seth?" the doctor asks.

He blinks several times and drops his hand from his head. "I'm...fine, I guess. Dizzy though. Very dizzy. Light-headed."

"That's it?"

"You were unconscious," I interject.

Seth leans past a nurse to look at me. He waves a hand dismissively. "That was just for a bit."

"So you were sleeping?"

He nods and yawns, stretching his arms above his head. Then he chuckles at everyone still watching him intently. "I'm fine now." He snaps his fingers, eyes lighting up. "Hey, am I on the news?"

Dr. Bailey releases a tense chuckle, patting Seth's shoulder. "You've been on the news almost every day, Mr. Calvin. Though you did give us a little scare."

So he *was* worried.

Seth seems so normal, but the tension in my chest barely eases. What had happened just after the injection? Why had he passed out like that?

Dr. Bailey turns toward all of us. "I'm glad to see you all

doing well. It's late, but I want you to get outside for a bit. Okay?"

Nods all around. The doctor nods then leaves Seth's unit, followed by the nurses. Guards take their place to escort us to the outdoor grounds.

A slap of biting November wind smacks my body and stings my exposed skin. My body quakes with shivers and I hug myself as I make a beeline for the garden, eyes on the small patch of dying plants. A hand grabs my arm and jerks me back. I stiffen at first. Has a guard or even the doctor sent to monitor us noticed something? My heart pounds.

"Act normal," Ares' voice brushes my ear. He moves past me, casually striding toward our tree.

I take a deep breath and follow him, forcing my steps to be slow and even. I falter halfway there as a thought takes me unawares.

I didn't feel Ares' overwhelming cold.

Nadia and Ares lower weakly to the ground and lean against the tree trunk. Seth flops on the ground again, staring at the sky.

I almost pass them on my way to the garden, but pause, eyeing Seth. The grey evening light makes his skin look even paler as his ribcage lifts with each weak breath.

"Seth?" I say. "You okay?"

He lifts his head and the corner of his mouth curls faintly. "Yeah, I think so." He looks at the others and huffs a chuckle. "Did I scare you guys?"

Nadia lets out a breath. "A little bit."

A gust of wind hits me and I brace against it, muscles stiffening as cold air slips down my jumpsuit. I shiver. Bone-chilling cold seems to have overtaken my whole body. How can my fire still live in me?

I crouch and the others turn their gazes to me, obviously having expected me to go to the garden. I rub my thumb along my palm. "Your powers...are they still...?"

I want to search for the warmth in my core, but something

stops me. What if it's not there? What if all I find is more icy cold? Fear squeezes my throat.

Ares closes his eyes and tips his head back. For a brief moment, that pale complexion returns to his face, then fades as rosiness takes over his cheeks again. He drops his gaze to the ground. "Yeah, it's there," he says. But his shoulders sag weakly as he lifts a hand to stare at his palm.

Nadia casts a frown at him before closing her eyes too, setting her hands flat against her legs. I watch them closely, and as soon as her fingers start to tremble, she stops, drawing her hands closed. She swallows hard and chews her lip.

The fear in their eyes and their diminished powers makes my stomach knot. But I dig for my fire anyway. I reach into my core, searching for the warmth and the energy in my veins. Like a dying candle flame, a pulse of heat blooms in my core, chasing away a fraction of the cold in my bones. Another gust of wind hits my back and the warmth flickers out.

I chew my lip and rub my palms together, trying to warm my stiff fingers. So maybe the serum is successful. I recall a time when I would've been overjoyed at that. But now...it's like a part of me is slipping away and I don't know how to get it back.

I shift my gaze to Seth, who stares at the sky, eyes dazed. "Seth?"

He flinches and blinks at me. "Huh?"

"Your powers...are they still there?" I ask softly.

He shrugs and looks away. "I don't feel like trying."

I tilt my head. "Why not?"

He coughs into his fist and angles away from me. "I just don't want to, okay?"

I hesitate. "Okay." Why doesn't he want to test his powers? Does he still hope the serum will take it away? The thought makes me wonder again if he's really on our side.

I take one more look at Seth before standing again to continue to the garden, measuring my steps. Even though the back of my neck tingles with the guards behind me and my heart quickens its pace, I do my best to act natural. I stretch my arms above my head with a groan, then sit with my knees under my chin at the edge of the garden. I face with my side toward the garden, watching the guards from the corner of my eye.

They don't seem to be doing anything other than their normal rhythm, so I reach my hand into the dirt, smoothing here and there, pulling more dead weeds. My fingers still near the patch of dying flowers. There are no weeds here. Every harmful plant has been removed, and the pile I started before has grown.

Someone's been here. I just hope it was Ivon.

I shift to sit on my knees, using one hand to dig for the note, and the other to continue rearranging soil and pulling weeds. Finally, my fingers brush against paper. A bead of sweat dribbles down my temple. I suck in a breath and let it out slowly, then pull out the paper with one hand and quietly unfold it among the thick flower stems and grass.

I keep my head down and glance at the guards once more. Then, I let my eyes drop down to the dirt-smudged paper.

There's a response.

Small, hurried writing follows my barely-decipherable scratchings. My eyes dart to the end, where Ivon's name is scrawled. I let out a breath, then go back to the beginning of the message.

The only reason I'm trusting you now is because I know Rez once did. I'll go along with your plan... What do you have in mind? -Ivon

My stomach clenches painfully as I glance where the others still sit underneath the tree, shoulders slumped weakly from the effects of the serum, talking softly. Nadia catches my gaze, then stands and strides toward me.

"Want some help?" she says as she crunches over the grass toward me.

"Sure," I reply with forced cheerfulness. "I'm just getting some of the weeds out of here."

Nadia crouches behind me and reaches for a particularly

sturdy weed. "Note?" she whispers. She yanks the weed out with a grunt, and I take it from her to put it on the growing pile.

"Yeah," I whisper back, barely moving my mouth. "He's in. Asks what our plan is."

Nadia's hand trembles a little as she reaches for another weed farther into the garden. She doesn't have to say anything, because I know we're thinking the same thing. We don't exactly have a plan yet.

I dig for the pen and quickly write on the dirt-smeared paper, still hidden among the grasses.

We're thinking. Any ideas would be appreciated. -S

My hands shake and I want to look over my shoulder, but I keep my head down and stuff the note and pen in the dirt and cover it with soil. Then I lean back and swipe my hands together, forcing my shoulders to relax.

Nadia follows my motion, brushing her hands together. But she glances nervously at me. I force a small smile, then bend to pick a dainty purple flower. I twirl it between my fingers to give them something to do and motion for her to follow me back to the boys.

We lower onto the grass when we reach them and they both look at us. Ares raises an eyebrow in question. I cast a quick glance at the doctor monitoring us, but he's busy with his tablet again.

I lean a little closer into our circle, picking at a leaf on the flower's stem. "He's in. Wants to know what our plan is."

Seth sits up, brow furrowing. "What'd you say?"

I shrug a shoulder. "I told him I'd keep him posted."

Ares chews his lip and picks dry blades of grass from the ground. "We need to come up with something. Fast."

I nod, studying the way his brow furrows faintly and his sharp jaw clenches slightly. How did I not see before how much he looks like Dr. Bailey?

Movement over Ares' head catches my attention, and I look up to see the monitoring doctor watching us.

I shake the tension from my shoulders and lean back on the tree trunk. "Quit whispering. Talk about something else." The doctor continues to watch. My heart knocks against my ribs and I force my breaths to be even.

Seth shifts to glance over his shoulder.

"Don't," I say before he can turn around.

He chews his lip, hands trembling slightly as he runs them through his hair, but he keeps his eyes forward.

Ares looks up at the branches in thought. "Right. Conversation topics..." He smirks. "Nice weather we're—"

"We're not doing that again," Seth says, sitting up.

Ares' smirk doesn't leave. He straightens his shoulders and clasps his hands in front of him. "How are you feeling?" he says, imitating Dr. Bailey's voice. It strikes me again how much he resembles his father when he does that.

Seth swings an arm at him, but Ares leans away just in time. Their banter loosens a little tension in my chest, but my stomach still clenches painfully. I rub it, working my brain for some solution, some plan that will get us and the supers out of this place. But the harder I think, the only result I get is a quickening heartbeat rather than ideas.

I close my eyes and take a deep breath. The note is safely hidden. Ivon knows where it is and will be ready for the escape plan. With the four of us, we'll think of something. Everything will be okay. I lean back against the tree with a sigh.

"We need a plan," Nadia whispers, watching Ares and Seth go on about food again. "Any ideas?"

Before I answer, I scan the grounds briefly. The guards stand still as statues, diligently watching us and our surroundings. My gaze snags on the doctor. He still stares at us. I quickly avert my eyes and pretend to be closely examining the flower's petals.

I clear my throat, drawing the boys' attention. "Seth, it's time for your favorite cover-up game."

He grins and hops to his feet, but staggers until he regains his balance. My brows knot at the way his skin turns a shade paler. His frame pokes sharply against his jumpsuit. Is he thinner?

But he still keeps his eager grin. "Great! Guys against girls again?"

Ares frowns at him as he stands, and Nadia and I follow suit. "Eh, no. I want a new teammate," he says.

"What? Why?"

"They beat us last time."

Seth sighs dramatically. "Fine. Who do you want?"

He doesn't miss a beat. "Nadia."

I gasp and grab her arm. "No! She was the reason we won last time. I'm not giving her up."

"Aw, come on! You have to share the skill."

Nadia hides her laugh behind her hand as I pull her closer. "She stays on my team." I deepen my voice. "Or face my fiery wrath."

Seth steps between us, holding up a finger. "I'd rather see an ice versus fire fight than play basketball, actually."

We all fall silent for a moment. I rub a thumb on my palm as a breeze makes me shiver. Are our powers even still there enough to do more than just warm or chill us slightly? I share a look with Nadia and Ares. Nadia's forehead wrinkles as she stares absently at the clouded sky. Ares' jaw clenches slightly as he stares at his hands, rubbing his palms together.

My stomach knots painfully, and I give my head a shake before my thoughts can run wild. I miss the cheerful mood we just had. In the midst of everything, a little happiness is good, right? Especially if we're losing our powers.

I throw a fist at Seth's arm, but he twists away. "We're not gonna fight."

Seth grabs Ares' wrist and drags him toward the court. "Then come on, let's play already."

Ares stumbles, trying to keep up with Seth. "Wait, are we on the same teams or not?"

Seth shrugs. "I dunno, let Nadia decide."

Nadia chuckles as she looks between me and Ares.

"I'm fine with that." I lean closer to Nadia, crossing my arms. "I trust she'll make the right decision."

Obviously trying to fight back her grin, she nods and winks. "I'll stick with Scarlett."

Ares rolls his eyes. "Should've known. Girls."

Seth picks up the ball and tries to balance it on one finger. "You girls ready to get beat?"

I snatch the ball from him and jog a few steps away. I'm not even going to attempt to dribble. "I think the better question is are *you* ready to get beat *again*?"

Seth raises his eyebrows. "Oh, it's game time now." He reaches for the ball.

I hold it away. "Winners get the ball."

He smirks. "Starting to like basketball, are we?"

I change my mind and fling the ball at him. "No, so don't get any ideas."

We're a pretty pathetic sight as we spread out on the court, resting on the balls of our feet while our legs shake weakly from the effects of the serum. But before we can even get started, the doctor approaches us, followed by several guards.

I swallow hard and turn around, heart beating in my chest. Do they suspect something?

"Dr. Bailey wants you back to your units to rest," he says in a nasally voice. He beckons the guards and they surround us and guide us toward the exit door.

Seth huffs, then narrows his eyes at me. "You were saved. This time."

I look over my shoulder at him. "I think it's the other way around, buddy."

We march through the doorway, our symphony of footsteps echoing through the halls. Even over our noise, I catch the sound of more footsteps from another hall, these slower, shuffling. I glance down each hall we pass, looking for the source.

We pass a short hallway. A string of grey jumpsuits pass in a parallel hall, traveling in the opposite direction. Drooping shoulders, eyes glued to ground. But I recognize these sun-tanned, hardened faces.

They're Rapid supers.

A large, hulking form appears in the line, towering over the rest. Thick cuffs encircle his wrists, lights glinting off his bald head. I lock eyes with Ivon's steel-grey gaze. His jaw shifts slightly under his rough stubble, then he looks ahead again. More Rapid supers follow behind him, barely lifting their feet off the floor with each dragging step.

The wall cuts off my view, forcing me to look forward again. I clench my hands, eyes stinging. They look so tired. Hopeless. Weary. My nails dig into my palms, pressing through flesh against bone.

I'll get them home. If it's the last thing I do, I'll get them home.

CHAPTER TWENTY-SIX

Ignore them. Stay inside yourself.

I tell myself those two things over and over again as nurses prepare us for another injection. Sometimes it's just a whisper in my head. Sometimes I feel like screaming it when the chatter gets too loud, when the reporters press closer. I either close my eyes or stare at my knees while people blur past my peripheral vision.

My breaths are even, controlled. *Ignore them. Stay inside yourself.*

A touch on my arm makes me flinch.

Dr. Bailey frowns at me. "Are you feeling well?"

I nod. "I'm fine."

He hesitates and I can feel him studying me. "We'll begin shortly."

I nod again, taking a deep breath before closing my eyes again. But something bumps the viewing window, and the clank rings through the glass. I flick my eyes up and panic flutters in my chest at the crowd, the cameras. I force my eyes back down. But the image of the cameras, their lenses intent on me, is branded into my mind.

What if my family is watching again? The thought only makes my knee bounce nervously. What are they thinking? How has my neighborhood reacted to seeing me on the news? Are they shunning my family? Anger flares in my chest at the thought, but quickly fizzles out. There's nothing I can do. The distance separating me from my family presses against me, crushing my chest. I struggle to take in a breath past the building pressure.

I don't even flinch at the prick on my bruised inner arm as Dr. Bailey injects the serum. The sounds of nurses, reporters, and scuffling footsteps dim as I tip my head back to rest against the headrest. I close my eyes, focusing on my family. But the ache for them chokes me. After all this is done, will I ever see them again?

I miss them so much. I want to tell them about everything that's happened, how I've changed. I don't want them to be afraid of me, or misunderstand me. My mind locks onto the image of Ivon's steely gaze as I passed him in the hall, then to the note buried in the garden. If I explained everything to my family, about my powers and what Rez told me, what I believe in now, they'd understand. What wouldn't I give to tell Dylan or Ian that they were right, that I shouldn't have turned myself in so quickly, that maybe I could've found another way. They tried to tell me that night, but I was so sure, so determined to block out their pleas.

The familiar ache spreads from my arm and through my body, settling into my bones. My breath quickens, but that's all. But when the cold comes, layering on top of the chill already in my muscles, my hands clench. A shiver trails up and down my body. Someone covers me with a blanket.

As the cold intensifies, I almost open my eyes but I squeeze them shut again at the last moment. If I open them I'll just see all the people again, all the watching eyes. My thoughts move back to my family, my childhood. For a fleeting moment, I wonder if, after all this, I could go back home. Pick up music again and chase those dreams that seem like they're from so long ago, another life. My fingers twist, aching to play one of my instruments. Feel the smooth gloss of my guitar or smile at the happy tune of my ukuleles.

I give my head a hard shake. Forget about that. Just focus on getting the Rapid supers home. That's more important. Leave the music to Ian.

Instead of making me feel better, more focused, that thought just magnifies the ache inside me. An ache that has nothing to do with the serum. I won't be able to go home, not after this. I'll really be a wanted criminal. Like Rez. I can't get rid of the image of him sitting in a damp, dark cell in the basement of this facility. Cut off from his family. Alone. Hope lost, crushed under a cruel heel.

My hands clench again. *I'll fix everything. I promise.*

"Scarlett?"

My eyes fly open to meet Dr. Bailey's concerned stare. He studies me, eyes narrowing. "Are you feeling all right?"

I swallow and nod. "I'm okay."

"You're sure?"

"Yeah, I'm fine."

He nods, then moves away to go to Nadia's unit to perform her injection. Every eye follows the doctor's movements. Even Ares and Seth nervously watch as he injects the serum into Nadia's bloodstream. My gaze moves past the doctor to Seth. His skin seems paler than before. Maybe it's just the white lights, but dark circles hang under his eyes. He stifles a cough.

My almost-constant headache renews its intensity, pulsing through my skull while my vision blurs. I close my eyes against the dizziness. The drowsiness follows, tugging me, pulling me, pressing down on me. Worries about Seth try to fight the sleep, but it's too strong. It engulfs me, pulling me under.

The hum of conversation wakes me and sparks irritation in my gut. Has it ever occurred to them that we'd just like a little peace and quiet sometimes? I grimace as I sit up, rubbing my fingertips over my temple. As soon as my eyes open, I scowl, sending a glare at the reporters that makes them take a step back. Dizziness presses me back down to the bed.

I roll to my side so I face the other units. Nadia still sleeps, forehead slightly wrinkled. I wonder what's going on in her head, making her frown in her sleep. My heart twinges. I hope it's not her past.

Ares waves at me. I try to smile and wave back, then press the button on the bed railing to raise the bed to the upright position. I motion toward Seth—who lies still—and mouth, "Is he okay?"

Ares looks over his shoulder for a few moments, then says something into Seth's unit I can't hear. He turns back around and nods. "He's awake. Says he's fine." Something on Ares' face tells me he doesn't believe him. He chews his lip and looks over at Seth again.

A buzz echoes through the units as Seth's door swings open. Nadia stirs at the sound and rubs her eyes as she slowly sits up.

All the attention shifts to Dr. Bailey as he strides in. He nods a greeting to the reporters, then checks Seth over, asking questions in a low murmur I can't quite catch. Seth's skin seems paler than ever, even though he still has his lop-sided grin. Then the doctor moves on, spending only a couple minutes with Ares and Nadia.

When he enters my unit, I don't let him bother asking the question. I'm tired of hearing it. "I'm fine," I mutter.

He pauses. "Okay. Good." He turns to face the other units, raising his voice. "Glad to see you all awake, after only an hour. Your bodies seem to be holding up well."

Seth stifles another cough with his fist.

I bite my lip to hold back my questions about Seth's health

because I know I'll just get the same answer as always. I ask a different question instead. "Can we get some outdoor time?"

He turns back to me and holds up a hand. "Not just yet. We have some tests to run." He slips his tablet out, taps a few things, then drops it back into his pocket. The unit doors open and guards step into our units.

I purse my lips. We need to plan, and the best place to do that is the outdoor grounds. "Now?" I can't even feel my fire anymore without digging deep. Just icy cold. We're running out of time.

"Yes, now." He passes my bed to leave, then guards take his place and flank me as I slide out of bed and step through the doorway.

At first the path we take is unfamiliar, confusing. But soon we travel familiar halls, familiar doors, and down an elevator. The guards prod us through the basement halls until we reach the large concrete powers-testing room we'd been in before. Once we all step inside, they leave us, locking the iron door behind them.

This time Dr. Bailey isn't the only one standing behind the high viewing window. Behind a string of rope barriers, reporters and cameras crowd close, all shoving for a view of the superhumans down below. The all-too-familiar black painted target stares at us from the other side of the room. And another concrete slab propped up on blocks. I slide a glance to Nadia. She stares at the target, stiff. Hands shaking.

The speakers crackle before Dr. Bailey's voice comes through. "This should feel familiar to you."

Except we may not have powers anymore. I rub my stomach, brow knotting as I try to feel my fire. A warmth so small that it could be my imagination flares in my gut before fizzling out. My heart lurches.

"So far your results after the injections have been promising," he continues. For the first time I realize two men in dark suits flank him. "Scarlett, would you be our first?"

I wrap my arms around myself. So cold. How could I ever summon my fire through all of the ice in my veins? Still, with a gulp, I nod and step toward the target. I stop in the middle of the room. My fire couldn't possibly be strong enough to shoot from my hand, so I'll just try it from here.

I lift my hand and stare at my palm, trying to ignore the pressure of so many eyes on me. I swallow past my parched throat and take a deep breath to calm my speeding heart. I close my eyes, focusing on the pit in my core where my fire usually burns, trying to wake it, visualizing it flowing through my veins and channeling toward my hand. My fingers tremble. For a moment I think warmth touches my skin, but even that fizzles out.

I clench my jaw and try again. Harder.

I drop my hand, sweat running down my temple. My heart still beats wildly as I look up to the viewing window.

"Try once more," Dr. Bailey says. His voice is calm even as murmuring increases behind him.

I know trying again won't change anything. But still, I hope. I lift my hand again, closing my eyes to focus on coaxing my fire. My hand begins to shake violently, but I keep going as more sweat breaks out over my body.

A small, thin flame blossoms on my palm.

My eyes widen as the flame grows slightly. But I can't maintain it. My trembling hand drops again and I suck in breath after breath. My muscles tremble, but it seems some of the chill in my bones has diminished a fraction. Relief seeps through me and I release a gasping breath. It's not too late. The fire is still there, though buried deep as though it's hibernating through this winter within me. If I keep pushing, keep testing it and feeling for the fire...Will it stay alive and survive the serum?

Murmurs run through the crowd of reporters, carrying through the speakers. They hurriedly bring mics to their mouth, talking excitedly to the cameras and the country.

One of the suited men leans toward Dr. Bailey and says something in his ear. The doctor nods, but holds out a hand, as if calming him. "There are still more tests to be run." He clears his throat, turning his attention back to us. "Ares, if you please."

I eye Dr. Bailey, but he doesn't watch Ares, instead staring at his tablet. Is he so ashamed that he can't even look at his super-human son? On trembling knees, I turn and make my way back toward the others. When Ares passes me, it hits me again that I don't have to recoil from his chill. I glance over my shoulder at him. Faint rosiness covers his cheeks and nose. Is it because he's getting warmer or I'm getting colder?

Ares stops in the middle of the room. He lifts his fist and just stares at it for a long minute.

"Go on," Dr. Bailey prods.

Ares throws a glare at him, but says nothing. He rolls his shoulders back and takes a deep breath, hand clenching tighter. His body tenses, shoulders rising and falling with uneven breaths. A faint frost creeps over his hand, swirling in crackling patterns over his skin. But just as quickly as it appears, it fades like melting snowflakes. His hand drops against his leg and he sucks in a breath.

"I can't do anymore," he mumbles, words trembling. He swipes the back of his hand on his forehead and pushes up his sleeves.

More murmurs. More frantic voices skittering back and forth through the crowd. The suited men shift from foot to foot, glancing at each other.

Dr. Bailey doesn't seem to notice any of it as he stares at his son for a long moment. "Ares..." When he breaks off, I look at Ares. He moves his gaze away from the doctor to stare at the wall.

Dr. Bailey shakes his head and clears his throat. "Seth, are you ready?"

Seth nods, shuffling past me to the middle of the room. He barely lifts his feet off the ground and I frown as I watch him. He's exhausted and slow. There's barely anything left of the fast, wind-sped boy from a few weeks ago. He stops and spreads his feet for balance. Sweat already beads on his forehead when he lifts his hands. Then he starts scooping the air, as if urging it upward.

I wait for even the faintest breath of wind to brush my cheeks. But the air is still. I bite my lip, pulse quickening. Why is the cure affecting him so differently?

Seth's arms drop and he staggers, then rights himself. He presses a hand to his head. "I don't...think...I can," he says between breaths. He sways again. I rush forward and grab his shoulders to steady him, then help him back.

"Nadia." Dr. Bailey's voice comes through slow, but firm, a warning tinging his tone.

Nadia licks her lips, fingers nervously drumming her thighs as she stiffly steps forward. As I pass her, still supporting Seth, I give her shoulder a light squeeze. She catches my eye and pulls in a deep breath, then she strides to the cement slab.

She stares at the surface for a long minute. Dr. Bailey, finally getting some sense, doesn't rush her.

Seth still wobbles on his feet, so I sling his arm over my shoulder and grab him around the waist to keep him standing. He still breathes hard, sweat sticking his hair to his forehead. I glance at him, but he stares at the ground, eyes slightly glossy. Worry stirs my gut. Why's the serum doing this to him?

I bite my lip as I turn to watch Nadia. Now that I know the nightmares that must resurface every time she uses her powers, I want to protect her from the eager eyes staring at her, pressuring her. She quivers, so small and alone beneath all those watching eyes.

She presses her palms on the concrete, leaning her weight against them. Her shoulders hunch and her arms begin to shake. She gasps in a breath with the effort. I watch the concrete for the slightest movement. A faint quake tremors through the slab, coupled with a soft rumble. Then it cuts short and Nadia staggers back, panting.

Again, the infernal murmurs. This time they're louder and

last longer. I would cover my ears if I wasn't keeping Seth from falling. Ares, Nadia and I share a glance. I can see what they're thinking from their eyes. Our powers are weakening. Will they be gone altogether by the time we form the escape plan?

We have to endure several minutes of the excited chattering of reporters to the cameras while Dr. Bailey types on his tablet. My muscles tremble and stiffen under Seth's weight and the cold of this room. But a slight note of warmth moves through my veins. It may be my imagination, but I latch onto it. Maybe my fire hasn't given up after all. Maybe it'll fight back.

Seth shifts to put more weight on his feet, leaning on me less, but stifles a cough behind his fist. Are his powers fighting back?

Finally, Dr. Bailey leans toward the intercom. "Please take them back to their units—"

"Wait." I gulp when all eyes swivel to me. "Can we go outside?"

The doctor pauses. "You seem to like going outside."

I shift nervously. "It's better than being cooped up all day."

He nods, sighing. "Fine. Take them to the outdoor grounds."

The iron door clangs as it's unlocked and swings open. Guards filter in and surround us to guide us back into the hall. Seth pulls away to stand on his own, nodding his thanks. He shuffles out of the room ahead of me. I glance over my shoulder at the viewing window. Dr. Bailey has his back toward us, saying something to one of the suited men beside him. Did he even notice Seth looks sick? Is he so distracted by the cameras?

A guard nudges me forward and I step out of the echoey room. The trek is longer, having to march all the way from the underground levels to the outdoor common grounds instead of to our units. But Seth's steps strengthen with each turn we take, releasing some of the tension in my middle.

We step outside and I'm disappointed to see thick grey clouds cloaking the sky again. My body craves warmth, heat that will reach my very bones and feed my lingering fire.

But I'll think about getting warm later. My gaze wanders to the swaying garden of flowers and grasses. I follow the others to our usual tree. My knees tremble beneath me as I sit against the tree trunk. The four of us share a look.

Time to brainstorm the escape plan.

CHAPTER TWENTY-SEVEN

The air hangs heavy with tension, weighing down our shoulders as we cluster under the tree. Seth lies on his side, tucking his arm underneath his head, and stares blankly at the dead grass, skin looking even paler under the grey afternoon light.

Ares rubs his fingertips together, staring at the skin losing its frosty complexion. "I guess the cure really is working, isn't it?" he says softly.

I chew my lip, staring at my own hands too.

Nadia reaches across me to give Ares' hand a squeeze. "It's not over yet." She glances over her shoulder toward the garden. "We'll figure this out soon."

Ares barely looks at her as she sits back again. Despite what she just told him, I can see the same fears written on her face.

I try not to let the same mood crush me. I take a deep breath and lean back against the rough bark, double-checking that the doctor isn't watching us too closely.

"We need to come up with a plan," I say softly. "How are we going to everyone out of here?"

Our gazes wander to the tall building surrounding the grounds on all sides. A seemingly impenetrable cage. We'd need something big to get out of a place like this...

My gaze shifts to Nadia, remembering a time when she used her powers so effortlessly. There's power in those hands. Power that might be just what we need.

Unless the serum has taken too much. Or her nightmares.

Just as Nadia shifts to look at me—maybe sensing my gaze—I avert my eyes.

"Look," I begin. "This place is strong. We need something powerful, something big to get out of here."

Seth frowns as he props himself up on an elbow. "What, you want to bring the whole place down? There are kids here."

I grimace. "No, that's not what I mean." What do I mean? But Seth has a point. There are children supers in the SCF. I don't want them hurt or fighting for their lives. How are we going to get them out safely?

I rub my chin. "Maybe the thing we need to get out of here is not something big, but some*one*...as leverage." With the right person, we could access the units to let the supers out.

Ares tilts his head. "What do you mean?"

I chew my lip as I study him and I can't help that Dr. Bailey comes to mind. Maybe...he's what we need. "Maybe your father..."

He stiffens. "What about him?"

"Maybe we can use him as leverage. He's an important man and if we can get a hold of him, threaten him somehow to keep guards away, get a weapon..."

"What?" Seth squeaks, sitting up.

I hold out a hand. "We don't have to use it—"

"Then why get it? This isn't gonna work." He rubs his hands over his face.

"Seth, just calm down and hear me out." I take a deep breath, gathering my thoughts before continuing. "If we can do that, then we get his ID card to open the units. The more supers we can free, the more unstoppable we'll be." I know by now that the SCF can't handle large numbers of superhumans.

"But the kids." Nadia's soft words slow some of my momentum. She meets my eyes. "What about the kids?"

My stomach knots tighter. "I know, I know." I press a fist to my head, mind spinning. The children will need to be protected. Maybe we can gather a group of supers to do just that. I turn toward Nadia. "You and I can gather a group of other supers to protect the kids as much as we can."

Nadia nods. "Okay, go on."

"Maybe with Dr. Bailey as leverage, we can keep the guards at bay and get outside the building."

"What then?" Seth interjects. "The building's surrounded by a wall."

Ares leans forward with furrowed brows, stroking his chin. "The most likely weak spot would be the gate. If we can somehow break that down..."

"Then we're back to needing something big," I say, sighing at the ground.

Ares catches my gaze then glances at Nadia. I follow, studying her out of the corner of my eye. Can she do it? Are her powers strong enough? *Will* she do it?

"Nadia..." I say softly.

She keeps her eyes on the grass. "Hmm?" she responds flatly, as if anticipating my request.

I hesitate, chewing my lip and working my brain for another alternative. But the fact remains that she has the most powerful gift out of all of us, and it just might be what we need to combat the SCF's forces and break down that gate. Still, the words are reluctant to form as I wonder how she'll react. I think of the Rapid supers hopeless in their cold cells. I'll just have to take a chance.

"Nadia," I begin again. "We need you."

She bites her nail, still not meeting my eyes, and sighs heavily. "Me?"

Her voice comes out weak and small and my heart pinches. "Only if you're willing." The least I can do is give her a way out, the option to refuse. She told me about her past, and I don't want to make things worse for her.

She doesn't say anything for a few long minutes. Just stares at the grass and bites her nail, brow knotting tighter. I don't know what wars behind her dark eyes, but I resist the urge to interrupt her thoughts. But as the moments pass, my mind already tries to think of another alternative.

Finally, Nadia lifts her head and takes a long, deep breath. "Okay. I'll do it." Her words tremble slightly but she looks at me and forces a weak smile. "For the Rapid supers. For all of us."

I let out a breath and grab her hand to squeeze it gently. "Thank you, Nadia," I breathe. She's got to be the bravest person I know.

Nadia's hand trembles, so I continue to squeeze it. "Okay, Nadia can break down the gate, and she and I can try to get the children through right away."

"While the rest of us hold off the guards so you can get through," Ares finishes.

I nod. "Right. Then everyone can follow after us." Or whoever's left. Tension clutches my chest. I can't pretend everyone will make it out of this.

I meet each of their gazes. When I reach Seth, he looks away. I take a deep breath. "That's the plan, then?"

Nadia and Ares meet my eyes and nod. I turn to Seth. "Seth?"

He only meets my gaze for a moment before looking away again, fingers knotting in his lap. "I don't know...all those supers free..."

I let go of Nadia's hand to lean over and squeeze Seth's shoulder. "It'll be okay, all right?" I need everyone to be strong, do their part. But he worries me, the way his fingers fidget and his eyes dart around. He's afraid—we all are. But will he let his fear turn against us?

He finally meets my gaze and nods weakly.

I let go of his shoulder. "Okay, good." I stand and stretch, glancing briefly at the doctor monitoring us and the nearest guards. "I'm going to tell Ivon," I whisper. I don't know when we'll get a chance to carry the plan through, but all Ivon needs to know is to be ready. And tell others the same.

I round the tree toward the garden. Seth trips after me. "Scarlett, wait."

I slow until he catches up, but I don't stop. "What is it? Are you feeling okay?"

He waves a hand, but I catch his fingers trembling. "Yeah, yeah." He bends nearer, lowering his voice. "You're checking the note?"

"Yeah," I whisper back, frowning at him. "That's what I just said."

His fingers fidget with the neck of his jumpsuit as his eyes dart around the grounds.

Still eyeing him, I crouch at the edge of the garden, on the opposite side of where the note is, so I don't go to the same spot every time. There aren't as many weeds on this side, but I find a few to pull out

Seth sits beside me, glancing at the line of guards behind us. "Are you absolutely sure this is a good idea?"

I wish he'd stop looking at the guards like that. "Hey, relax." I step to the side to get more weeds.

"But—"

"Seth." I turn toward him, looking at him until he meets my gaze. "Are you with us or not?"

He blinks at me and hesitates. "Yeah."

I go back to weeding, working my way around the garden toward the note's location on the other side. The closer I get, the more fidgety Seth gets. Eventually, he stands and goes back to Ares and Nadia.

I watch him leave, hand stilling over a weed with prickly leaves. He said he's with us, but...is his past too strong, too painful? Will he turn on us in the end?

I reach the patch of dying flowers and wilting grasses. There aren't many weeds left, so I work quickly to find the note with my right hand while leisurely pulling the remaining weeds with my left. The back of my neck warms, thinking of the line of guards behind me. It takes every bit of strength I have to relax and keep my breaths slow and even.

My fingers scratch against the edge of the paper. I move aside the soil, pluck out the folded note, and spread it out among the grasses. I grab the pen, ignoring the dirt collecting under my nails, and write as fast as I can, in as few words as possible, the plan we just formulated. At the end I add, *We don't know when, but soon. Just be ready. Tell others.* I pause, then scratch out my first sentence, writing above it: *Tomorrow.*

I jump when the door to the grounds clicks open. My heart lurches in my throat and I crumple the paper in my fist and stuff it back into the hole. I suck in a deep breath as I stand and look toward the doors, brushing dirt from my hands and the knees of my jumpsuit.

Dr. Bailey's shoes crunch on dry grass as he strides toward us.

Dr. Bailey? Out here? Why is he here? My heart thuds faster. Does he suspect something? I bend quickly to scrape more dirt off my hands on the grass, then walk back over to the others.

Ares and Nadia stand stiffly as the doctor approaches, while Seth stays on the ground, glancing between Dr. Bailey and Ares. When I reach them, I glance at Ares too. His jaw is set, eyes cold as he stares at his father. Nadia and I share a look, and I see the same worry in her eyes. Why is the doctor here?

He stops when he nears us, holding his hands behind his back. He smiles at each of us, rocking happily back on his heels. "I'd say today was pretty successful."

We glance between each other. Maybe successful to him. I resist clenching my hands as I eye him. Did he come to gloat?

"Depends on your standards of success," Ares states. His hands curl into fists.

The doctor's smile falters for a split second. "I trust you're all still feeling well?"

Now my hands clench. Did he already forget about Seth in the midst of the attention of the press? I glance at Seth to see how he'll answer, but he nods. Our heads bob in response.

"Good, good." He clears his throat, looking around the grounds uncomfortably.

Dr. Hiram Bailey at a loss for words? This gives me more satisfaction than it should.

He turns his focus to Ares, lips pressed together. "Ares, I..." He trails off and flicks a glance at the rest of us.

"Whatever it is, I don't want to hear it," Ares snaps. He crosses his arms and sits back down on the grass, glaring at the ground.

Dr. Bailey's cheerful mood fades altogether as he stares at his son and he clears his throat again. "Yes, well, I..." He clenches his jaw and shakes his head, then beckons to the nearest guard. "Take them back to their units."

Fire engulfs me. Surrounds me. Pressing in on me until I can't breathe. The roar of the flames fills my ears. I turn in frantic circles, looking for an escape in the ring of fire. But it's thick and angry, reaching its tendrils toward me. The heat crowds closer, closer...

I burn.

My skin burns. The flames lick over me, agonizing pain searing through my entire being. Screams—my screams—echo around me. I can't get away from it, can't escape it. Suddenly I'm curled up on the ground, a small thought deep in my mind wondering...wondering...

About a time when I didn't burn. When the fire was mine. When I was the fire.

Now I burn.

I flinch awake, panting. I rub my hands over my arms, where the charred skin was. My skin tingles beneath the touch and the vivid memory of the lingering dream. My heart beats frantically and I rub a hand over my face, finding sweat slick against my skin. Fingers tremble as I press them against my mouth, trying to forget the nightmare.

A low, whispered voice makes me freeze. I open my eyes to find myself facing the other units, the white light glowing beneath the glass walls. Everything else is cast in the shadow of night.

In Ares' unit, a tall figure stands over his bed.

Alarm blares in my head and I almost snap upright. But something about the posture, the voice, is familiar.

Dr. Bailey.

I tug the blanket to cover most of my face, just leaving my eyes free. I half close them and strain to catch the low voices.

"Why do you care?" Ares hisses, throwing his blanket off and sitting up to glare up at his father.

Dr. Bailey's missing his usual pristine lab coat, revealing a simple button-up shirt and tie. He rakes both hands through his hair. "She's my daughter, Ares."

"Yeah. So why did you—"

"I didn't have a choice!" He smacks the mattress.

Seth groans in his sleep and stirs. They both go silent, breathless until all is quiet again. Dr. Bailey takes a deep breath, lowering his voice again. "I've explained this to you and your mother a million times—"

"I guess you don't understand what family is supposed to be, *Doctor Bailey*."

Even in the dim light, I can see the muscle in the doctor's jaw bulge as he clenches it. "I'm not the one who left you. Your mother was the one who ran away—"

Ares shoves him. "I would've left too if I was old enough. But I didn't have a chance to grow up, did I? Unless you call living ten years in this place a good childhood."

Dr. Bailey's hands flex at his sides and his shoulders shudder with breath after breath. He growls and turns away toward the dark viewing window. His next words come out strained and shaky. "Ares, will you just tell me if you found her?"

With his father's back turned toward him, Ares quickly swipes a hand across his eyes. "If I found her, you wouldn't have heard from me again."

Dr. Bailey lifts a fist as if to punch the glass. Slowly, he forces it back down to his side. "Did you...find out anything? About where she might be?"

Ares wipes his hands across his eyes again. "I was trying. My time was cut short."

Slowly, the doctor turns around, eyes on the floor. "I thought maybe...it was enough time."

"It wasn't."

Dr. Bailey straightens his shoulders. When he lifts his gaze to his son, he plasters that familiar composure over his expression. Indifferent, cold, controlled. "Well, that wasn't the main goal anyway—"

"You've got to be kidding." Ares shakes his head and scoffs sharply. "You took her to the SCF, lost her to some supers, then took out your revenge on all superhumans? You would've lost her anyway if you got her into the SCF." He pauses, spine weakening. "Just like you've lost me."

The doctor's composure cracks and a shudder runs through him, but he plasters his mask back together in only a moment. "I..." He clears his throat and straightens his tie. "Excuse me." He brushes past Ares and leaves the unit. The door clicks closed behind him, then the units are blanketed in silence.

Ares slumps, wiping the heels of his hands over his cheeks. He sniffs hard then falls weakly back on the mattress. But he doesn't sleep. His eyes remain wide open, staring up at the ceiling, and his breath hitching every now and then.

I blink back the sting behind my eyes. I can't imagine being locked up here for so many years, let alone my own father acting like he doesn't know me. I clench my fist. I'll help him find his sister. After all this is over, I'll help him make his family whole again.

After overhearing the conversation between Ares and his

father, I barely sleep. A few minutes of dozing here and there. Mostly I stare at the dark ceiling, rubbing my fingers on my palms, willing warmth into them. I try to coax my fire despite my exhaustion, and it barely responds. My body feels weak, lacking in the warm energy that usually flows through it.

My foot taps in rhythm with my pattering heartbeat. We're running out of time. If we don't have enough of our powers left... that might complicate things with the escape.

I look over to Nadia's unit, where she still sleeps, curled into a ball. She said she was willing to use her power for the escape plan, but I can't help but remember what she told me about her cousin, her powers, that building...

Like Seth's, is her past too heavy for this task?

I'm already sitting up in bed by the time morning comes and the lights flick on in the units. Still huddled under the blanket, I try to savor the short time of quiet before the reporters start arriving.

My mind goes numb as the morning's regular activities progress. Nurses come in to check on us, Dr. Bailey comes later. Reporters and cameras fill the viewing room. We're given breakfast. I go through the motions without a word, mind on the note crumpled in the dirt and the mountain of a task that stands before me.

I can't fail. I *won't.*

The busyness around the units spins tightness in my chest. But finally, guards come to escort us to the outdoor grounds. As soon as I step onto the dry grass I suck in a deep breath of fresh air. The units can get so stuffy sometimes. The late morning sunshine casting beams of golden light over the grounds tries to lift my mood, but it's like tying a single balloon to an anvil. I scan the building looming above our heads as I follow the others toward our tree. We don't seem to have enough energy to do anything else.

As soon as we settle on the crunching grass, Seth leans forward to whisper, "Are you sure we can do this?"

"It'll work," Nadia says immediately.

I swallow. I hope she's right.

Ares, without moving his head, scans over the line of guards at the perimeter, to the doctor by the exit door. "I think we have a good plan. It'll work—"

Seth sighs. "But how can you be sure? Maybe we shouldn't do it, huh? It's pretty risky."

Ares nods. "I know, but we have to try—"

"Things could go wrong. *Very* wrong."

I gnaw my lip and share a look with Nadia and Ares. Yes, it could go wrong. But like Ares said, we have to try. We have to give the supers that chance.

Nadia grimaces and rubs the back of her neck. "Let's talk about something else for a minute or too, huh?"

Ares and Seth blink at her while I study the way she takes quick, shallow breaths and her fingers tremble. Is she nervous about her part in the plan? Can she do it? Images flash across my mind. Nadia standing like a frozen statue as we were attacked by Mikey's gang. Then again later when Rez was stopping them from leaving Rapid. She just stood there, afraid.

But she wouldn't do that again, I tell myself. She believes in this cause as much as I do. She wouldn't let us down.

Ares raises an eyebrow. "Sure, I guess." Silence follows as he tries to come up with something to say. "So...everyone get good sleep?"

I blink, eyes stinging after the night I had. I flick a glance at Ares. Dark circles rim his eyes and exhaustion pulls at his face.

Seth waves a hand dismissively, seeming to be able to breathe better with the topic change too. "Boring topic."

Ares crosses his arms. "Think of something better then."

Seth taps his chin. "Maybe...Oh!" He snaps his fingers. "What's your favorite ice cream topping?"

Nadia groans and rubs her stomach. "Does everything have to be about food with you?"

Seth shrugs and proceeds to give us a list of toppings he'll accept on his frozen dessert. But I barely hear him. His question took me back to that summer night at the ice cream shop. I tuck my knees under my chin and wrap my arms around myself. That familiar ache blooms in my chest. Eating ice cream with Dylan and Hannah, talking about music with Ian. And the attack in the alley. I shudder thinking of those flames again. Those roaring, devouring flames. My own fire tries to awaken at the thought, and pulses a faint spark of energy through me.

All conversation stops when the guards step forward from their posts. As we stand to be taken back to our units, my mind darts to the note stuffed in the dirt and my breath quickens. Can we really do this? I square my shoulders. Yes. We can do this. We *have* to do this. I do my best to hang on to this new resolve and confidence as we march through the hall to our units.

As I settle onto my upright bed, I catch Nadia looking at me, worry etched on her brow. I straighten my spine and offer a reassuring smile. She takes a deep breath and some of the worry leaves her face as a slight grin lifts her lips.

I barely notice the nurses bustling around, checking on us, making sure we're comfortable. Reporters and cameras crowd the viewing window. My recent confidence seeps away, replaced by frustration at the noise, the people. My breath comes quicker, as if the crowd presses the oxygen from the room. I rake a glare over them all. They shrink away from my gaze, reporters and guards alike. All...except one.

I freeze. Through the crowd, a pair of familiar green eyes meet mine.

Ian.

CHAPTER TWENTY-EIGHT

My breath stills in my lungs as my jaw goes slack. My mind spins painfully, questions knocking against my skull like rocks.

How...how is *he* here?

Suddenly there's no one else in the room, just one of my best friends, the boy with the big music dreams that he was going to chase no matter what. Dressed...

As a security guard.

My fingers dig into the mattress. Questions coil on my tongue, ready to hurl through the glass. So many questions, so many things that don't fit. Why is he here, let alone as a guard? He doesn't break eye contact, even as Dr. Bailey comes into my unit.

"Scarlett, how are you feeling?"

I blink. Ian. Here. What happened to—

"Scarlett."

I jolt, finally looking up at the doctor. But my gaze keeps trailing back to Ian. "What?"

"I asked you how you're feeling."

"Oh. Fine."

Ian's face morphs into a frown as he looks around the room. Reporters begin to glance between us, confusion written on their faces. Redness creeps up Ian's neck and face. He looks away from me.

Is he...embarrassed?

"Are you sure you're fine?"

How is he here? Why *is he here?* What happened back home that he has a job at the SCF?

A sharp sigh. "Scarlett—"

"I'm sure." I grab his sleeve, resisting the urge to point. "Who..." I break off. No, I can't ask him. Something tells me that if others realize that Ian and I know each other, it could complicate things, though I don't exactly know how.

"Who what?" Irritation hardens the doctor's voice.

I let go of his sleeve and he straightens it. Ian still won't look at me. "Nothing. Never mind."

Dr. Bailey leaves to go to Nadia's unit, nurses following him. I force my gaze away from Ian, yet I can't help but flick a glance at him every so often, willing him to look at me again, to tell me he isn't ashamed. But he doesn't budge. Some reporters continue to look between us. The last thing I want is to cause Ian trouble, so I look away too, trying my best to smooth out my frown and act like the crowded room opposite me is only stuffed full of strangers.

But that's not true. And my mind keeps spinning because of it. Why would he work for the SCF? What happened to college, to music? I press a hand over my chest as my gaze sweeps to him again. With the escape plan unfolding tomorrow, he might get caught in the middle. He flicks his eyes to me for a split second before they dart away again. I don't want him to get hurt in the middle of this. Why, why, *why* does this have to happen *now*?

His SCF security guard uniform glares at me. Whether I like it or not, Ian has already been pulled into this simply by being here. His clothes and posture say he works for the SCF but...he'd help us, right? When the fight comes, he'd help me...

Right? Suddenly I'm not sure if I know this boy as well as I thought I did.

Sleep is a foreign thing tonight.

I lie under the layers of blankets, staring at the ceiling. My body lies still but my mind moves, spinning at dizzying speeds. With each nervous heartbeat a question flies through my head.

Why is Ian here? Will this change things?

Will the plan work? I hope Ivon sees the message.

What if someone suspects something and stops us? What if—

A rustling of sheets and a sigh halt my thoughts. I roll over to my side to see Nadia blinking up at the ceiling, hands tucked behind her head.

I sit up. "You awake?"

She jumps at my voice, then sits up when she sees me. "Nope. You?"

I chuckle. "Sound asleep." I grow sober again, stomach twisting as if I'm on a stage about to perform the most important song of my life.

Nadia slides out of bed and kneels in front of the glass separating us. "Nervous?"

I join her on the floor, trying to ignore the way the coldness of the tiles make my joints ache. "Yeah." I rub my middle. "Stomach's all in knots."

She nods, sighing. "Mine too." She shakes her head. "I just keep thinking. What if...what if..."

"I know. I—" A pulse of warmth flares in my core, silencing my words. I frown and stare at my stomach.

"What's wrong?"

"I don't know. It kind of felt like..." Like that familiar fiery energy, when it wakes up after lying dormant for a while. I wait, but nothing more happens. "It's probably nothing."

Nadia studies me. "You sure?"

"Yeah, it's probably something I ate." As I try to chuckle, another wave of heat pulses through me. Faint, but unmistakable as tingly energy zips through my arms. I rub my fingers together. They're no longer numb and stiff from the cold.

"Scarlett?"

I stare wide-eyed at my hand. "I feel it, Nadia."

She leans forward, worry in her eyes as she looks back and forth from my face to my hand. "Feel what?"

"M-my fire. I think..." A warning blares in my head to not grab onto hope. Don't set myself up for a let-down. But I can't deny the soft pulse of heat in my veins. It's faint, but I've become familiar enough with my fire to know what its energy feels like.

Nadia presses a hand against the glass. "Is it...coming back?"

I dig deep for the remnants of fire in my core. It responds to my beckoning, growing and warming underneath my skin. A smile grows on my face when I look at Nadia. I press a fist to my heart. "It's there. I can feel it. It's fighting against the serum." The more I try to coax it to flow through my veins, the stronger it seems to grow. I release it, letting it retreat to my core again before it gets too strong.

A smile splits my face, but falters. Will it be enough for tomorrow?

Nadia grins. "That's great, Scarlett," she whispers.

My smile just gets wider. "Try yours."

She hesitates. "That's okay. I'll do it later." Her smile fades altogether as she looks over her shoulder at the boys' sleeping forms. "What about the tests?"

"What do you mean?"

"They'll run more tests to see how strong our powers are. What do we do? If they see it's coming back then they might use more serum."

My hands fall to my lap as I chew my lip in thought. "We can fake it."

"Fake it?"

"Yes. Ares said they can detect that we have powers in our bodies using their tech, but they may not be able to tell how strong they are unless we use it against the sensors. We'll just only use very little, keeping with the success pattern so far."

Nadia nods slowly, biting her lip. "Could work. Let's do it." She glances over her shoulder again. "I'll tell the boys, in case theirs are starting to come back too."

I nod. "Okay." I hesitate. Besides once in the testing room, Seth has never tried using his powers after the injections. I chew my lip. Why is the cure affecting him so differently? I just hope that once we get out of here, he'll be himself again.

I turn my attention back to Nadia to find her staring at her hands. "Hey, you sure you don't want to try yours?"

She rubs her hands together, giving me a weak grin. "I'm sure. I'll do it later." She flicks a brief glance at the ceiling and the walls, as if surveying their strength. Are her memories plaguing her again?

Before I can ask, she moves on. "So...tomorrow, huh?" Her voice trembles slightly.

I nod, stomach twisting tighter again. "Yeah...tomorrow." I squeeze my eyes shut, determined not to let the doubts and fears start swirling in my mind.

"We can do this."

I open my eyes to find Nadia smiling gently, shoulders squared. She gives a sharp nod.

I smile back and straighten my spine, returning her nod.

She stands. "Better get some good sleep. Good night."

The cold reminds me of its presence as I stand. "You're right. G'night."

I climb into bed and shiver as I pull the layers of blankets over me. Settled under the covers, I look over my shoulder at her curled form facing away from me. The blanket rises and falls with her even breaths, but I know she's not sleeping, not yet. What tomorrow holds seems to keep my own eyes open too. Maybe neither of us will sleep tonight.

My eyes sting from lack of sleep when morning comes. I expect another morning filled with the rush of nurses and doctors preparing us for another injection, reporters and cameras crowding closer than ever, making it hard to breathe.

The reporters are still watching behind the viewing window, but no nurses. No Dr. Bailey. No syringes filled with blue liquid. I scan the faces. No Ian either.

We're left pretty much alone with our breakfasts. My twisted stomach doesn't want to accept the food, but I eat anyway. As I fork scrambled eggs into my mouth, I cast a glance at the others. They poke at their food, barely eating.

It's not until after the nurses take away our food trays that Dr. Bailey steps into my unit. More nurses follow him, the familiar sensor equipment in their hands.

I swipe my sweaty palms on my jumpsuit pants and climb back into bed. Even though we all stare at him, wondering why there isn't another injection, Dr. Bailey says nothing as he prepares me for the test.

When I clear my throat, he jumps and looks at me like he didn't even realize I was in the room.

"Oh." He clears his throat. "Just tests today. No injection." I watch him as he goes through the motions, slipping out his tablet and frowning at the screen. His eyes are red and dark circles frame them.

I venture to ask the same question he asks us a million times. "You okay?"

He jolts again and blinks at me. The nurses glance at me. "I'm...fine," he says, still seeming surprised by my question.

I'm not convinced. "Are you sure?" I say, mimicking his voice.

He raises his eyebrows, but this draws a light chuckle. But he doesn't answer, instead making sure the egg-shaped sensors are secure in my palms. "Go ahead."

I almost forget. I almost throw all my effort into drawing my fire into my hands. I stop myself just in time, closing my eyes, concentrating on the output of my fire. Just a faint glimmer of warmth reaches my veins, then I release.

"Hmm." Dr. Bailey's grunt makes me open my eyes again. He frowns at his tablet. "Once more."

I do the same again.

He raises an eyebrow, nodding at the screen, grunting again. "Interesting." He takes the sensors off me and moves to Nadia's unit.

As soon as he's gone, I let out a breath. Just to make sure that it wasn't my imagination last night, I try to draw the fire from my core. Soft, tentative heat warms my limbs, driving away the cold in my bones from the serum.

While Dr. Bailey goes through the tests with Nadia, my foot bounces impatiently. I twist to look at the clock displayed on the screen by the door. *10:00am.* We should be scheduled for outdoor time soon.

My stomach twists and I suck in a breath. Sweat dampens my brow and I knot my fingers together beneath the bedsheet. I swipe a sleeve across my forehead. Just stay calm. Everything will work out fine.

My gaze swings to Nadia again. Her eyes meet mine for a fraction of a second, then bounce away. She chews her lip again, rolling the egg-shaped sensors in her palm. Dr. Bailey places a hand on her arm to stop the nervous fidgeting. She takes a deep breath and nods at something he says. Even though I know she will hold back her powers, I still hold my breath until Dr. Bailey takes the sensors away.

The doctor doesn't say a word while he tests Ares, who stares straight ahead at the reporters. I find myself holding my breath again, hoping Nadia was able to get the message to them to use only a small amount of their powers. But Dr. Bailey's reaction to Ares' test is no different than mine and Nadia's, so I assume he got the message.

Once finished with Ares, Dr. Bailey moves on to Seth. It only takes him a few minutes to finish the test. Then, as the nurses carry away the equipment, he taps on his tablet a while more then slips it back into his pocket. Our unit doors open to let in guards.

I sit up straighter. "Are we going outside?"

Dr. Bailey moves toward the door. "No. We have another test to run downstairs. Shouldn't take long, but it's important."

My jaw clenches. I hope it'll be quick. Even though my stomach knots as tight as a taut guitar string, I itch to get outside and go through with the plan. It's time for the Rapid supers to be free.

We march through the SCF facilities in silence, traveling down to the underground levels and through familiar low-ceilinged hallways. The guards leave us in the large concrete testing room again.

We stay nervously clustered near the door. Ares leans toward us. "Be happy," he whispers.

Seth frowns. "Huh?"

Ares keeps his eyes on the viewing window, where Dr. Bailey stands with an army of reporters and cameras behind him. "After we act like our powers are almost completely gone, celebrate like you're happy."

We all nod subtly, then turn our attention to the doctor. He turns to whisper something to one of the suited men standing next to him, then back to us. "Okay, we'll just run through the same routine. Anyone up for going first?"

Seth raises his hand. "I will." He makes his way to the middle of the room then sets his feet apart for balance before raising his hands. After a deep breath, he begins the same waving motion, trying to coax a breeze from the stagnant air. Nothing happens. No brush of wind against my skin.

I frown. Didn't Nadia tell them to use only a small amount of their power? I glance at her, but she just shrugs.

That same excited murmur reaches us from the crowd of reporters, but I barely notice this time as I stare at Seth. His skin pales and a bead of sweat glints in the light as it slides down his temple.

Does he have powers left?

Dr. Bailey rubs his jaw, gesturing toward us with the other hand. "Next."

Ares shrugs. "I'll go." He passes Seth to the center of the room, then lifts a fist to his face. I can't help but glance between Ares and Dr. Bailey, hoping his fascination with the cameras' attention will keep him from suspecting anything.

A faint frost creeps over Ares' fingers and some of the rosy hue fades from his cheeks. Before the frost can reach his arm, he drops his hand with a released breath.

Dr. Bailey drops his hand from his face and steps closer to the viewing window. "Scarlett, if you please."

I gulp and pass Ares to take his place. As he passes my shoulder, I detect the slightest chill emanating from him. When I reach the center of the room, I lift my palm upward, my other hand fidgeting with the leg seam of my jumpsuit as all eyes turn to me.

First, I press all my fire down, letting the cold of the room shove it to the depths of my core. Then, slowly, I let a trickle of the energy seep out. A whisper of a flame pools in my palm. Before it can grow, I drop my hand, turning my attention back to the doctor, pretending to be breathing hard.

"Hmm." He steps even closer to the glass. The murmuring of the reporters has stopped, replaced by rapt silence. I feel every person in the room inching forward, vying for a better look.

They think history is being made. They think the cure is working. That our powers are all but gone.

Nadia passes me on the way to the concrete slab on the other side of the room. Her shoulders are set as she strides toward the concrete, but I catch the faintest wrinkle of her forehead. I try to draw from her strength despite the nerves.

I reach the boys and turn to join the rest of the people intently watching Nadia as she places her hands on the concrete.

After a deep breath, she hunches her shoulders over the surface, pressing the heels of her hands into it. Faintly, with the rhythm of a ticking clock, pulses of vibrations tremble the concrete.

The quake doesn't even reach my feet when Nadia steps back from the concrete, arms hanging limp at her sides.

Dr. Bailey lets out a breath and the sound echoes through the whole space. The murmur of the reporters resumes in full force, growing into elated shouts and rushed strings of words as they relay information to the cameras. I imagine the country, watching from their TVs at home, applauding the success. The suited men give Dr. Bailey firm handshakes and hearty claps on the back. He gives smiles to them all, waving at the cameras like a celebrity.

Nadia walks back over to us, a tight smile plastered to her face. My lips purse before I manage a smile. We're supposed to be celebrating.

Seth gives a whoop that makes us all jump. Nadia gives me a quick hug and a pat on the shoulder. Ares grins, though forcefully. Seth turns to him. "Well, I ain't hugging you." He extends a hand.

Ares huffs, then returns the handshake. "Thanks."

Cheers and laughter from the viewing room echoes through the speakers. It takes all my strength not to let that plastered smile fall. Every bit of willpower not to let my fire flare in anger at their celebration. Celebration because they think they've gained control.

But the doctor has no idea how we're about to shatter his world.

CHAPTER TWENTY-NINE

Once Dr. Bailey remembers that we're still present, he orders the guards to take us to the lab down the hall. As I step into the same lab where Dr. Bailey tested me after I got back from Rapid, the lingering guilt of my betrayal tickles me. I swallow it down and settle into one of the four chairs facing the stuffed viewing room. Nurses step forward to secure the restraining straps.

I tug against the straps, shifting back and forth to see over the heads of the reporters to the line of security guards in the back. I plop back into the seat with a sigh. No Ian. I want to talk to him before we attempt our escape, but I don't know how.

I calculate how much time we've lost running these tests so far. My foot bounces nervously.

Dr. Bailey barely looks at us as he places sensors on our bodies. Watching him walk around, drunk on the applause of the reporters, nurses, other doctors, and mysterious government men makes my fire want to surface. I stuff it down, letting the cold of this basement lab claim my muscles instead. Still, my heart beats a wild tempo against my chest.

Dr. Bailey can't seem to stop grinning or glancing at the viewing window as he conducts the test. He finally tears his eyes away from the cameras to type on his tablet.

A door opening echoes behind us, followed by the clip of high heels. "Dr. Bailey, you're needed for an interview."

The doctor hurriedly slips the tablet back into his pocket. "Oh, yes, of course. I'll be there right away."

I purse my lips. "Dr. Bailey?"

He turns to hand a nurse the testing sensors and gives her some instructions I can't hear.

"Dr. Bailey?" I repeat, louder.

He turns, irritation breaking through the entranced grin. "What?"

"Can we be let outside?"

He waves a hand. "Sure, sure."

Guards step forward, unstrap us, then escort us up the snaking path to the outdoor grounds. When we step onto the grass, I watch the guards out of the corner of my eyes as they settle into their usual posts. Again, a doctor takes up his position near the door, tablet in hand. I force myself to take even steps toward our tree, but my hands still shake, betraying me.

Seth jogs toward the basketball court, making a beeline for the ball sitting in the grass. "Wanna play a game?"

We whip frowns at him.

"Seth," I hiss. "Not now."

He balances the ball on his head, arms spread wide. "Why not?"

"Seth, get over here," Ares practically growls.

The ball tips off Seth's head as he returns our frowns. He looks at the basketball again, but slowly strides over to us.

We lower to the grass under our tree, but I twist to look toward the garden. "Should I check the note? In case Ivon said something?"

Ares shoves to his feet. "I'll check it."

He disappears and tense silence blankets us. It takes all my concentration not to act nervous. Nadia sits beside me, taking slow, even breaths. Seth on the other hand, fidgets with his sleeves, his hair, and glances repeatedly at the guards and doctor monitoring us.

"Calm down, Seth," I say quietly. If he's not careful, he could draw unwanted attention our way.

Seth barely looks at me, but at least he stares at the grass instead of the guards. I eye him, lips pursed. I just hope he's been telling the truth. I hope he really is going to help us.

A few moments pass before Ares comes back, pale hands streaked with dirt. He sits then scrubs his palms on the grass. "Ivon said they'll be ready."

I take a deep breath and nod. They're ready. We're ready. It's time.

I suck in another breath and rub the knot forming in my stomach. "Okay." I pause to meet each of their gazes. "You guys ready?"

They pause to swallow, take deep breaths, gather themselves. Ares and Nadia nod. I look to Seth to find him looking over his shoulder at a guard.

"Seth, are you listening?"

He blinks at me. "Huh? Me?"

I purse my lips. "Yes. Are you ready?"

He hesitates, gulping. But he nods, although shaky.

"Okay. So here's how we're going to get Dr. Bailey's attention...We're valuable at this point, and he thinks the cure is working. What would get his attention is if one of us were not to feel well." I pause, glancing at Ares. "Ares, this is where you come in. You'll fake being sick and we'll get Dr. Bailey out here."

A hint of panic flickers in Ares' ice blue eyes, but he takes a deep breath and sets his jaw, then nods. "Got it."

"I'll try to get to Dr. Bailey." I lift a hand to stare at my palm, urging my fire to warm. A wispy flame tickles my fingers. "I'll use him as leverage to get us to the units to open them. Things might be easier when our numbers are larger."

They nod. Some of my readiness washes away in the face of the nervousness clawing at my chest. I look each of them in the eye. When Nadia squeezes my hand, I realize how much they're shaking.

"Okay, guys," I say, breaths already coming quicker. "This is it. Just...do your best. I'm sure everything will work out." It feels like a lie, because I have no way of knowing how this will turn out. But they all nod. They're ready.

"I still think this is a bad idea," Seth mumbles.

I huff a frustrated sigh. "Yeah, I already know you think so."

He sits up suddenly, looking intently at me. "I think we should call it off. Maybe we're wrong—"

"Seth," I hiss. "It's fine. Everything will be fine." I raise an eyebrow. "Okay?"

He looks away, brow furrowed.

I study him a moment later, sighing again, then turn to Ares. "Okay. Then let's do this. Ares, you're up."

He nods again. Then he presses a hand to his head, feigning light-headedness and leaning to the side.

"Ares?" I say loud enough for the doctor to hear.

Nadia, Seth and I crowd around Ares, propping his limp form against the tree.

"Got the doctor's attention," Nadia whispers.

I look over my shoulder to see the doctor's face twisted with concern as he strides toward us. He motions toward a couple guards and they flank him.

"Get Dr. Bailey!" I yell at them. "Quick!"

A guard breaks off to run back into the building, while the other guards crowd closer. The doctor shoves past them to get to Ares first.

It's as if doctors, nurses and guards descend from the sky. In no time at all, Ares is surrounded by people. They hover over him, press against him, checking his pulse, asking questions. I crowd with them, plastering panic and concern on my face, Seth and Nadia close by my side, as Ares still feigns sickness. I scan the faces of the doctors. Where's Dr. Bailey? Why isn't he here yet?

A few of the guards grab us by the elbows, pulling us back from the crowd toward the exit door. I tug against the guard's grip on my arms, still trying to get a look at Ares. But something doesn't feel right. The hands gripping my arms should be hard and firm. These are loose, unsure. The guard shifts from one foot to another, then clears his throat.

I twist to face him, heart fluttering. "Ian?"

The black helmet stares at me, then he jerks a hand up to flip the visor away. "I can hardly breathe in that." His blond brows furrow over those familiar green eyes as he looks at me. Faint stubble shadows his chin. Is he taller?

My eyes fly wide. "Ian!"

"*Shh!*"

My heart pounds against my ribs at finally seeing him here, face to face. I lower my voice to a whisper, but can't help the questions that flood out. "What are you doing here? Is everything back home okay? Why—"

"*Shh,*" he hisses again, glancing at the crowd still huddled over Ares. "I can't explain everything now."

I frown at the look in his eyes, because I can't read it. He keeps his gaze on the commotion, jaw tight. Again, he won't look at me, no matter how long I stare at him. "Ian...why are you working at the SCF?"

He still doesn't meet my gaze. He stares unseeing at the commotion around Ares, chewing his lip, forehead wrinkled. "Things...changed. After you left."

Panic twists my stomach. Things changed? How? "Is everyone okay?"

"Yes, everyone's fine," he says, but a note of frustration laces his tone.

My mind jumbles in knots, trying to make sense of this boy and why he's here, why he won't tell me more, look me in the eye. What happened to my best friend who had big dreams in music, his future all planned out to reach his goals? What made him give that up for this?

Nadia casts a concerned glance at me from nearby, a guard holding her from behind. As much as I want to sit Ian down and demand he tell me what's going on, I need to finish what I started here. But I will find out. There's something he's not telling me. That thought makes my stomach twist tighter.

I scan the doctors again. Still no Dr. Bailey. Where is he?

My eyes trail down to the handgun at Ian's side. His hand only loosely holding my elbow, I stretch for it, keeping my gaze on the nearest guards who might see.

His hand snaps around my wrist. "What do you think you're doing?"

My fingers still stretch for the weapon, even as his grip makes my fingertips go numb. "Ian, listen to me—"

"Scarlett, this isn't—"

"Listen. I need to do this. I have to get the Rapid supers back home."

Finally, he looks at me, eyes wide, mouth forming an O. "You've got to be *kidding*, Lettie!"

"*Shh!*"

His jaw clenches. "That's crazy." Will he try to stop us?

My heart stutters. "I know it sounds crazy. Look, I can't explain everything right now. Maybe someday. You don't understand everything that's going on here. I need you to trust me." I pause. "And let me take the gun."

Now he stares at me, studying my face. He opens his mouth to speak, then closes it. His face twists with confusion and concern as he looks around the grounds. When he looks back at me, his brow is still knotted and mouth set in a hard line. But he gives an almost imperceptible nod.

I let out a breath. Maybe he still trusts me, maybe he's still on my side.

His grip on my wrist loosens. "Don't get hurt, Lettie," he says softly with a deep frown.

I smirk. "No promises."

The doors to the grounds fling open. Dr. Bailey storms through. "What's going on?"

As soon as I see the doctor, warm energy zips through me. I snatch Ian's gun from the holster and lunge for Dr. Bailey. I wrap my arm around his neck from behind, cutting off any further words beneath the pressure on his throat. Guards yell, lifting their guns to me, but they can do nothing else. The doctor grunts, grabbing for my arm.

He stills when I touch the gun to his temple.

My stomach roils and I feel like I'm going to throw up. My finger trembles, not daring to even touch the trigger. Surely Dr. Bailey will see through me, knowing that I'd never actually use this thing, but he stays still, bent backward against my shorter height.

Guards start toward me, then stop, glancing nervously at each other.

"Stay right there," I order. I back toward the exit door, dragging Dr Bailey awkwardly with me.

The guards shift toward Nadia and Seth, fingers twitching for weapons. Do they intend to use them as leverage to get me to drop the gun? I open my mouth to warn them against it, but Dr. Bailey cuts me off.

He flings an arm out at the guards. "No, don't hurt them!"

Realization dawns on me. By "them" he means his human science experiments. The ones with millions of dollars worth of research pumped into their bloodstream. My arm tightens a fraction as I continue backing away toward the door. "Guys, come on."

Ares hops to his feet and hurries toward me as nurses and doctors gape at him. Nadia and Seth slip out of the guards' limp grips and pass me into the building. I scan the watching people, frozen to the spot as I drag the world-famous doctor into the facility by gunpoint.

"None of you move," I say as the doors close in front of me.

Dr. Bailey shifts, but I don't loosen my grip. "That goes for you too, doctor."

"What do you think you're doing?" he growls.

"Saving the supers." Even as I say it, my voice shakes. My whole body shakes.

Nadia steps forward to dig through the doctor's pockets. Reaching into the inside pocket of his suit, she whips out an ID card. "Got it."

"Okay." My wild heartbeat knocks around my words. I tug the doctor farther down the halls, the others trailing behind me, until we reach the first row of unit doors. I nod at Seth. "Here. You watch him."

I tighten my arm around the doctor's neck, and he grunts in protest, and I hand the gun over to Seth. Then I let go of Dr. Bailey, staying close to make sure he doesn't try to run off. But he stays put, face red as he rubs his neck and shifts his fiery glare from me to Seth and the gun.

Seth stares blankly at Dr. Bailey. "Hands behind your head, doctor." His voice trembles.

Nadia stares at the ID card in her shaking hands. Gulping, she jerks it toward me. I don't know why she thinks my nerves are any better, but I take the card from her and my trembling hands fumble to keep it in my grip. "You keep him with us, Seth. If anyone threatens us, remind them who we have at gunpoint. Got it?"

His jaw clenches as he nods.

ID card between my fingers, I turn toward the first unit and swipe the card on the scanner by the door. It releases a harsh buzz and flashes red. Hands shaking, I swipe it again. Same thing.

A number pad flashes on the screen. The code.

I beckon to Seth, who stares numbly at the gun in his hands. "Seth, bring him over!"

Seth flinches then weakly gestures with the weapon at the doctor. Glaring sharply, Dr. Bailey slides along the wall toward me.

I point at the pad. "Code."

His face just hardens. I look at Seth, but he says nothing, glancing over his shoulder. I gesture toward the gun. My fire surges through me, and I settle a fiery gaze on the doctor. "You're in no position to refuse, remember?"

He stares at the weapon for an agonizingly long moment and his face pales. I never knew the doctor was capable of feeling that.

Fear.

His hand trembles violently as he reaches for the pad. A trickle of sweat catches the white light from overhead as the bead drips down his brow. He glances at us, down the hall, then at the gun, before typing the code. We all watch intently, memorizing it.

The door buzzes and swings open. I don't have time to wait to see who's inside. I just call a "come on!" and keep moving down the wall to let out more supers. Swipe, code, open. Swipe, code, open.

Every time I swipe, I look behind me to see who emerges from the last unit, scanning for Ivon's hulking form. No sign of him yet. Something in the back of my mind reminds me of Rez. I have to look for him too. Another part of me wants to avoid that meeting as long as possible.

Some supers tentatively step out into the hall, others practically trip over themselves as they leave their units. Still others only peek their heads out.

A middle-aged super grabs my arm. "Hey, what's going on?"

I smile and wave the ID card. "Rescue mission."

I turn to keep swiping. Somehow Nadia must've gotten her hands on another card, because I hear more buzzes down the hall. Supers pour out into the hallway, flooding it, pushing, shoving, almost knocking me off my feet several times.

I hop on my toes, trying to see over heads to get a view of where Seth and the doctor are, but I'm too short. And still no Ivon. Or Rez.

I wave my arm at the river of supers pressing against the walls. "Come on. We have to hurry."

I expect the supers to flow down the hall in unison, but some scatter in different directions while most just mill about the hall, their anxious and confused murmurs echoing off the walls. A super flies over our heads and I duck before his shoe smacks me in the face. I can feel—almost *taste* the panic swelling in the crowd. More flying supers circle the air above our heads and some yell angrily up at them. A thread of lightning crackles, streaking up into the air and shattering a lightbulb. People scream and cover their heads against the debris. Someone with super speed zips through the crowd, knocking people over. I get an elbow to the stomach and I grunt as I fall back against the wall.

My heart beats painfully fast, blood rushing in my ears. No, no, no. I didn't plan for this. How can I get control of this crowd of supers? I scan the faces again for Ivon. Instead I spot Nadia, eyes wide as she frantically searches in the crowd. I shoulder through the milling supers and grab her arm.

She flinches at my touch, then lets out a breath when she sees me and grabs my arm too. "I'm gonna find the kids," she yells over the noise.

I nod before she disappears again, melding in the grey jumpsuits. I get jostled against the wall again and it rattles my teeth. Frustration sparks my fire to warm, flowing energy through me.

Hard, fast footsteps sound over the nervous scramble of the supers. Yelling and screaming escalates at the right end of the hall. I jump on my toes to try to see what's going on, my ears filling with the sounds of panicked screaming.

Gunfire splits the air.

More screaming. More yelling. Supers duck, some run. Those crouching, covering their heads and shaking in fear, leave me a path to see to the other end of the hall. Black-clad guards press against the crowd, pointing their weapons, yelling, threatening. Most of the supers freeze with fear. With some, I only catch a glimpse of their snarling faces before they unleash their powers on the guards.

Gunfire again. I clamp my hands over my ears, but it stops almost as fast as it started. I drop my hands and scan the crowd again. Where is Nadia? Did she find the kids? I should go help her, but I also have to find Ivon so we have more help.

Over the heads of supers still ducked under their arms, I see a boy in grey with brown tousled hair, watching the wild commotion with wide eyes and slack jaw. His arms hang limply at his side, no gun in his hand. Seth.

But where's Dr. Bailey?

Something tells me we've lost our one point of leverage, and my stomach sinks. Did Seth let him go? I set my jaw, blocking out the sounds of the crowd as I elbow my way toward Seth, hands shaking for the nagging fear that more guards will come any moment.

I reach the edge of the crowd, but Seth is missing. A few more supers break away from the group, running down halls, letting their powers loose. I don't have time to try to call them back before they disappear.

My hands reach up to grab my hair. I need to keep the supers together, but how? Voices reach me from around the nearest bend in the hall. I can't catch the words, but I recognize Ares' voice. It's different, strained.

I round the corner to find Ares and Seth facing each other. Ares has his icy gaze leveled on Seth, hands flexing at his sides as frost crackles off his skin. "Seth, just calm down," he says.

Seth shakes his head, taking slow steps backward, fear flashing in his gaze. "No, no, this was a bad idea."

I step to Ares' side, his chill keeping me from getting too close, and eye Seth. "What's going on?"

Seth roughly swipes the sweat off his forehead with a sleeve, then points an accusing finger at me. "I told you this wasn't going to work."

My fire pulses through my veins, coiling for the fight. I suppress it, keep it calm. For now.

"I told you this was a bad idea." His voice trembles as he continues to back away.

I take a step closer to him, holding my hands out like I'm calming a skittish animal. "Everything's going to be—"

"Stop telling me that!" he spits. "Didn't you see them out there?" He gestures in the general direction of the hall that's still crowded with panic-stricken supers. My fingers fidget with the urge to go back to them, to get them out of here.

It hits me that no more guards have come. Maybe that's good, but my stomach sours. Something's not right. They should be trying to stop us right here. Where are they?

"They've gone crazy," Seth continues. He's stopped moving backward, but the fear still twists his face and sweat sticks his hair to his forehead. "If they get out of here, they're just going to do exactly what supers do. Hurt people."

I quickly scan the hall. "Where's Dr. Bailey?"

"Are you even listening?" He stifles a cough behind his hand. He clenches his jaw but his voice still trembles. "Call all this off."

No, no, no. I should've seen this coming. He wasn't really with us, was he? He's turned against us. Or maybe he planned this all along. My chest aches. Is this some of what the Rapid supers felt after I betrayed them? "You know I can't do that."

"I don't know why I let you convince me to go this far. We belong *here.* The cure was...working." He coughs again, harder this time, a grimace twisting his face.

I frown, feeling the fire and warmth pulse through me. It gets stronger by the moment, shaking off the cold grasp of the serum. The cure hasn't taken my fire...Has it taken his powers? "Seth, what's wrong? Are you feeling okay?"

His gaze sharpens. "Don't act like you care, like you're my friend..." His voice trails off, weakening as his eyes grow distant. "I thought you were my friends...but...you're leaving." He shakes his head sharply. "You don't understand." Another cough racks him. More sweat drips down his face, glistening under the harsh white light.

I venture a step forward, still holding out my hands. "Seth, there's something wrong with you. The cure—"

"No! I'm fine. There's nothing wrong with me. Dr. Bailey is fixing—"

"Where is the doctor?" Ares interjects, stepping beside me.

Seth staggers on his feet and presses a hand to his head. "You don't understand...you don't understand..."

I take another step. When Seth's eyes snap up to meet me, my fire flares energy through my body. This time, I let the heat grow, pulsing into my palms. "Seth, stop this. We can help you. Figure out what's wrong—"

"Nothing's wrong with me! Not anymore. The cure worked."

Ares and I exchange a frown. Why did our powers survive while Seth's didn't? Is the serum making him sick? Worry stirs my stomach as I remember him passing out after that one injection. Since then he hasn't quite been the same.

Before I say anything else, Seth points a finger at us. "Call it off. You have a chance here. To be normal again."

Those words hit a deep part of me. A piece that was part of me not so long ago, a piece that I rooted out. I venture another step. "Seth, I know how you feel. But we don't want to fight you."

A pulse of cold behind me makes me stiffen. Ares steps forward. "But we will if we have too."

Seth huffs sharply. "Fire and ice. A winning combination."

Ares and I exchange a glance, then step away from each other as far as the hallway walls allow.

Seth's face darkens, wet clumps of hair hanging over his eyes. With a growl he lunges for me, head ducked. I lift my palm toward him, heat coiling in my hand. But I can't bring myself to unleash the flames.

Seth collides with my stomach. I grunt and we tumble backward, rolling across the floor. When I finally get my bearings,

Seth is on top of me. Before I can try to get him off, Ares slams into him from the side and they roll across the floor.

Seth gets the high ground again, sitting on Ares stomach. Ares lifts a palm toward Seth's face. Before any ice can shoot from his hand, Seth smacks it away and lands a punch on his jaw.

I scramble off the ground and grab Seth from behind, wrapping an arm around his neck like I did with Dr. Bailey. Seth jabs a hard elbow into my ribs. I yelp, but keep my grip.

"Hold him!" Ares picks himself off the ground, and rushes to my side. I let go of Seth's neck as Ares grabs his wrists and yanks them up his back. Seth yelps at the pain as Ares pulls him to his feet and shoves him against the wall.

Seth grunts, snarling as his cheek presses against the wall. Ares still holds his arms at an odd angle, but sadness softens his face. I share a look with him. Neither one of us wants to hurt Seth. But it hurts me that things have come to this.

I sigh. "Seth, we—"

"Just shut up," he rasps. His eyes glisten. "You don't understand. You'll never understand."

My own eyes sting as I step away. "Ares, I need to..." My voice trails off as I stare at Seth, a roiling mixture of anger, fear and sadness twisting his face. What's happened to him? Why—

"Keep going," Ares says, snapping me back to the present. "I'll keep an eye on him."

I nod, head still spinning. "I'll send help as soon as I can." I cross the hall on wobbly legs to pick up the ID card I dropped on the floor.

When I turn down the halls, frustration flares in me again. The supers still mill around, grey jumpsuits blending together, confusion and fear keeping most frozen. Is it just my imagination, or are there fewer? How many broke away from the group? A million more questions hurl through my mind. What has the cure done to Seth? Where's Dr. Bailey? Was Nadia able to find all the children?

And where are the guards?

CHAPTER THIRTY

I swipe the card and punch in the code as fast as I can on unit after unit. I need to find Ivon. Eventually the faces peeking out of the opening unit doors look familiar. Hardened, sun-tanned faces. Rapid supers. Ivon must be close.

Maybe Rez too?

"Scarlett!"

The booming voice that echoes down the hall above all the noise makes me jump. I whirl around and let out a breath to see Ivon striding toward me, face hard as stone. The crowd of supers parts easily for him, while I'm jostled on every side. When he reaches me, I grab his thick arm to just stay on my feet.

"Ivon!" I yell to be heard over the noise of the crowd. A question rolls off my tongue almost without me noticing, "W-where's Rez?" My voice wavers. What will he do when he sees me? My fingers knot together.

Ivon doesn't hear my question. "We have to get out of here," he yells back, scanning over the heads of the supers.

"Wait." I press the ID card into his hand. "I need to check something."

I turn, but he grabs my arm. "What are you doing? We need to leave *now*!"

"I just need to check on someone." There's no time to explain about Ian now. That'll have to wait.

His jaw clenches as his frown deepens. "Make it quick."

As soon as his grip loosens, I slither through the crowd.

"Scarlett?" Nadia's voice is almost lost in the noise.

I turn in a circle, looking for her, but I don't see the familiar long, dark braids between all the heads and shoulders. "Go to Ivon, Nadia! Get the kids to him!" Hoping she hears me, I resume my struggle through the bodies.

Finally, I break free of the most congested area. Every beat of my heart pulses warm energy through me as I run through the halls, searching for...

I skip to a stop. "Ian!"

Sitting against the wall of the empty hallway, unit doors wide open all around him, Ian lifts his head when he sees me. "Scarlett?" he says weakly.

I run to him and pull him to his feet. "You need to get out of here." I don't know if Nadia's powers will reach the building, but I don't want anybody hurt, whether it's SCF employees or the supers that broke off from our group.

He jerks free of my grip. "Wait. You need to tell me what's going on here. You wanted me to trust you but this is—" He breaks off, running a hand through his honey-colored hair and looking at the empty units.

"I don't have time to explain now."

His gaze sharpens, almost to a glare, and I take a step back. Ian never glares except in jest, but there's no humor in his eyes now. "Do you realize what you're doing? How dangerous this is?"

I nod, not trusting my words to be strong enough. Silence passes between us as we stare at each other. Sentences form in my mind, but fall apart to form others as I try to figure out what to say.

Before I can say anything, he looks away. Again.

My jaw shifts and I consider walking away, so he doesn't have to look at me and be embarrassed or ashamed. But I need to make sure he's safe. I grab his arm again. "Ian, listen to me. You need to get out of the building. Do you understand?"

His eyes flick to me then to his boots. He nods weakly.

I shake my head. What's wrong with him? My mind still hasn't come up with a scenario that would land him here in the SCF. I want to talk to him, ask all the questions spinning in my mind, make sense of it all, but there's no time now.

I pull him to his feet and push him down the hall. "Go. Hurry. Get to safety."

With barely a glance over his shoulder, he trudges down the hall then turns out of sight.

I turn to find Ivon again, but stop. My hands clench at my sides as I look over my shoulder where Ian disappeared. I hate leaving him like this. Things feel odd and I don't know why.

Could it be that he's ashamed of me? Because I'm a super? Is my family ashamed of me too?

The thought threatens to crush me, so I shove it away and sprint down the hall. The chaotic noise of fearful supers reaches my ears before I collide with the dense mass of people. I shove my way through until I reach Ivon's side again. I grab his arm as grey jumpsuits threaten to knock me off my feet.

"Scarlett!" Nadia appears behind Ivon, clutching the hands of two kids. A small army of children follow her, crowding around her legs, grasping each other, eyes wide. I let out a breath of relief and draw near two of the youngest, who whimper fearfully, tears rolling down their cheeks.

Ivon doesn't even seem to notice us here, instead frantically searching over the heads of supers.

I tug his wrist. "We gotta go!" I turn, and slam into a human wall.

I look up into a pair of mismatched eyes. One brown. One emerald blue. My throat constricts. "R-rez..."

It's so weird to see him in the light grey SCF jumpsuit, numbers stamped above his heart. His broad shoulders don't hold the same confidence. His face hardens as he looks at me, gaze sharpening. His jaw clenches and I brace myself, ready to receive what's coming to me.

But the words don't come. Instead confusion wrinkles his forehead as he scans the children at my feet and the panicked crowd, as if in a daze. "You..." he begins weakly. "*You* did this?"

I swallow, noting a scabbed-over cut on his cheekbone. What did they do to him? "Yes," I rasp.

I'm surprised he heard the soft-spoken word as he looks back at me. He says nothing, shifting his jaw to the side, as if thinking.

I take a deep breath and step closer to him so he can hear me over the crowd. We're running out of time, but this needs to be said. Suddenly my throat grows thick and I can't swallow past the lump clogging it. I blink back the sting in my eyes. "I'm sorry, Rez." My voice scrapes past my parched throat, words trembling. "I'm so, so sorry."

His face softens slightly, and that seems to only bring more tears to my eyes. I don't bother wiping them away. He takes a slow, deep breath, then lifts a hand, hesitates, then places it tentatively on my shoulder. He swallows as his eyes glisten. "I know."

I grasp his hand, still on my shoulder, with mine, as if holding onto the small hope that he could forgive what I've done. "I'm... I'm different now. I understand." I pause to swallow hard again. "Rez, can you ever forgive—"

"Scarlett," he says gently, almost like a warning. As he gives my shoulder a squeeze, some of that old joy sparks in his eyes. He gives me a small smile, then looks over the crowd again. Despite their numb confusion and panic, he nods as if in approval. Then he looks back at me.

"I already have," he says, squeezing my shoulder again. "I'm proud of you. Even if this doesn't work out."

Joy and relief mix and warm my chest as more tears stream

down my cheeks. I swipe my sleeve across my face as Rez drops his hand. "Thank you," I rasp. I open my mouth to say more, apologize more, explain more, but he lifts a hand, cutting me off.

"It's time to lead," he says.

I blink. "Of course. We'll follow you—"

"No." He looks intently at me. "You."

"W-what?" I sputter.

He grabs my shoulders firmly. "You need to lead them out."

"What?" I gasp again.

He looks over the group of kids surrounding us. "I'll help watch the kids." Rez looks at me again, eyes piercing, urgent. "Get them out of here to the front gates."

My lungs forget how to breathe. "But...I can't, I..." Did I expect that I'd find Rez or Ivon and they'd take over for me? But I'm no leader. I'm nothing like Rez.

He swallows and takes a deep breath. "Use your powers. *Their* powers." He gestures to the confused supers still frozen with panic. "They won't be able to stop all of us if we work together."

I shake my head and open my mouth, but no words come. "Rez...Rez, I can't do this."

He gives my arms a squeeze before letting go. "Yes, you can." He pauses, and I can see that he struggles with his next words. "I believe in you."

I wonder if he's still trying to forgive me like he said he already has. Already has? While he sat alone in a cold unit? He could've been hating me, not forgiving—

I shake my head sharply. *Focus*. "Right. Okay." I've got this. Everything will be fine. I grab his wrist again. "Wait. Ares is holding Seth. Can you help him?"

He frowns. "Holding him?"

"Things...went wrong."

Ivon steps forward. "I'll go." Rez gives him a nod, and Ivon turns and shoulders into the crowd, calling over his shoulder. "Get moving!"

Rez claps me on the shoulder and I flinch. "I'll make sure everyone follows." He turns away into the crowd before I can say anything else.

I grit my teeth as I watch him disappear. My heart beats a panicked pace and my breathing shallows. Shadows blur the edges of my vision. I jerk my head. *Get it together.*

"Hey!" I wave my arms to get the crowd's attention. "Hey! Listen up!"

Several heads turn, starting a domino effect until everyone's staring at me. I gulp. "We've got to get to the front gates." Adrenaline makes my voice tremble. "We've got to go quickly—"

"What do we do when we get there?" A teenage boy with unruly red hair twists his hands nervously.

I clench my hands into tight fists and inject confidence into my voice. "We're going to take down the gate to get through. But we have to clear the way for Nadia" —I nod to her— "to get the kids through first." There's enough of us. We can do this. I swallow and square my shoulders. "Follow me."

To my surprise, they do. I have to push through the thick crowd to reach the front. But as soon as I start running down the halls, their thunderous footsteps follow. We spill through the SCF like a roaring river, collecting more supers along the way and keeping the children clustered in the middle of us. Without breaking pace, I look over my shoulder, hoping Rez got to Ares to help him.

We tear through the building then barrel outside into the growing darkness. Our large numbers split between several exits, spilling through every doorway in rivulets of grey-clad supers. Like magnets, we draw back together on the wide stretch of ground in front of the wall encircling the SCF. The main gate looms ahead.

We skid to a stop, as if to keep from falling over a cliff edge.

It's like the entire force of the SCF has come to meet us. A sea of black uniforms lines the concrete wall. At least three men to each watchtower glare down at us, bright white searchlights trained on our group. Some supers in the back of our crowd start a panicked murmur. I turn to catch glimpses through the crowd of another sea of guards filtering out of the building from behind us. Where have they all come from?

And they've all got guns. Guns pointed at us.

My heart beats in my throat. Fear reaches its icy fingers around my throat and chokes me.

A door flings open and a tall figure stumbles from the building, white coat flapping, blonde hair hanging over his face. Dr. Bailey shoves through the guards, eyes wild and panicked as he glares at them. "No!" he screeches. "Don't hurt them! Don't shoot!"

Several guards look at him like he's crazy, some in fear and confusion as they glance from him to us. They shift, not sure what to do. Leave us be and potentially let us escape, or shoot America's scientific breakthrough?

I can barely feel the chill from the serum in my body anymore, but I thank it. It may have just bought us some more time. I face the front again, squaring my shoulders and shoving away fear's clutches.

The early evening sunlight casts the scene in still, grey tones. The silence stretches taut, ready to snap with the first movement. A faint breeze, like a whisper, slithers through the supers. I shiver.

I look over my shoulder and catch Nadia's wide gaze in the midst of the other supers' pale faces. Rez stands near her, keeping his eye on the children, trying to calm them. I give her a nod. Her lip trembles for a moment before she sets her shoulders. She returns my nod and turns toward our rear, calling for half the supers to join her.

I just hope her powers are strong enough.

"Listen everybody!" I wave my arms at the fear-stricken supers. They slowly tear their attention from the guards and pin it on me. I straighten under the weight of their panic-gripped gazes. "Half go with Nadia to attack the rear while we rush the front with all we've got. Keep the fire away from the kids as we try to get to the gate."

They give no response, but they slowly shift to stare forward again, straightening their spines and fists clenching. But they're scared, eyes wide as they stare at the weapons. They dart glances at me. As if I'm their leader.

I take a stride forward and brace myself. The wind shifts my messy hair and it tickles the bruise on my cheek from Seth's attack. Warmth spreads from my core as evening darkness steadily devours the light. The growing shadows course confidence through me. My fire will shine all the brighter. I look down at my open hands. Golden, flickering fire dances in my veins, fueling the flames balling in my palms.

It's in me, this fiery creature that breathes warmth through my veins. It *is* me. This is who I am.

I lift my eyes to face the foe. They shift, glancing between each other. It's as if not a soul breathes.

A deep rumble shakes the earth beneath me. I spread my feet to keep my balance. The rumble increases to a brain-jarring earthquake. My vision blurs and the sound of earth splitting behind me pushes me forward. Pushes all of us forward.

We charge, screaming our throats hoarse. I've never seen such a beautiful mix of powers. Several launch into the sky. I blink against flashes of crackling lightning. A teenage boy hurls balls of blue energy at the enemy. A woman with a wrinkled face crouches down to press her palms to the ground. Thick vines rise from the dirt and shoot toward the soldiers.

They want to be free. They want to live their lives like everyone else. They want to make their own choices for their own lives. And I'm with them.

Gunfire pierces the air and my throat constricts. *The kids. Find the kids, get them to safety.*

I glance over my shoulder to find Nadia and Rez ushering the children right behind me. Nadia heaves in heavy breaths, her hands trembling as she rushes the kids forward. I look beyond her to see cracks splitting the earth, a fissure separating us from the soldiers at the rear. Black-clad figures lie sprawled across the ground or scrambling for weapons they've dropped. I turn to face the front again to see most of the supers drawing the soldiers away from the front gate.

I look over the fear-stricken faces of the children as they press close together, clutching each other's hands. "Stay close!"

I surge toward the gate. My fire shakes off the final cold remnants of the cure, roaring inside me like a dragon. Flames encase my hands, lighting my veins and sparking in my eyes. I bring my hands forward to create a wall of fire as we sprint toward the gate. It's as if the cure never happened, like that cold never settled into my bones and almost robbed me of my powers. It's like it's just been waiting to be released, to be accepted. It's freeing. It makes me feel light and invincible.

We're halfway to the gate looming high above us. More supers join our sprint, keeping the soldiers and guards away. I want to clamp my hands over my ears against the gunfire and screams, but I press on. I need to get the kids through.

"Stop!"

We're still a good distance from the gate when Nadia stops us. She squeezes past us to face the gate, then crouches to rest her palms on the ground.

As much as I want to see the walls of this place crumble to the ground, I turn my back toward her, keeping the kids between us, and watch our rear for attackers. Most of the battle still churns in the middle of the grounds.

That bone-jarring shake returns, pulsing through the earth. The children cry out and try to find their balance, some falling to the ground. Then the ear-splitting crack brings me around. Tiny fissures spiderweb across the huge wall and the whole grey structure shudders, trembling for a moment, then it crumbles.

Stone and dust spray outward as the wall collapses before Nadia's powers. SCF soldiers cry out, stumbling from the wreckage. Nadia doesn't waste a moment, shoving to her feet and grabbing the nearest kids' hands. "Come on!"

We run across the remaining stretch of ground. Rez scoops a couple kids into his arms and carefully steps over the rubble. A rock shifts and he trips. I gasp but he gains his footing again and disappears on the other side. Nadia and I follow him, holding the hands of the youngest and getting the oldest to help the others. As we crest the mound of rubble, I can hear supers behind us still fighting back soldiers to let us get through.

I hop down the last boulder and help down two little girls whose hands I'd been holding. Rez gathers all the children toward the edge of the crumbled debris, and they huddle against the wall behind the protection of a large boulder.

Nadia grabs my shoulder and nods toward the wall opening. "Come on."

She lifts her foot to step on a piece of wall, but I pull her back. "No, you're staying here."

She blinks. "But I want to help."

I look into her dark eyes, usually soft but now intensely holding my gaze. My ears filter through the sounds of the fight and find the noise of gunfire. I know she wants to help, but...I don't know what I'd do if she got hurt.

I grab both her shoulders. "I know, Nadia. But the kids need you."

Her gaze softens as she looks past me at the kids, cradling scraped knees, wiping tearful eyes, and hugging themselves with pale fear plastered on their faces.

She takes a deep breath and nods. "Okay, I'll stay with them."

I nod in return and hoist myself up on the first boulder. A hand grabs my arm and pulls me back down to the ground. I turn to find Rez holding my arm.

"I want you to stay here too," he says.

I gently pry his hand off, shaking my head. "No, Rez. I need to be out there. I want to help them."

He purses his lips, but his eyes soften as he studies me. "Fine. But stay close to me." He turns to climb up on the rubble.

I grab his sleeve. "Wait."

His forehead wrinkles as he turns toward me, glancing once over his shoulder at the wall opening. "What is it?"

"I just..." Why did I stop him? "I just...wanted you to know that..." I swallow and force myself to get the words out without stopping again. "I understand now. Everything you tried to tell me—"

I jump as a super suddenly scrambles over the rubble, tripping over the rocks as he flees into the darkness. The supers are trying to get through. We need to help them. I move to climb up the boulders, but Rez places a hand on each of my shoulders.

He grins, though strained as the battles rages behind him. "I knew you would. Someday."

I start to smile back when the sound of bullets spitting the ground nears the opening. We instinctively duck, then Rez waves for me to follow him over the wall.

I scramble after him as more supers climb over the debris, some with blood stains on their grey jumpsuits, holding hands against cuts, gripping bruised sides. Rez surprises me by stopping near the crest of the hill of rubble and turning back to me, catching me by the shoulders again and looking intently at me. "Listen, no matter what you've done, Scarlett, I still mean every word I said to you when you were in Rapid. None of that has changed. You're on this earth for a reason. I know God can use you for great things." He glances at the fight again. "I think He already is."

He gives me one last sad smile, then launches back into the fray. I watch him leave, bullets hitting the ground around his feet, exploding dirt into the air. Watching him disappear into the battling crowd makes my stomach clench. Like somehow, in the back of my mind, I know he might not come out of this alive. I knew people would get hurt, but now that I'm here, in this moment, with bullets flying and supers fighting and the noise of it all drowning me...My chest aches at the pain and destruction on both sides.

As more supers scramble over the rubble into freedom, I force myself to face the fight once again.

CHAPTER THIRTY-ONE

I scrape my shins, my knees, my palms on the wall debris as I climb over the mound of rubble. The noise of the battle hits me full force and panic squeezes my throat. I growl and shove it away, my fire sparking through my body and lighting my fingers.

Like a changing tide, the thick of the fight has shifted from the middle of the grounds to creep closer to the crumbled wall as soldiers try to stop supers from getting through the opening. An array of superpowers rise up to meet the SCF's forces even as they beat back the supers toward the opening. Several supers break away to scramble through. Bullets still pierce the air, dropping many grey jumpsuits to the soil. Each fall squeezes my heart tighter, and I drop to shelter behind a jagged concrete boulder. My eyes widen when I spot some soldiers firing on their own. That's when my gaze catches Rez, fighting back a guard before he could get to a fallen woman super. Is he using his mind-manipulation on the soldiers or have some turned of their own accord?

My gaze drifts to the still bodies on the grounds. What if my friends are among the fallen? Nausea stirs my stomach and flames flicker around my fingers as I scan the crowd for familiar faces.

The energy in my body moves me forward out of my shelter, drawing fire from my core. Flames gather around my clenched fists, growing, pulsing with hot energy as I enter the fight. I step to Rez's side and create a wall of flames again, forcing soldiers back from the heat.

Rez looks at me and nods in approval, a slight grin lifting the corner of his mouth despite the bruise blossoming on his jaw and the sweat dampening his uniform.

I take a step forward, spreading my hands to push back as many soldiers as possible as the fire follows my motion. Some supers step away from me too in the face of the intense heat. Seeing the roaring flames pouring from my hands takes me back to that night behind the ice cream shop. The moment this fire entered my body and became a part of me. The moment I became superhuman.

I trip over a rock and my flames falter. Rez grabs my arm and helps me find my balance.

The supers surge forward again and the jostling almost knocks me over. I grab Rez's sleeve. "Where are they?" I yell over the noise.

"Who?" he yells back.

We duck under a flying super streaking through the air. "Ares, Ivon, Seth!" My throat grows hoarse from trying to be heard. "Have you seen—"

"Duck!"

A cold shock covers the top of my head as a hand presses me to the ground. Bullets smack the ground around us.

I turn my face to the left, keeping my body plastered to the grass. "Ares!"

He has a bruise on his jaw and a cut on his cheek, but he seems fine otherwise. He points toward our right. "They're over there."

I follow his finger and find Ivon's hulking form moving toward the wall opening. Seth hangs limply over his shoulder, skin pale even in the dark.

I shove off the ground and sprint across the distance toward them, keeping my head down in a crouching run. I can feel Ares' cold presence behind me as he follows.

I reach Ivon just as he bends to help a middle-aged woman over the debris. I rest my hands on my knees to catch my breath. "What happened to him?"

Ivon looks at me only a moment before making sure the woman gets over a large boulder. "I don't know. He just passed out."

Ares looks over the rubble at the open countryside. "Where do we take him?"

The question hangs in the air and my mind spins as I study Seth's pale face, sweat-dampened hair sticking to his skin. I look toward the looming SCF building. Do we leave Seth here, where he wants to be? Or do we take him with us? My hands clench. I can't just leave him here. I can't let him waste away in this place. I need to help him see the truth about himself and his powers.

I grab Ivon's arm and push him toward the opening. "We'll take him with us." I grab Ares' arm too, then suck in a breath at the icy chill of his skin and pull away. Still, I wave him toward the opening too. "Go. Hurry."

Ivon climbs over the rubble, but Ares doesn't budge as he frowns at me. "What about you?"

"I'll follow soon. I..." I look over my shoulder to scan the remaining fighting supers. Where's Rez? I frantically search the grey jumpsuits still facing the black-clad soldiers, but can't find him. I dive back into the fray.

I shove through the crowd, searching for Rez. A trio of supers break away from the fight and stampede toward the opening. They knock me down in the process, and dirt flies into my eyes as more feet follow the three supers streaking toward the opening. I quickly swipe it away and press my hands to the grass to get up. But the crowd presses too close. A knee to my ribs knocks me to my side. I groan and clutch my side. Clenching my teeth, I press my free hand down again so I can shove myself up. Someone steps on my hand and I yelp.

Through the tangle of legs, a bright white searchlight passes over a figure nearby on the ground.

A light grey jumpsuit like everyone else. But there's something else, something familiar.

Wavy, chocolate brown hair. Broad shoulders. Sun-tanned skin.

And blood.

Rez.

CHAPTER THIRTY-TWO

My lungs seize. *No, no, no. He's got to be okay.* Dazed, I scramble across the ground, clawing the dirt. Crawling my way through the supers. I get kneed in the temple, and my vision darkens and blurs. I press on.

He has to be okay. He has to be okay. Please be okay.

I grab a fistful of his jumpsuit and scoot myself as close to him as I can get. I try to shield him from the crazed supers stampeding around us. Bullets still fly through the air, screams accompanying them, but I barely hear them. More people fall in my peripheral vision. Each body that falls, each thud on the earth, every image of red-stained jumpsuits adds to the gaping hole rending my chest.

With a grunt, I roll Rez onto his back. He groans and grinds his teeth. Bloodied fingers clutch his stomach.

"Rez!" My voice quakes. No, this can't be happening. He's got to be okay. Rapid needs him. They need their leader. Guilt prods me and my stomach roils, threatening to empty itself. This is all my fault.

I clamp my mouth shut and swallow hard before taking a deep breath. I have to stay calm, stay controlled. Rez needs help. I gently pry his blood-stained fingers from his middle. Blood seeps from a hole in his flesh. I gasp and press his hand back over it. I look around, frantically. Everything sounds muffled, like it's underwater. All I'm aware of is Rez's writhing body and my heart beating rapidly inside my chest. My breathing quickens. I need help. He's got to be okay. I don't know what to do. I press my hand over his. Apply pressure? I don't know. I need help. Anybody...

A hulking form collapses to his knees on the other side of Rez.

"Ivon!" I try to scream, but it comes out all choked. "Help him!"

Ivon's eyes dart from Rez's face to the blood staining his middle. He pulls my hand away from Rez's and checks the wound. He pales. Rez pales. The muscles in Ivon's jaw bulge and his nostrils flare. Fear shines in his eyes.

This isn't good. I grab fistfuls of my hair as I continue to heave in gasping breaths. *Please be okay, please be okay. Rapid needs you.* I want to ask if Rez will make it. If he will live. But the words don't make it past my tongue for fear of the answer.

The noise of the battle dims. I tear my eyes from Rez.

The last remnants of the supers climb over the rubble to freedom on the other side of the wall. Guards and supers alike lie still in the dark. But soldiers still shoot at the supers escaping through the hole. Soon we're going to be the only ones here. I'm surprised we haven't been shot already.

"Ivon..." Rez breathes.

Ivon shifts Rez into his arms in one swift movement. Rez releases a scream through clenched teeth. I grimace, still gripping his sleeve.

Ivon looks at me, his steel eyes stormy, churning. "We have to go. Now. Lead them to Rapid."

I swallow, finding my throat scratchy. "Okay."

We run, melding with the trickling stream of supers. Gunshots follow us, urging us on faster, faster. It takes everything I have to keep up with Ivon's long strides. As we climb over the rubble, Rez pales from the jostling and he groans.

Somehow, some of the supers got a hold of some SCF vehicles. Ivon takes over a shiny black sedan, setting Rez carefully in the back seat. He instructs me to sit beside him and apply pressure to the wound while he drives.

I crouch beside Rez's prone figure, my hands shaking as I press against the bloody mess of his side. Something slaps against the backseat window and I jump.

Ares waves through the glass and I quickly wind the window down. He peeks his head in. "A couple guys and I are gonna take Seth—" His eyes land on Rez and he freezes.

"Ares!" I reach for him, but he's too far. I try to gather myself. "I need you to lead the supers to Rapid. We need to take Rez to a hospital."

Ares nods and takes off running.

"No hospital." The whispery, weak voice snaps my attention to the man lying on the seat.

"Rez..."

He licks his chapped lips, eyes closed, forehead wrinkled. "No...hospital..."

Ivon frowns over his shoulder before the engine roars to life and we accelerate with a jolt.

I press a hand to the leather seat to steady myself. "Rez, what are you talking about? You need medical attention!"

He shakes his head and grimaces. "Take me...home."

"Rez." Ivon's deep rumble makes me jump. "You need professional help. We can't give you that kind of help—"

"Take me home." His head lolls to the side.

Ivon grips the steering wheel harder. Something cracks. "Rez, trust me..."

A sharp squeeze on my hand makes me suck in a breath. Rez's hand grasps mine, blood slick between our skin. He opens his eyes a crack. His eyes roll around then find me. They lock on. His grip falters for a moment, then squeezes harder than before.

"Take me to Rapid." His breath hitches and he coughs. Pain twists his face.

"Ivon..." I say without taking my eyes off Rez. "Go to Rapid." Maybe...maybe there's not time for a hospital anyway. My chest clenches painfully and I bite my lip hard, desperately casting the thought aside. He needs home.

"Scarlett, he's not thinking straight. He needs—"

"He needs home. Go to Rapid."

I almost don't notice the crowd of battle-weary supers filling the warehouse as I follow Ivon carrying Rez inside. I remember how empty this space seemed after the Rapid supers were taken away, and the familiar guilt sours my tongue. But now the space fills with supers in SCF uniforms, the light grey stained with dirt and blood. Nadia stands near a cluster of children, eyes wide when she sees Rez. I spot Ares rising from a crouch near the corner, where Seth is propped up against the wall. Everyone quiets as they watch us come in.

I snatch the nearest blanket and throw it on the ground, and Ivon sets Rez on it. He hisses from the jostling, his skin growing ever paler. How is he not passed out by now?

Ivon hurries toward the shelves. "Bandages. I'll get bandages."

I kneel at Rez's side, feeling others gathering around behind us.

Rez groans again. I grab his hand as he coughs and press my other hand against the wound, wincing when he gasps at the touch. Warm blood seeps over my fingers from the wound, and sticks his hand and mine together as I grip it tighter.

"Scarlett..." His voice is just a wisp.

I swallow unshed tears. "I'm here."

"Wh-where's Ivon?"

"He's trying to find bandages."

He twists his neck to see around him, looking for his friend. "Ivon..."

I lean closer. "He's coming." I bite my lip and twist toward the shelves. "Hurry, Ivon!"

"I'm trying!" he barks.

Rez slowly shakes his head. "Too...late..." he mumbles.

Tears blur my vision and I fiercely blink them away. "No. No, it's not." I squeeze his hand harder. "Just hang on. You're gonna be okay." *You've got to be okay.*

He cracks his eyes open and glances numbly around. His eyes land on me. Weakly, he squeezes my hand back. "Scarlett."

I lean forward to catch his words. "Yes?"

"I want you to promise me something."

I shake my head as a tear escapes. "You're fine, Rez. Just hang on."

He shakes his head again, closing his eyes while he tries to swallow. I glance around. Water. He needs water.

"Scarlett, listen to me." His chest barely rises. His grip on my hand weakens.

Where's Ivon? "You're gonna be okay, Rez." I say through gritted teeth.

Rez throws his other arm across his body and grabs my sleeve. I wince at the force of his grip, despite the trembling overtaking his body. His eyes open fully and his mismatched gaze locks firmly onto mine.

A few more tears slide down my face as I hold his mismatched gaze.

"Scarlett...I need you to promise me something."

This time, I nod.

"Take care...take care of..." His grip loosens for a moment as he glances around the warehouse and the supers watching him. "Take care of them...for me."

My throat constricts. I blink but nothing can hold back the tears spilling from my eyes. "Rez..." I choke.

"Promise?" His grip tightens again. His skin is like paper.

I suck in a shuddery breath and give him a firm nod. "I promise. I'll take care of them."

I think he's trying to smile, because the corner of his mouth twitches. He lets go of my sleeve and rests his arm back at his side.

Ivon finally returns with an armload of bandages. They're just ripped fabric.

"Oh, Ivon." I squeeze Rez's hand with both of mine. "Can't you help him?"

Ivon takes a long look at his friend, the silence twisting my gut. He lifts my hand to check the wound once more, then studies Rez's face. His face sags as his eyes glisten. He slowly shakes his head, dropping the bandages to take Rez's other hand.

My chest trembles beneath the sobs that I'm desperately trying to contain.

Rez glances drowsily between the both of us. An attempted chuckle makes him wince again. "Thanks for...everything, Ivon."

Ivon swallows hard, muscles in his jaw bulging, his eyes rimmed with red.

Rez looks at me again. I think he tries to squeeze my hand, but all his fingers do is shake. "You'll...you'll remember everything I told you, right?" A faint smile lifts one corner of his mouth.

I nod, losing more tears down my cheeks. "Of course, Rez. Of course."

He coughs. "The Bible. You keep that. Read it...okay?"

"Of course. I promise."

He's so still. His chest barely moves beneath his shallow breaths. "And Scarlett?"

I lean closer. "Yes?"

He shifts his glazed eyes to me and they bore into my soul. "Don't lose your fire."

One more hand squeeze. Weak and trembly.

One more shallow breath. Thin and raspy.

His eyes slide closed.

His hand falls out of mine.

Ivon digs the grave. We stand around the mound of fresh dirt, silence thick and heavy like a wet cloak. I bite my lip, only stopping myself when I taste blood.

Blood.

I squeeze my eyes shut and turn my head away. But the image of the grave and Rez's blood is seared into my memory.

A soft touch on my arm makes me open my eyes. Nadia's soft brown eyes meet mine, watery and red-rimmed. I wrap my hand over hers and squeeze.

Ivon holds a board of rough wood he nailed to a stake, frowning at the blank surface.

I shuffle to him and finger the wood. "May I?"

He looks at me, confused. But he lets me take the board from him.

I kneel beside the freshly turned dirt, breathing in the earthy smell, and place the board in my lap. I lift my finger and hesitate just a moment, hoping this'll work.

Then I press the tip of my finger against the wood. Heat builds under the pressure until the wood smokes. I trace my finger across the board, ignoring the scrapes and splinters. I carefully craft each letter, each word.

Once I'm finished, I hand it back to Ivon. He looks at it for a long moment, then lifts red eyes to me and nods. He moves, stiff and numb, to hammer the make-shift grave marker into the earth with the back of the spade.

I can feel the others crowd closer to read what I wrote.

Rez

Superhero

Nadia sniffs and takes a deep breath. Ares swipes his nose and stares at his shoes.

I turn away, my feet taking me from the peaceful, grassy spot just outside Rapid, back into the city. Rez's city. The city I promised to take care of.

I don't even register where I am until I stop in some damp alley. I lean against the brick wall of an apartment building, relishing the firmness. It's strength. How did Rez think I could do this? I close my eyes as my throat constricts. I lean my head back against the wall and press a hand to my chest against the ache. How am I going to do this? The future is as dark as the receding shadows.

Rusty stairs crawl criss-cross up the opposite wall to the building's roof like a stubborn vine. My foot finds the bottom step. One foot in front of the other. I barely notice the echo of my footsteps and the scrape of the edge of the building on my leg as I climb onto the roof.

The rising sun spreads its soft morning light across Rapid. A small flock of birds flit across the sky, their feathers catching the warm glow. Wispy clouds streak the gentle hues of soft pink and orange. A breeze lifts my hair and I close my eyes and let the warmth grow on my face.

"Lettie?"

I flinch, and whirl around. Only my family—

Nadia climbs over the edge of the roof. Ares follows. I don't know what to say, what to do. Ask them to leave me alone? Do I want to be alone? My hand trembles as I raise it to rub the back of my neck. Seeing their red-rimmed eyes makes the lump in my throat grow.

Nadia moves to stand beside me. She doesn't ask if I'm okay. No one's okay. She just takes my hand. Fresh tears well up in my eyes.

"Scarlett," she begins, softly. "I want to tell you something."

I swipe the back of my hand across my face and meet her steady gaze.

"I'm with you," she says. "You don't have to do this alone."

I curl my toes in my shoes as hard as I can, but nothing stops the tears. I open my mouth, but my throat spasms. I can't form words. I can't...

Ares lifts his eyes from staring at his shoes. The dawn's light adds a contrasting warmth to his ice-blue eyes. "Me too, Scarlett. We're all going to help you."

I swallow hard. Once. Twice. A raspy "thank you" passes my trembling lips. I reach for Ares' arm, despite his coldness. "Ares, I promise to help you find your sister some day." I squeeze, hoping he knows I mean it. I want to mean my promises.

He nods, blinking rapidly. "Thank you."

Now we're just missing one person...

"I'm sure Seth will come around," Nadia says, glancing back in the direction of the warehouse. "Don't worry."

I nod and shrug one shoulder. But she's right. I need to hang on to hope for him. For all of us.

The weight of responsibility settles on my shoulders like a drenched quilt, pulling me down. My knees feel weak, trembling beneath me. I look toward the sunrise and take a slow breath.

I'll keep my promise to Rez. I'll take care of his Rapid supers.

And I'll never lose my fire. Not ever again.

I stride down the narrow hall of small storerooms in the back of the warehouse. Ivon stands in front of one, feet spread shoulder-width and hands gripping his belt. But his shoulders sag, and he stares at the floor.

"Ivon?"

He looks up.

I clear my throat. "Can I see him?"

He glances at the door, then back at me. He nods, then unlocks the door and opens it, mumbling a "be careful."

I slip inside and Ivon closes the door behind me.

"Seth?"

He sits slumped in the corner on a crumpled blanket, knees

drawn up under his chin. His forehead rests on his knees. The single white lightbulb overhead buzzes and flickers. An unopened bag of potato chips sits against the wall.

I clear my throat. "Seth?"

He lifts his head. His gaze slowly slides across the room until it lands on me. He lifts his pale face. Dark circles accent his eyes. His head slumps back down. "What do you want?" he mumbles.

I look around the room and grimace. It's barely bigger than a closet. I take a step closer to him. "How are you feeling?"

He huffs. "Why do you care?"

I sigh and stare at my hands. "We're all worried about you. Y-you don't look well."

He looks at me, his glare like a knife. "Leave me alone."

I take a half-step closer. "Seth, I want to explain."

"What, are you going to apologize?"

"No. That's not it. I want to explain why I did...what I did."

He stares at me, glare only sharpening.

"We *had* to stop you, Seth," I say gently.

"You were the ones that needed stopping," he snaps.

I purse my lips. "Let me explain—"

"Don't waste your breath." His head falls back to his knees.

I frown and reach for his shoulder. "Seth, what's wrong? I mean, you don't look well."

"Leave me alone!" He jerks away from my outstretched hand.

I snap my hand back. I wait a moment, though I don't know what for. For him to say something, for me to think of something to say? Silence fills the room. What's happened to this once-cheerful boy?

I turn back toward the door. I won't give up on him. Not yet. Someday I'll figure out what's wrong with him and what the cure is doing to his body. Why is it affecting him like this and not us? I chew my lip. Maybe it's just a matter of time.

After I rap on the door, Ivon lets me out. I nod my thanks and walk back down the hallway. When I step back into the main space of the warehouse, I'm met with confused murmuring conversations. Supers mill about, obviously unsure what's next. Some rifle through the shelves, finding old stores of food. Some adults give the children food, while others greedily hoard granola bars and crackers. Most children huddle in corners, watching everyone else with wide eyes, hugging themselves against the chill. Others cradle wounds, hands clamped over bloody cuts and wincing against bruises. A pale shock covers everyone. I feel it too, squeezing my throat.

What in the world did we just do? What happens after this? Will I live in Rapid permanently now? What will that be like? To be surrounded by supers, doing good in the world, making a difference?

Maybe that's what I'm here for. To do more good for supers.

Nadia elbows through the crowd until she reaches me. "Scarlett, they need to know what's next."

She should lead them, not me. She's kind and strong while my knees quake beneath me. Still, I straighten my shoulders. "Okay." I make my way toward the firepit where I know most of the empty crate-seats remain. I stack two on top of each other and scramble to the top. It wobbles a little under my weight, then settles.

"C-can I have everyone's attention, please?" My voice gets lost under the hum.

Nadia taps my shoe. I look down at her and she gives an encouraging nod.

Come on. I can do this. If Rez thought I could...I clear my throat and take a deep breath, then clap my hands. "Hey, listen up, everybody!"

It takes a few moments, but soon their attention swivels to me.

My palms dampen with sweat and I wipe them on my jumpsuit pants. I survey this beaten, tired group. It's such an odd image of pale grey SCF jumpsuits against the dusty backdrop of the old, worn warehouse. Our group is so much smaller than when we first escaped, yet still larger than the original Rapid supers. I wonder who broke off, hoping they're okay.

I jolt. Stop thinking. Speak. They're waiting. "Okay, we need a plan now. There are wounded here that need tending. We have some medical supplies...er, I think..."

Nadia taps my shoe again. She points across the room. Ares holds a rickety first-aid kit over his head and jabs his finger at a pile of bandages—mostly just ripped cloth—on a shelf.

"Okay, yes, we do have medical supplies. So here's how we're going to do this. If you're not injured, then help gather all the wounded over here, by the fire." I point to the firepit then realize it's black and cold. Heat flushes the back of my neck. "Uh...I'll get a fire going here soon." I lick my parched lips. *Keep going. You got this. They need you.* "Once we get the wounded settled, some of us will tend to them while others get food together for everyone." I hope we have enough. My mind spins with the thought of stealing food like Rez did. I fidget with the hem of my hoodie. I don't want to do that. I guess I'll have to cross that bridge when I come to it. "So, um..." I clap awkwardly. "Let's get going."

Before I can make more of a fool of myself, I jump down from my crate stage. To my surprise, the supers get to work immediately. The healthy help the limping, wincing, and groaning toward the side of the warehouse closest to the firepit. I watch in a daze as they work together like a team.

Wake up, Scarlett. Concentrate.

I jog over to the firepit and toss some logs on from the wood bin, which is half empty. I'll have to fill that soon. For now, flames spit from my hands and spark over the logs. They catch and start to crackle.

It's a good thing I have fire powers because I wouldn't know how to start a fire otherwise.

As the hours pass, my confidence swells. At first, we're all tentative. Strangers. But bound by the fact that we're all special. Different. We're all supers, all gifted.

Soon we have the wounded taken care of, everyone fed—although meagerly—and most everyone settles down for sleep. Some of the anxious children are too upset to sleep. They lie in the corner of the warehouse, whimpering as they clutch their blankets. Their worry sparks an idea in my mind. I quickly slip from the warehouse, relying on my memory to navigate the streets in the dark. I reach Mikey's grocery store, but all is silent. My brow knots as I wonder where they are now, if they got out with everyone else.

I step inside, shoes crunching on wrappers and bumping into cans until I reach the back closet Crynn showed us before. I feel across the wall and flip a switch. A yellow, flickering light illuminates the shelves. My gaze latches on to the beat-up ukulele and a smile spreads across my face as my fingers curl around the instrument.

I hurry out of the closet and back out onto the street. Half-running, half-walking, I rush back to the warehouse and tune the old uke on the way. When I step back into the warehouse, the children sit up, golden firelight flickering across their faces as they look with curiosity at the instrument in my hands.

I take a deep breath and settle down in the midst of them. At first my fingers tremble, as if afraid I might've forgotten. But once I start plucking the strings, I settle into a simple rhythm, playing snatches of lullabies I remember. Some of the younger kids crowd closer to lean against me, sighing as sleep begins to take them. I let out a breath as I watch them relax, glad I can distract them from whatever plagues their minds.

At the end, I'm exhausted. I'm sore. I can barely keep my eyes open as I tuck the ragged edge of a blanket around a small boy fast asleep beside me. But I feel good.

And there's not even one scorch mark on the ukulele.

CHAPTER THIRTY-THREE

I knock on the back door of my own house. I feel foolish. I could just walk in, but...I sigh and glance over my shoulder.

Nadia peeks her head out from behind a thick bush. I can just barely see her outline in the dark. "Go on," she whispers.

I knock again.

The steps come, slow and tentative. Maybe going to the back door wasn't such a good idea. But the front seems too exposed. I'm a wanted criminal now.

The door slowly opens, just a crack. One eye studies me.

"Mom?"

The door flies open. Mom gapes at me with wide eyes. Tears pool in her eyes and spill over her cheeks. "Lettie!"

Suddenly I forget about spying neighbors, SCF soldiers, and being wanted by the government. I collapse into her arms and she wraps me into the tightest hug, kissing the top of my head. Her tears wet my hair.

She pulls me inside and closes the door. "Dylan! Hannah!"

She doesn't ask how or why I'm here. She just holds me. Face against her shoulder, tears wetting her sweater, I soak in her familiar embrace, her familiar smell. I want to smile, but I can't, knowing I don't have long. I don't want to endanger them with my presence here.

Hannah collides into me before I even see her. I laugh and kneel so I can wrap my arms around her. Is she taller? I bury my face in her shoulder, not wanting her to see that I can't stop crying. Mom wraps her arms around the both of us.

"Honey, what—"

Dad's warm, deep voice makes my head jerk up. His eyes widen, jaw slack, as he rushes down the hall and envelopes us all in his arms.

"How did you get back?" he whispers into my hair. "The news...we saw..."

I take a deep breath and gently pull out of the group hug. "I'm not exactly...back."

"What do you mean?" Mom's voice hitches.

I shake my head and swallow hard to keep back another onslaught of tears. I need to keep it together, for their sake as much as mine. "I can't stay."

They just stare at me.

I take another deep breath. "There are supers in Rapid City. And they need me. And the SCF—"

Dad's brow furrows. "What? Honey, you're not making any sense."

How do I explain all this in limited time? I look intently at both of them. They need to know I'm serious. "There are superhumans in Rapid, people who are realizing things about their powers. Wonderful things. And the government has no right to take that part of us away. These supers are trying to live a normal life, and they're trying to do good with their powers. Trying to help people. I..." That now-familiar weight of responsibility tugs on me again. "I need to take care of them."

Mom blinks rapidly. "But, how...why...?"

"I made a promise to someone. I need to keep it."

"Scarlett. Please. Can't you stay just a little while?"

I shake my head. "It's too dangerous for you all if I stay here.

They could be looking for me." I refuse to let my eyes roam around the house. Too many memories. I may change my mind. "More dangerous than it was before. Please understand."

They both study me deeply and more tears spill onto Mom's rosy cheeks. She inhales, her breath shaking, then she smiles sadly and strokes the side of my face. "Oh, Lettie..."

Dad clenches his jaw as if that will hold back the wetness in his eyes. "We...we'll try."

I nod and smile back. They follow me when I stand, Hannah clutching my sleeve. "Is...Is Dylan here?"

Mom sniffs and nods. "Dylan!"

"Coming!" Dylan's muffled call from the basement makes my heart clench.

His thundering footsteps pound up the stairs and he rounds the corner into the hallway where we stand. He freezes. "Lettie?"

I press my hand to my mouth as I look at my best friend. His eyes meet mine and widen, glossy with tears. He collapses into my open arms.

I wrap my arms around him and squeeze hard. He's gotten taller. I can no longer put my chin over his shoulder. I bury my face in his chest and feel his strong heartbeat against my cheek as my tears soak his t-shirt.

He clears his throat. "Are you...?"

"I can't stay."

He pulls away, holding me at arms-length. He looks over my shoulder at Mom. She nods. "I'll explain it to you, dear."

"Hello? What's going on?"

I suck in a breath at Mrs. Henley's voice. Her thin frame rounds the corner from the living room, TV remote in hand. She stops dead in her tracks when she sees me, gasping and slapping a hand over her mouth.

"S-Scarlett." She glances over her shoulder toward the living room. For the first time I notice the low noise of the TV. Probably the news. "We just...we just saw..." What happened at the SCF is probably plastered on every news station in the country. Part of me wants to see what the reporters are saying about it.

"I know." I clear my throat, hoping it'll lessen the thick wetness in my voice. Flashes of vivid images, like nightmares, make my throat constrict. The deafening sound of gunfire, grey jumpsuits lying still on the ground, Rez's blood on my hands.

I bite my lip, studying her green eyes so much like Ian's. "Mrs. Henley...I...I saw Ian—"

"Can you stay, dear?" she cuts me off. "Are they after you?"

Her words, coupled with a soft tap on the back door make my chest tighten with urgency.

Mom frowns at the door. "Who's that?"

"A friend. She's just reminding me."

"Of what?"

I try to take a deep breath, but weight crushes my chest. "That I should go."

Silence falls on us. I need to leave. For their safety. The SCF knows where my family lives and they could come here to ask questions.

No words are spoken. They just all lift their tear-filled eyes to me. My heart threatens to tear in two. Trying my best to be strong, I give them each one more long embrace. Mom hugs me the tightest, the longest. When I finally gently pull away, I try to give her my best smile. "I promise I'll come back again to see everyone." I look up at Dad and give his hand a squeeze."Some day."

I look them each in the eye one last time. They watch me turn toward the back door. My shaking fingers grab the knob and I swing it open.

"Lettie..."

I look over my shoulder to meet Dylan's gaze.

He swallows. "Come back sooner rather than later, huh?"

Even as more tears sting my eyes, I smile. "I will. You can bet on that."

He pauses, then a twinkle lights in his eyes and a small grin lifts the corner of his mouth. "I'd better see you on the news. Saving people."

A chuckle bubbles up. "You can bet on that too, Dylan." The weight lifts a little as we share a smile.

I hesitate. "If you see Ian—"

"Don't worry about it. We'll explain things to him."

He doesn't know about our encounter at the SCF. Do they know why he was working there? I try to swallow, casting a glance at Mrs. Henley. She looks away, hand pressed to her mouth. What is she hiding about Ian?

"Thank you." I take one more good look at them, studying every bit so I can treasure them in whatever hard days I know are coming. "I love you all."

They say it all in their eyes, their sad smiles. Sometimes words aren't needed. I give them my best smile before I turn away.

My heart feels lighter. A lifted weight and a piece left behind.

I wake up with the sun. It's weird. I feel like, as a leader, I should wake up early, before anyone else. I think part of being a leader means being ready whenever someone needs help.

No one's awake when I force myself out of my blanket nest. I carefully step over sleeping bodies and make my way to the firepit. All that's left on top of the ashes are a few smoldering embers. Ares lies on the ground near the pit, sound asleep, fire-stoking stick still in hand and snoring softly. He volunteered to tend the fire all night, although he can barely stand its heat.

I carefully take the stick from him and quietly set the last few logs in the pit and get the fire going. I'll restock the wood box as soon as I'm warmed. It's hard to coax my fire to warm my body fast enough in this cold, so the flames will help. I sit on the nearest crate and let my eyes scan the warehouse. My gaze lands on a pile of folded blankets propped against a shelf.

And a thick, leather-bound book sitting on top.

My breath stops for a second. With a sigh, I walk over to the blankets and bend over. My fingers curl around the thick book. Rez's Bible? How did it get here?

My heart squeezes. That was part of the promise too, wasn't it? To read this book. I suddenly feel lost. Rez isn't here to help me understand what's inside this, and I don't even know where to start.

With Mark. That's what Rez said.

I begin to flip through the whisper-thin pages. In the latter half, I find the book of Mark, but tears blur the words in front of my eyes. I snap it closed and press the book against my chest. Not here, not right now. I stand and scramble over people and out the door.

The wind hits me and hushes my anxious thoughts. I take a few steps away from the warehouse, pretending I'm leaving the weight of responsibility behind. But I'm closely tethered by my promise.

I suddenly feel very alone. It crushes me like an impossible burden on my shoulders, making my legs weak. Nadia and Ares said they'd stick with me. Even Ivon pledged loyalty. But it's still all so much. How will I lead these people? These people I once betrayed. What happens if the SCF comes after us again? How will we fight them off? How did Rez ever think I could handle this?

I find myself walking around the warehouse to the small patch of garden basking in the morning sun. I kneel at the edge and finger a young plant wriggling through tangles of weeds. I don't even know what it is, but it's beautiful. This city is so full of broken and damaged, but between the cracks and the rubble things new and growing and thriving are beginning to emerge.

I set the Bible on a thick patch of grass and begin pulling weeds. It feels good to have something for my hands to do, like I know what I'm doing, like I have a plan.

Soft footsteps swish across the grass and stop beside me.

Nadia crouches by my side. After a moment, she reaches toward the soil and begins plucking weeds.

I thought I wanted to be alone, but I'm grateful for Nadia's quiet presence next to me. I take a deep breath.

Nadia piles her pulled weeds in the grass. "Thank you, Scarlett."

I stop, my hand hovering over a bright dandelion. I almost don't want to pull it out. "For what?"

She rests her arms on her knees and shyly glances at me. "For being a leader. For showing me that my powers...my gifts can be used for something good. To defend."

I can't help the tears beginning to prick my eyes. I blink. Do I say "you're welcome"? I feel like I didn't do anything. I just changed. My heart changed. I nod, allowing myself a small grin.

She smiles back, her eyes glistening in the early morning light. We both turn back to the upturned soil and its earthy scent, pulling the weeds to make room for the young plants.

"Scarlett." Nadia breaks the silence. She drops a wrinkly weed in her pile and stares at the sky thoughtfully. "I have an idea I've been mulling over..."

"Yeah?" I brush dirt off my hands. "What is it?"

She stares at her hands, picking at her nails. "I want to study superpowers. I want to be able to help the supers that come here learn more about who they are. I don't want them to think of themselves as mysteries."

I grab her hand. "That's beautiful, Nadia. You'll be the smartest superhuman doctor in existence." Better than that Dr. Bailey any day. Because Nadia Farlan truly cares.

Nadia smiles wide and bright, then nods and turns back to the garden. We fall into comfortable silence again.

As the sun climbs higher over the horizon, I shove to my feet. I wipe the dirt from my hands onto my jeans before picking up the Bible from the grass. "We'd better be getting back inside."

Nadia nods and follows me into the warehouse.

Ares is missing from his post by the fire, but only a few

people are awake when we enter. Others are stirring or sitting up to yawn and stretch. As soon as I find a crate by the fire again, the warehouse door opens.

"Scarlett." Ares' call comes a bit too loud for this hour.

I glance at the children still sleeping in the corner. They curl tightly under worn blankets, some sucking their thumbs. "What is it?"

He strides toward me, stepping over still forms. A little girl with dirty cheeks and a mess of wavy hair tries to follow his long strides, hanging onto his hand for dear life. The pair stop by the fire.

She stands stiffly, looking all around her. Ares gestures to the girl. "I found her at the edge of the city. She's hungry."

The little girl's lip quivers. She swipes a tear from her eye and wipes it on her pale grey jumpsuit. She's from the SCF. I wonder how long she's been alone. I guess she must be hungry, and thirsty too.

I lean forward and smile for her. "Hi. What's your name?" A series of numbers are stamped on her uniform but I refuse to look at them. That's not her.

She sniffs. "Madelyn," she whispers.

"Nice to meet you, Madelyn. That's a pretty name."

She almost smiles.

"Would you like something to eat?"

She hesitates, then nods.

Nadia's a step ahead of me, pressing a banana into my hand. I smile at the girl again and pat my lap. She can't be more than four years old.

She cautiously steps toward me, then climbs into my lap. I peel the banana and hand it to her. She takes a bite bigger than I thought capable of her small mouth. When half the banana is gone, she shifts and rests her head on my chest, letting out a weary sigh.

I wrap my arms around her, wanting her to feel safe, hoping she does.

"I'm scared." I barely catch her whisper.

I lean a little to see her face. "Scared? Of what?"

She sniffs again, holding her banana loosely. "Of myself."

Oh. I hold her tighter. "Want to talk about it?"

She pauses. "I don't know what I am." Her voice is steady, though soft, but I can feel tears wetting my shirt. "I...can hurt people."

I don't know what her powers are, where she came from, or what they told her at the SCF. All I know is one thing that Rez told me. Something I think I am at least beginning to understand, and even to believe.

"You don't have to be scared." I stroke her unruly, blonde curls and bend near her ear. "You're special, Madelyn. Gifted. God doesn't make mistakes."

ACKNOWLEDGMENTS

Years ago, I thought writing was a solo job. I was so wrong. Taking *Ignite* on my first foray into the publishing world, I see just how much other people's support, encouragement, and help are so important to the process. There are so many people I couldn't have done this without. So, many heartfelt thanks...

First, to my family. To my mom and dad for supporting me, encouraging me, being my mentors, and helping to make my dreams come true. Thanks to my siblings who endured random rants about story science and my characters. You guys are the best.

To the community of Kingdom Pen. You guys are awesome. My writing growth skyrocketed when I joined this amazing like-minded community. I love your encouragement, your amazing stories, and jokes. I know God will do big things with your storytelling. (I'm a kapeefer, 'til we're old and grey!).

To *Ignite*'s beta readers: Mariposa, Nicole, Penny, Chelsea, Abigail, Valerie, Alia, and Anisa. When I couldn't figure out how to take my story further, your feedback was just the thing I needed to take it to the next level. Your fangirling about characters made me smile and your helpful comments have made me a better writer.

To my editors: Nadine, it was truly a dream come true when I managed to get one of your editing slots that summer in 2020 (seriously, you have no idea how much I was internally squealing). Your excited comments and helpful feedback fired up my creativity to take the story to the next level. Not only that, but it also helped me grow as a writer for my future stories. And to Jane: your feedback was invaluable to me, and helped me identify my strengths and weaknesses as a writer. You were a delight to work with and your excitement about this story really helped get me through those hard edits. Thank you for all you do for authors.

To Ebook Launch for making my long-held dream of having an epic book cover come true.

To my street team. You guys are epic. I'm so thankful for all your support and encouragement. You make me so excited to be an author. (Avengers, assemble!)

To all the wonderful authors who inspired me with their stories and faith, who showed me what great Christian fiction looks like and how it can impact the world. You inspired me (and continue to) in my own writing journey. A special thanks to Allen Arnold for his book *The Story of With*, which made me realize what a beautiful, wild and free journey to creating God was invited me to join with Him. That changed everything.

To my readers, for picking up this book and reading Scarlett's story. Thank you.

And finally, to my Heavenly Father, who's been there all the time, even when I forgot. You've given me a passion for storytelling from the beginning, and a love for the impact of art on people. You've made my dreams come true, which is way more than I deserve. I look forward to the years we will continue to create stories together.

COMING SOON

Ignite Duology Book 2...

EMBERS

The SCF has discovered their new serum isn't working... just making supers deathly ill. It'll be harder to get rid of superpowers than they thought.

But the cure wasn't the only thing they've been working on in secret for years. They have one more tactic up their sleeve. But they need to test it out. So they target Rapid City once again.

Scarlett desperately tries to balance her new life as a leader in Rapid and keep everyone happy, which she seems to be failing at. And now the SCF's new scheme looms on the horizon. Will she learn what it means to be a leader, or fail and risk everyone's lives?

BONUS CONTENT

Visit igniteduology.wordpress.com for *Ignite*-themed bonus content like:

- ***Fan art***
- ***Playlists***
- ***Reviews***
- ***Merch & more!***

If you enjoyed *Ignite*, please consider leaving an honest review on Amazon, Barnes & Noble, or Goodreads. Thank you!

ABOUT THE AUTHOR

Jenna Terese believes stories are powerful. That's why she's dedicated to creating fiction that will impact the world. You can find this INFP dreaming about the future, fangirling over her favorite books, geeking out about Marvel, playing piano, or sipping a chai tea latte as she writes sci-fi novels.

For more information and updates:
www.jennaterese.com

CPSIA information can be obtained
at www.ICGtesting.com
Printed in the USA
BVHW081053230621
610212BV00002B/32